Song of the Dark

Song of the Dark Series

Book One

BRYN SUDDARTH

For my family.
Thank you for always loving me no matter who I discover I am.

Chapter One

I can't even die right.

Thomas lay flat on the deck of the recently wrecked ship, left alone with only his thoughts. The scratching at the hull sounded in time with the discordant song that drifted on the wind. The roar of an occasional wave crashing against the ship gave him a quick break from the depressing music, but he could always count on it to return once the ocean calmed. It was a fitting end for him.

Why won't they just kill me?

Hours ago, he had helplessly watched each member of the ship's crew throw themselves into the sea in a desperate, final act to reach the source of the music. Thomas was the only sailor unaffected by the deadly chanting, and now he was all alone. The wind had pushed the unmanned ship into a cluster of jagged rocks; Thomas could do nothing but watch it capsize. A dark part of him had hoped he wouldn't survive the wreck. Unfortunately for him, the ship didn't sink. It had merely parked itself on the boulders. Only the starboard hull and main mast took damage, leaving the ship completely inoperable.

Maybe I should just get it over with.

It was a dark thought, but there was no way he could sail this ship on his own. His fate was sealed the moment the sirens found the ship. Thomas took a deep breath and pushed himself up from the wet floorboards. The harsh wind blew over him as he stood upright, causing him to shiver in his damp clothes.

He dug in the pocket of his sea-soaked pants, pulling out a silver cigarette case. He hoped the case was protective enough to keep its contents dry, but with his luck, the case was already empty. He hadn't the heart to look inside.

He traced his thumb along the images sculpted into the silver: a fox sneaked through the grass beside a stream, proudly holding a bird in its mouth. The fox had probably spent days hunting that poor winged creature, plotting and scheming its downfall. Catching the bird must have been important to the fox. Why else would he bother?

Thomas frowned at the imaginary story and flipped open the case to stop himself from thinking about it. Three carefully rolled cigarettes waited in their slots, all dry. It took him a few moments to work up the courage to pull one out. He put the cigarette in his mouth and dug for his matches. Unlike the cigarettes, the matches were very damp. Hopefully, they would still light.

It took a few tries, but eventually, he had a lit cigarette. With reckless determination, he took a deep drag of the hot smoke. Intense heat prickled at the back of his throat, worsening by the second. He choked on the smoke, coughing and hacking to get the fire out of him. Tears burned his eyes, but he didn't know if it was from the pain or the smell. He welcomed the cold wind, sucking in deep breaths of the chilly air to soothe the damage in his throat. He released a ragged sigh and waited to try again. He was careful not to overdo it the second time.

"Ugh," he groaned as he exhaled another cloud of smoke. "I should have known I would die like this, slowly and alone." He frowned, wondering what point there was to talk out loud when he was the only person around for hundreds of miles. Then again, why not? "I shouldn't have expected any better."

Peering over the side of the ship, he watched the watery monsters that had stolen his crew. Each of them frantically clawed at the hull with long, sharp blades for fingernails, mindlessly ripping splinters from the wood and throwing the shards to the sea. They intended to do the same to him.

At least thirty sirens pushed themselves against the ship in a futile attempt to reach the deck above. The sirens looked like regular women if regular women had blue skin and fishtails. Their eyes were a pale milky shade of white that thinly masked the empty violence behind them. The somber song grew louder and more urgent at the sight of him. The song was lovely, but it was nothing to die over.

"Isn't it sad?"

The unexpected sound of another voice sent a surge of panic through Thomas. He scrambled away but only managed to create a foot of distance between himself and the new entity. Clinging to the bulwark, Thomas peered up at the large woman who had suddenly appeared.

A blue tint sparkled from deep beneath the translucent surface of her figure. Cloudy white fabric clung to her in a way that resembled a dress, if dresses could be made of mist. Two sapphire eyes watched him from beneath a turbulent pile of waves that cascaded from her head with an inhuman elegance. He would have almost been convinced that she was human had it not been for the unnatural sea-blue hair and her towering height of at least eight feet.

Thomas gawked at her, rubbing his eyes several times in an attempt to make her disappear. "Am I hallucinating already?"

In one powerful motion, the tall woman whipped her head around to look behind her. Her elegant blue waves rolled over her shoulders with a liveliness that made him wonder if her hair had a mind of its own. She looked at Thomas again and shrugged. "I don't know, what do you see?" Her voice sounded like pouring water and surfacing bubbles. Her blank expression hid laughter behind it, as though she were waiting for him to laugh so she could join in.

Thomas didn't laugh. He tightened his grip on the edge of the ship, his jaw clenched shut. *Was she joking*? "Um... you."

Her laughter broke through, dancing across the waves and echoing over the horizon. "You're not hallucinating. I forgot how easy it is to scare humans," she said with a grin.

"Humans?" Thomas asked. He pushed himself away from the edge and took a step back.

The tall woman approached Thomas to stand close beside him. He took another step away. Her gaze remained on the sirens below as she spoke. "I am curious. How did you resist the sirens' song? I don't understand why most men jump overboard, but you're still here."

Thomas's stomach tied itself in a knot as he thought about the answer to that question. "If you're going to kill me, will you please get it over with?" he asked, wishing for an end to this bizarre encounter.

She laughed again. "I'm not here to kill you, I would like to help you."

Thomas sighed. "Who are you?"

"I have many names, but in this form, I go by Mariana. You probably know me better as the ocean."

Thomas scoffed. "The ocean? You are the entire ocean?" He spread his arms to gesture all around him. "As in, the sea? You?"

"What? You don't believe me?" she asked. Without waiting for an answer, Mariana hopped onto the ledge and dove into the swarm of sirens, becoming nothing but a stream of water before she hit the surface with a splash.

Thomas stepped away from the edge of the ship and looked over the horizon. The landscape of the sea slowly shifted, and a large hill of water grew nearby. It looked like a normal wave, but there was something ominous about it. It was huge. Thomas watched carefully as it silently raced toward the ship, growing with its rapid approach. Just as he had suspected, he was soon faced with a massive wall of water.

The reality of the situation sank in. He ran as fast as his feet would carry him to the narrow hatchway that led below deck. He slipped at the edge of the stairs, clumsily falling to the lower deck just as the wall of water came crashing down with a deafening roar. He wondered momentarily why he didn't just let the wave kill him. It would have been a better death than the one that awaited him below.

The roar of water beating against the sturdy wood died down. A river of icy seawater streamed in from the open hatchway, drenching Thomas. Just as she had departed, Mariana returned, forming her human body from the water of the sea-soaked floor. Thomas watched, more irritated than amazed as he realized that she had caused that deadly wave just to make a point.

"Do you believe me now?" she asked, a smug smile poised on her perfect, almost human face.

"No." He glared at her from under a mess of drenched blond hair, salty water streaming down his face. Truthfully, the gigantic wave had convinced him that there was something otherworldly to her, but he hated the smug look in her eyes. "Are you some kind of magus? There's no way you are the entire ocean, you would have to be a deity."

"Yes, some people recognize me as a god. It's a term humans made up, but I've always thought it was fitting." The smug expression did not leave her face.

Thomas rolled his eyes. "If you're a god, what do you want with me?"

Mariana's smile remained on her face, but she hesitated before speaking. "I need your help."

"I thought you wanted to help me," Thomas said dryly.

"Of course I do, but I'm not going to help you for free. If you help me out, I'll get you home."

Thomas stood up. "No thank you. I don't want to go home." He turned around and ascended the dripping staircase. The bright sunlight stung his eyes as he emerged. He squinted as he tried to get a sense of the damage done to the deck by Mariana's wave. Not that it mattered.

She stood in the same spot in which she had first appeared, waiting for him. "I can give you anything you want. What do you want? Immortality?" she asked.

Thomas grimaced. "Absolutely not. I would rather die."

"What do you mean? Don't you want to live?"

Thomas shrugged. "Not really." He thought for a moment before he continued. "Actually, no. Just leave me here." Mariana gaped at him as he walked across the deck and perched himself on a barrel that had been tipped on its side. He pulled out his cigarette case once more and lit another cigarette, finding more success this time.

"What?" Mariana asked, dumbfounded. "That goes against human nature. Every time I think I understand you humans, you do something completely backward."

Thomas shrugged again and inhaled the hot smoke.

Mariana frowned at him. "Fine," she said. She stepped overboard and jumped back into herself, leaving Thomas all alone. As he slowly burned his way through his second cigarette, he wondered what a deity could offer him that he might want, but he couldn't think of a single thing.

Suddenly Mariana appeared at the side of the ship, leaning in from the outside and somehow suspended in mid-air. Thomas raised his eyebrows. "Please help me," she begged.

"You seem pretty desperate for an all-powerful deity. What can I do for you that you can't do for yourself?" he asked.

She released a bubbly sigh. "It's not that simple. I'm not able to interfere with the lives of the creatures that live within me. For years, countless colonies of merpeople have flourished all across the earth in many bodies of water. The largest group lives inside me, of course." She paused to flash a proud smile.

Thomas rolled his eyes.

"Recently a plague has spread through my colonies, and it's spreading fast," she continued. "There's something strange about this disease, but I can't intervene. I hadn't met a survivor of a siren attack until I found you. I need your help. Please."

"Aren't you intervening at this very moment? How is saving me different from saving them?"

"You don't live in the sea, you live on a boat. You're a creature of the land."

"Oh, that makes sense," he said sarcastically. "Why can't you find a woman to help you?"

"What do you mean?" Mariana asked.

"Nothing," he said. Mariana watched him closely, waiting for an explanation. "So this 'plague' only affects mermaids? I don't think I've ever heard of a male siren."

"That's right, as far as I've seen it's only ever affected mermaids, and it's irreversible. I'm afraid if I can't stop it soon, all the mermaids will die. My ecosystem can't handle such a largescale disruption. The consequences of this sickness will be felt across the planet. I need your help."

Thomas inhaled the cigarette one final time as he considered her request. The entire planet was in danger, and *he* could do something about it. His depressing life was not nearly as important as the well-being of an entire species, let alone the entire planet. He flicked the cigarette butt overboard. Mariana's eyes followed the path of the smoking bundle of paper until it fizzled on the surface of the water. She frowned at him, but he ignored the look.

"All right. I guess I can help you," Thomas said. "But I want something better than survival as a reward. I was content to die here until you selfishly stuck your nose in my business and offered to save me."

"I don't have a nose," Mariana said.

Thomas stared at her.

"What would you like as your reward? Your own ship? Magic? Wealth?" she asked.

Thomas grimaced. "Magic?" he asked. Why would anyone *want* to be a magus? "No. I don't know. Let me think about it."

Mariana grinned at him. "Well hurry up, I don't have all eternity." The moment she finished speaking, she threw her head back and cackled into the open air. It took her a few moments to compose herself before she spoke again. "It's funny because I do have all eternity. But you don't. Why aren't you laughing?"

Thomas's blank stare had become an irritated glare. He already regretted agreeing to help her. "Should we get started?" he asked.

Mariana excitedly jumped into the ship and landed on the deck with a watery thud. She ran to him and wrapped him in a cold, wet hug. "Yay! Thank you!"

Thomas groaned. "Don't make me change my mind." Mariana released him and the familiar chill of evaporating seawater stung his skin. He thought he would never be dry again.

"First, we need to figure out what's causing it," Mariana said.

"You don't know what's causing it?" he asked. "This is going to take forever."

"Yes, it is. That offer of immortality is still on the table," she said, throwing her head back to laugh again.

Thomas shook his head. That offer was going to stay on the table. *Forever.*

Blackwater Academy – Six Months Earlier

The muffled chatter of students' noisy conversations enveloped the silence of the empty classroom. Thomas has been the first to arrive in the classroom on the first day. His eyes ran along the pages of text in the book before him, but the words had no meaning. He didn't even know which class he was waiting for. History, maybe? He laid his head down on the pages of his book. His attention was somewhere far away from this classroom, and he was powerless to bring it back.

Students trickled into the room around him, bringing their noisiness with them. When he lifted his head, a page of his book briefly stuck to his face before falling back in line with the other pages. He took a moment to look around the classroom. At the front of the room, the usual dusty green chalkboard was placed beside a wide desk piled high with old books. An older man with a short gray beard sat at the desk, focused on his work. The desks were divided into three sections. Two large oak doors waited at the back of the room. Thomas had chosen a seat in the back corner of the room for an easy escape.

Thomas did his best to keep to himself, but his reputation was inescapable. Some people had tried to befriend him for their benefit, and some had despised him for his name, but most students only gave one knowing glance and decided they didn't care to talk to him at all. It was the beginning of the year, and he was receiving those glances all over again. He sighed and, to his dismay, accidentally made direct eye contact with the person who undoubtedly despised him the most: Charles Southworth.

The Southworth family was the largest competitor to Thomas's family, the Hambletons, in the industry of global maritime shipping. The Southworths' fleet of ships was almost, but not quite, as large as the Hambletons' fleet, and they were almost, but not quite as wealthy as the Hambletons. Naturally, the two families did not get along very well.

Thomas and Charles were only two months apart in age, Thomas being the older of the two. Charles had always hated Thomas much more than Thomas hated Charles. Thomas found their rivalry petty and exhausting.

Upon realizing that Charles had noticed him, Thomas nodded once. Charles returned the greeting with a scathing glare. Thomas narrowed his eyes, wondering what he had done to anger Charles, aside from existing.

It was painfully obvious that Thomas wasn't a real threat to Charles. Charles was much more put together than Thomas. Thomas could not even manage to button his shirt correctly, while Charles was practically flawless. His dark brown hair was always perfectly styled, and his posture was invariably excellent. Their school uniforms were identical, but Charles's uniform looked much better on him. He was the image of perfection. There was no chance that Charles's hatred for Thomas was born of jealousy, but Charles always seemed to have a perpetual judgmental glint in his eyes.

The students had settled into their seats before the clock at the front of the room struck eight. The bearded man stood beside the chalkboard, silently demanding the attention of his new students. "Good morning, students. I would like to introduce myself before we begin. I am Professor Quincy Franklin." He turned around to write *Professor Franklin* on the chalkboard, hastily underlining his name before he continued. "Welcome to *The History of Tinera*, your new home Monday through Friday from eight to nine-thirty for the next four months. Now, I'm sure you all have some knowledge of your home country already, at least I hope you do. Can anyone tell me who led the first expedition to Tinera?"

The room was silent and still. Nobody bothered to raise their hand. Thomas was surprised that nobody would answer the question. He couldn't tell if it was because they didn't want to speak or if it was because they didn't know the answer. Thomas raised his hand.

"Uh, yes. Mr. Hambleton, please." Professor Franklin gestured toward the back of the classroom where Thomas sat.

"Starla Waye," Thomas said.

"Good guess, but that is incorrect. Anyone else?" Professor Franklin asked.

Charles was quick to raise his hand this time. Before the professor could call on him, he spoke. "Actually it was Edwin Baine. Waye and her crew died at sea."

"That is correct. Thank you, Mr. Southworth." Professor Franklin turned once again to his chalkboard to write down *Edwin Baine.*

Thomas noticed Charles watching Thomas from his peripheral vision. Thomas offered Charles a blank stare in return for the smirk Charles shot in his direction. Thomas shook his head and decided he would try to ignore Charles for the rest of the class period.

Charles made himself hard to ignore. Every question Professor Franklin asked was promptly and correctly answered by Charles, who seemed to be trying to make a point that Thomas did not care about. Eventually, Professor Franklin checked his watch and informed thirty extremely bored teenagers that they were dismissed.

The quiet classroom erupted with the sound of shuffling papers and chair legs scraping against the hard stone floor. The majority of the students filed out of the classroom at the quickest pace their crowding would allow. Thomas waited for the crowd to die down before leaving his seat. When the classroom was nearly empty, Thomas silently shuffled out of the room behind the last of the students.

Charles had once again placed himself in plain sight across from the classroom doorway, where Thomas could not avoid running into him. "Nice job in class today, Hambleton," Charles said. Three other students stood around Charles, snickering at Thomas. Thomas sighed. The day had barely started and he was already tired of their imaginary rivalry. "You would think a Hambleton would know something about the history of sailing."

Thomas nodded. He didn't have the energy to argue that Starla Waye had been wronged by historians. "Yeah, you would think so."

"That's pretty sad," Charles said, then he laughed.

"Are you done?" Thomas asked. "Can I go?"

"Sorry, Hambleton. I'm afraid it won't be that easy to get rid of me." He flashed his perfect smile as he dug into his coat pocket, retrieving a silver cigarette case and a small box of matches.

Thomas rolled his eyes. "Goodbye, Charles." He turned to leave as Charles lit a cigarette, preventing him from spouting off any rude parting words. He only watched Thomas walk away.

CHAPTER TWO

PANTHEA SEA

Mariana walked across the deck, observing the capsized ship. For a long time, her attention was on the fallen mast. The rigging had kept it mostly in place, but it had been snapped in half and tilted at a noticeable angle. Thomas wondered if Mariana could fix it somehow. He didn't know what she was capable of. Then, she turned to him and asked a question that destroyed all hope of divine intervention. "Can you fix this?"

Thomas laughed. "Me?"

Mariana waited patiently for an answer.

"No," he said, suddenly realizing that Mariana probably didn't understand humans that well. She clearly didn't understand human transportation vessels.

Mariana peered over the starboard side of the ship, where the ship had landed on the boulders. "What about this?" she asked, her head buried in the wreckage.

"No," Thomas said. "You didn't think about this before asking for my help? How am I going to help you without a ship?"

Mariana pulled herself back onto the deck and turned to face him. "I might have a few ideas," she said with a sly smile.

Thomas hesitated to ask for clarification. "What do you have in mind?"

Mariana did not hesitate to answer. "There's another ship passing nearby. If I can pull it over here, the sirens will take care of the crew and it will be all yours!"

Thomas stood up from the barrel. "What?! You're going to murder an entire ship's crew? That's horrible!"

The excitement in her eyes vanished. She shrugged and turned away from him. "I'm not the one killing them."

"Please don't do that. Not only would I not be able to sail the ship on my own, but you would be killing an entire crew of men who want to live just to keep alive someone who doesn't," he pleaded.

"What? Who?"

Thomas frowned. "Me."

"What? You want to die? You can't die, you're the most important human in the world!" Mariana grinned at him.

Thomas glared at her. "Well, you're the only..." he trailed off, trying to think of the correct word. Gesturing in the air, he said, "*Being* in the world who believes that."

"Oh, I'm sure that's not true, uh..." She paused. "What's your name again?"

The conflicting nature of her statement and question together stole a laugh from Thomas. She hadn't bothered to ask his name and now she was trying to claim that he was more important than anyone else so she could commit murder. "This crew knew me as Felix, but my real name is Thomas."

Her excitement returned. "Felix! That's a perfect name for you! Do you know what it means?"

"No."

"It means happy and lucky!" She clasped her hands together and stared at Thomas with admiration.

Thomas grimaced and looked around at the wrecked ship. He was sure he hadn't genuinely smiled at Mariana one time since they met, and he was certainly not lucky. He did not understand why she thought that name was perfect for him. "Yeah, it's very fitting," he said.

"Oh!" Mariana exclaimed and shifted her attention to the open sea. Thomas tried to follow her line of sight out to sea but saw nothing interesting. "Felix, they're here!"

He wasn't bothered that she used his fake name. It had been his name for the last two months of his life aboard this ship. He didn't quite care for his birth name anyway, so he didn't correct her. "Who is? I don't see anything."

Suddenly Mariana stood right beside him. Her unexpected appearance startled Thomas. She extended one glimmering arm toward the middle of the horizon and pointed at something almost indiscernible and far, far away.

It was another ship.

His heart sank. "Mariana, I'm begging you not to do this, there has to be another way. I don't want to be responsible for the death of these people."

"What are you talking about? You're not killing anyone, the sirens are," Mariana said as though it were a simple solution.

"Isn't there something else we can do?" he asked desperately.

"Nope!"

Thomas broke away from Mariana and began to wander around the ship, looking for something else to solve this problem. A pile of rope near the stern caught his eye, and for a brief moment, he believed that he could fix the damage. He quickly disregarded the thought and continued searching, becoming increasingly panicked as the ship on the horizon grew larger.

Finally, a lifeboat caught his eye. He ran to Mariana, who eagerly watched the approaching ship.

"What if I took one of the lifeboats instead? It's a working boat that only needs one person to operate. I don't need an entire ship."

Mariana watched him closely for a moment before throwing her head back to cackle into the air. Thomas crossed his arms. When she finished laughing, she said, "Do you *want* to die, Felix?"

"I get the feeling you haven't been listening to me," Thomas said as she continued to laugh.

BLACKWATER ACADEMY

The school courtyard bustled with activity on an early Thursday afternoon. Most students chose to study outside on rare sunny days like this one, but Thomas found the noise too distracting. One look at the crowded yard sent him right back inside to find a quieter place to study. He settled for the floor inside a quiet hallway with little traffic. This hallway held most of the classes he attended, but the students in his year had their break at the moment, which meant it would be empty. He chose the best spot in the hall, just beneath an open window.

Thomas cracked open a fresh book, eager to get his reading out of the way for the week. The book was titled *Eternality*, a story about a man who wastes his life searching for the secret to eternal youth. Why would anyone waste their time in search of *more* time? He unsuccessfully read the first paragraph four times before the sound of a door's latch clicking into place echoed through the hallway, breaking him from what little concentration he had managed. He instinctively looked toward to source of the noise, but the sound had come from an unseen hall around the corner. Thomas heard the hall's occupant before he saw him. The stranger sang somber lyrics, which Thomas had never heard before. His voice was well-practiced and pleasant. Thomas was surprised to see Charles Southworth round the corner.

Charles took a few steps in time with his song before he noticed Thomas and stopped. He stared blankly at Thomas for one long moment, and Thomas thought he saw a hint of embarrassment on Charles's face. His expression quickly darkened to accusatory anger. "What are you looking at?"

"You, obviously," Thomas said. He had been staring, but he couldn't help himself. It was rare to catch Charles in any mood except angry.

"Why?" Charles asked as he approached.

"I guess I'm just surprised to hear something pleasant come from your mouth."

Charles paused. "What is that supposed to mean?"

Thomas tossed *Eternality* to the side and stood up to face Charles without the disadvantage of being on the floor. "It's a compliment. You have a nice voice."

Charles pulled his silver cigarette case from his pocket and withdrew a cigarette, lighting it as he scrutinized Thomas. "Are you making fun of me?"

"No. I'm not rude like you."

Charles's perfect dark eyebrows twitched upward for a moment but quickly reverted to anger. "I'm not—" he stopped himself. "Why are you being nice to me? What are you doing?"

Thomas sighed. Why *was* he being nice to Charles? "I don't understand why you have it out for me. Have I done something to you?"

A thick cloud of smoke escaped Charles's mouth before he spoke. "You're a Hambleton, I'm a Southworth. We were born to hate each other."

"I don't hate you."

Charles surrendered his expression to complete surprise. "You don't?"

"Do you hate me?"

Charles tilted his head to the side and fixed his gaze on the ceiling as he considered the question. "No," he finally said after a great deal of thought.

Thomas offered him a small, brief smile before picking *Eternality* up from the floor. He leaned against the windowsill and attempted the first paragraph one more time, but Charles broke his concentration again. "Do you like to sing?"

Thomas shook his head. "I'm not a musician."

"That's not what I asked."

"No, I don't like to sing," Thomas said.

Charles watched Thomas for a moment as he inhaled from his cigarette. "What's your secret talent, then?"

Thomas scoffed. "If I have a secret talent, then it's been kept a secret from me as well."

"I don't believe that. Everyone is good at something."

"I'm good at being bad at everything."

Charles laughed, and Thomas was surprised to hear it. Until now, he had never had a pleasant exchange with Charles Southworth, and Thomas had just drawn a laugh from him. It was nice. "So you're funny," Charles said.

"Funny looking, maybe."

"You're not very nice to yourself, are you?" Charles asked.

"Why should I be? No one else is," Thomas said.

Charles frowned. He waited a long moment before speaking again. "I'm sorry."

Thomas suddenly felt very uncomfortable being pitied by Charles. He pretended to read his book again, suppressing a grimace as he stared at the dark crease down the book's center.

Footsteps echoed down the long hallway from the end of the

hall opposite the direction Charles had come from. Thomas and Charles looked toward the sound to find Professor Redmond, a notoriously strict professor at the school, approaching them. Her typical disappointed frown contorted her mouth. The moment she spotted the loitering students, her pace quickened.

"Mr. Southworth!" she yelled as she approached them.

Charles flinched and lowered his hands to his sides in an attempt to hide his cigarette. "Hello, Professor Redmond," he said with a relaxed grin.

"Put that out right now! You know better than to smoke on school grounds," she said.

"Yes, I know. I'm very sorry." Charles reached through the open window behind Thomas to put his cigarette out on the sill, leaning close to Thomas as he did so. Up close, Thomas could see that Charles's school uniform was the same quality as his own. Why did it look so much better on him? Charles made brief eye contact with Thomas as he leaned away. His eyes were dark amber flecked with gold.

"If you were already aware that you were breaking the rules, why would you allow yourself to continue? This is the third time I have spoken to you about your actions this month. I think it's time to contact your father, don't you?" the professor asked.

The fingers of Charles's right hand skimmed the cuff of his left sleeve. He wore a confident smile, but there was a faint glimmer of fear behind his brown eyes. The threat had shaken him, and Thomas knew why. Thomas had met Charles's father before, and he was not a nice man. Charles was probably in for something terrible. "Aw, come on professor. I don't get a fourth chance?" Charles asked.

Professor Redmond shot him a stern look. She did not think he was funny or charming.

"I gave it to him, Professor. I'm sorry," Thomas said.

The professor eyed Thomas suspiciously. "Give me your bag,"

she demanded. Thomas reached to the floor where his book bag sat and handed it to her. She ripped it open and aggressively rifled through its contents. As quickly as she had started, she stopped. "Shame on you, Mr. Hambleton." She pulled a box of matches from the bag and dropped the bag to the floor again. It seemed to be enough evidence for her. "You know better. I'm confiscating this. If I see either of you smoking on school grounds one more time *both* of your families will be hearing from me." She paused to give them each one last deadly glare over her spectacles before continuing down the hallway again.

Charles sighed a breath of relief. "Why did you do that?"

Thomas shrugged. "I would hate to see you get sent home over something as simple as smoking in the hallway. Especially on the day we finally set aside our differences." He smiled weakly.

Charles scoffed. "I wasn't aware that we had."

Thomas raised an eyebrow at him. "You owe me a box of matches."

Charles reached inside the pocket of his coat and retrieved a box identical to the box that had just been taken from Thomas. "Why do you need matches, anyway? I've never seen you smoke," he asked as he handed the box over.

Thomas shrugged. "I don't smoke."

Charles shot him a suspicious look. "Right, well... Thanks, Hambleton."

"You're welcome, Charles."

PANTHEA SEA

The sound of scratching at the hull slowly quieted as the new ship approached. Thomas didn't want anything to do with

Mariana's horrible plan, but there was nothing he could do to stop her. He had tried calling after the sirens to get them to come back and briefly thought about jumping into the water to distract them. The moment Thomas realized they couldn't be stopped, he hid in the captain's cabin and covered his ears so that he wouldn't have to witness it again.

After an eternity of waiting, Mariana's voice broke through the silence he had been fighting to maintain. "It's over, Felix. You can look now," she said with the cheerful voice of someone who hadn't just murdered thirty men.

Slowly, he crept back outside to peek at the aftermath of the siren's attack. An empty ship slowly drifted closer. The sirens seemed satisfied now and did not return to Thomas's ship. He let out a heavy sigh and stood up on shaky legs, preparing himself to board the other ship. There was no point. It would be impossible for him to sail it alone.

The two ships made contact with a loud crack and stayed together by an unseen force. The ships should have been damaging each other, but instead, they floated together as though they were docked in still waters. It must have been Mariana's doing. Thomas looked to where Mariana had been standing to find that she was gone. He took one glum look around his old ship before climbing aboard the new one.

His feet hit the boards of the deck with a clumsy thud, and he looked up to find himself on a much different ship. He turned around to compare the two only to find that they were already drifting apart. His heart sank when he turned his attention back onto the new ship. This ship was just as familiar to him in ten seconds as the last one had been in two months. He was on a Hambleton ship.

Every Hambleton ship was decorated from bow to stern with the emblem of the Hambleton shipping company. There wasn't a place on this ship Thomas could look to avoid seeing it. Painted onto the center of the mainsail was a dark crimson "H" behind the black silhouette of a crow. Thomas suspected the Hambletons' bad reputation came partially from their lack of humility.

Thomas cautiously approached the center of the deck. It appeared he was the only person left aboard the large cargo ship. The loss of the crew was very disturbing, but a very small part of him was relieved. If anyone on this crew saw him, there was a chance they would recognize him. He wasn't sure how high that chance was, but it was there.

A cold gust of wind blew over his damp clothes and he shivered. He quickly made his way out of the cold breeze and into the captain's quarters, knowing that the captain always had spare clothes. The door hung open, swinging along with the bobbing of the waves. He gently pulled it open and walked in. At the center of the room was a table built into the floor with a map of the world lying on top. To his right was a small bed, also built into the ship, big enough for one person. A circular porthole window dusted the room in dim sunlight from above the bed. The somber interior reminded Thomas of the room's previous occupant, who was probably dead. Thomas tried to shake the thought away by turning his attention to a wide chest at the left side of the room. Despite his grief, he didn't hesitate to raid it.

The captain was a larger man than Thomas, and understandably so. Thomas had always been slim and could never quite catch up to his peers regarding his height. He was only seventeen years old, at least half the age of most ship captains. Thomas managed to put together an outfit that was much too large for him, but still much warmer than the seasoaked clothes he had been wearing. The one thing he hated most about living at sea was being perpetually damp. There was nothing he could do to stay dry. It didn't seem to bother the other sailors, but sometimes Thomas felt like the sea targeted him.

He stepped back onto the deck much warmer than before, wondering what he was supposed to do now. Mariana was still away and there was no way he could sail this giant ship alone. Did Mariana know that? He recalled telling her, but he also remembered telling her many things that she had promptly forgotten. She might have forgotten about him entirely. His old ship was already a speck on the horizon. Mariana was either moving the ship on her own, or it was stuck in a strong current. The difference between the two concepts wasn't very clear.

Since Mariana had not shown herself to give him any more instruction, he made his way toward the main hatchway that led below. This lower deck was where the crew slept and ate and did anything but work. Rolled-up bundles of fabric hung bolted between two points, one on the wall and one on a support beam, where the sailors would sleep and store their belongings. He meandered through the space of dead men, carefully looking at their things, but respectfully leaving them alone as if they were still alive to know that Thomas had messed with their stuff.

He made his way down another level to the cargo hold, which was filled with dozens of stacked boxes. The smell immediately told him that they were carrying tobacco. Great. He had hoped that this ship would be full of something useful, but unlike his fake name indicated, he was not that lucky.

"Hello?" a muffled voice from behind him called out. Thomas jumped.

He wasn't alone.

"Hello?" he called back.

No response. He wondered again if he was hallucinating. He thought about how strange it would be for this to be the hallucination and not the giant woman made of water.

"Hello?" he asked again, pushing open the door behind the hatchway stairs. It was the brig.

The brig was a narrow room lined with smaller rooms

protected by vertical bars. This ship had an unusually high number of cells. Thomas counted eight. There were rarely more than three on an average ship, especially a merchant ship. "Is there someone here?" he asked. He heard harsh whispering at the other end of the room and slowly walked toward the sound. The last two cells at the end of the room were occupied.

To his right was a young woman, probably a few years older than him, sitting against the far wall with her elbows on her knees. She had long, bright orange hair pulled back into a frizzy ponytail and a light spatter of freckles across her pale face. Her dark brown eyes watched him with curiosity. She appeared to have been dressed for colder weather but she had removed some of the layers, which were now in a pile in one corner of her cell.

To his left was another woman, maybe ten years older than him. She stood tall with her arms crossed. She glared at him with a ferocity stronger than any look he had ever received. Her eyes were the deep golden yellow of a fire and just as fiercely hot. Her straight, dark hair fell down both sides of her face, coming to a point just below her chin, which she held high as she scrutinized Thomas. She was tall, which added to her intimidating aura. Everything she wore was dark crimson, which complemented her tawny sun-kissed skin tone. Unlike her companion, she was dressed for hot weather, which exposed her strong muscles. He couldn't imagine how anyone managed to imprison her.

Thomas didn't know what to say. There were so many questions running through his mind but he couldn't settle on any of them. He took too long, and the tall woman spoke first. "Well?" she asked. That was a good first question. It was vague.

"Are you all right?" he asked. The two women exchanged puzzled glances.

"Who are you?" the sitting girl asked, leaning forward. Her words were cloaked in a familiar accent. Thomas quickly realized she was from Dufonn. That explained the warm clothing.

"My name is–" He stopped, thinking that he shouldn't use his real name on a Hambleton ship. "Felix," he said quickly, trying to make up for the lost time he spent considering the lie. The tall woman raised one suspicious eyebrow. Before she could interrogate him, he asked, "Who are you?"

The women exchanged the same puzzled look one more time. The tall woman didn't say anything, but the sitting girl stood up and approached the bars of her cell. "My name is Fiona."

Thomas nodded once at Fiona, then turned to the other woman. "And you?"

The woman continued glaring at him but said nothing.

"That's Faya. She just got here," Fiona said.

Faya exhaled forcefully. She probably didn't want to share her name with him. He sympathized with her. "What happened?" Fiona asked. "We heard singing, and scratching, and a lot of splashing. And then nothing."

Thomas grimaced and scratched his head, silently cursing Mariana. "Sirens."

"Sirens?" Fiona asked. "Why didn't they get you?"

Thomas shrugged. "I guess I'm immune." It felt like a lie.

"Oh, wow. That's lucky," Fiona said.

Thomas politely smiled, thinking about how this was probably the second worst day of his life and he had been called lucky twice. The day wasn't even over yet. "Can I help you out of those cages?" he asked. He couldn't leave them in their cells, especially not when he lacked a crew.

"Why would you do that?" Faya's voice pounced from the left. Her voice carried with it the intonations and sharp edges of another language. Thomas could almost place the accent, but it escaped him at that moment.

"*Faya!*" Fiona hissed. "I think what she meant to say was *yes.*" Fiona smiled sweetly at Thomas.

"Where are the keys?" he asked.

"One of the crewmen always had them on his belt..." Fiona trailed off. The crewmen weren't around anymore. "Maybe he left them somewhere?"

Thomas sighed, knowing better than to rely on hopeful optimism. "The captain usually has spares. I'll be right back."

Chapter Three

Blackwater Academy

It was a cold morning, and it had been a particularly hard one for Thomas to pull himself out of bed. As he filed into the dining hall with his classmates, he was aware that his sloppy appearance made him stick out from the crowd. His classmates threw casual glances his way, but he knew they would eventually stop as the year went on. Thomas always looked a little disheveled. He shuffled to an almost empty table and fell into a seat. Two other students chatted at the other end, but they didn't seem to notice Thomas at all.

Thomas yawned and used his arm as a pillow in an attempt to get a few more moments of rest before the day began. The events of the previous day played back in his head for the hundredth time. Somehow, he had managed to strike up an unlikely acquaintanceship with his longtime adversary, Charles. Thomas wondered briefly if Charles was in the dining hall yet and lifted his head to check the tables behind him.

Sure enough, Charles occupied his regular seat, chatting with his usual group of friends. Charles made talking to people look easy, but Thomas had never found that to be the case. Thomas admired the way Charles composed himself, from his casual hand gestures to the expression on his face as he talked. Charles had a natural charisma that Thomas lacked, and Thomas envied him for it.

For reasons that Thomas didn't understand, he always seemed to know where in the room Charles was. Maybe it was the wariness he had been trained to feel around a Southworth, but that reason didn't feel right to Thomas. He might have been more uncomfortable with the feeling if he hadn't suspected that Charles had the same sense for him too. On the first day of classes, Charles shot Thomas a dirty look without even searching the classroom for him. Thomas thought a lot about how Charles had already known where to look. He thought about the dirty look, too.

At that moment, Charles turned his attention away from his friend and locked eyes with Thomas. Thomas gave him a small smile and quickly turned back around. His face burned as he realized that he was thinking about how much he stared at Charles *while staring at Charles*. He rubbed his eyes and groaned quietly. This was exactly why he didn't have any friends.

After several agonizing moments of self-loathing, the bench creaked beside him with the weight of a new occupant. Thomas was too busy with his scornful inner monologue to look up.

"You're a bit of a loner, aren't you?" said the pleasant and familiar voice.

Thomas finally looked up at Charles sitting beside him. He quickly glanced at Charles's regular seat to make sure it was really him. Charles's comment wasn't funny, but Thomas couldn't help smiling in response. "Yeah. I try to make friends by staring at them from across the room, but it's never worked until today," Thomas said.

Charles laughed, and Thomas's smile grew wider. It wasn't often that someone laughed at something he said. To be ignored was usually the best response he could receive.

"That explains it. You have to talk to people if you want to be their friend," Charles said.

"I see. Is that why you're talking to me?"

Charles smiled. "Yes." Thomas felt a pleasant uneasiness shift inside him. Was it nausea? He couldn't tell. "You were right. We don't have a reason to hate each other except for our names. But that can end with us, right?"

Thomas nodded. "Absolutely. You probably can't tell by looking, but I've never cared much about my name."

Charles looked him over once. "I can tell."

Thomas frowned and fumbled with the buttons on his shirt, hurrying to fix the ones he had missed that morning.

"I think it's charming," Charles added. Thomas stopped fumbling with his clothes and stared miserably at Charles. He couldn't tell if Charles was making fun of him again. "I wish I had the courage not to care."

"I wouldn't call it courage," Thomas said. "I don't know what to call it. It's not good."

"Whatever it is, I like it. It looks good on you."

Thomas's smile returned along with the strange nausea. It had been a long time since Thomas smiled this much. He wasn't sure how to respond. He decided on an awkward, "Thank you." He continued to fumble with his shirt, suddenly very aware of his sloppiness. The contrast between himself and this handsome, well-groomed rich boy sitting next to him made Thomas feel more unkempt than usual.

"You're welcome." Charles paused. "By the way, I'm, um... *sorry* for the way I've treated you in the past." He spoke the second half of the sentence quietly like he didn't want anyone but Thomas to hear him. "It's hard to shake old biases."

"It's okay. Trust me, I get it."

"Yeah, you probably understand better than anyone," Charles said. "You should come sit at our table. I'll introduce you to everyone. You won't even have to stare at them from across the dining hall first."

Thomas laughed, but it was short-lived. He didn't know how well he could handle a large group of people he didn't know. "I don't think your friends like me very much."

Charles frowned at him. "Any dislike they have for you is completely my fault. They're quite nice." Thomas turned to look at Charles's friends as he considered the offer. All of them were watching Thomas and Charles with astonishment. Thomas quickly faced forward again. "Come on," Charles said as he stood up, pulling Thomas up with him.

Charles dragged Thomas across the dining hall. Everyone quietly watched them move through the room together. Charles took his regular seat again and pulled Thomas down to sit beside him. The bench had been crowded before Thomas arrived, and now it was packed. Thomas was squished between Charles and one of his friends. Charles wasn't bothered by it, but his friend seemed annoyed.

"Everyone, this is Thomas," Charles said, placing a hand on his shoulder. "We're friends now."

A brief silence passed over the table, and then, "*What?*"

Charles ignored the question. "Thomas, this is Louis, Walter, Roland, Jeremy, Francis, and Leonard."

Thomas didn't think he would ever remember any of their names. "Nice to meet you all," he said.

There was another longer silence.

"You're Thomas Hambleton, right?" asked Walter, who sat on Charles's other side.

"That's right," said Thomas.

"Why?"

Thomas scratched the side of his face, unsure how he was supposed to answer. "That's just the way I was born, I guess."

A couple of Charles's friends snickered at the answer. Thomas felt the familiar heaviness in his stomach that he felt when someone laughed at him. "He's funny, isn't he?" asked Charles. Suddenly the bad feeling was gone.

"Are you trying to piss off your dad?" asked Roland, who sat on Thomas's other side.

Charles shrugged. "What he doesn't know won't hurt him."

"He's always pissed off," said Thomas. His answer was met with more laughter.

"It's nice to officially meet you," said the boy who Thomas thought might be Jeremy. Thomas nodded at him.

"Can I ask you something, Thomas?" asked Walter.

"I guess so," said Thomas.

"Is it true that you–" Charles elbowed him before he could finish his question.

"*Walter*," Charles said.

"What?" Walter asked.

"You're going to get me in trouble," Charles whispered.

"I just want to know if it's true."

"*Stop.*"

Thomas watched the conversation unfold with pure bewilderment. After a tense moment of silence, Thomas cleared his throat. "I don't have the slightest idea what you were going to ask me, so the answer is probably no."

"Don't listen to him," Charles said with a smile. "He doesn't know anything."

"Probably because you don't let him ask any questions," said Thomas.

Walter laughed. Charles narrowed his eyes and smiled. "Trust me, it's not a question worth answering."

Thomas wanted to trust Charles, but he knew he shouldn't. It went against his instinct as a Hambleton. Thomas decided he was letting his paranoia get the best of him. The students at this school loved to pass around silly rumors, and they were almost always baseless accusations. Charles was probably just protecting him from hurtful gossip. It probably really wasn't worth answering.

Thomas shrugged. "Okay."

Charles raised his eyebrows and stared at Thomas.

"I'm sure there are a lot of stupid rumors about me. You're right. They aren't worth hearing," said Thomas.

Charles cleared his throat. "Yeah."

"Yeah, but they were all started by—" Walter began again.

"Walter, I swear to Dei if you don't stop talking right now..." Charles said.

Walter stopped talking.

"By you?" Thomas asked Charles.

Charles smiled guiltily. Thomas laughed at him.

"You're not angry?" Charles asked.

Thomas shrugged. "If we're going to be friends, we're going to have to learn to forgive each other."

"Wow," said Charles. "Are you sure you're a Hambleton?"

Thomas laughed. "Unfortunately, I am."

PANTHEA SEA

It had taken longer than he thought it would, but Thomas finally found the spare set of keys hidden in the captain's cabin. As he once again approached the brig, he could hear Faya and Fiona arguing with each other, but he couldn't understand them through the wall. They fell silent when he entered the brig. He quietly walked to the back of the room where their cells were located.

Fiona and Faya were pressed up against the bars of their cells. Whatever they had been talking about must have been very captivating. They watched him apprehensively. He lifted the ring of keys and lazily jingled them to show that he had found them but got no reaction from either of them. Faya's gaze burned a hole in the side of his head, so he decided to unlock her cell first. He quickly realized his mistake.

The moment she was free, Faya grabbed the keys from him and pushed him into her cell, locking him inside. It happened so fast Thomas didn't have time to react or to understand what had happened to him until he was staring at her from the other side of the cell door.

In hindsight, he probably should have asked them why they were in the brig.

"Why did you do that? I was trying to help you," Thomas said.

Faya scowled at him. "I don't believe that you were doing that out of the kindness of your heart. If you were on the crew of this ship, you don't have a heart." She turned to help Fiona out of her cell.

For a moment Thomas considered telling the truth, that he was from another ship and had come aboard this one with the help of a god, but he didn't think that would go over well.

Fiona joined Faya outside her cell, watching Thomas with fretful curiosity.

"I'm sorry for whatever the crew did to you," Thomas said. "I really am." Although he wanted to earn their trust, he meant what he said. He knew that he was partially responsible for the actions of anyone who worked on a Hambleton ship because he was a Hambleton himself. There was obviously no escaping it.

"But?" Faya asked.

"What?" Thomas asked, not sure what she meant.

Faya narrowed her eyes at him. "You're a strange young man."

Thomas sighed. "I know." He sat on the floor and rested his elbows on his knees, staring at his feet. After a prolonged moment of silence, the latch to his cell clicked. Thomas peered up at them through the open door.

"I thought you were a threat but you're just..." Faya tilted her head. "You're just a kid."

Thomas had not expected such a docile remark. It was refreshing to hear, even if she hadn't meant it as a compliment. Thomas stood up. Fiona and Faya watched him carefully. "Thank you," he said quietly.

Without another word, Thomas slipped out of the cell and squeezed past them. They followed him to the top deck of the ship, where they happily bathed themselves in the sunlight that they had probably been missing for many days.

Mariana waited for him at the center of the deck. Thomas looked at Fiona and Faya to gauge their reactions to this strange blue woman, but they did not seem to care that she was there.

"Who are these people?" Mariana asked.

"Prisoners," Thomas said. "They survived because they were locked up, but they probably would have survived anyway."

Mariana watched Fiona happily admire the sea from the starboard side of the ship. Faya had escaped out of sight somewhere. "Why?" Mariana asked.

"Because they are women," he said.

"You aren't a woman and you survived," Mariana said.

"Thanks for reminding me," he said. "Where is this ship going?"

"I thought you knew how to sail," Mariana said.

Thomas sighed. He had been right about her disregard for his warnings. "I do, but sailing a ship of this size takes at *least* eight people, and that's the bare minimum. Eight people would be a struggle. *Like I said before*, I can't sail this ship on my own."

"Hey!" Fiona shouted at him. "Who are you talking to?"

Thomas turned his attention to Fiona, relieved that she had finally acknowledged Mariana. "This is Mariana, she's the god of the ocean," he said bitterly, remembering how he hadn't believed it at first.

Fiona slowly approached, her eyes darting back and forth between him and the space in front of him. "What?"

"I don't know how else to explain it. She is the sea, but she looks like a human," he said, looking Mariana over again.

Fiona gave a polite laugh. "There's nobody there, Felix."

Mariana grinned at Thomas. He narrowed his eyes and considered for the millionth time that day if Mariana was a hallucination. Maybe he had lost his mind. Fiona clearly thought so. There was no way he could have boarded this ship without Mariana's help, so he decided he wasn't hallucinating. Fiona just couldn't see her.

Lying would be just as useless as telling the truth, so he chose the truth. "I guess you can't see her," he said. As soon as he finished speaking he regretted his honesty.

"Okay," she said. She threw him a skeptical look before wandering off to find Faya.

"What was that about?" Thomas asked. "Why can't she see you?"

Mariana giggled with a voice full of bubbles. "She's not helping me. I don't need her to see me."

"Okay, but now she thinks I'm insane, and she's going to tell Faya and they are both going to ostracize me."

Mariana shrugged. "Oh well. So you were saying you don't have enough people to sail?"

Thomas glared at her, growing more annoyed by the second. "*Yes.*"

"Why didn't you tell me that before? You will have to figure something out. I can't help you."

Thomas sighed heavily. There was no way to explain to her that it wasn't possible. Without her help, he would just die. His life was insignificant to this ancient deity. She knew she could just find someone else, but would she? She didn't seem to understand the sirens well enough to know who to look for. Even if she did, how often would she come across someone like him?

If he didn't find a way to get this ship going, he would die, and the mermaids would die too, and the rest of the planet would suffer for it.

He had to get this ship sailing.

BLACKWATER ACADEMY – FIVE MONTHS EARLIER

It was a cool afternoon on the grounds of Blackwater Academy. A chilly breeze rustled the leaves of trees and pushed the blades of grass into a steady sway. Thomas meandered around the small lake at the edge of the school grounds. Other students sometimes swam in the lake on the weekends when it was warm, but Thomas had the lake to himself on this breezy evening.

The sun had started to set, setting the thin layer of clouds alight with peachy tones. It was beautiful, but Thomas preferred to watch the sunset from the reflections that flashed against the ripples on the water's surface. The reflections in the water were much more beautiful than their material counterparts. He leaned over the water at the shore to look at his reflection, which he always thought to be the exception to the water's beauty.

Thomas turned away from the lake, getting the strange sense that the water was disappointed to see him. Across the swaying lawn was the familiar shape of Charles, who left a thin trail of smoke behind him as he walked in Thomas's direction. Thomas usually preferred to be alone, but lately, he found that he didn't mind having company, as long as that company was Charles.

"What are you doing out here? I've been looking everywhere for you," said Charles as he walked up, flicking the butt of his cigarette into the water.

"Why?"

Charles shrugged. "I wanted to talk to you."

"Is something wrong?"

Charles smiled at Thomas before shifting his gaze across the water. "No. I just think you're better company than the rest of the morons at this school."

Thomas raised his eyebrows. He was surprised to hear Charles talk negatively about his peers. "What about your friends?"

Charles waved a hand in the air dismissively. "Oh please. They don't care about me. They just like me because I have money."

Thomas stared at Charles, at a loss for words.

"That's why they hang around you too, by the way," Charles added.

"You don't really believe that, do you?" asked Thomas.

Charles smirked at Thomas. "Not only do I believe it, I *know* it's true. I've heard them talking when they thought I couldn't hear."

"That's very sad."

Charles shrugged. "That's why I wanted to talk to *you*."

Thomas got the same strange nauseous feeling that he had been struggling with ever since befriending Charles. "Now you know where I go to be alone."

Charles smiled at Thomas, then looked out across the water again. "So," Charles said, "now that it's just the two of us, tell me about your life back home."

Thomas felt queasy at the personal nature of Charles's request. There was something about being alone with Charles that made Thomas feel special in a way he had never felt before. "What would you like to know?"

"Do you have a girlfriend?" asked Charles, watching Thomas closely.

Thomas was surprised at the question, both at its private nature and the quickness with which Charles had asked it. "A girlfriend?"

Charles nodded.

"I've never really been interested in... that," Thomas said.

"Really?"

"Do you have a girlfriend?" Thomas asked.

"No, not anymore. She broke up with me over the summer," Charles said.

"She broke up with *you*?" Thomas asked.

Charles gave him a sly smile. "You sound surprised."

"I am surprised. I would have thought you would be the one ending relationships," Thomas said.

"Oh? Why is that?"

"Well, because–" Thomas hesitated. He didn't know *why* he thought that, but it seemed obvious. Charles was handsome, smart, funny, charming, and rich. "Because you're rich," he said.

"Hmm..." Charles said with a frown. "Well, you may not be interested in dating, but I bet you've got girls lined up to try."

Thomas laughed. "Are you kidding? Me? No."

"Why do you say that?"

"I'm ugly and awkward. Girls don't like me."

This time Charles laughed. "That is completely untrue. You are the most handsome boy in this entire school. And I think you're very charming."

Thomas's face warmed. His heartbeat was audible. "Thanks," he mumbled, "but I think you left yourself out of that ranking."

"Oh, you think I'm handsome?"

"It's not a matter of opinion..." said Thomas. His scattered mind prevented him from finishing his thought.

"Are you telling me it's an objective truth that I am handsome?" Charles asked with a grin.

"Y-yes."

Charles looked very pleased with himself. "That's quite a compliment."

Thomas stared at his feet and said nothing. The conversation was harmless, but Thomas had the feeling that he was doing something wrong. Of course, the act of talking to Charles Southworth itself would get him in trouble, but that wasn't what bothered him. He bit his lip as he thought about it.

"Is everything all right?" Charles asked.

Thomas brought himself back to reality and looked up into Charles's hazel eyes. The sight sent a strange sensation from his stomach through his heart. He turned away again. "I, um..." Thomas cleared his throat. "Do you ever feel like..."

"Yes?"

Thomas shook his head. "Never mind."

"That's not fair. You can't start a question and then back out halfway through. You have to tell me."

Thomas scoffed. "I don't have to tell you anything, Southworth."

Charles crossed his arms and threw an amused glare at Thomas. "Fine, then I'll go back to my dorm." He began to walk away.

Thomas laughed. "Okay, enjoy your dull conversation with the other 'morons.'"

Charles stopped walking and turned around. "Come with me."

Thomas pretended to think hard about the invitation. "All

right, but I was going to leave anyway. It's not because I want to talk to you."

Charles rolled his eyes. "Shut up," he said. "You love me." As Thomas walked beside Charles, Charles slung his arm around Thomas's shoulders. Thomas *did* like Charles, more than he probably should have. The smell of cigarette smoke was strong on Charles's clothes, but Thomas didn't mind. He was starting to love it.

Chapter Four

Faya and Fiona chatted at the bow of the ship, while Thomas struggled to find a solution to the problem. How could he sail this ship with only three people? It was impossible, and Mariana was no help.

Faya and Fiona spoke to one another discreetly, and Thomas suspected he knew what they were talking about. He headed to the bow to join them before they said too much.

Their conversation fell quiet as he climbed the stairs. Thomas tried to smile at them, but he had forgotten how. His smile felt like a grimace. He decided to stick to comfortable stoicism after receiving uncomfortable smiles in return. "We're going to be spending a lot of time together on this ship until we dock, and I'm afraid we got off to a rocky start. Can we try again?" he asked.

Faya and Fiona looked at each other and then back at Thomas. Neither of them spoke.

Thomas reached his hand out to Fiona first. He was wary of

Faya after the incident in the brig. "My name is Felix. I'm from Tinera. Where are you from?"

Slowly, Fiona reached out her hand and shook Thomas's. She gave him a polite smile and said, "I'm from Dufonn." It wasn't anything he didn't already know, but it was a start.

Thomas turned to Faya and offered his hand for her to shake. Faya didn't acknowledge it. "Where are you from, Faya?" Thomas asked, dropping his hand back to his side.

"Chratan," she replied. He tried not to look surprised, and he shouldn't have been. Everything about Faya told him that she was Chratanian. The origin of her accent was suddenly obvious. It fit inside his mind like a missing piece to the puzzle that was Faya.

"Right," Thomas said.

Faya cocked her head to the side and narrowed her eyes.

An awkward silence passed between the three of them while Thomas tried to decide what to say next. "If you don't mind me asking, why were the two of you in the brig?" It might not have been an appropriate time to ask, but it seemed important.

Fiona gave a short, curt laugh. "Are you serious? There's no way you don't know who we are if you were a crew member of this ship."

Thomas scratched his head and looked past them at the horizon. "I'm not from this ship."

Faya's skepticism bled onto Fiona's face. "I don't believe that at all," Fiona said.

Thomas shrugged. "It's true. Both of our ships got stranded in the same area and I was lucky enough to board this one instead. I was on a Southworth ship." Thomas tried not to cringe at the name *Southworth*.

"Southworth?" Faya asked, throwing a look at Fiona.

Thomas frowned. There were too many ways to explain that name, but he didn't think they wanted to hear his definition. "It's a..." Every definition of the name battled in his mind until the simplest one finally escaped. "Shipping fleet."

"I *know* who the Southworths are," Faya said.

Fiona spoke up, trying to ease the tension between Faya and Thomas. "It doesn't matter. If he doesn't know why we were in the brig, he doesn't know." She didn't wait for Faya to respond, instead turning to address Thomas. "We are magi. We were arrested and sent away from home."

Thomas took a cautious step backward. "You're magi?"

Fiona tilted her head and frowned.

Faya scowled at him. "Is that a problem?"

"Um, no—I just, uh..." Thomas stammered. It *was* a problem, but he couldn't say that to her. He was not comfortable being alone with two magi. They could have been arrested for anything.

"Really? You seem nervous." Faya took a step forward. Thomas took another step back.

Fiona grabbed Faya's arm. "Faya, stop. He is uncomfortable. This isn't helping anything. This is exactly *why* people are scared of us."

Faya whipped around to face Fiona. "Why, Fiona? Because they try to kill us and then get angry when we retaliate? I don't know about you, but I have never hurt anyone with magic. I hardly ever *use* my magic."

Fiona watched Faya carefully for a moment before speaking. "You're right, but he's right too. We are stuck on this ship together and we need to do our best to get along despite our differences." She paused. "He *did* release us from the brig."

Faya slowly faced Thomas again and looked into his wide eyes with deep disgust. "He wouldn't have released us if he knew we were magi."

Thomas leaned back against the edge of the ship, which Faya had backed him into. He crossed his arms. "Of course I would have." Thomas had saved Faya and Fiona without question, and now they were mad at him for the same reason. "If you're magi, why couldn't you get out of the brig on your own?"

Fiona furrowed her brow and smiled. "Are you joking?"

Thomas shrugged. "No."

"The cells are magic-proofed," Fiona said. "We could have easily overtaken the ship if they weren't. Right, Faya?"

"Right," Faya answered without looking at either of them.

Fiona's answer scared Thomas, but he tried to put aside his fear of magic for the sake of their journey. "Wow, that's... good for you."

Faya scoffed and shook her head. "We may share this space, but we *do not* have to be friends," she said, clenching her fists tightly at her side. "You will never understand what it feels like to have your entire life thrown away by someone you love, all for something entirely out of your control." Her voice broke at the end of her speech, and she took a step back. Her hands uncurled slowly. The air around them lit up as small flames rolled off her fingertips. Thomas tried not to stare.

Faya took off to the other side of the ship, leaving Fiona and Thomas alone together. Thomas stood glued to one spot, unable to do anything but watch Faya leave. Small flames continued to ignite from her fingertips and roll up her forearm before disappearing at her elbow. Thomas had never seen anything like it in his life.

As she walked away, Thomas could only think that they were much more alike than she thought. He knew exactly how that felt.

BLACKWATER ACADEMY – FOUR MONTHS EARLIER

Charles Southworth struggled to focus during Professor Franklin's monotonous lecture on the history of Brenton. He was already familiar with the history of his hometown, so it didn't matter much. Instead, his attention was stuck on Thomas, who completely ignored the lesson altogether.

Thomas was also from Brenton, and one of the top students at Blackwater, so he didn't need to pay attention either. Instead, he doodled on the paper in front of him. Charles wished he could see what Thomas was drawing. It was probably something weird because Thomas was a little weird. Charles was fascinated with him. He didn't know why he had spent all these years taunting Thomas when Thomas was the most interesting person in the entire school.

Charles and Thomas had grown very close in the first couple of months of the term. They spent all of their free time together, and they tried to spend as much school time as possible together. Charles wished he could sit closer to Thomas in class, but the seat they had taken on their first day had become their permanent seat.

Professor Franklin snapped Charles out of his academic neglect by asking the class a question. "What is the population of Brenton?" The professor focused on Thomas before anyone could offer an answer. He had spotted Thomas's inattention. "Mr. Hambleton?"

"Huh?" Thomas asked, quickly looking up and straightening his posture. "Yes?"

"I'm waiting for an answer." The professor would not repeat the question.

Charles felt a smile creep onto his face. The rest of the class snickered at Thomas as he stared straight ahead and tried to figure out what the question was. Charles laughed with them.

The professor faced Thomas, waiting patiently for him to answer. Charles sat behind the professor, outside his line of sight. Thomas caught Charles laughing and narrowed his eyes. Charles raised his hand to spell out the answer for Thomas. He extended his fingers to show the number two, then closed them together in a circle to create a zero, then mouthed the word *thousand*.

Judging by the look on his face, Thomas didn't get it. "Twenty," he said.

Charles covered his mouth in an effort to stop the laughter. The rest of the class was not as successful.

"The population of Brenton is twenty? Are you sure?" Franklin asked.

Thomas stared at Professor Franklin with his mouth hung open. "I meant twenty-thousand. Isn't that what I said?"

"No," the professor said as he turned to glance in Charles's direction. Thomas had gotten a wrong answer from somewhere, but Charles's laughter absolved him of guilt. Professor Franklin turned toward Thomas again. "Pay attention, Mr. Hambleton."

Thomas nodded. When the professor turned away, Thomas threw an amused scowl in Charles's direction and mouthed the word *thanks*.

Charles grinned and winked at him in response. Thomas's smile grew wider and he averted his eyes, but Charles kept his gaze on Thomas. What did it mean? Why would Thomas respond that way?

After class, Charles met up with Thomas in the hallway. "Twenty people? Really, Hambleton?" Charles asked as Thomas approached him at their usual spot by the window.

Thomas rolled his eyes with a reluctant smile. "I'm beginning to suspect you don't know my first name."

"Of course I do. It's Timmy."

Thomas raised his eyebrows and stared at Charles like he couldn't tell if he was joking.

Charles laughed. "I'm kidding. I know your name, Toby."

"You're stupid," Thomas said, laughing with him.

When the laughter died down, Charles said, "Hey, um..." but he stopped when the rest of the words wouldn't follow. Thomas patiently watched him struggle. "Can we talk later? Alone?" Charles glanced around the hall wondering if anyone heard the stupid way he had asked the question. There was nothing wrong with being alone with Thomas, except that Charles could get in a lot of trouble if the wrong people found out. "I'll meet you at the Eastern perimeter of the school grounds," he added.

Thomas's face fell. He watched Charles carefully. "You can't talk to me right now?"

Charles frowned and glanced around the hall one more time, stuffing his hands inside his coat pockets to hide his nerves. "No," he said, smiling at Thomas again. "Why? Do you have plans tonight?"

Thomas rolled his eyes and smiled. "I'll be there."

"Great, I'll see you then." Charles grinned at Thomas, but it quickly fell away when he turned to leave. He had been trying not to think about having this conversation. It would be hard, but it was necessary. Charles hoped Thomas would understand.

PANTHEA SEA

Faya, Fiona, and Thomas did not get along as Thomas had hoped. The three of them stayed as far away from each other as the ship would allow. Faya tried to calm herself at the stern while Fiona sat at the base of the mast. Thomas stayed where they had left him. He leaned over the side of the ship and stared into the deep sea, resting his head in his hands. His attempt to mend things with Faya had only made everything worse. He had no idea what to do.

Thomas needed to ask Faya and Fiona how much they knew about sailing, but his last attempt to talk to them hadn't gone well. He wasn't eager to try that again, but if he didn't, they would all be stuck on this ship going nowhere. The sun had started to set on the horizon, leaving bright orange streaks of light across the inky sea. It would be dark soon. Time was running out.

He took a deep breath and slowly exhaled before proceeding to the middle of the deck where Fiona sat. She sat quietly with her eyes closed, legs crossed, and her back against the mast. Thomas wasn't sure if she knew he was there. Without opening her eyes, she smiled and said, "Hi, Felix."

Thomas stared at her in silent awe. How could she know it was him? Then again, who else could it be? Faya wouldn't have willingly spoken to either of them. "Hello, Fiona," he said, dropping himself to the floor beside her at a safe distance.

"Is something wrong?" Fiona opened her eyes and watched him carefully.

Thomas struggled to find a polite way to pose the question. "Do you know anything about sailing?" he asked.

Fiona slowly looked around the ship, stopping at the mast that towered high above her. She looked at Thomas again. "I have never sailed a ship myself, but I've been on them and I know a few things."

"How much do you know?"

"Only the basics." She stood up, observing the jungle of ropes that stretched over them. "It doesn't matter how much I know about sailing without a crew, though."

"Yeah. I don't know how we're going to get back to land with only three people." He raked his fingers through his hair and tried to imagine how three inexperienced sailors could run a ship, but he only imagined running it aground.

"How many people do we need?" Fiona asked.

"At least eight. This ship is huge."

Fiona rubbed her chin. "I might be able to make something that can help us out." Her eyes drifted up to the dimming sky as she lost herself in thought.

Thomas didn't know what she could make that would take the place of a ship's crew. "What are you going to make?"

"An enchantment," Fiona said without losing focus.

Thomas had not been around very much magic in his life. Anyone who appeared to be a magus was run out of Brenton. He had always thought keeping magi away was necessary for the town's safety, but now that he had spoken to a few magi, he was starting to question that fear. So far he had met three magi, and none of them had tried to harm him in any way. The first magus he had ever met had helped him, and another was trying to help him at that very moment. But he still didn't trust magic. What if something went wrong?

Thomas's stomach turned as he realized magic was probably the only option. "What kind of enchantment?" he asked, not entirely sure what an enchantment was.

Fiona finally looked at him. Her gaze was invasive, as though she could read his mind. For all he knew, she could. "I may be able to get this ship to sail itself. I just need a few things to make it work. We probably have everything I need." She spoke with passion in her voice. Her focus returned inward as she stood up and made her way to the lower decks.

A self-sailing ship didn't seem terribly dangerous, and Fiona had just offered to fix his biggest problem with her magic. He let out a sigh of relief. So far Fiona had been smart, kind, and helpful. She wasn't scary.

Thomas watched the spot she had been sitting in, wondering what she had been doing before he interrupted her. He probably wouldn't have understood whatever it was.

A shadow fell over him. The strong, angry figure of Faya loomed above him. "Where is Fiona?" she demanded.

Thomas stood up to face her, forcing himself not to back away out of fear. Sitting on the floor beneath her made him feel very small. "She went below deck. I think she's looking for ingredients to make a..." He had forgotten the word already. "Enchancement."

Faya frowned at him. "Enchantment," she corrected him.

"Oh. Uh... Yeah." Thomas scratched his head and looked away.

Faya sighed and walked to the edge of the deck, watching the darkening sea with a somber frown on her face. This was the first time Thomas had seen her looking anything but angry. The wood creaked beneath his feet as he joined her at the side of the ship.

"Faya..." He paused, wondering if he should even try to talk to her again. He continued anyway. "I'm sorry about earlier... I've always thought magic was strange, but I'm starting to think someone lied to me. Every magus I've met has been nothing but helpful and kind." He paused again, remembering how Faya had not been helpful or kind to him, but he wasn't going to say that. Faya continued to stare at the sea. He couldn't tell if she was listening to him. "I'm not going to say I know how you feel because I don't know what you've been through, but I can say that I know what it's like to be mistreated by people I love for reasons beyond my control. That's why I'm out here, too."

Faya finally looked at him. "What happened to you?"

Thomas shook his head. He should have known the question was coming. It was stupid of him to bring it up if he didn't want her to know. "It doesn't matter."

She eyed him suspiciously, but to his relief, she didn't push it. He pulled the cigarette case from his pocket for the fourth time that day to find that he only had one cigarette left. If he was probably going to die soon anyway, why waste it? He pulled the final cigarette from the case and put it in his mouth. The matchbox came out next. It was lighter than usual. Upon opening it he found that it was empty. He pulled the cigarette out of his mouth and sighed.

"What's the matter?" Faya asked.

"I'm out of matches," Thomas said. Faya inspected the empty box like she had never seen a matchbox before. Maybe she hadn't. With a flourish of her hand, she produced a small flame that hovered just above her index finger. She held it out to him, and Thomas stared in awe. It was not fed by any energy but the energy from Faya. "Wow, thank you." He lit the cigarette with her fire.

"Anytime." She smiled at him. It surprised him. He hadn't thought she was capable of smiling. He smiled back as he inhaled the cigarette. All three magi he had met so far had been kind and helpful to him.

"Wow. I didn't think you were capable of smiling," Faya said.

Thomas laughed. It was one more thing they had in common.

Chapter Five

The sun hid behind the trees of the forest that surrounded the perimeter of the school. A cool afternoon shadow fell over the expansive lawn, framed by the illuminated treetops. Wet grass squished underfoot as Thomas walked the stretch of lawn that reached the eastern edge of the school grounds.

Thomas scanned his surroundings in search of Charles as he walked. He clenched his teeth to fight the nerves he felt. Why was he afraid to speak to Charles? He spoke to Charles every single day without issue, so why was this different? Maybe it was because Charles asked to talk alone. Every time Thomas thought about Charles's request to be alone, he got that pleasant nausea again. Maybe Charles had that feeling too. Maybe he would explain it to Thomas.

Finding Charles didn't take long. He was sitting on an old wooden fence that separated the school grounds from the forest. A long trail of smoke drifted toward the sky. His eyes were fixed on the yellow clouds. The usual smile he wore was nowhere to be seen, but there was an idle contentedness in his eyes.

Thomas had come close enough to smell the cigarette smoke before Charles caught sight of him. The absent smile quickly returned, and Thomas suspected it hadn't arrived voluntarily. "You made it!" Charles said as he hopped off the fence.

"Of course," Thomas said, unable to contain a smile of his own.

"Would you like a cigarette?" Charles offered, smoothly withdrawing his silver cigarette case from his coat pocket.

Thomas looked at the cigarette case. He had never noticed it until then, but the decoration was an engraving of a fox with a bird in its mouth. He frowned at the image and said, "No thank you." Charles shrugged and returned the case to his pocket. "What did you want to tell me?" Thomas asked.

Charles smirked at Thomas. "Right to business, huh?"

"Yeah, it's pretty cold out here. I don't understand why we had to come outside to talk," Thomas said. It *was* cold outside, but truthfully, the curiosity had been eating at him all day. He was dying to know what Charles had to say that was so special it warranted a meeting away from the school.

"It's not that cold out here," Charles said.

Thomas shivered. "I think I see ice forming on that fence post."

Charles turned to look at the post in question, lazily brushing rainwater from the top of it. "You must have superhuman vision."

"You must be blind."

Charles laughed. "I don't need eyes to feel how cold it is."

Thomas raised an eyebrow at him. "Yes, it *is* cold. Now tell me why we're out here so we can go back inside."

Charles's demeanor immediately switched from relaxed to uneasy. Whatever he was going to say was difficult for him, which was why he postponed it by pretending he wasn't cold when he was visibly shivering. Charles sighed. "Okay…" he hesitated, trying to find the right words. "Please don't take this the wrong way. I value the friendship we have, and I don't want to do anything to jeopardize it, but I think we both know that our friendship is unusual." Charles stared at the ground as he spoke.

"What do you mean?" Thomas asked. He didn't want to assume anything, but he thought he knew what Charles meant.

Charles looked at him. "We're not supposed to be friends. We're not supposed to like each other at all." Thomas did not understand until Charles spoke again. "My parents are visiting tomorrow."

Right. Their friendship was unusual because they were supposed to be enemies. Thomas got a sinking feeling in his stomach that he once again struggled to understand.

"Oh," Thomas said. "I see."

"I'm sorry, but while they're here I can't talk to you. If they knew that we spent *any* time together they would probably withdraw my enrollment from the school entirely. And we spend *all* of our time together." Charles looked away.

"I understand," Thomas said, but he didn't really. If he were in that situation, he wouldn't hide their friendship at all. Charles cared more about his parents' opinion of him than Thomas did.

"Thank you," Charles said. Thomas leaned against the wooden fence beside Charles and stared at nothing. Charles frowned at him. "Are you all right?"

"Oh, yeah…" he trailed off. "I guess I was just expecting you to say something else."

Charles gave a short laugh. "What were you expecting me to say?"

Thomas forced a smile. "I don't know," he said. There was a long silence before he spoke again. "Can I ask you something?"

"Of course."

"That first day I sat with you in the dining hall… Walter tried to ask me a question, but you wouldn't let him. What was he going to ask me?"

Charles glanced sideways at Thomas and then shrugged. "I don't know. It probably wasn't important."

Thomas narrowed his eyes at Charles. He knew that Charles's father, Alfred, was a notoriously good liar, but he wasn't sure if the same was true of Charles.

Thomas shook his head and sighed. He hated that he still thought about Charles as an adversary. Charles was his best friend. It was just as likely, if not more likely, that Charles simply didn't remember whatever stupid rumor he had started about Thomas. If he did, he was probably just too embarrassed to share it.

"That's too bad. I've been curious about that ever since it happened."

Charles nodded lazily. He squished the remainder of his cigarette against the wooden fence post. "You know what they say about curiosity."

"I'm not a cat."

Charles smirked at him. "I'll see you on Sunday, okay? Enjoy your Saturday, Hambleton." Without waiting for Thomas to reply, Charles walked away toward the school.

"Bye Charles," Thomas said, knowing that Charles was too far away to hear him.

Charles's reaction to Thomas's question had been very strange. Thomas stood alone for a long time, thinking about it. He had hoped that breaking it down in his mind would reveal that he was just paranoid, but he only managed to convince himself that Charles had lied to him. If Charles still felt the need to hide Thomas from his parents and lie to Thomas, then he still considered himself a Southworth before he considered himself Thomas's friend.

Thomas pulled his coat around his shoulders and shivered. It suddenly felt much colder outside.

PANTHEA SEA

Fiona soon returned to the upper deck with an armful of various items, none of which seemed to be related in any way. Among them was an empty glass bottle, a torn sheet of paper, a small burlap sack halfway filled with an unknown substance, and a tricorne hat. She sat in the middle of the deck and unloaded the contents of her arms to the floor before her, observing them in silence.

Thomas and Faya exchanged confused looks. Faya didn't know what Fiona had planned any better than Thomas did. "Should we offer to help her?" Thomas asked quietly.

Faya shook her head. Thomas wondered if talking would somehow disrupt Fiona's magic, so he remained quiet and still. It was painfully obvious he was the outsider here in the world of magic.

Eventually, Fiona opened the bag, and Thomas was surprised to see her scoop a handful of tobacco out of it. He had assumed that the bag contained some kind of magical substance. "You can come over here to watch if you'd like," Fiona said without looking up from her work.

Thomas and Faya glanced at each other before quietly approaching Fiona's workspace. They sat across from her and watched. Under the quickly dimming sunlight, Fiona began stuffing the tobacco inside the glass bottle. She paused halfway through to roll up the sheet of paper and push it carefully into the bottle, then she continued filling the bottle with tobacco until the paper was completely covered.

"What is the tobacco for?" Thomas asked.

"Tobacco is known for its stimulating properties. In witchcraft, it can be used for automation. We are very lucky that this ship is carrying so much of it," Fiona said.

"What was on the paper?" he asked.

Fiona smiled sadly. "I found it among the crew's personal belongings. It's a page from a journal. It doesn't matter what's written on it. It only matters that the person who wrote it knew a lot about sailing. Let's hope he did."

Thomas frowned. He had been trying very hard not to think about the fate of the ship's previous crew. "What about the hat?"

Fiona looked up from the bottle to glance at the hat. She seemed surprised at its presence. "Oh," she said, reaching for the hat. "I just thought it was neat." She placed it on her head. "How do I look?" she asked with a grin.

Faya shook her head. The hat looked very silly on Fiona, but she seemed happy to be wearing it. Thomas didn't say anything. Their negative reactions didn't faze Fiona and she immediately got right back to work, still wearing her ridiculous hat.

Fiona held the bottle in her hands, closed her eyes, and began speaking in a language that Thomas didn't recognize. Several of the tattoos on her arms emitted a faint white light while the rest remained a faded gray.

Tattoos? Thomas hadn't noticed them before that moment. How long had they been there? He could have sworn her arms were bare, but maybe he simply hadn't been paying attention. Symbols covered her arms, but Thomas didn't recognize any of them.

As soon as Fiona stopped talking, the boat creaked and stretched like it was waking up from a long sleep. Thomas watched in awe as the ropes moved on their own. The areas of the ship that usually required constant supervision operated smoothly without sailors. Fiona opened her eyes to grin at

Thomas and Faya. His astonishment must have been apparent because she laughed at him when he finally peeled his eyes away from the automated rigging to look at her.

"The only thing I can't help you with is navigation. Please tell me that one of you can navigate, because I can't," Fiona said.

"Sorry, no," Faya said.

"I know a little," Thomas said.

"Great!" Fiona said with a smile. "Navigate us to York, Dufonn!"

"No, no, no. We are going back to Chratan," Faya said. "We're only *two* days away, and I need to go back."

"I need to go home too!" Fiona said. "You think I don't have things I need to take care of? I've been on this ship longer than you!"

"We're closer to Chratan!" Faya argued.

"Why would you go back to a place that doesn't even want you?" Fiona asked.

"Why would *you?*" Faya asked.

"Because I need to find my brother," Fiona said. "I need to know what happened to him, and every day that passes decreases my chances of finding him."

"I have family too, Fiona. My daughter is only six years old. I can't leave home without her," Faya said.

Thomas's jaw dropped. *Faya had a daughter?* He shut his mouth before either of them could see his surprise. Faya did not seem the motherly type to him, but he would never tell her that.

Fiona crossed her arms and frowned at Faya.

"I am all she has left. Her father was taken by those horrible sea monsters," Faya said, gesturing to the water. "She is a magus like me. She could barely control her magic after we lost him. There's no way she can control it without me. Please," she begged, the anger on her face melting into grief.

"Your husband was taken by sirens?" Thomas asked without thinking.

Faya nodded. "Yes," she whispered. "Most of the men in my town were."

"*Most* of them?" Thomas asked.

Faya covered her face with one hand and turned away. Thomas quickly realized he had been more inquisitive than sympathetic.

"I'm so sorry, Faya," Fiona said.

"I'm sorry, Faya," Thomas added. "I didn't mean to upset you."

"I wish he had been immune like you, Felix. You're lucky," Faya said.

Thomas shook his head and looked away. She had no idea what she was saying. She wouldn't have wanted that. "I'm not lucky," he muttered, thinking about his fake name. It wasn't fitting, but Faya somehow wasn't the first to call him lucky that day.

When he looked up, Faya was watching him closely. They made eye contact, and he recognized a glimmer of understanding in her gaze. He looked away again. There was no way she knew what he meant. How could she know?

"All right, Faya. We'll go back to Chratan," Fiona said, "but as soon as we find your daughter, we're going straight to Dufonn."

Faya smiled. "Of course. Thank you."

"I'm sure your daughter is just fine," Thomas said.

Faya frowned and shook her head. "I hope you're right."

BLACKWATER ACADEMY

It was Saturday morning. Thomas had been instructed by Charles to stay away, but he was spiteful of those instructions.

Thomas meandered through the halls as he made his way to the dining hall, taking the scenic route. The sights weren't very interesting, but it was certainly better than sitting alone in his room all day.

Upon arrival at the dining hall, he sat at his usual table with Charles's group of friends. Charles did not care for them much, but Thomas thought they were all right. Only a few of them were seated at the table this morning. Everyone else was probably still asleep. Louis, Walter, and Roland greeted him warmly.

"Hey, Thomas! Rough night?"

Thomas smirked, "Shut up," he said. "You wish you looked this good in the morning." They laughed at him, but it quickly died down. They threw shifty glances at each other and averted their eyes. "What?" Thomas asked, suspecting that he already knew exactly what.

"Well, Charles told us that his parents were going to be here today, and, uh..." Roland started but looked at Walter for help.

Walter continued, "They hate you."

"Yes, they do," Thomas said.

"If they see you with us, they're going to know something is up," Louis said.

"I don't care," said Thomas.

A tense silence filled the space between them. "Thomas," said Walter, "can I ask you something?"

Thomas leaned forward, hoping that Walter would try to ask the question Charles had kept from him. Charles wasn't here to stop him. It was the perfect opportunity. "Yes," said Thomas.

"Why are you friends with Charles?"

Thomas leaned back again. "What?"

"He's a jerk. He's just using you," said Walter.

"He's after your money," said Roland.

"I don't think that's all he's after," said Louis. Everyone laughed.

Thomas scratched his head. He had no idea what they were talking about. "I don't understand."

"You haven't heard?" asked Walter.

"Obviously not," Thomas said, arching an eyebrow impatiently.

"Well, word around the school is that Charles's girlfriend dumped him over the summer because she caught him with another boy," said Roland.

Thomas stared at Roland. "She didn't want him to have other friends?"

"No. He was cheating on her, Thomas. He likes men."

Thomas stared wide-eyed at Roland for a long moment, and then he laughed. Walter, Roland, and Louis laughed with him, but their laughter was not the same.

"Are you saying that Charles wants to...?" Thomas trailed off, not knowing how to finish the question. "He wants... *me?*"

They laughed again at the question. "Yeah. If I were you, I'd stop hanging around him before he tries something," Roland said.

The conversation made Thomas feel nauseous, but he didn't think it was disgust. It was the same weird feeling he always had around Charles. Did he *want* Charles to try something? The thought of it made him feel queasy and all the other horrible, confusing feelings he had been having since he befriended Charles.

Could this be the answer?

"Wow," Thomas said as he stood up. "You guys are terrible friends."

"Where are you going?" asked Louis.

"Please don't say anything to Charles," said Roland.

Thomas shook his head and walked away. Charles was right about them. They *were* morons.

After that enlightening conversation, Thomas didn't feel quite so spiteful. He decided he would go back to his room to be alone for the rest of the day. He turned a corner in the main hall, only to find that he was too late. Three Southworths stood before him, two of them eyeing him judgmentally and the third desperately trying to hide his panic. The sight of Charles sent a surge of electricity through Thomas. How had it taken him so long to realize what it meant?

Charles's father, Alfred Southworth, was a tall, thin, and severe man. His dark piercing eyes commanded the attention of everyone who spoke to him. His black hair was parted neatly down the middle and fell lifelessly to either side of his head.

His mother, Lucille Southworth, was a quiet, sharp woman. Not only did she dress sharp, but one got the feeling that they would be cut if they looked at her too long. Her long chestnut hair fell over one shoulder and her narrow hazel eyes watched him carefully. It was obvious Charles got his good looks from his mother.

"Well, well, well," Alfred said. "What a surprise. Hello, Thomas."

Thomas nodded at him. "Mr. Southworth."

Thomas tried to walk past them to avoid more unpleasant small talk, but Alfred put a hand on his shoulder before he got too far. "Where are you going? Didn't you learn that it's rude to leave without saying goodbye?"

Thomas shot a glance at Charles, trying not to think about what his friends had just revealed. Charles didn't acknowledge the look, remaining as stoic as a statue. "I didn't want to interrupt your tour, but I would love to stay and chat if that's how you would like to spend your morning."

"Oh, yes. Nothing would give me greater pleasure," said Alfred.

Thomas was suddenly aware that he was extremely underdressed and unprepared for an encounter with almost the entire Southworth family. He should have listened to Charles. Alfred would not show Thomas any mercy. "I apologize for my appearance," said Thomas. "I was not expecting to see you today."

"Oh, don't worry about it. I wouldn't have expected any better from you," Alfred said. Charles kept his eyes glued to his feet.

Thomas did not know what to say. Alfred wanted to talk to Thomas in the same way he spoke to Thomas's father, but Thomas never really cared for their unfriendly back and forth. Thomas wanted to say many things to Alfred that were just as rude and condescending, but Thomas didn't want the Southworths to hate him any more than they already did, because he was very fond of their son. It was pointless and futile, but he would try.

"My apologies," Thomas said.

Alfred scowled. "It's okay if you don't know what to say. It's hard to walk and talk at the same time."

Charles brought his hand up to cover his face but quickly straightened up again when his mother shot him a look.

"Yes, it is," Thomas said.

"You're not very bright, are you?" Alfred asked.

Thomas shrugged. "It is kind of dark in here," he said in an attempt at a joke. Alfred thought Thomas was simply stupid.

Alfred forced a smile and said, "Thank you for your time, now I know to tell the headmaster where he should be directing our funds."

Thomas smiled. "Always a pleasure, Mr. Southworth." He nodded at Lucille and Charles. A glint of amusement hid in Charles's eyes. Lucille did not remove her harsh gaze from Thomas. Thomas wondered how these two terrible people could have created Charles.

Charles nodded once at Thomas, acknowledging that this was the only appropriate time to interact with him. He was careful not to look too pleased to see Thomas but did not take enough care to look as hateful as his parents. Thomas winked at Charles as they walked past one another and saw a smile threatening the corner of Charles's mouth.

Thomas took one final look behind him as he parted ways with the Southworths. It bothered him how pleasing the sight of Charles was. Was it true what Roland had told him? The possibility was thrilling. Thomas could not wait to see Charles again.

Charles glanced behind him and made brief eye contact with Thomas. His eyes widened guiltily and then scanned Thomas from head to toe. When they made eye contact again, Charles's eyes held something other than guilt. Thomas didn't know if Roland's rumor was true, but he did know one thing for certain; no one had ever looked at him like that before.

Charles walked several steps behind his parents as they made their way to the entrance of the school. A heavy silence filled the air. Charles could not stop thinking about the unkind way they had spoken to Thomas. He had been helpless to stop it from happening. This wasn't the first time Charles had seen Thomas become the victim of unfair insults, but it was the first time Charles had witnessed it as his friend.

"That boy is not much of a threat to our future, is he?" Charles's father asked.

"Not at all," said his mother.

Charles stared at the floor.

"How is he doing in school, Charles? Does he have low grades?" his father asked.

Charles didn't know what to say. Of course he knew the answer, but he shouldn't have. "I don't know."

His father watched him through narrowed eyes. "You don't know?" The question was a threat. "You should know everything about him, Charles."

Charles nodded.

His father paused briefly before speaking again. "I want you to find out how he is doing in his classes, but you should know more than that."

"What do you mean?" Charles asked. His father's cryptic demands usually made sense, but at that moment, Charles did not know what was being asked of him.

"It is not helpful to know that he is doing well in school. If he is a good student, keep searching until you find something worth knowing." His father turned away from him again, preventing Charles from asking any further questions.

Charles didn't need to ask any more questions. He knew he was being asked to embarrass his best friend. The consequences he would face if he ignored his father would be extreme. His chest felt tight and he struggled to breathe.

Charles already knew that Thomas was a very good student.

CHAPTER SIX

CHRATAN

The short journey to Chratan had been relatively uneventful compared to the crew's first day together. Faya and Thomas both agreed that Fiona should be the captain since she had created the enchantment that moved the ship. On several occasions, Thomas had tried to get Mariana's attention when Faya and Fiona weren't looking, but he did not succeed. Mariana did not seem to enjoy talking to Thomas very much.

The trip to Chratan took two days, as expected. The ship's previous crew had not made it very far before the siren swarm overtook them. The ship's new crew eventually found themselves preparing to dock in Faya's hometown, lovingly known as Widow's Cove to nearby locals, which Faya spitefully explained.

Chratan was a very large, tropical country. It was bountiful in resources, which made it a popular place to trade, but shipments had been stopped in Widow's Cove. Sailors would not risk passing through the siren-infested town.

The sun blared from above while the thick humidity in the air slowly suffocated them. Faya could tolerate the brutal environment, but Thomas and Fiona struggled with the deadly heat.

Faya stood tall at the bow of the ship, watching her hometown widen on the horizon. Nearby, Fiona and Thomas took off as many layers of clothing as possible without becoming indecent and stood at the edge of the ship, hoping to catch a breeze.

Finally, Mariana appeared to Thomas, confidently strolling onto the deck. Fiona was too distracted by the heat to notice Thomas watching the empty air like it was a person. "Chratan? Interesting choice. What are you doing here?" Mariana asked.

Thomas was reluctant to speak to her in front of Fiona, so he remained silent.

"What's the matter with you? Did you forget how to talk?" Mariana asked.

Thomas glared at her and crossed his arms. He shook his head before giving a subtle nod at Fiona, who was now leaning over the side of the ship in an attempt to reach the cool water far below her.

"What?" Mariana asked.

The nod was more emphatic this time.

Mariana stared at Fiona for a moment. "Is that the girl from earlier?"

Thomas nodded.

"If you're going to refuse to talk to me then I'm not going to help you," she said.

"Right, because you were *so* helpful before," Thomas said, his indignance overpowering the fear that Fiona would hear him.

"Did you say something?" Fiona asked, turning to look at him.

"No," Thomas lied.

Fiona shot him a skeptical look before facing the sea again.

"Why are you here?" Mariana asked.

Thomas stepped toward Mariana so Fiona wouldn't hear. "There are sirens here. Faya's husband was killed by sirens. She might know something we don't know," he said in a hushed voice.

Mariana nodded thoughtfully and rubbed her chin. She looked at Thomas and narrowed her eyes. "Who is Faya?"

"The other woman on the ship."

"Ah! The human."

Thomas squinted at her. "We're all human."

Mariana laughed like he had made a joke and slapped one damp hand on his shoulder. "Let me know what you find out! Good luck!" she said and disappeared from the deck as fast as she had arrived. Thomas scowled at the empty air where she had been standing.

Thomas tried to brush the water off his shoulder, but it had already soaked through his shirt. He groaned, once again wishing Mariana had just left him on the Southworth ship.

The quiet creak of footsteps from his left told Thomas that Faya had finally decided to join them. She stared at the ground as she walked, paying no attention to Thomas or Fiona. Thomas had only known Faya for two days, but he had not yet seen her like this. The ferocity in her eyes was gone, replaced with stifled fear. She stopped beside Thomas and Fiona.

"Are you ready?" Fiona asked.

Faya nodded. Her expression slowly took the shape of the comfortable anger Thomas had become used to seeing on her. "I can't be seen here, or I'll be arrested again," she said, looking back and forth between Thomas and Fiona. "Will you help me?"

"Of course we will," Fiona said. "Right, Felix?" She looked to Thomas for affirmation, but he was distracted by quiet music on the wind. "Felix?" she asked again.

The repetition of the still-unfamiliar name told him that he was being addressed. He whipped his head in their direction and took a moment to replay the archive of their voices in his head. "Of course. Whatever you need." He hesitated. "Do you hear that?"

"Sirens!" Faya said.

"Felix, plug your ears!" Fiona said.

Thomas shook his head. "I'll be fine."

Fiona clamped her hands over his ears and held on tight. He pushed her away. "Get off me!"

"I don't want you to die!" Fiona said, releasing him from the auditory shield, but hanging onto his arm like he would make a run for it at any second.

Thomas frowned at her and pulled his arm away. "Stop it. I'm not going to die," he said. "Unfortunately," he added under his breath.

"What did you say?" Faya asked him.

"Nothing." He looked away, embarrassed at expressing his desire for death in front of someone who couldn't get away from it.

The singing grew steadily louder until it was all they could hear. Fiona watched him closely as the scratching and tearing at the side of the ship began. Her face slowly changed from worried to curious. Eventually, she let go of Thomas's arm.

"Anyway," Fiona yelled over the singing, "I can create a cloaking charm for you. That way you can show yourself without the risk of being noticed. I need more supplies, though."

Faya distractedly wandered toward the edge and peered down at the sirens.

Fiona and Thomas exchanged a confused glance. "Do you think she heard me?" Fiona asked.

Thomas ran to join her at the edge, worried that she would throw herself in. The captivated look on her face was very familiar. Thomas had seen that look on men who were no longer alive. The singing increased in volume when he came into sight. "Faya!" he yelled.

Faya's dazed expression sharpened with focus as she looked at him. "What?" she asked.

"Fiona is going to do magic for you, but she needs to go into town for supplies," Thomas said, glancing at the sirens below. Their lifeless eyes locked onto him, every one of them clawing each other and the hull directly below him. The sirens weren't here before they showed up. If all the men in this town were gone and the sirens were gone, that must mean that the sirens only sought men. How close could he get to a siren before they noticed he was there?

"I can't go into town," Faya said.

"That's the purpose of the magic. Were you even listening?" Thomas asked.

Faya frowned at the sirens. Did their song work on her? Was she like him? Maybe that's why she had understood his immunity so quickly. "I hate them," she said quietly. She wasn't the same as him. She was just angry.

"It's not their fault. They're sick," Thomas said.

Faya narrowed her eyes at him. "They took my husband."

Thomas nodded and looked away. "I know. I'm sorry."

"You don't know. You have no idea," Faya snapped.

Thomas stared at her. Had she forgotten how they met? "They took my whole crew, Faya. I know it doesn't compare to losing your husband, but I have lost people to the sirens too. Beneath the dead eyes and the blue skin, there are mermaids, and those mermaids have families and lives of their own. If we don't help them, they will continue to kill people."

"Who said anything about helping them?" Faya asked.

"Me. I want to help them so that nobody else has to die," Thomas said.

Faya shook her head. "That's very noble of you, but right now I just want to find my daughter."

"Right. Yeah," Thomas said, scratching his head. Of course Faya wouldn't want to help him. What was he thinking?

Faya frowned at him before walking away, leaving him feeling very silly for trying to talk a widow from Widow's Cove into helping him cure the sirens.

The ship slowly made its way toward the empty harbor while Faya disappeared below deck. Thomas held his head in his hands as he stared down at the angry monsters that swam in the ship's wake, gurgling their song at him as they slithered through the sparkling water.

"I'll help you, Felix."

Thomas lifted his head. Fiona had appeared beside him without warning. "You will?" he asked.

She nodded with a smile. "I think it's terrible. These poor mermaids are innocent, and most people don't realize they're just sick. Besides, I..." She frowned and looked at the water, the face of fear peeking through her happy façade. "I would hate to lose my brother that way."

"Is he a sailor?" Thomas asked.

Fiona shook her head. "No, but he might be on a ship. I don't know what happened to him."

"Why would he be on a ship?" Thomas asked.

Fiona furrowed her brow and smiled. "What do you mean?"

"If he's not a sailor, why would he be on a ship?"

"Because he's a magus," Fiona said.

Thomas rubbed his neck and frowned at the sea. "Oh, right. So, your brother is a criminal too?"

Fiona reeled back, as though his comment were a physical slap to the face. "We aren't criminals, Felix."

Thomas stared at her. "But you were arrested. You were in the brig."

"I was in the brig for being a magus," she said.

"That's not illegal."

Fiona rolled her eyes and stared into the water with him. "You would think it was, the way people treat us."

Thomas didn't say anything. He wasn't entirely convinced that Faya and Fiona weren't criminals. Saying something didn't make it true. He had learned that the hard way.

"You don't believe me," Fiona said.

"What?" Thomas asked.

"You think I'm a criminal."

Thomas stared at her with his mouth open. He didn't know what to say.

Fiona sighed. "I get it. Typical magus, getting locked away for committing dangerous and violent crimes. Do you want to know what they caught me doing?"

Thomas stared at her with wide eyes. "Um... okay."

"I made a healing salve for a friend, and she turned me in."

"Your friend turned you in?" Thomas asked. "That's horrible."

"Yeah," she said as she nodded. "It is. I was trying to help her, but she couldn't look past the fact that I'm a witch, even to save her own skin."

"Is that... is that a joke?" Thomas asked.

Fiona smiled. "Yes, but I'm not lying to you."

"That's what liars say," Thomas said.

Fiona exhaled heavily. "All right... I clearly can't convince you of my innocence. Go ahead and trust your instinct that I practice evil magic and worship Tetra, but we'll have to trust each other if we're going to help each other."

Thomas frowned at her. She was right. He wanted her help but refused to believe she wasn't a criminal. It wasn't exactly fair, but her argument was just convincing enough to make him skeptical. He nodded and cleared his throat. "What is Tetra?" he asked.

Fiona stared at him with a flat look. "You're joking. You claim you've spoken to Mariana, but you don't know who *Tetra* is?"

"You know who Mariana is?" Thomas asked.

Fiona laughed. "You're cute, Felix. You really don't know anything about witchcraft, do you?"

The extent of his knowledge of witchcraft was that it should be avoided at all costs. He had also heard somewhere that witches always wore dark clothes and had long hair, a stereotype that Fiona had so far proven correct. "No," he said. "Sorry."

"Don't be. I'm glad you're just ignorant instead of actively hateful. Maybe if you learn about magic, you'll start to believe me. Would you like me to teach you?"

"You can teach me magic?" Thomas asked.

"Well, yes, I can teach you how to do magic, but you can't actually do magic unless you were born a magus. I'm afraid you'll just have to observe."

"Aren't there different types of magic? Like, um... shapeshifting and... fire?" Thomas asked, forcing the question out. He sounded so stupid. Fiona would surely laugh him out of the magic world.

"Yes. Faya, for example, is a fire elementalist, but she could do witchcraft if she wanted to," Fiona said. Thomas was grateful for her gentle response. "You may have heard her say she doesn't often use her magic. A lot of magi these days don't, because they don't want to get caught. But she could be as powerful as me if she tried."

"I heard that!" Faya yelled from somewhere beneath them.

Fiona snickered. "Anyway, yes. All magi can do witchcraft."

"What kind of magic were you born with?" Thomas asked.

"I can read minds," Fiona said, narrowing her eyes and smiling.

Thomas felt a surge of panic as his brain rudely reminded him of every uncomfortable secret he didn't want Fiona to know.

He took a step back, painfully aware of the blush creeping onto his face.

Fiona cackled. "I'm kidding! Wow, Felix! What's on *your* mind?" She continued laughing.

Thomas covered his face with one hand. "That's not funny."

"You believed me!" she said, laughing harder.

Thomas crossed his arms and stared out at the sea. As Fiona continued laughing at him, he watched the shoreline and spotted one single siren, clawing the sand of the beach but struggling to pull herself out of the water. Why was she on the shore instead of chasing after him with the rest of the sirens? There were only women left in Widow's Cove, which meant that particular sirens went after women instead of men.

Interesting.

BLACKWATER ACADEMY

It was Saturday night, and the common area was full of noisy students with nowhere else to be. Thomas sat on a soft red sofa, failing to focus on the book in his hands. Since befriending Charles, Thomas had not gone an entire day without him. He had so much to say to Charles, and he desperately wanted to catch Charles walking back to his dorm for the night.

Thomas had no idea what book he was holding. As far as Thomas was aware there was only one line in the book, because it was the only line he could read, and he had already read it about a hundred times. He shut the book and set it in his lap, finally admitting that it wasn't going to happen.

The common room door opened with a shrill creak, and Thomas whipped around to inspect the room's newest occupant.

He had been doing this all evening hoping to see Charles, but so far, he had been disappointed every time. This time was different.

Charles slowly ambled through the doorway. His hair fell against his forehead in an uncharacteristically messy manner and his skin was pale. He looked ill. He stopped in front of the door and rubbed his tired eyes. His visit with his parents must have been exhausting. His feet dragged slowly across the carpet as he moved in the direction of the dormitory hall. He didn't notice Thomas.

"Hey!" Thomas called out.

Charles flinched. As soon as his eyes landed on Thomas, he flashed his classic, perfect smile and changed course to be with Thomas instead of his bed. Charles sat down close beside Thomas, leaving plenty of extra sitting room on the other end of the sofa. "Hey," he said, draping an arm behind Thomas on the backrest of the couch. There was something strange in Charles's voice. Was it sadness?

"Is everything okay?" Thomas asked.

Charles's smile faltered as he stared into the fire that blazed in the large stone fireplace beside them. He quickly smiled again and nodded. "Yeah, I'm just tired."

Thomas had heard that line before. Not from Charles, but from himself. He would say that to people when he thought they didn't want to hear that everything was not okay. Thomas frowned. He knew what Charles looked like when he was tired, and this was not it.

"I'm sorry about earlier," Charles said. His smile vanished again. Charles was genuinely upset about Thomas's interaction with his parents. Maybe that's why he looked unwell. Thomas's stomach turned as he remembered his spiteful attitude at the beginning of the day. He should have listened to Charles from the start.

"It's okay. I barely remember what they said to me. It's not a big deal," Thomas said. It was a lie, but a small one. He remembered everything the Southworths had said to him. He had been replaying it in his head all day.

Charles lifted his head to look Thomas in the eyes. Normally Thomas would have felt that they were uncomfortably close, but he was not uncomfortable with their proximity. Charles smiled at him, and Thomas couldn't stop himself from smiling back.

Thomas quickly turned his face away, remembering what Roland had told him that morning. There were a lot of other people in this room, and he didn't want them to get the wrong idea.

Would it be the wrong idea?

"What's the matter?" Charles asked.

Thomas scanned the room and then faced Charles again. "Can I talk to you? Alone?"

Charles smiled briefly. "You can't talk to me right here?"

"Ha-ha," said Thomas, remembering their conversation from the day before. "No, I can't. But I know you're tired. It can wait."

Charles frowned. "No. I want to hear what you have to say." He stood up, pulling Thomas up with him. He nodded toward the room's exit and walked away without another word. Thomas followed him.

They walked together in silence down the dark deserted halls of the school. It was late and the moon was high in the sky, casting bright white light through the windows and illuminating the walls. After a couple of minutes of walking, they wound up at the very same hall under the very same window where they had first struck up an acquaintanceship.

Charles leaned against the windowsill and watched Thomas carefully. "Well?"

"Well," said Thomas, "I saw your friends this morning..." Thomas had no idea how to continue. "I don't think they are your friends."

"I know. I've told you that already," Charles said. He pushed himself away from the window and stood up straight. "What did they say?"

Thomas scratched his head. "They told me that you're using me," he said, pausing to watch Charles for a reaction.

Charles shook his head. "Of course I'm not using you. We're friends."

"Yeah," Thomas said. A long silence passed between them.

"That's not what you wanted to tell me," Charles said. "You wouldn't bring me out here just to tell me that."

"You're right," said Thomas. He let the words linger, unable to continue. He could feel his heart pounding in his chest. His hands were damp with sweat, so he shoved them in his pockets.

"What else did they say?" Charles prodded.

"They told me why your girlfriend left you."

Charles took a deep breath and closed his eyes on the exhale. "It's not true."

"I haven't even told you what they said."

"Did they tell you she caught me cheating on her?" Charles asked.

"Yes... but—"

"With a boy?" Charles demanded.

Charles was angry. Thomas hesitated, afraid of upsetting him further. "Yes."

Charles shook his head. "It's not true."

Thomas's heart sank to his stomach. "Okay." He felt stupid for feeling disappointed. He didn't want to be disappointed over this. Charles was his friend. That was all he should ever be.

"Would that be so terrible?" Charles asked, staring out the window.

"Cheating?" Thomas asked.

"No."

Thomas stared at Charles. Charles refused to look at him. "No," Thomas said.

"I don't understand why everyone thinks it's so funny."

Thomas shrugged. "Me neither. To be honest, I..." Thomas couldn't finish his thought. His brain paralyzed his tongue.

Charles finally looked at him, waiting for him to continue.

Thomas cleared his throat. "I was hoping it was true," he said quietly.

Charles stared at Thomas for a long time. Thomas averted his eyes and looked through the window at the pale lawn. His heart beat fast and he struggled to keep his breathing steady. He messed up. He shouldn't have said anything.

"Why?" Charles finally asked. "So you could tell your father? So you could embarrass me?"

"What?" Thomas asked. He stared at Charles, horror-struck. "No! Why would you even think that?"

"Why would I think that? Are you serious?" Charles ran his fingers through his hair. "Because we are enemies."

"We aren't enemies. We're friends," Thomas said. He couldn't believe what he was hearing. This conversation had spiraled out of control.

Charles was quiet for a moment. He shook his head. "I don't think we should be friends anymore."

"What?" Thomas asked. "You don't want to be friends?"

"That's not what I said."

"I don't understand... Was it something I said?" Thomas asked.

"No."

"Then... why?" asked Thomas.

"Because I don't trust you. And you shouldn't trust me."

"But I do trust you. And you have no reason not to trust me," Thomas said.

"You trust me? Did you honestly think it would be that simple? I had no idea you were so naïve."

Thomas stared at Charles, desperately trying to understand. "I had no idea you were so mean," he finally said.

"Yes, you did," said Charles. "You've always known."

"Charles," Thomas pleaded, but he couldn't think of anything else to say.

Charles shook his head. "I'm sorry. I really am." Without another word, Charles walked away from the window, leaving Thomas alone.

Chapter Seven

CHRATAN

It had been a long time since Thomas felt the steadiness of the earth beneath his feet. His legs had made themselves at home on the waves, and they had trouble keeping their balance now that the rhythm of the ocean was gone. Walking to the other end of the long dock was challenging, but he did it.

Fiona had decided Thomas needed to come with her to get the ingredients for the cloaking charm since he was attracting the sirens to the ship. She assumed they would leave if he went into town. The sirens clamored over each other, splashing noisily beneath the dock as Thomas and Fiona made their way across.

An angry woman stood at the end, waiting for them. Thomas smiled at her as he approached. "Good afternoon," Thomas said. She continued scowling. He never could win people over with just a smile like stupid, perfect Charles always could.

"This port is not accepting shipments or visitors. Please leave immediately," the woman said.

"We just need some supplies and then we'll be on our way," Thomas said.

The woman shifted her attention to Fiona. "Do you realize the risk you are putting your husband at by bringing him here?"

Thomas laughed out loud at the thought of being married to Fiona. Fiona glared at him. Nobody seemed to understand the sirens, or him, at all.

"He's immune to the sirens," Fiona said, gesturing to the flailing fish monsters around them. "He'll be fine."

"He's *immune* because he's with you. We all thought the same of our husbands until we parted ways, and they ran for the shore," the stranger said.

"They weren't affected until they were alone?" Thomas asked.

"That's right."

"Hmm..." Thomas rubbed his chin. "Let me assure you, I have been alone with sirens before and I'm still here."

"I will not let you risk your life for a few supplies. There is another port city around the bay where you can restock, but you are not welcome here."

"Let's make a deal... I'll give you 100 cabills if I die, that way we both win," Thomas suggested.

The woman shot him a confused look but quickly settled back into anger. "I'm not falling for that again."

Thomas raised his eyebrows. *Had someone tried that on her before? And it had worked?* Not for them, obviously. "Are there any men here?" he asked.

"A few."

"*Really?*" Thomas asked. "How is that possible?"

"They live far enough up the hill that the sirens can't detect them, and they can't hear the sirens. Many of them stay with their wives all day."

"They stay with their wives all day? Every day?" Thomas asked.

"It's the only way to keep them from dying."

"Right..." Thomas said. "If those men are still alive, I think I'll be all right as long as my lady stays with me," he said, grabbing Fiona's hand as though they were married.

Fiona smiled and lovingly leaned against Thomas as if they hadn't just met three days ago.

The woman sighed a long and drawn-out breath. "All right," she finally said. "I'll let you in, but if I see you without him at any point during your visit, I expect you to pay up," she said, pointing at Fiona.

"Right," Fiona said, glancing nervously at Thomas.

"Thank you," Thomas said. The woman stepped aside and glared at them as they passed her, making their way into the quiet town. A few women strolled along the shore-facing street, watching Thomas and Fiona warily.

"Felix, I don't have 100 cabills. Do you?" Fiona asked.

"Did they take all your money when they arrested you?" Thomas asked.

"Shh!" she hissed. "No, but 100 cabills is a lot of money."

Thomas tried not to look surprised, and forced himself not to ask, "*It is?*" He cleared his throat and said, "Right. No, um... I don't have 100 cabills. It doesn't matter anyway because I'm not going to die." He did have 100 cabills. He had a lot more than 100 cabills, but he now knew that was not normal.

Fiona raised an eyebrow at him. She didn't believe him. "So how do you plan on helping the mermaids? What could you possibly do for them without getting yourself killed?"

Thomas glanced at the shore as they walked along the beachfront path. The sirens had moved away from the ship and now clawed at the surface of the beach, dragging themselves no further than the waves. He wondered which of these sirens he had seen earlier alone at the shore. "I don't know. Maybe I *will* die," he said.

"Felix," Fiona said in a stern tone.

"What?"

"I'll make you something to help. It won't be much more work than the cloaking charm I'm making for Faya," Fiona said.

"Oh yeah? What are you going to do? Turn me into a woman?" Thomas said with a dry laugh. That would probably not even be enough, considering the lone siren he had seen earlier.

"No, but I can turn you into a merman."

Thomas stared at her. "How?"

Fiona dragged him away from the sea and down a sunny street that sang with the force of the wind. The whole city looked abandoned. Few people were outside, and it didn't seem like many people were inside, either. "I'll make you an enchanted bracelet. You're not opposed to jewelry, are you? Is that too ladylike for you?" Fiona prodded.

Thomas rolled his eyes. "No."

Fiona laughed. "Good. Maybe I'll make you a necklace too."

"Go for it," Thomas said.

Fiona giggled and let go of his hand. Thomas hadn't even realized they were still holding hands. "Oh, look!" Fiona said, pointing at something in the distance.

A wooden sign hung over a doorway that read *Apothecary* in dark red paint. Apothecaries typically stocked medicine and various other cures for sick people. Why would Fiona need one now?

"Most apothecaries are witches," Fiona said with a big smile. "If we walk into that shop and the owner has long hair, I guarantee she's a witch."

"They'll have what you need?"

Fiona nodded and walked into the shop without him. He followed her in, taking slow, deliberate steps as he took in the unfamiliar surroundings. The shop was lit by dim orange candlelight. The whole place smelled strongly of a mixture of herbs and thick aromatic smoke. If the rest of the unmagic world knew as little about witchcraft as Thomas did, there was no question why apothecaries went unnoticed. Thomas never would have guessed that apothecary shops were run by magi.

Fiona was already chatting with the shop owner, who had waist-length black hair, as Fiona had predicted. The shop owner stopped talking to eye him warily. She wasn't old, but she was older than either him or Fiona.

"Oh, it's okay. He's with me," Fiona said.

"I've never seen you around here before. Are you...?" the woman asked.

"Am I what?" Thomas asked.

"He's not," Fiona said.

The woman crossed her arms. "What relation is he to you?"

"My husband," Fiona said. She seemed to enjoy lying about the status of their relationship.

"Yes, I am her husband," Thomas said, reluctantly playing along. "My name is Felix Warren, and that's my wife, Fiona Warren."

"You took an unmagic last name?" the shopkeeper asked Fiona.

Fiona laughed nervously. "He's a Warren. Even the unmagic in their line are powerful."

The shopkeeper raised her eyebrows like she knew what Fiona was talking about. Was that true, or had Fiona just made that up to get out of the lie? Thomas decided to keep his mouth shut because he didn't know what he was talking about. "Well, Felix and Fiona, it's a pleasure to meet you both. My name is Kassandra. What can I do for you?"

Fiona started listing off ingredients that Thomas had never heard of and explaining what she would use them for. It seemed like an interview, as though Kassandra wouldn't give Fiona the ingredients if she didn't explain herself correctly. Maybe that's how it worked between witches.

Eventually, the shopkeeper gathered the ingredients and asked for payment. "Fifty-seven cabills for everything."

"Fifty-seven cabills?" Fiona asked. "I don't have that much money. Damn. I need this stuff. Felix, dear? Which of the enchantments do you think are more important?"

"Fifty-seven cabills for a bunch of dried plants and oil?" Thomas asked. "Why? All of that should cost thirty at the most."

"Oh, Felix, no," Fiona said, standing in front of him and raising her hands in the air. "Forgive me, he doesn't understand these transactions."

"Isn't he a Warren?" Kassandra asked.

"He is," Fiona said. "But he's not familiar with witchcraft."

"But you're married to him?" Kassandra pried.

Thomas dug in his pocket and pulled out sixty cabills. "Whatever, fine. Keep the change," he said, handing it to Kassandra.

Kassandra stared at Thomas like he had insulted her. "I will not keep the change, Mr. Warren. If this transaction does not end in seven, the protection spell is broken."

Thomas dropped the money in Fiona's hands. "I'm out of my element. Just do what you need to do." Thomas shot Kassandra a flat look.

Kassandra stared at him for a long moment, then gasped. "Thief! Liar! Get out of my shop you wretched man! Destroyer of souls! May nothing but harm fall upon you and your family! Out!"

Thomas gawked at her. "What?"

"Out! Both of you!" Kassandra yelled.

"What are you talking about?" Fiona asked.

"How dare you bring the likes of him into my sacred space?

How dare you tell him our secrets, young witch? You should be ashamed!"

"The likes of him?" Fiona asked.

Kassandra pointed to the exit, and an overwhelming force pushed Thomas forward toward the door. Fiona stumbled after him.

They tripped through the door together and it slammed shut behind them. Thomas caught Fiona before she fell. "Are you okay?" he asked.

"Yeah," she said, steadying herself against him. "That was weird. Why would she say that to you?"

Thomas shook his head. "I have no idea."

Fiona sighed and took a step away from him, brushing a lock of orange hair away from her face. "Some witches have no respect for the unmagic. I'm sorry."

"It's okay. Most unmagic have no respect for witches," Thomas said.

"That's true," Fiona said with a laugh. "Oh well. I guess we'll have to do this the hard way."

"What's the hard way?" Thomas asked.

Fiona grinned at him. "Get ready to learn some magic, Felix."

BLACKWATER ACADEMY

On Sunday morning, Thomas was nowhere to be seen. Charles's eyes scanned the sleepy dining hall whenever his friends weren't watching. Thomas wasn't at the empty table he had once occupied.

Nobody commented on the fact that Thomas was gone, but they all seemed to know something had happened.

Charles was distracted for the entire day. In the halls, he

peered around every corner. Outside, he searched the lawn tirelessly. His heart was heavy, and his stomach felt sick. He had never had a friend like Thomas before, and he probably never would again. Thomas understood him like no one else did. He was the only person who didn't desperately want Charles to like him, but Charles liked him more than anyone.

Thomas wasn't in the dining hall at lunch. At dinner, Charles started to worry. Was he okay? Obviously not, but had anyone seen him? Who was his roommate? Thomas had mentioned him before. He shared a room with someone Charles didn't know very well. His name was Richard. Or maybe it was Robert.

"Charles?" Walter asked.

Charles returned to the moment, suddenly aware that he had been biting his nails and staring at nothing. He folded his hands in his lap. "What?" he asked.

"Where is Thomas?"

"I don't know or care," Charles said, narrowing his eyes at Walter. "Go ask Robert if you're so worried about him."

"You mean Richard?" Walter asked.

Damn it. "Whatever," Charles said.

"Did something happen?" Roland asked.

Backstabbing bastards. "Yeah. He doesn't want to be my friend anymore," he said. Maybe he could get them to believe it was their fault. They were the ones who outed him to Thomas, after all.

"That's weird," Roland said. "I thought he liked you."

Charles frowned at him. "You thought wrong."

"But... okay," Roland said, scratching his face. "Anyway, have you guys seen Professor Franklin's daughter? She's nothing like her stodgy old dad."

Charles tuned out Roland's stodgy old conversation to watch who he thought was Richard walk into the dining hall. Charles stood up and walked off without saying anything. As he made his way toward Richard, he could hear his friends snickering. He could only imagine what they were saying now that he was gone, especially considering the conversation he had walked away from.

Richard eyed Charles as he approached. When Charles reached him, Richard stepped aside as though he were in Charles's way.

"Are you Richard?" Charles asked.

"Yes...?"

"You're Thomas Hambleton's roommate?" Charles asked.

Richard sighed and looked away. "Yes."

"Is he okay? Have you seen him today?"

"Why do you care, Southworth?" Richard asked, raising one eyebrow.

"Have you seen him?" Charles asked again. He didn't need to justify his concern.

"Yeah, I've seen him. He's been in bed all day."

"Is he okay?" Charles asked.

"I don't know," Richard said. "I don't talk to that idiot."

"Don't talk about him like that," Charles said. "He's better than you think."

"You are Charles *Southworth*, aren't you? Why are you defending him?" Richard asked, crossing his arms.

"Have you ever tried talking to him?" Charles asked. "I think you would be pleasantly surprised."

Richard rolled his eyes. "It must be nice to be so wealthy that you have the luxury of ignoring the state of the world when it's convenient for you. You should really stop to think about the impact your actions have on the rest of us."

"What does that mean? How does my friendship with Thomas affect you?" Charles demanded, even though they weren't friends anymore.

Richard narrowed his eyes and held Charles's gaze for a

moment before speaking. "You honestly don't know?" he asked. "You're supposed to be helping us. You can't let him get away with anything, and I'm afraid you will."

"*Us?*" Charles asked. "Richard, are you...?"

Richard looked away. "No, and I wouldn't tell you if I were."

Richard was lying. "I won't tell Thomas," Charles said.

"There's nothing to tell. Leave me alone, Southworth." Richard pushed past Charles and sat down at a table nearby. Charles watched him, but he ignored Charles and carried on with his day.

Maybe Richard was right. There was a reason Charles had never spoken to Thomas before. There was a reason no one else spoke to him. Their friendship would be bad for everyone. Thomas probably wasn't the nice guy Charles thought he was, anyway. Charles couldn't give up on the world over one silly fixation.

It was for the best.

Chapter Eight

Professor Franklin's monotonous voice rambled on, lulling Thomas into a dull state between sleep and wakefulness. Thomas stared straight ahead, seeing nothing. It took everything in his power not to look across the room at his former best friend.

The last week had been the longest and most excruciating week of his life. Charles refused to talk to him, look at him, or acknowledge him in any way. Thomas hadn't tried talking to Charles or his fake friends. The rejection had hurt so much that he didn't want to relive it.

Thomas hadn't been paying attention to the lesson, but the sound of Charles's voice brought him back to the classroom. "Four," he said.

"That is incorrect. Anyone else?" asked Professor Franklin. "Mr. Hambleton?"

Thomas stared dully at the professor. "What was the question?"

"How many major nautical trade routes are connected to Tinera?"

"Five," said Thomas, resisting the urge to look at Charles. Was he serious?

"Well done," said Professor Franklin before continuing his lecture.

Against his better judgment, Thomas glanced at Charles to find Charles scowling at him. It was the first time Charles had acknowledged him since their friendship ended, and it was a scowl. Thomas stared straight ahead again.

It was Friday morning. Thomas just wanted the week to end. He didn't think he could tolerate sitting through the rest of the day's classes, so he decided he wouldn't.

After class, Thomas walked in the opposite direction from his usual route. He passed Charles in the hall talking to his regular group. Charles stopped talking to watch Thomas walk by. Thomas ignored him.

Thomas crossed the school grounds and walked until he reached the isolated lake. He would have to stay here all day to avoid getting caught skipping class, but he didn't mind. This was his happy place. It didn't feel very happy anymore, but it could still be his less-sad place.

He followed the forest trail to the far end of the lake and sat down at the grassy shore. The wind rippled the surface of the water and shook the leaves of the trees around him. An occasional snap of a twig from the nearby woods told him that he had been sitting still long enough for the wildlife to forget he was there. He rested his head against his knees and closed his eyes. After several minutes of silence, he heard footsteps approach. He lifted his head just as Charles sat down beside him.

Thomas stared at him. "Did you follow me?" As hard as Thomas tried to put the anger behind his words, they fell out lifeless and monotone.

Charles shook his head. "I didn't have to. I know where you go to be alone."

Thomas looked out at the empty lake again. "I guess I'll have to find a new place." He stood up.

"Wait." Charles grabbed Thomas's hand to keep him from leaving. "I'm sorry."

Thomas stared at Charles with raised eyebrows. "For what?"

"I—" Charles paused. "I miss you."

"I wouldn't have guessed that by the look you gave me," Thomas said, pulling his hand away.

"I didn't mean it."

Thomas didn't understand how Charles could claim to not mean anything through a scowl. "Why are you here?" he asked, sitting beside Charles again.

"I don't think it's possible for us to not be friends. Nobody understands me like you do," Charles said.

Thomas shook his head. "I don't understand you, Charles. How could you make it this far in life as a Southworth without knowing there are five major nautical trade routes connected to Tinera?"

Charles had been watching Thomas closely, but when Thomas finished speaking, Charles let out a laugh Thomas hadn't heard before. It was unrestrained and unusually happy for Charles's typical demeanor. Was this his real laugh? Had Thomas never heard Charles genuinely laugh before?

"I can't keep up with you, Thomas," Charles said, averting his eyes as he spoke.

Thomas couldn't find his words for a moment. Something electric struck him at his core when Charles said his name. "So, you *do* know my first name," he finally said.

"Of course I do," Charles said quietly.

Thomas scowled at Charles, but Charles wouldn't look at him. How could he be so infuriating and so enchanting at the same time? Thomas wanted to walk away from Charles as much as he wanted to stay and interrogate him more. "How can you be friends with someone you don't trust?" Thomas asked.

"I do trust you."

"I had no idea you were so naïve," Thomas said, looking out at the water again.

Charles sighed. "I'm sorry I said that. I was scared."

"You have no reason to be scared of me. I don't care enough about the Hambleton fortune to sacrifice you to it."

"I know that. I'm not scared of you."

"Then what are you scared of?" Thomas demanded, watching Charles.

"I was scared of what you were going to say that night. And I'm scared…" Charles fiddled with the cuff of his sleeve.

Thomas waited for Charles to continue, refusing to speak until he finished his thought.

Charles finally looked into Thomas's eyes. They were beautiful and brown and wide with fear. "I'm scared of how much I like you."

Thomas's eyebrows shot up. "Oh."

Charles focused on the button of his sleeve again. "It's true, Thomas. What they say about me."

"That you, uh…" Thomas didn't know how to continue the conversation. He wanted Charles to say everything. It was the least he could do after the week Thomas had.

"I like boys."

Thomas stared at Charles for a long time, his heart racing. Charles refused to look at Thomas, his face becoming more panicked with each passing second. Thomas knew he should say something, but he was at a loss. He had not been expecting this.

Suddenly Charles sat up straight and forced himself to look at Thomas. "I didn't cheat on my girlfriend," he said, pausing uncomfortably. "I just told her about... my preferences, and she didn't take it well. She was a bad confidant."

"Me too," Thomas finally managed to say, but Charles had already moved the conversation forward without him.

"You're a bad confidant?" Charles asked, his panic quickly changing to surprise and confusion.

"No..." Thomas grimaced at himself. Could he be any more awkward?

"Oh," Charles said with a relieved smile. "Good." He moved closer to Thomas until there was no space left between them.

Thomas's face burned. "I like you too," Thomas muttered, focusing on the rocky ground. "I can't get you out of my head. It's not fair that you came into my life, introduced me to this side of myself, and then just left."

"I'm sorry." Charles lifted his hand to Thomas's face and gently turned it toward his own. "How can I make it up to you?"

Thomas made a sound that he didn't recognize. He quickly realized it was the sound of giddy laughter. Charles grinned at him. He leaned forward and kissed Thomas tentatively. It was over before Thomas had time to react. Charles's eyes scanned Thomas's face. Thomas smiled and then pulled Charles into another kiss. Charles smelled and tasted like cigarettes, but Thomas didn't mind. He loved it.

A twig snapped loudly behind them. Before the sound had even registered in Thomas's mind, Charles pushed Thomas away and scanned the tree line. The firmness of the push stung with the same rejection Thomas had felt all week. Charles peered into the forest for a long moment before returning his attention to Thomas, who was frowning at the lake again.

Charles quietly reached forward to hold Thomas's hand. "I'm sorry," he whispered.

The reality of their situation hit Thomas. It was easy to deal with his thoughts when they were friends, but now that he knew the feeling was mutual, it felt impossible. Thomas shook his head. "This isn't going to work."

"I'm sorry," Charles said again. "We can keep this a secret. It will work." He lifted Thomas's hand and kissed it. Thomas wanted to believe Charles, but he wasn't the one who had just shoved the other away out of fear of being caught. Charles draped an arm around Thomas and pulled him close. Thomas leaned his head against Charles's shoulder. The feeling of being close to Charles overtook everything else, and all of his doubt melted away.

This could work. It had to.

Chratan

"I found everything we need for your enchantment, Faya!" Fiona said, exploding through the doorway of the main cabin. Thomas ambled in after her, silently taking a seat in the wooden chair beside the map table.

When Fiona had said, "Get ready to learn some magic," what she meant was, "Get ready to dig through mud and leaves for hours to find what *I* need to do magic." Thomas was exhausted and irritated.

Faya sat on the bed with her feet up, looking bored. "Finally," she grumbled. Thomas rolled his eyes. She had no idea.

"It's not my fault it took so long. The Apothecary went crazy on Felix and kicked us out. We had to find everything ourselves," Fiona explained.

Faya raised one eyebrow and scrutinized Thomas. "Kassandra?" she asked.

Thomas nodded.

"I have never heard of her kicking anyone out of her shop before. What did you say to her?"

Fiona waved away the question and sat beside Faya on the bed, forcing Faya to make room for her. "It doesn't matter. He's not a magus and he's a bad liar. What *does* matter is what you plan on doing once you have this cloaking charm." Fiona pulled bundles of crumpled flowers and leaves from her pockets, dropping them onto the bed beside her as she waited for Faya to answer.

"Plan?" Faya asked.

Fiona stared at her. "You don't have a plan? What have you been doing all day?"

"Waiting for you to come back," Faya said.

"All right then, where is your daughter?" Fiona asked, tugging the drawstring from the front of her shirt loose.

"Ametta is probably with my husband's brother and his wife," Faya said.

"Ametta? Is that your daughter's name?" Fiona asked.

Faya nodded.

"Your husband's brother lives here?" Thomas asked.

Faya looked firmly into his eyes. "He's immune. Like you."

"Like me?" Thomas asked. "We were told that men won't be affected if they stay with their wives."

"Most men weren't affected around their wives. Most men couldn't stay by their wife's side for very long. It's been a year, Felix. Every man still here is immune. *Like you*," she said again, shooting him a pointed look. She definitely knew.

Thomas shot a nervous glance at Fiona to see if she had caught on, but she was busy braiding flowers around the drawstring. She didn't seem to be listening at all.

"I didn't think—" Thomas stopped himself before he said too much. "So Ametta's fine, right? She's with family, she'll be okay."

Faya shook her head and fixed her eyes on the ground. "They're the ones who turned me in."

"*What?*" Thomas asked. "Your own family turned you in?"

Faya lifted her gaze to meet his eyes. "They're only family by marriage, and I'm widowed now. They are not my family."

Thomas shook his head as he tried to understand. "Dei, Faya. That's terrible. I'm so sorry."

"It is terrible. My former sister by marriage was my best friend until she found out I was a magus. She turned me in because she was scared for Ametta..." Faya clenched her fist, stifling flames in her palm. "But Ametta is a magus too. Knowing how she handled her father's death, I doubt it's a secret anymore."

Thomas didn't know what to say. He couldn't believe Faya's own family had sent her away. He shook his head silently, wishing he could find the words.

"Well, I have good news for you and Ametta," Fiona said, holding up the braided loop of string and flowers. "We're one step closer to finding her."

"Is it done?" Faya asked.

"Nearly. I just need to cast the spell, and we'll be set. Care to put this on for me?" Fiona asked.

Faya ducked her head, allowing Fiona to drape the braided rope around her neck. Fiona continued to hold onto the back of it, keeping her eyes closed as she did. She began chanting in the same mysterious language as before, and Thomas once again remembered that she had tattoos when a symbol on her forearm glowed white against her skin. How could he have forgotten? Fiona traced her fingers around the length of the necklace toward the front until the chant was complete, then she opened her eyes.

"Done," Fiona said, then her face fell. "Oh, um... Who are you?" she asked the stranger sitting beside her, her hands recoiling from the stranger's neck.

"Are you kidding?" the stranger asked. "It's me, Faya. You *just* made me this cloaking charm," the stranger said, tugging at the rope around her neck.

Thomas squinted at the strange woman. She definitely had all the same qualities as Faya, but he didn't recognize her. Her words were already escaping his memory as he tried to process them.

"I'm sorry, who?" Fiona asked.

The stranger shook her head. Fiona looked at Thomas for a clue but Thomas only shrugged. He was just as puzzled. The stranger pulled the thin rope necklace over her head, and suddenly Faya sat where the stranger had been. Thomas couldn't understand how he ever saw anyone else.

"Oh! That's right. Faya, of course." Fiona laughed nervously. "I think I made that charm a little too potent."

Faya rolled her eyes. "This isn't going to work. Neither of you can even remember who I am. What are we going to do?"

"Give me the necklace." Fiona snatched the necklace from Faya before Faya could offer it to her. With a quick motion, she plucked a few petals from the rope and handed it back to Faya. "Try it now."

Faya threw the charm around her neck again and she was gone. Thomas didn't recognize the person sitting beside Fiona anymore, but he knew it was Faya. "Well?" Faya asked.

"I remember her. Do you remember, Felix?" Fiona asked.

"Yes, that's Faya."

"Wonderful, what's the plan, Faya?" Fiona asked.

Faya shook her head. "All I can think is to burn their house down, but that's not productive."

Fiona laughed nervously. "No, it's not. Aren't you worried about hurting Ametta?"

"Fire won't hurt her," Faya said quietly. She sighed. "That's the least of my concerns."

"I'm sure she's fine. We'll find her," Fiona said.

"What if we don't?" Faya asked, her voice cracking on the last word. She cleared her throat and stared at the ground. "I can't stand the thought that she might be alone in a prison cell somewhere."

"Who would lock a child in a prison cell?" Thomas asked. "That's horrible."

Faya looked at him, the fire in her eyes now doused with tears. "Come on, Felix. We already know exactly who would lock a child in a prison cell," she said, gesturing to the room around her.

Thomas looked around, not understanding what she meant. "Who?"

Faya and Fiona exchanged a brief bemused look, just like they had on the first day. "The same people who locked *us* in a prison cell," Faya said.

"The police?" Thomas asked.

"Wow, you *weren't* a crew member of this ship, were you?" Faya asked.

Thomas let out a short, nervous laugh. "What does the crew have to do with it?"

"You seriously don't know?" Fiona asked.

Thomas shook his head.

"It's the most feared name among the magi, and you're on their ship," Faya said.

Thomas stared at her, slack-jawed. She had to be mistaken. "Wh—what?" Thomas asked. "You don't mean...?" He glanced around the room, quickly fixing his eyes on a Hambleton emblem painted onto a nearby barrel just to be sure he understood. His blood ran cold with the sense he was about to learn something he didn't want to know.

"Yes," Faya said. "The Hambletons."

Thomas struggled to keep his cool at the sound of his name.

"The Ha—The family who... The *Hambletons?*" he stuttered. "This Hambleton?" He pointed at the ceiling, knowing the question didn't make any sense. Faya had completely stalled his brain.

"Yes," Faya said again.

Thomas continued shaking his head. It couldn't be true. Why would the Hambletons want a six-year-old girl? The Hambletons only shipped goods between countries. And prisoners, apparently. Magus prisoners like Faya and Fiona. In a brig that was much too large for a merchant ship.

Oh. Oh no.

BLACKWATER ACADEMY – THREE MONTHS EARLIER

On a chilly autumn afternoon, Thomas lay in the lakeside forest with his head in Charles's lap, staring into the cover of trees above them. Sunlight beamed through the branches and landed on them in warm patches. The cold wind carried the sweet floral scent of the wildflowers that bobbed in the air around them. Charles leaned against a tree with a cigarette hanging from his mouth and idly ran his fingers through Thomas's hair, lost in thought.

Thomas had never known it was possible to feel this way about anyone. He had always assumed married couples were only pretending to love each other. As it turned out, love was real, and he had proof. For the first time in Thomas's life, he was happy.

Charles and Thomas had decided that their relationship needed to be a secret. Being friends had been risky enough; a romance between them would never be tolerated. The only place at Blackwater where they could spend time alone was by the lake. They had both decided that it was worth fighting the harsh autumn cold to be together. They spent every weekend at the lake and usually hid in the nearby woods to avoid potential visitors.

Thomas sighed happily. "I'm so lucky."

"Hmm?" Charles brought his attention back from whatever introspection had consumed him. "Why?" he asked, pulling the cigarette from his mouth so he could talk.

"Because I get to be here. With you."

Charles smiled at him, and the warmth of it could have melted the frost on the grass. "I'm the lucky one. Trust me."

"Maybe we both are," Thomas said. "Think about it. What are the odds that we are both... like this?"

Charles raised his eyebrows at Thomas and put the cigarette back in his mouth. After a short moment of contemplation, he shrugged.

"And of all people, a Southworth and a Hambleton," Thomas continued. "It all seems very, very unlikely, doesn't it?"

Charles thought for a moment before responding. "Yes, but it's *unlikely* because it's not impossible. The odds are low, but not zero. It was bound to happen to someone at some point, right? Why not us?"

"Yeah," Thomas said. "This isn't new, is it?"

"What do you mean?"

"I mean, I understand now I've liked you for a long time, but I didn't know it." Thomas paused. "I'm sure it was one-sided. You were never very nice to me."

Charles frowned. "I'm sorry. It wasn't one-sided," he said. "I was conflicted about it because I wasn't supposed to like you. I was supposed to be better than you. It annoyed me that you were so carefree but still superior. And it drove me crazy that you never retaliated when I insulted you. In hindsight, it's obvious I just wanted your attention."

Thomas laughed again. "I am *not* superior."

Charles grinned at him. "You are. I'm sorry you can't see that. If I had known you liked me back, I probably would have been a lot nicer to you."

Thomas rolled his eyes. "I don't believe that. Why did you finally decide to befriend me anyway?"

"You were nice to me," Charles said.

"I've always been nice to you."

Charles was quiet for a moment. "Wow. You're right. I'm sorry."

"I forgive you."

Charles laughed. "Honestly Thomas, I think the day you took the fall for me in front of Redmond was the day I realized I had feelings for you."

"Really? Why?"

Charles stared at Thomas for a moment as he raked Thomas's hair away from his face. "It was the first time you ever smiled at me. I've been completely obsessed with you since then. I've made it my life goal to see your smile as often as possible."

Thomas grinned, but not because Charles wanted him to. He couldn't help it. "Your life goal, huh?"

"Yeah," Charles said with a smile, running his fingers through Thomas's hair one more time.

They sat together in silence for several minutes, listening to the rustle of the leaves above them and the sound of the wind dancing through the tall, unkempt blades of wild grass. Thomas's life, as it was at that moment, was perfect, but a question stuck in the back of his mind. He often tried to ignore it, but it always came back louder than before. This was one of those moments where that question skipped the queue of thoughts and sat directly at the forefront of his mind. Now that the world around was silent, the question screamed for an answer. Maybe it was time to give it a voice.

"Charles..."

"Thomas."

Thomas tried to swallow his nerves, but it didn't help. Now they were in his stomach, and he felt nauseous. He frowned and looked up at Charles.

"What's wrong? Are you okay?" Charles asked.

"Yeah." Thomas hesitated but decided it would be best to get it over with. "I just can't help but wonder what the future will look like... for us."

Charles thought about it quietly. The silence in the air now was different from the silence from seconds earlier. It was heavy and uncomfortable. "I don't know," Charles finally said. It wasn't what Thomas wanted to hear.

The heavy silence returned, but Thomas fought against it. "Will we always have to pretend we don't like each other?" Thomas asked. "Do you think we could change things?"

Charles shook his head. "I don't know, Thomas. I'm sorry."

Thomas sat up to face Charles. "You haven't thought about this?"

"Of course I have, but it's a hard question to answer. There is no answer. Only time will tell."

Thomas frowned at him. "Can't you speculate?"

"Can't *you*?" Charles asked.

Thomas felt frustration growing inside him. Charles was avoiding the question. It was just like a Southworth to dance around the answer. He tried to push the thought out of his mind, angry with himself that it was ever there in the first place. Charles wasn't his enemy anymore. "Yes, but I wanted to hear your opinion," Thomas said, trying very hard to be patient.

Charles sighed a spiraling cloud of smoke. "I'd like to be optimistic about it, but to be honest with you, I don't think either of our families will *ever* be okay with this. Even if they were okay with their firstborn children being with someone of the same gender, they would never allow it to be with a *Hambleton* or a *Southworth*." He said their surnames with mock hatred, imitating the typical tone he would hear them in.

Thomas laughed at his impression of their silly rivalry.

Charles stared at Thomas for a quiet moment. "Thomas, can I ask you something?"

"Of course."

Charles narrowed his eyes and sucked on the cigarette again. "We've never talked about... magi," he said, looking away.

Magi? The conversation had taken a turn that Thomas was not expecting. "Why would we?" Thomas asked.

Charles arched an eyebrow and examined Thomas. "Seriously?"

Thomas scratched his head. "Do you know any magi?"

Charles shook his head. "Nope," he said quickly. "We don't need to talk about it."

"I don't understand. That has nothing to do with our future," Thomas said.

Charles eyed him again. Thomas did not understand the look. "Okay," Charles said, looking away with a muted scowl.

Thomas stared at Charles, but Charles would not look at him. "Charles..." Thomas said.

Charles finally looked at Thomas. Even under the pressure of this uncomfortable conversation, his pretty brown eyes still gave Thomas butterflies. Thomas smiled at Charles, and Charles's anger loosened from his features.

"That's not fair," Charles said. "Now you know my weakness."

Thomas laughed. "I'm going to use it against you every chance I get," he said.

"Good," Charles said, pulling Thomas closer so they sat side by side underneath the tree. "I hope you do."

Thomas laid his head against Charles's shoulder. "We have a lot of time to figure this out," Thomas said. "Everything will be okay."

"Yeah," Charles said, and he kissed the top of Thomas's head. "Everything will be okay."

Thomas hoped it was true.

Chapter Nine

"You've never heard of the Hambletons?" Fiona asked, tilting her head and frowning at Thomas. Like it was common knowledge. Like everyone in the world already knew.

Thomas shook his head, struggling to keep his breathing steady and normal. He wished he could say he hadn't heard his name before, but he couldn't believe the context he heard it at that moment. It couldn't be true. The way Faya and Fiona looked at him like he was stupid told him it was. No wonder his peers had always treated him like he was a powder keg near a lit match.

It was true. Somehow, for some reason, he hadn't known.

He should have known. Why didn't he? Why didn't his parents tell him? It seemed like a massive oversight.

"I didn't know," Thomas said. He didn't know if he was talking to himself or Faya and Fiona.

Fiona shrugged. "Why should you? It doesn't affect you."

Thomas just shook his head again. He felt extremely out of

place. He had no right to share a space with these magi. They had no idea who they were traveling with. He stood up. "I'm so sorry..." he said. "I'm sorry that's happening. I had no idea."

"You did think we were criminals," Fiona said with a lighthearted laugh.

Faya scowled at her. "Why is that funny?"

"It's not..." Fiona said, sobering from Faya's harsh gaze. "I'm just glad he knows the truth now."

"Excuse me, I need to..." Thomas tried to think of a normal, non-Hambleton-related reason to leave, but instead, let his sentence die as he walked through the cabin door.

The cool breeze blew over him, a welcome escape from the dark humidity of the cabin. He walked to the bow, taking deep breaths of salty ocean air.

How could he not know?

It explained a lot. It explained why his peers had always avoided him. It explained why Charles Southworth had been so *mean* to him his entire life, even when they liked each other. He deserved it. He had always lived right at the center of one of the world's worst conspiracies, and he was *completely oblivious*.

Thomas gripped the bulwark, holding himself steady against it as he took deep breaths. He couldn't seem to catch his breath, but he had hardly moved.

"Felix?" Mariana's crystal voice asked as she appeared at the side of the ship. "Are you all right?"

"Mariana," Thomas gasped. "I'm... I think I'm dying," he said. He deserved to die. He wanted to die. He was a *Hambleton*.

Mariana swung her legs over the side of the ship and walked toward him, grabbing his shoulders. She watched him desperately breathe. "Are you drowning? You're not underwater."

"I don't know. I don't know," Thomas said, holding onto her. She soaked through his clothes, but he barely noticed.

Mariana pulled him up and pushed him off her. His wet

clothes stuck to him where he had been clinging to Mariana. "You're not dying. Have you learned anything about the sirens?" she asked.

Thomas stared at her, trying to process the question. "What?"

"The sirens?"

Thomas glanced at the cabin, struggling to move past the horrible news he had just learned. Mariana didn't care that he was having a crisis. The merpeople depended on him. He had gone long enough selfishly ignoring the problems of the world for his own stupid issues. He was here to help her. It was the only reason he was still alive. "They appeared a year ago," he said. "That's all I know right now. I'm sorry."

"Why are you sorry?" she asked.

Thomas shook his head. He was sorry for existing. Sorry for ignoring the world. Sorry for being stupid enough to somehow *not know.* "Did anything notable happen a year ago?" he asked.

Mariana placed a finger against her mouth and looked into the sky as she thought about it. "The Pantheon."

"The what?"

"The decennial Pantheon meeting. The gods get together once every ten years to discuss our problems and conflicts. It usually lasts days because there are so many of us and we can't seem to get along... some of us more than others. I can't think of anything notable that happened during the meeting this time, except..." She looked at him again. "We were permitted to give mortals eternal life. The offer still stands, by the way."

"No. Stop asking," he said. "I would rather drop dead where I stand."

"The point of immortality is to *not* die," Mariana said, tilting her head.

"I know."

Mariana laughed like he had made a joke. "You're funny,

Felix. Acting like you want to die all the time. That's very unhuman of you."

Thomas frowned. He had never felt human, and he felt less human by the day.

Mariana shrugged. "Anyway, that correlation means nothing to me. What else have you learned?"

"I haven't learned anything else. Fiona is going to help me, so I'll have more information for you tomorrow."

"All right, let me know what you find out," she said with a smile, then collapsed back into the ocean as a column of water.

Thomas gripped the bulwark and stared at the darkening horizon. The sun sank beneath the ocean, casting bright orange reflections across the water. It was beautiful, but it was wasted on him. The world felt dead and tired no matter where he was. He didn't deserve to witness the beauty of the world when he was a source of evil in it.

He turned around but couldn't bring himself to face Faya and Fiona again. He decided to retire for the night instead.

Thomas couldn't sleep all night. He waited impatiently for the sunrise to spare him from the tossing and turning, but Fiona came first, appearing above him as a black silhouette in the early morning darkness of the living quarters.

"Felix," she hissed.

"Fiona," Thomas said grimly.

"I finished your bracelet."

Thomas sat up and tried to focus on the frizzy shape that was Fiona, but she remained a dark blur. It was probably better that he couldn't see her. It would be hard to look her in the eyes. "The mermaid bracelet?"

"Merman."

Thomas sighed. "Yeah, whatever. Great."

"What's wrong? Are you scared of using magic?"

"No!" Thomas insisted a little too quickly. "Not at all. Thank you, Fiona. You're amazing."

Fiona giggled. "Come on, let's go try it out!"

"Right now?" Thomas asked.

"Of course! This is the best time to do magic. When no one is around to see you," she said.

Thomas was grateful Fiona couldn't see his face. If she knew he was the reason she had to get up early to do what she loves, she wouldn't be sharing it with him. "Okay," he said.

"Are you all right?" Fiona asked, offering her shadowy hand for him to take.

"What?" Thomas asked, staring at her hand. "Why?"

"You seem down."

Thomas took her hand. She pulled him up, and he noticed for the first time that he was noticeably taller than her. He wasn't very tall at all, but he felt bigger than ever. Too big. "Is this better?" he asked.

She pushed him playfully and laughed. "You're hilarious. Come on," she said, dragging him toward the hatchway and up to the top deck.

The sun wasn't up yet, but the pale light slowly crept across the sky opposite from where it had disappeared the night before. Fiona held out her hand, revealing a pile of small clam shells weaved together by one long piece of twine.

"May I?" Fiona asked, reaching for his hand.

Thomas pulled away, holding his hand against his chest. "Isn't it going to turn me into a mermaid?"

"Mer*man*. And no, not right away. I wouldn't do that to you," she said with a smile. "May I please see your hand?"

Thomas hesitantly offered it to her. She gently held his arm as she slid the bracelet onto his wrist, the insides of the shells facing outward. She pulled a string, fastening the bracelet tight against his wrist.

He held his wrist up to observe her work. She had somehow knotted the twine in a way that made it adjustable. "It's inside out," he said, moving to flip it the right way.

"No!" Fiona said, grabbing his other wrist to stop him. "Sorry," she said, immediately letting go. She tucked a piece of curly ginger hair behind one ear and smiled apologetically. "That's how it works. If you flip it the right way, you'll turn into a merman. You don't want to do that right here."

She guided him to the edge of the ship, where the sirens had been tirelessly clawing at the hull all night. He wondered if the noise had kept Faya and Fiona up all night too. Fiona patted the top of the gunwale. "Sit here," she said.

Thomas peered down at the sirens. Their singing became frantic when they saw him. He shrugged. "All right," he said, hopping up onto the edge. He toyed with the idea of letting himself fall overboard, but Fiona caught him by the waist to steady him before he could commit.

"Whoa! Careful, Felix," she said with a nervous laugh. "You don't want to go down there as a human."

He did, but he wouldn't argue with her. Keeping her arm around his waist, she started working his bracelet right side out. "Wait," he said. Fiona stopped and looked up at him. "Should I take my clothes off?"

Fiona's eyebrows shot up. Her pale skin flushed pink, and a smile hid behind her forced stoicism. "Do you want to take your clothes off?"

"Not particularly."

Her expression cracked as she laughed at him. "You won't usually need to get naked for a transformation," she said.

"Usually?"

"Yeah," she said without elaborating, but even in the dim morning light, he could see that she was blushing to her fingertips. She silently worked the bracelet right side out, making sure the bracelet fit tight against his wrist when she was done.

In a wave that moved from his hips to his feet, his legs fused to form a fishtail with glimmering emerald scales. His feet flattened and expanded into translucent green fins.

Thomas hadn't realized he was clinging to Fiona until she spoke. "Are you all right?" she asked, wincing from his grip.

"Sorry!" he said, releasing her and almost falling backward.

Fiona caught him again but with less urgency. The sirens weren't singing anymore. They had dispersed when he became a merperson.

Thomas turned around to look at the empty water beneath him, still rippling from the sirens' departure.

"Felix!" Faya called from below deck. Her footsteps thundered across the length of the ship, then up the hatchway. Her face contorted with concern until she saw him sitting with a fishtail. She exhaled heavily. "Gods, I thought you were dead."

"Why?" Thomas asked.

"The sirens stopped singing. That's never a good sign."

"Well, not *never*," Fiona said with a proud smile.

Faya nodded, approaching them. "This is impressive, Fiona. Maybe now we can get some damn sleep."

"Ugh, I'm sorry, Faya," Thomas said, rubbing his eyes. "I didn't sleep last night either."

"It's not your fault, Felix," Faya said. "But you *are* sleeping with that tail tonight."

Thomas exhaled a short, involuntarily syllable of a laugh. "Sure, if it helps," he said.

"Hopefully we won't have to stay another night," Fiona said, looking back and forth between them. "We'll find Ametta today, we'll figure out the sirens tonight, and then we'll leave."

"Maybe we should split up and get it all done at the same time," Faya suggested.

Fiona twirled a long curly strand of hair around her index finger. "I don't know. That doesn't seem safe."

"Did you make more than one of these?" Thomas asked, lifting his wrist to show off his bracelet.

"Eh... No," Fiona said with a miserable frown.

"It would probably be better if he stayed here," Faya said. "He doesn't provoke the sirens in this state, and no one wants to hear that."

Thomas stared at the ground. "Yeah," he said quietly. "I'd probably just slow you guys down anyway." He wanted to help Faya get her daughter back. He wanted to redeem himself as a Hambleton, but he couldn't. These powerful, magical women didn't need his help.

"Oh, Felix, I didn't mean it like that," Faya said. "It's just... the situation isn't—"

"It's okay, Faya," Thomas said. "I understand. You two go find Ametta, and I'll try to find the sirens."

Fiona tugged at a clump of hair at her neck. "Will you be okay?"

"Yeah, I'll be all right," he said. "Be safe, okay?"

Faya and Fiona exchanged a nervous look before nodding at him. "You too, Felix," Faya said.

He offered them a short nod and a small smile in return. "Good luck," he said and then pushed himself over the edge into the dark water below.

CHAPTER TEN

Charles was unwell. The tight knot that had made itself at home in his stomach years ago grew ever tighter by the day. Sometimes by the hour. He wanted to think that he didn't know what caused it, but he knew. He wished he could ignore it, but it was part of him now. The only time it ever eased up was when he was with Thomas. Thomas was the most wonderful person he had ever met, and he hated that Thomas couldn't see it himself.

Charles and Thomas spent every single day together, but usually only as friends. Only on rare occasions could they truly be alone together. Normally it was during the weekend when nobody cared or worried about where they were, and they would spend the entire day in the forest by the lake. Those days were nice. But this was not one of those days. It *was* the weekend, but he had to stay on the school grounds because his parents were visiting again.

Thomas had learned his lesson the last time the Southworths

visited, and this time he stayed far, far away from Charles. Charles appreciated the lengths Thomas would go to for him but wished for nothing more than to be with him that day. It was only a matter of time before his parents started speaking ill of the Hambletons, specifically Thomas. It was impossible to visit with them without having at least one conversation about their biggest adversaries.

Charles did his best to hide his misery, but after a while, he struggled to mask it. His mother noticed quickly. "Charles, my dear, are you all right?" she asked. He realized he had been grimacing and quickly threw on a smile.

"Yes. I'm fine," he said in the most reassuring tone he could muster. "I'm just feeling nervous for the end of the term."

"You have nothing to worry about. You are the most academically minded student here by far," his father said. It wasn't a compliment. There was a difference between being academically minded and being smart. Compliance versus intelligence. It wasn't a compliment, and Charles suspected his father knew that.

"Thank you."

"You know who should be worried," his father said.

Oh no. Here it comes, Charles thought. He felt himself grimacing again and tried to swallow his discomfort.

"The headmaster. If he doesn't do something about these horrible sconces, we are going to have to withdraw some of our funding." His father drilled a look of disgust into an innocent light fixture on the wall above them.

Sconces? What a ridiculous thing to be upset about. At least he wasn't talking about Thomas. Charles nodded. "Yes, they are ugly." He didn't think they were ugly, and he wouldn't have cared if they were, but his father needed someone to agree with him, or his bad mood would only get worse. It could always get worse.

Everything could always get worse.

His parents had no idea how bad it could get. They would probably find out soon. Charles tried not to think about that. Instead, he looked at the artwork that hung on the walls and tried to find something to criticize, which was evidently what they were there to do. Now and then a student would amble by in their messy weekend attire, catch sight of the Southworths, and quickly try to straighten themselves up. Charles wondered what it was like to only have to worry about that once in a lifetime.

The next person to wander down the main hallway was not a student, but Professor Franklin. Professor Franklin was not particularly friendly, and he was quite dull, but he was one of the more agreeable teachers at the school. He stopped to greet the Southworths. "Ah, hello Alfred. Hello Lucille. How are we doing today?" he asked with a polite smile.

"Just fine, Quincy. How are you?" Alfred said. *Quincy?* Charles had spent almost every day of the last four months with this man but didn't know that his first name was Quincy. Strange.

"Glad to hear it. I'm great, thank you for asking." He nodded at Charles. "I don't mean to tell you that which I'm sure you already know, but your son here is a perfect student. We're very lucky to have him here at our academy."

That was a lie. Charles was smart and did his schoolwork, but he tended to be disruptive. Quincy was letting his fear speak for him. Nevertheless, Charles flashed a smile and said, "Thank you, professor."

"Yes, of course. I will also admit, it's nice to see a Southworth and a Hambleton getting along so well. I thought that feud would never die," he said with a hearty chuckle.

Charles felt his heart in his throat. He was in trouble. He did everything in his power to keep a calm demeanor, but he felt his eyes widening in fear despite his efforts. He fixed his gaze on the scarlet rug that ran the length of the hallway to delay the confrontation.

"I beg your pardon?" his father asked. Charles could hear the quiet fury in his tone, which probably wasn't audible to Professor Franklin.

Professor Franklin looked between the three of them before his eyes landed back on Alfred. "My apologies, Mr. Southworth. I thought you knew." Professor Franklin pawed at his hair and gave a nervous laugh. "Charles and Thomas have become quite close during the term."

Charles winced. It hadn't occurred to him that a teacher would tell his father about their friendship. He should have known. It was a stupid slip-up that he should have foreseen. His father said nothing. Charles could see in his peripheral vision that his father's eyes were now glued to him, and they would not become unglued until this was settled.

"Well, it was nice catching up with you. Have a nice evening," Professor Franklin said. He knew what he had done and left before he took any collateral damage.

"Goodbye, Quincy," Lucille said.

Charles kept his eyes on the ground for as long as he could. Hours seemed to pass before his father said anything. "Charles. Look at me." Charles slowly turned to face his father, his calm expression crumbling under the weight of his anxiety. "Is it true? Is Thomas your friend?"

"No. I hate him," Charles tried to lie, but the truth about his feelings for Thomas was louder. His father wasn't convinced.

"*Charles,*" his father scolded. Charles flinched but remained silent. "Don't lie to me."

Charles swallowed his fear. "Yes," he finally managed to say. "We are friends." It was still a lie, but an easier one.

His father released a lengthy, disappointed sigh. "This can't continue. It should never have happened in the first place," he said. "Do you remember the conversation we had in October?"

Charles's eyes fell to the floor again. How could he possibly forget that conversation? He remembered every painful moment of it. That was the day that everything changed. When everything got *worse*. "Yes."

"Please tell me that your," he paused, "*friendship...*" The word was displaced from the rest of the sentence like an outcast, as Charles would surely soon be. "...is just a cover?"

Charles swallowed nervously. He thought about the conversation he had recently had with Thomas. The conversation about uniting their families and changing the whole dynamic of the industry. Charles wanted to admit everything to his parents right then and there, but he knew he couldn't. It would ruin his life. He looked his father in the eyes again. His father wasn't asking him a question, he was telling Charles what the situation needed to be. His father's opinion of him was important whether Charles wanted it to be or not, but Charles wasn't sure that he would be able to do this.

"Yes, it is," Charles said. More than ever before, it was clear to him that he had a decision to make. This time the odds were not in his favor. It was bound to happen to someone at some point, but not him, and not now.

Chratan

Thomas had not anticipated the terror of falling twenty feet into the dark sea. The cold morning water engulfed him as he hit the surface, flailing to gain control. His instinct was to kick his legs, but his legs were gone, replaced with a tail that he did not know how to use. He flapped his fins in an attempt to propel himself forward and found that it was harder to swim with a tail than he had expected. He desperately clawed the water to keep steady as his tail moved him through the strange dark world below.

His body quickly began to crave oxygen. He had been holding his breath since he hit the water, and he would have no air left in his lungs soon. He had swum too far down. There was no way to reach the surface in time.

Suddenly, he took a deep involuntary breath of water, but it didn't go into his lungs. The frigid water traveled down his throat and outward through the side of his neck. He instantly felt relief. He touched his neck to feel the new anatomy that had saved him from drowning. There was a slit in his neck where smooth skin had been before. He inhaled another deep breath of water and felt the water filter out of his neck, recovering his reserves of oxygen.

Now that he wasn't as focused on his survival, he noticed that the sirens were still lurking around the cove. They swam away from the ship in slow, lurching movements. His skin prickled at the sight.

The world around him was very clear, not at all like when he had tried to open his eyes underwater in the past to a mild sting and blur. The colorful fish swam past him like he was a natural part of the environment. Darkness blanketed the seafloor, keeping the bottom out of sight.

Something about the darkness filled Thomas with deep dread. Logically, he knew he should explore it for Mariana, but instinctually he did not want to go anywhere near it. He forced himself to swim down, knowing it was the reason he was there. Investigating the sirens for Mariana was his only remaining purpose.

He descended deeper toward the horizontal wall of darkness, surprised at its unwillingness to reveal what hid beneath. As he got closer, he found that it *was* like a wall, unlike any darkness he had experienced before. He could reach out and touch where the darkness began, sitting stark against the clear tropical water above. Taking a deep breath of water,

Thomas pushed himself down. Even after crossing the inky threshold, he couldn't see.

His presence in the watery underworld started a chaotic clamor among whatever was down there. A loud hissing echoed from below and around him. He blinked hard, desperately trying to force his eyes to adjust. The pitch-black world slowly began to reveal blurry shapes below. The first thing he saw was sharp, snarling teeth and pale, angry eyes.

He was surrounded by sirens. Unlike his previous experiences, they did not try to attack him. They sat curled up around other dark, blurry shapes, hissing like scared cats. They wanted him gone.

He hovered around the entrance of this strange underworld, watching the sirens hiss until his eyes allowed him to see what they were protecting. When he finally realized what he was seeing, panic rose in his throat. He exhaled a strangled gasp as he flailed his tail in an uncoordinated attempt to swim away. The sirens were clinging to dead bodies. After a year underwater, they were mostly skeletons, but some were not quite as tolerable a sight.

Thomas did not stay to investigate more. He swam upward as fast as he could, breaking the surface and taking deep, desperate gulps of air. He shut his eyes to escape the too-bright, too-disgusting world, but the nauseating image remained burned to the back of his eyelids.

"Ugh!" he groaned, rubbing salt water into his eyes. "Mariana!" he yelled.

Mariana was at his side in an instant. She sat perched on the surface of the water like it was solid ground. "Felix! What did you find?"

"Why do you need me to go looking inside the ocean for you? Can't you see everything down there?" His voice wavered as he spoke.

"Can you see what's happening inside *your* body?" Mariana asked.

Thomas sighed, dropping his face into the water, but quickly pulled it out again when he remembered what waited underneath. He shook his head. "No," he croaked.

"What did you see?"

Thomas took a deep breath, preparing himself to say it out loud. "Dead people. So many dead people at the bottom."

Mariana nodded like it was normal. "The men from Widow's Cove?" she asked.

"Yes," Thomas coughed the word out.

"What's wrong?" Mariana asked, lying on her belly to investigate him closer. "You didn't know the sirens were killing people?"

"I've never seen a dead person before," Thomas said.

"Oh..." she said, tilting her head like she still didn't understand. "But you know that everyone eventually dies, don't you?" She smiled. "Except you, if you change your mind."

"Of course I know that!" Thomas snapped. "I don't want to live forever!"

Mariana frowned at him. "So, the sirens are hoarding dead men?" she asked.

A faint remnant of the siren's song drifted from the direction of the shore. Thomas looked toward the music and found the lone siren from yesterday, still clawing at Widow's Cove.

"That siren is trying to get to the women," Thomas thought aloud.

"Why?" Mariana asked.

"She probably likes women," Thomas said.

Mariana stared at him until understanding flickered in her eyes. "Oh," she said, carefully considering his face. "I see."

"I'll talk to you later," Thomas said, diving under to swim away from Mariana. He stayed entirely underwater as he swam but remained as close to the surface as possible. He didn't want Mariana to ask any follow-up questions, but he also didn't want to see the sea floor again.

When the blanket of darkness disappeared from beneath him, he knew he was close to the shore. The waves pushed him forward and reeled him back aggressively. He lowered himself onto the cool sand several feet behind the lonely siren, slowly pulling himself toward the surface.

The air warmed his skin as he crawled up onto the sandy beach beside the monster, who didn't care about his presence at all. He had never been so close to a siren before. Her skin was dark blue, and her hair fell around her in tumbling black curls. She clawed the sand of the beach with long, sharp nails and sang beautifully at the passing women with a desperate look on her face. It was almost like she was calling for help.

Now that he was here, Thomas didn't know what to do. How could he help her? "Hello," he said.

Her pale milky eyes landed on him for a careless moment before she turned her attention back onto the people of Widow's Cove.

Thomas tugged at the seashell bracelet on his wrist. He couldn't do much with a tail, but he wouldn't be able to help her as a human either. What was the point? He watched her scramble through the sand for a minute until he got an idea.

He loosened his bracelet and then grabbed the siren's arm. The siren did not allow it. She stopped singing and snapped at Thomas, sinking her sharp teeth into his arm.

"Agh!" he yelled, pulling his bleeding arm away from her. Maybe this wouldn't work.

She looked much more frightening with his blood on her mouth but went back to ignoring him as she clawed at the beach.

Thomas wouldn't give up. He took a deep breath, then pulled his bracelet off. He grabbed the siren's arm again, slipping the bracelet onto her wrist and tightening it before she could take another chunk out of him.

The siren slowly stopped singing. She blinked hard a few times, and then rolled onto her back, pushing her head into the sand with a scratchy, pained groan.

Shit. He had messed up. The enchantment didn't work both ways. He reached for her arm again, but before he could pull it off, she rolled back onto her stomach and coughed up something dark black. Was it blood? Was she dying? Thomas reached toward her but stopped when she groaned again. It sounded so human that he had to check to see if she still had a tail. She didn't. She had two human legs. Her skin was no longer blue, but a lovely shade of dark brown.

"Hey, are you all right?" Thomas asked, clutching his bleeding arm in his hand.

She looked up at him with two bright golden eyes and a desperate open-mouthed frown. She was beautiful. "What happened? Where am I?" As she spoke, the black matter she had coughed up squirmed away, slinking into the ocean like some kind of disgusting unknown deep-sea creature.

"Did you see that?" Thomas asked, staring into the incoming wave where the black creature had disappeared. Over the rush of the waves, Thomas heard a familiar sound. The sound of singing.

He only realized his mistake when it was too late.

A wave washed over him, bringing with it dark, clawed hands to grab him and pull him in. Thomas grabbed handfuls of sand, desperately trying to pull himself back onto the beach, but the sirens were stronger. Images of the underwater graveyard flashed through his mind. He couldn't die among the corpses in that nightmarish place. "Help! Help me!" he yelled at the girl, but she had that distant look in her eyes. The look that meant she was probably about to die with him.

The mermaid moved toward the sirens, crawling forward

slowly as she reached out her hand. Walking with human legs did not come naturally to her.

The sirens dug their claws into Thomas's legs. He yelled in pain as he reached for the mermaid. If he could just get that bracelet back from her, he could fix this. The sirens didn't want mermen. Maybe a mermaid wouldn't want the sirens either. Maybe she was only affected by their music because she was human at the moment.

Her arm was just out of reach. She dragged herself toward him just as the sirens dragged him back, digging sharp nails into his skin as they pulled him in further.

The mermaid crawled forward a few more inches, and it was enough. Thomas desperately lurched forward, grabbing onto her arm. The sirens pulled him back again, matching his energy. His grip slipped, but he caught the bracelet on the way down, holding onto it with all of his strength as he pulled it off of her.

Thomas prayed to Dei that she wouldn't turn back into a siren now that he had the bracelet. He tried to slip the bracelet back onto his wrist, but he couldn't wrestle one arm from the sirens long enough to reach the other. They had dragged him under completely, and now they were fighting over him.

He struggled against the sirens, fighting hard to turn himself back into a merman. No matter how hard he tried, he could not break free, and he was running out of air. Panic filled his chest. He suppressed a desire to inhale, but his instincts took over. He inhaled a deep lungful of offensively salty water. He coughed to get the water out, which only caused him to inhale more water. His lungs were on fire. Moving became difficult, and his vision began to darken at the edges.

This is it, he thought. *I'm going to die.*

Chapter Eleven

Blackwater Academy

It was a gloomy Saturday afternoon. The cold wind beat against the shuttered windows, fighting to reach the warm interior of the building. The end of the term was fast approaching, with final exams starting at the beginning of the week. Many students at Blackwater Academy spent the weekend cramming as much information into their heads as would fit to prepare for their exams. Most chose to study in the warmth of the library, surrounded by other students who could help them. Thomas preferred the solitude of his dorm room. Studying with others was far too distracting for him. That didn't stop him from studying with Charles, of course, but Charles was spending the day with his parents.

It was getting late, and Charles would be returning soon. The door to Thomas's room was propped open so that he could keep an eye on the hallway. Charles's room was near the end of the hall, so Thomas would see when he walked by. At that moment Thomas was occupied with a final essay for his literature class.

The mental strain of composing each sentence slowly drained him. Eventually, he gave up and rested his head against the wooden desk.

The sound of his door clicking shut and a gentle hand on his back pulled him from his academic stupor. He sat upright and looked at the tall figure that stood alone in the room with him. "Charles!" Thomas grinned, internally scolding himself for sounding too excited to see a person who was only supposed to be his friend.

"Hey, Tommy." Charles smiled, and suddenly the room didn't feel quite so cold. Charles looked like he hadn't slept for a week. His visits with his parents always seemed to drain the life out of him. "You look like you're having fun," Charles said sarcastically.

"Yeah, so do you," Thomas said. He leaned back in his chair. "How did it go?"

Charles shrugged and his smile disappeared. "You know how they are."

"Yeah," Thomas agreed, not entirely sure what he meant.

Charles looked around the room. "You got the room to yourself, huh?" he asked.

Thomas looked behind him at the empty beds that occupied the limited floor space. Looking back at Charles he said, "I *did* have it to myself..." Charles looked around the room again, not catching on, and then threw a quizzical look at Thomas. "Up until a few moments ago," Thomas added, snickering at Charles.

Charles's confused expression immediately changed to mock surprise. "Oh! I'm so sorry. I'll just show myself out." He took a few steps toward the door before Thomas threw his hand forward to grab Charles's hand.

"No, wait!" Thomas said. Charles stopped, turning to smile slyly at Thomas. Thomas stood up, still holding his hand. He looked from the closed door to the back of the empty room to make sure that they were alone. "I like being alone, but I'd rather be alone with you."

Charles's smile became sad. "Thomas…"

Thomas let go of Charles's hand and took a step away from him. "I know, I'm sorry. Not here."

"No, that's not what I was going to say." Charles grabbed Thomas's hand and pulled him close again.

It was risky for them to be so close in Thomas's room, but Thomas didn't care. In his opinion, they spent too much time apart, and this was long overdue. "What were you going to say?" Thomas asked. The butterflies in his stomach flapped their wings to the beat of his pounding heart.

Charles took a deep breath and frowned at Thomas's hand in his own before speaking. He exhaled and looked into Thomas's eyes. "I love you," he said. Without waiting for a response, Charles slid his arms around Thomas and held him in a tight embrace. "I love you, Thomas Hambleton."

A wide smile broke across Thomas's face. Nothing could ruin this moment. Thomas had been nervous to hear what Charles had to say, but it was better than anything he had expected. He wrapped his arms around Charles and squeezed him tight. "I love you too, Charles."

"Thomas…"

"Yes?" Thomas asked. He broke away from the embrace to look at Charles, who remained silent. Charles looked exhausted and uncomfortable. Something was wrong.

"I don't think we can change anything," Charles said. "I don't think we have that power. It's either us or them."

"Oh," Thomas said. He considered Charles's words for a moment before he spoke again. "I'd rather be with you than live the life that's expected of me."

Charles nodded. Thomas could see that rejecting his future was going to be much harder for Charles than it would be for

Thomas. "Me too," Charles said. "I don't care where I end up anymore, as long as you're there."

Thomas placed his hands on either side of Charles's face and pulled him into a kiss. Charles gently pulled Thomas closer. When they parted, Thomas's paranoid eyes darted to the closed door while Charles's tired eyes wandered to the empty bed.

"These beds are small, but I bet they could fit two," Charles said, his eyes glued to Thomas's small single bed. The beds at Blackwater Academy were very small since they were meant for only one person. Nobody ever expected to share.

"Oh, no, Charles. I don't think that's a good idea," Thomas said. "You're just tired." As he spoke, Thomas gently brushed aside the messy strands of dark hair that had fallen across Charles's forehead.

Charles hummed in disagreement. "I *am* tired. Do you mind if I stay here while you study?"

"I'm not studying, I'm writing an essay. But, yes, of course you can stay here."

"Oh. Do you want help with it? I finished mine already," Charles said blearily.

"No, thank you. You look like you need to sleep. You can take a nap if you'd like." Thomas said.

Charles frowned.

"What's wrong?" Thomas asked.

"We've been apart all day. I don't want to be so far away from you."

"It's not even five feet away," Thomas said, laughing because Charles was being ridiculous, but also because he was flattered.

"That's too far," Charles complained.

"Okay, fine. I'll come sit beside you until you fall asleep," Thomas said. Charles grinned triumphantly at Thomas, and Thomas couldn't help smiling back. Charles's smile was contagious. Charles shuffled across the small room and fell onto the single bed. Thomas dragged his desk chair to the side of the bed and sat down with a book to study from.

Charles tossed one arm over the edge of the bed. "Hold my hand."

Thomas laughed. Charles's demanding nature was starting to show now that all of his charisma had been used up for the day. "Okay." Thomas interlaced their fingers, flipping through the book with his other hand.

"Tommy," Charles's voice broke through the wall of focus that had begun to descend over Thomas. Thomas admitted to himself that trying to study would be a futile effort while Charles was there. Even when Charles was trying to sleep, he was a distraction.

"Yes, dear," Thomas said in a tone of fake sincerity, closing the book and setting it aside.

"This might be the last time we get to be alone together for a long time," Charles said. "This next week we're going to be busy with our exams and after that, we'll be home."

"Yeah, that's true." Thomas hadn't thought about it much. "It's a good thing we both live in Brenton."

"Right. Where both of our extremely loving and understanding families will let us spend all of our time together," Charles said.

Thomas sighed. Charles had a point. "It'll be okay," he said, but he didn't know if it would be.

"Can I have one last kiss?"

Thomas shot another nervous look at the doorway before leaning over the bed to kiss his boyfriend for what he sincerely hoped was not the last time. Charles hooked his arm around Thomas and pulled him onto the bed. Thomas pulled away from the kiss to find himself sitting on Charles. "Hey!" he said, offended at Charles's audacity. He whipped his head around to take another look at the door. "Somebody is going to see us."

"There's no one here. It's fine," Charles said, pulling him back down to kiss him again. Thomas decided that it probably was fine. Charles was usually right, and Thomas trusted him. He tried to relax. Thomas slid one hand under the lapel of Charles's school blazer and slowly began to slide it off his shoulders. It was stupid that he was wearing it on a Saturday, anyway. Charles sat up to help him get it off, and quickly threw it to the floor, an act that probably would have upset his parents if they knew. Considering what Thomas and Charles were doing at the moment, the coat would have been the least of their concerns.

Thomas slid his hands up Charles's chest, his fingers grazing the collar of Charles's shirt. He broke away from kissing Charles and took a deep breath. It took everything in his power to stop. Going any further than this would *definitely* get them in trouble. "It's okay," Charles said, holding Thomas's face in his hand and guiding their lips back together. Thomas knew that was a lie. It was not okay, but that was all he needed to hear to convince him to continue.

Thomas's fingers moved on their own, unbuttoning the first two buttons of Charles's shirt while his brain begged him to stop. He didn't get much farther than that before a sharp knock from the door echoed loudly through the room. Before either of them had time to react, the door opened, and the sound of footsteps entered the room. Thomas had never been one for prayer, but at this moment he prayed to Dei that his roommate would be understanding and discreet.

Charles pushed Thomas off him to the other end of the bed with such force that Thomas could only watch Charles with astonishment. Charles frantically buttoned his shirt, staring at the doorway in wide-eyed horror. Thomas's back was to the door, which gave him three extra seconds of blissful ignorance before he also saw who had entered the room. It wasn't his roommate standing at the door. It wasn't even school faculty. It was Alfred and Lucille Southworth.

A deadly silence filled the room as a similar horror enveloped Thomas. Surprise cracked through Lucille's usual stoic façade. Alfred glowered at his son with disgust. "*Ten minutes,*" he said. "It has been *ten. Minutes.* Since we spoke, Charles."

Charles scrambled out of bed and grabbed his coat off the floor. Thomas had been right about the blazer. It was the least of their worries. "I'm sorry," he said. His voice was small and scared.

"I came here to have a word with Thomas, about your... *friendship.*" The word was dirty in his mouth. "But it appears you got here before me."

"You told them?" Thomas asked.

"No!" Charles said.

The horrible silence returned. Thomas didn't know what to do or say to ease the tension. Nothing could be done. Alfred cut through the silence like a predator as he approached the bed. Thomas instinctively leaned backward, but Alfred struck at Charles, grabbing his arm and pulling him toward the door. Alfred eyed Thomas with disgust while Thomas slid off the bed and planted his feet firmly on the floor. Thomas looked from Alfred to Charles, expecting Charles to chime in any moment with an explanation. After all, they had just had this discussion minutes ago. Charles would rather be with Thomas in exile than live alone as a Southworth. Wouldn't he? His heart beat fast as the silence grew heavier. Thomas began to worry that he hadn't followed the first rule of dealing with a Southworth, and it was about to destroy him: *Don't believe anything they say.*

"Charles," Alfred said and slowly turned to look at his son. He kept his hand clamped firmly around Charles's arm. Charles refused to look at his father. "*Charles,*" he repeated more firmly. Charles flinched and made feeble eye contact with Alfred.

"Yes," Charles whispered. It was not a question, but a compliance.

"Did Thomas assault you?"

Charles's eyes grew wide at the question. He refused to look at Thomas, fixing his eyes on the ground instead.

Thomas felt his heart in his throat. Alfred knew exactly what was happening between him and Charles, and he was trying to turn it into something else. But Charles wouldn't take the opportunity to escape responsibility, right? Moments earlier, Charles had told Thomas that he loved him. He would do the right thing.

Wouldn't he?

"Charles," the desperate plea came from Thomas before he even knew he was talking.

"*Be quiet!*" Alfred scolded Thomas. Thomas swallowed his words. Alfred turned to his son again. "Well?" he asked. Charles pulled his arm away from his father, breaking free from his grip. Standing up straight, he cleared his throat and took one brief, detached look at Thomas. Thomas had a moment of hope, just as brief, that Charles would be honest. Until he spoke.

"Yes," Charles said quietly. "He assaulted me."

Chapter Twelve

Chratan

The world went dim. Thomas's lungs burned hotter than fire, screaming for air. There was no escaping the death grip of the sirens. He was going to die.

In his final moments, Thomas thought about home. He would never see his parents again. That was fine. They didn't want him around anyway. He would also never see Charles again, but he didn't know if that was fine.

Thomas didn't expect it to end like this. He had always thought he would go out on his own terms, not at the hands of a monster that wasn't even meant for someone like him.

It *couldn't* end like this. The mermaids still needed help. The magi still needed help. If he didn't get out of there, his entire life would be wasted. People would continue to suffer when *he* could do something about it. He fought and pulled against the claws that sliced into his skin, but their grip remained strong. His oxygen-deprived body didn't have much fight left, but he would use it all.

A pair of arms wrapped around his waist and pulled, wrenching him away from the claws buried in his skin. Thomas opened his eyes, but all he could see was a dark mess of curly hair.

His plan had worked. The mermaid came back for him. He was free from the monsters.

Before the sirens could attack again, Thomas slipped the bracelet over his wrist, impatiently waiting for the transformation to occur. The snarling faces of the sirens came into clear focus just as a siren lurched at him again. She stopped in place, no longer interested in him. Thomas gasped, desperately breathing water through his gills.

The mermaid marveled at his new tail while she held onto him. "How did you do that?"

"Maa—" Seawater traveled through his gills and out of his mouth so he could speak, and it was a sensation he was not used to. "Magic," he said, cringing at the unfamiliar feeling of water moving over his vocal cords.

The mermaid frowned at him. "Was I...?" She watched the dark shape of the sirens swimming away but didn't finish her question.

"Yes," Thomas said.

She looked at him again. "You saved me."

Thomas shrugged. "And you saved me."

She smiled sadly. "Thank you." Her smile fell away as she examined his tail. Small spirals of dark crimson blood escaped from the scratches where his legs had once been. "Are you all right?"

"I'll live," Thomas said. "What's your name?"

"My name's Fyavine. You?"

"Felix."

"It's nice to meet you, Felix."

"Likewise," Thomas said. Guilt tugged at his core. This

woman had saved his life and he couldn't even tell her his name. "I don't want to be down here anymore."

"No, me neither," the mermaid said. She released him, and he noticed for the first time that her tail was no longer blue, but the same beautiful sparkling gold of her eyes.

"Would you like to come with me?" Thomas asked. "It doesn't seem like there's much left down here."

Fyavine nodded sadly. "There's nothing left but death and loss."

"Come on, I'll let you wear the bracelet," Thomas said, lifting his wrist to show it off.

Fyavine stared at the bracelet, then at him. "I don't know if that's a good idea. The sirens affected me as a human."

"Right..." Thomas said. He stared at her for an uncomfortably long moment, struggling to find the right words to ask what he needed to ask.

"But they don't affect you?" she asked.

"I'll carry you," he said, desperate to get out of the conversation now that Fyavine had moved it forward.

"All right..."

Fyavine dragged him to the surface, where they emerged together. Suddenly, he was drowning again. He violently coughed water into the sea. His body refused to let him take a breath while it cleared the airways. Thomas clawed at his chest helplessly while he suffocated.

Fyavine pushed Thomas's head underwater again. "Breathe, Felix."

Thomas inhaled seawater until he wasn't suffocating anymore. "What is happening? Why can you breathe up there, but I can't?"

"You still have lungs, but you probably inhaled a lot of water. It will take a minute for you to be able to use them again. Don't forget you can breathe underwater," Fyavine said.

Thomas relaxed and allowed himself to catch his breath before surfacing again. It took him several long, painful minutes to clear his lungs, but finally, he could breathe air again.

Fyavine pulled him to the beach, doing all the work of swimming for him. They sat in the surf together, letting the waves wash over them as they collapsed into the wet sand.

"Gods, I'm exhausted," Fyavine said.

Thomas rested his head against his forearms and sighed. "This has not been my week."

Fyavine laughed gently. "I know what you mean."

Thomas turned to look at her. He didn't believe she knew how it felt to almost die, find a graveyard of corpses, and discover her parents have been destroying the world behind her back all within twenty-four hours, but he didn't say that. He didn't know what it felt like to be a man-eating monster.

Then again, maybe he knew it better than she did.

Thomas rolled onto his back, inhaling sharply as the gritty sand rubbed against the scratches the sirens had left. He finally realized the scratches weren't just on his tail. Red lines covered his chest and stomach. He couldn't see it, but he felt the sting down his back too.

"Are you all right?" Fyavine asked.

Thomas nodded. "Yep. I'm great." He pushed himself up, sliding farther up onto the beach so that he was entirely out of the water.

Fyavine followed him, dragging herself through the sand. "Seriously, that doesn't look g—"

"It's fine," Thomas said, yanking the shell bracelet off his wrist. All at once, his fins disappeared, replaced by his human legs, which continued to sting from the scratches. He groaned as he stood up.

"Felix—"

"I'm fine," he said again. He slid one hand under Fyavine's tail and the other around her back. "Ready?" he asked.

Fyavine slid her arm around his neck, hanging onto him tightly. "If you drop me, so help me—"

Thomas laughed and lifted her from the ground just as the sirens began to sing again. He watched her warily.

She rolled her eyes. "It only affects humans. I'm fine."

He smiled at her, wondering if she knew what that meant for her. He trudged across the beach, carrying her to a short stone wall near the pier that sat off to the side where they wouldn't draw too much attention. Each step hurt more than the last. By the time they reached the wall, his scratches burned like fire.

Thomas set Fyavine on top of the short wall and pushed himself up beside her. Her tail was much longer than his legs were, and it sparkled gold in the morning sunlight.

Thomas took a deep breath. "Fyavine, can I ask you something?"

"The answer is yes; I do think you should see a doctor."

Thomas glared at her. "I'm not sick."

"No, but you've been scratched to shreds," she said.

Thomas scratched his head. "Oh, yeah. Right... I'm okay." He pulled his wet shirt away from his abdomen in an attempt to stop the scratches from bloodying his shirt but wound up biting his lip at the sting of contact. Fyavine frowned at him and shook her head. He forced his pained expression into a smile.

"Hey!" a woman yelled as she ran down the beach toward them. It was the woman who had tried to stop him from entering town when he had first arrived. "You!"

Thomas pushed himself off the stone wall, wincing at the sting of salt and sand against his cuts. "Hello. Is there a problem?" he asked.

"Yes, there is. Did I see you doing magic? You turned her into a human!" she said, then eyed Fyavine. "And what are *you* doing out of the water?"

"I am *not* going back in there. Are you kidding?" Fyavine asked, crossing her arms as she watched the sirens roll over each other in the sand trying to reach Thomas.

"It's where you belong," the woman said.

"I think you belong somewhere else minding your own business," Fyavine snapped back. "I'm not hurting anyone out here. What's the problem?"

"I don't know how many men you've killed."

Fyavine's face fell. She glanced at Thomas, then at the sirens. "I haven't killed anyone," she said quietly.

"Sirens aren't welcome here. You'll return to the water if you know what's good for you," the woman said.

Fyavine's somber expression vanished as quickly as it had appeared, replaced with fury. "Excuse me? I am *not* a siren, and you aren't the only victims here. I lost my home and family because of the sirens."

Thomas leaned against the wall, taking this opportunity to give himself a break. He lifted his arm to examine the bite mark Fyavine had left. She had bitten him deep, and his wrist dripped blood onto the pale sand.

"Why are you bleeding?" the woman asked, noticing his apathy toward their conversation.

"Because I was attacked by sirens," Thomas snapped.

"And you survived?"

"*Obviously,*" Thomas said.

"Is there a doctor who can help him?" Fyavine asked.

"I'll see if Kassandra is available, but I'm also contacting the authorities. You can't be doing magic out here."

"I can't?" Thomas asked, too surprised at the legal restrictions on magic to defend himself against it.

The woman arched an eyebrow. "The Hambletons can help you," she said, then she turned to leave.

"The Hambletons?" Fyavine asked. "What a ridiculous name. Who are they?"

"Just some horrible rich family," Thomas muttered.

Fyavine nodded like she knew what he meant. "How will they help you?"

"They won't. They fucking suck. Let's get out of here," Thomas said.

Fyavine frowned at her tail, brushing the tips of her fins against the damp sand. "I can't move, and I won't let you carry me again."

"Like hell, you won't," Thomas said. "If she comes back, we're both screwed. We're swimming back to the ship." He raised the shell bracelet for her to see. If they were both merpeople, the sirens wouldn't bother them.

Fyavine sighed. "I don't know, Felix. What if I become a siren again?"

Thomas hadn't considered that. He didn't know what turned a mermaid into a siren, but judging by the black matter Fyavine had coughed up, it was some kind of illness. What did it take to get infected? "Maybe we should walk," he said.

Fyavine shook her head. "I don't know how. I'm sorry."

"Right. And the whole... siren song thing," Thomas said.

Fyavine cackled. "Would they even take me if I ran to them?" she asked. "Maybe that wouldn't be so bad..."

Thomas stared at her, trying to understand what she meant. She had to know what she was saying. Surely, she knew she was like him.

A scuffle of footsteps in the direction of town startled him. A team of three tall, tough-looking women approached him and Fyavine with angry frowns. Thomas grabbed Fyavine's arm, not sure what he planned to do with it. "Let me carry you," he said in a hushed whisper.

Fyavine frowned at him, glancing back and forth between him and the women who were clearly on their way to arrest them. "Are you sure you can handle that?" she whispered.

Thomas placed one arm around her back and the other under her tail. He lifted with all the strength left in him but could barely get her an inch from her seat before grunting in pain and dropping her back onto the wall. "Shit," he whispered. "Sorry."

Fyavine placed a gentle hand on his shoulder. "Let's swim back, that was a good idea."

Thomas breathed heavily, holding himself up against the wall beside her. He didn't know if he could get her to the water in time. He didn't know if he'd be able to swim all that way. He nodded. "Yeah, okay."

Before he could try again, a strong hand gripped his shoulder and whirled him around. "You're the magus?" an angry woman with dark hair and dark eyes asked him.

Thomas shook his head. "I'm not a magus."

"We heard a report of magical activity out here."

Thomas shrugged. "I've never done magic before."

The woman narrowed her eyes and then scrutinized Fyavine. "Why are you out of the water?"

Fyavine threw the salty look right back. "Would *you* want to get in the water right now?"

"Come on," the woman said, pulling Thomas by the arm toward the city. The sirens wailed desperately as he walked away. "Bring the siren! We've waited a long time to meet one..."

Thomas struggled against her grip as he watched the other two women take Fyavine under the arms and drag her through the sand. What were they going to do with her? What did that mean? "Let her go!" he demanded.

The woman ignored his pleas through the city, eventually

leading him and Fyavine into a wide town square with a large stone building as the central structure. She pushed Thomas toward the building, and Thomas got the sense that he wouldn't be leaving for a while.

Inside, the women led them through a back hallway and into a small room to present him to another woman in protective leather gear, who appeared to be a high-ranking official. She sat in a chair at a wooden table set against the wall, leafing through a large book. At their entrance, she looked up and scrutinized Thomas with suspicious, narrowed eyes. "Who is this?"

"We caught him doing magic," the woman holding him explained, then looked at Thomas. "What's your name?"

He glared at her.

The other two women dragged Fyavine in behind him and threw her onto the floor. She rolled onto her side and rubbed her elbow with an uncomfortable frown on her face.

"Your name," the woman repeated.

Thomas flinched. It wouldn't matter if they knew his fake name. As long as they didn't know the real one. "Felix," he said.

"Last name?"

"Warren."

"Who's the siren?" the seated officer asked.

"I'm a *mermaid!*" Fyavine spat, rolling onto her stomach to shoot them a hateful glare.

The officer rolled her eyes and stood up, approaching Fyavine. "Take her to the holding cell. I need to have a word with..." She narrowed her eyes at Thomas. *"Felix."*

Uh oh. Did she know who he was?

The three women left the room, dragging Fyavine behind them. Thomas lurched after them, unhappy with the way Fyavine was being treated, but the officer caught his arm and pulled him back into the room. She shut the door behind him and eyed the walls around her, where numerous weapons and other unfamiliar devices hung from nails. The officer approached the wall to her right and unhooked a rectangular contraption with a bulb sticking from the top.

"Have a seat, Felix," she said, gesturing at the seat she had previously occupied.

Thomas nervously glanced between her and the wooden chair, worried about what would happen if he did as she said.

"I'm not going to hurt you," she added. "I'm trying to help you."

Thomas reluctantly took a seat at the table, seeing no other way out of the situation.

"My name is Officer Caldera. Where are you from?"

Thomas fixed his uncomfortable glare on her. "Tinera," he said, unable to think of a plausible lie.

"Tinera? Where in Tinera?"

Thomas was silent for a moment as he struggled to think of an answer. "Wakefield." It was the farthest town from Brenton he could think of that was still in Tinera.

"Are you a magus, Felix?"

Thomas scoffed. "No."

Officer Caldera observed him for a moment and then nodded. "You know, that's what every magus says."

Thomas narrowed his eyes. "And what do the unmagic say?"

To his surprise, she laughed. "I didn't think it would be so easy to get you to admit it."

Thomas's jaw dropped. Her twisting of his words was a great injustice. He hadn't admitted anything.

"Words don't matter, anyway. I have this to help," she said, raising the contraption in the air for him to see.

"What is that?"

Officer Caldera squinted at him like it was a weird question. She hesitated a moment before she pointed the device at him and turned the dial. The bulb slowly brightened with a golden yellow light. She furrowed her brow. "Hmm..." She looked up at him. "They said you were doing magic? How is that possible?"

"I wasn't," Thomas insisted. "What does that light mean?"

"Did you work for the Hambletons?" Officer Caldera asked.

"What?" Thomas asked. What did this have to do with the Hambletons? How would she know that from this device?

"Answer the question."

It was a yes-or-no question, but neither answer was technically correct. *Just say no,* he told himself, but the word wouldn't come out. He just stared at Officer Caldera, trying hard to understand.

"They'll be wanting you back," she said before he could reply. "Let's go." She grabbed him firmly by the arm and led him out of the room.

"Wait!" Thomas called. "I don't want to go back, please! You don't understand!" He didn't know who she thought he was, but he knew what he was to the Hambletons. They wouldn't want him back.

But what was that contraption, and how did it connect him to the Hambletons? Why didn't he know the answer to these questions as a Hambleton himself?

Officer Caldera ignored his demands and dragged him out of the small room, across the main hall, and into a dark, narrow room lined with dingy jail cells. The only source of light in the room was through the small, barred square windows in the wall of each cell, casting an unhelpful beam of light into each tiny room. She unlocked a cell at the back of the room and threw Thomas inside, slamming the metal door behind him to quickly lock it again.

Thomas wondered how he managed to get himself thrown in a cell again. It must have been all of his good luck.

"Come back!" Thomas called after the soldier as she headed back through the main entrance. "I don't belong here!" Officer

Caldera ignored him, pulling the door shut behind her with unnecessary force.

Thomas sighed and rested his head against the bars of his cell. Things weren't going well for him. The Widow's Cove soldiers were going to send him back to Brenton. He couldn't think of a worse fate. He wished that Mariana had left him to die on the Southworth ship, or that the sirens had drowned him. He hoped Faya and Fiona were okay.

"Hey, Felix."

Thomas whirled around to find he wasn't alone. He had been locked in the same cell as Fyavine. She sat on a wooden bench attached to the wall by two rusty chains.

"Fyavine! Are you okay?" he asked.

Fyavine nodded somberly.

"Did they hurt you?" Thomas asked.

"I'm fine," she said. "Are you okay? How are your scratches?"

Thomas grimaced at his splotchy shirt and bloody wrist. "I think they've stopped bleeding," he said.

Fyavine shot him a skeptical look. "We have to get out of here."

Thomas nodded. He couldn't go back to Brenton, and he couldn't let Fyavine go back into the ocean.

Escape was the only option.

BLACKWATER ACADEMY

"Charles," Thomas whispered. He didn't know what to say. He couldn't believe this was happening. "Why?"

Charles refused to look at Thomas.

Thomas couldn't think. His heart pounded in his chest, begging to be freed before it shattered. He couldn't take his eyes off Charles, who had seconds ago told Thomas that he loved him.

Alfred grabbed his son by the arm again and yanked him into the hallway. "You are coming home with us. I don't understand how anything like this could have happened. This school is supposed to be safe." Alfred cast a deadly stare at Thomas. "You disgust me. You're worse than the monster that raised you. Expect to be home by the start of the week, Mr. *Hambleton.* Your time here is over."

Thomas had no words. Hot tears filled his eyes as he helplessly watched the Southworths walk away, taking his heart with them. "I'm such an idiot," Thomas whispered as tears ran down his face. "*Damn it.*" He took a deep shuddering breath and exhaled a heavy sob. He didn't care what people would think of him, or that he was getting kicked out of school. He could deal with anything when he had Charles on his side, but he didn't have Charles anymore.

Thomas fell onto the bed and buried his face into the pillow to muffle the sound of his crying. What else could he do but wait to be thrown out of school? A painful eternity passed as he drowned his pillow with tears. Nothing mattered anymore. The room could have been on fire, and he wouldn't have cared.

An idea suddenly struck him. He sat up.

Rage quickly replaced his despair. How could Charles betray him after everything he said? Thomas tossed the pillow to the side and slithered off the bed. It took tremendous effort to push himself up. He dragged his heavy feet through the room, wiping tears from his face before stepping into the hall. Thomas peered into the long, dim hallway and spotted his destination to his right.

Charles's room.

Charles wasn't there. He was probably already on his way home. In Alfred's theatrical haste, he hadn't allowed Charles to collect his things before leaving. If Alfred was going to claim that Thomas made the school unsafe, he might as well make it true.

Thomas dragged his bare feet along the cold wooden floor until he reached Charles's door. He gripped the icy brass knob and threw the door open to the surprise of Charles's roommate, Walter.

"Thomas!" Walter said, lifting his head from a book. Thomas ignored the greeting and walked past Walter to Charles's desk. "What are you doing?"

"Charles asked me to bring him his bag." Thomas tried to keep his voice level, but he could hear anger slipping through.

"Oh," Walter said. After a short pause, he asked, "Have you been crying?"

Ugh. Walter. Thomas picked up Charles's school bag and slung it over his shoulder carelessly. Rifling through the contents, he said, "No. What gave you that idea?" Everyone else was lying about obvious truths, why couldn't he?

"Your nose is red, and your eyes are puffy and watery."

"I'm sick," Thomas said. His fingers stopped at a thick packet of paper. *There it is,* he thought. *That damn essay.*

"Ew," Walter said, leaning away from Thomas as he headed for the door. "Feel better soon."

"I won't." Thomas slammed the door shut behind him.

Thomas hurried through the dorm halls and down the stairs to the main hall. The door to the sideyard was to his left. He pushed the door open and emerged into the cold winter night. Snowflakes stung his face as he waded through the snowy grass toward a large oak tree. The freezing pain in his feet did not register. He had a goal, and he would not stop until he had achieved it.

Thomas fell to his knees beneath the tree. Cold snow soaked through his pants, but he didn't care. He held Charles's bag tightly in his lap. The dorm hall loomed over him, its orange glowing windows speckling the wall that concealed all the happy, normal students. Thomas groaned. He shouldn't have been surprised at the disgusting person Charles turned out to be, but he *was* surprised.

Thomas forced himself to open the bag. His heart told him that he was about to do something bad, but why should he listen to his heart? It was broken.

As he rifled through the bag, his fingers brushed something smooth, and he pulled it out. A silver cigarette case with a fox and a bird. Nothing had changed since he first saw the engraving, and he wondered why he had ever thought it would. Thomas angrily threw it into the snow and searched the bag again, pulling out matches this time. The key to his plan.

Thomas struck a match and held it to the papers inside the bag until they lit. The fire spread fast. He pushed the smoking bag off his lap and stood up, taking a few steps back to watch the relatively tame nightmare he had created for Charles. If Thomas couldn't finish his final year at Blackwater, then neither would Charles.

Thomas shoved the matches into the pocket of his pants. A bright orange flash caught his eye from the ground. The cigarette case lay embedded in the snow several feet away. Thomas picked it up, wiped it on his pants, and shoved it in his pocket with the matches. Charles would die without his cigarettes. He might not even make it through the weekend. The thought gave Thomas some satisfaction.

Several minutes passed, and students started to open their windows. Thomas didn't move. It didn't make a difference whether anyone saw him. He would be in trouble either way. The orange flames licked the cold air, illuminating the shocked faces of people who would soon learn to hate him if they didn't already.

"Mr. Hambleton!" the familiar, shrill voice of Professor

Redmond echoed across the grassy lawn. The thin old woman kicked through the white snow to get to him. "What on earth are you doing?" she asked, gesturing harshly at the smoldering pile of nothing.

"I'm having a bonfire. Is there a rule against that?"

"There is a rule against vandalizing school property, Mr. Hambleton, which you are violating by setting the lawn on fire. Come with me." She grasped the sleeve of his shirt and pulled him back to the warm interior of the school. Fond memories of Charles tainted everything around him, making the inside feel just as cold as the winter storm that raged outside.

Professor Redmond dragged him to the headmaster's office where, to his absolute disgrace, Alfred, Lucille, and Charles Southworth were taking their leave. A dull pain throbbed in Thomas's face from the sustained pressure of clenching his jaw. He buried his fingernails into the palm of his hands until he was sure they were bleeding. Thomas locked his eyes on Charles, but Charles refused to look at him. Every step closer they came to one another, Thomas was sure Charles would look up, but he never did.

"Charles," Thomas said before Professor Redmond dragged him past the Southworths.

Charles ignored him.

"Charles!" Thomas yelled, straining against Redmond's grip to face Charles's shrinking silhouette. "Look at me," he pleaded.

Charles ignored him.

"Mr. Hambleton!" Professor Redmond scolded him. "Leave that boy alone."

"Good luck with your finals," Thomas shouted after him. "You're going to need it."

Charles stopped briefly, but his father yanked him forward. He was smart enough to know what that meant, but he couldn't acknowledge it.

Thomas trembled with anger. How could he have let himself trust a *Southworth*? He wiped his face with the back of his hand, and it came back wet. Charles was everything to him. The most painful part of it all was knowing that Charles had never felt the same way about him. Charles had never loved him.

"Why did you lie to me?" Thomas called out with a sob.

This time Charles stopped walking and turned before his father could stop him. He finally looked at Thomas with wide eyes. Thomas desperately wanted to understand the look. He wanted nothing more than to keep watching Charles, but he forced himself to face forward instead. Charles was nothing to him anymore.

Chapter Thirteen

Thomas searched the cell for something to help them escape. The midday sun bronzed the sky as it became afternoon, casting two bright squares of light on the floor between him and Fyavine through the small, barred window. Fyavine sat on the wooden bench hanging from the wall by two rusty chains. Two buckets sat in the corner of the room, one filled with murky water and the other empty. "Ugh," Thomas groaned. Nothing in this cell was useful.

Thomas closed his eyes and sighed, thinking of the worst-case scenario. If they didn't escape soon, he would be sent home. He would have to face his old life again. He would probably have to see Charles again, and he would have to see him very often for the rest of his miserable life. But it would be even worse to let Fyavine get turned back into a siren. Thomas would not let that happen.

"Felix, I think you need to rest for a minute," Fyavine said, sliding over on the bench to make room for him.

"I can't rest. I need to find a way to get us out of here!"

"Look at yourself." Fyavine gestured toward him with one hand. He looked down at his blood-stained clothes and his knees buckling under him as he leaned against the bars of the cell for support. He could barely keep himself standing, but he hadn't noticed until Fyavine pointed it out.

"All right," Thomas agreed. "Just for a minute." Thomas dropped himself onto the rickety bench beside Fyavine. It groaned reluctantly under the added weight.

Thomas stared at her fins lying dry against the stone floor. "Are you comfortable like that?" he asked. "Do you want to wear the bracelet?" Thomas dug in his pocket and fished out Fiona's enchantment. "I can't hear the sirens anymore, I'm sure you'll be safe."

"Oh, um..." Fyavine rubbed her neck. "Isn't that thing the reason we got thrown in here?"

Thomas shrugged. "Is your tail going to be okay like that for much longer?"

Fyavine frowned at her tail. "It should be fine."

Thomas didn't believe her. He placed the enchantment in her hand and closed her fingers around it. "Hold onto it for me, then. Just in case," he said.

Fyavine smiled at him. "All right. Thanks."

Thomas nodded and looked away. "Can I ask you something, Fyavine?"

"Oh... okay?"

"It's about the sirens," he said.

Fyavine dropped her gaze down to her tail. "I don't know if I'll be able to answer your questions but go for it."

Thomas nodded. Nobody seemed to know anything about the sirens. Not even the women of Widow's Cove, who should know better than anyone. "Do you know why it's usually men who run to the sirens?"

"Of course. Everyone knows that," she said with a laugh. She quickly stopped and stared at him. "Do *you* know?"

Thomas nodded. "Yeah. So, um... When you ran to the sirens, that meant...?"

"That I'm gay? Yeah."

Thomas stared at her. "What?"

"Oh, get over it. You're in no position to judge," she said with a dismissive shrug.

"What does that mean?" Thomas asked.

Fyavine's eyebrows shot up her forehead. "Oh wow. You humans don't have a word for it?"

"A word for what?" Thomas asked.

"Being attracted to the same gender. Gay," Fyavine said, like this part of him that he had been hiding from the world was just so simple it could be defined by a three-letter word.

Thomas's jaw dropped. "There's a word for it?"

"Apparently not where you're from," Fyavine said. "What have you been calling it?"

"What makes you think *I* need a word for it?" Thomas asked.

Fyavine shot him a dubious look. "You weren't even a little fazed that those crazy hot mermaids were singing you a beautiful song that most men would die for."

"Maybe I just have better self-control," Thomas suggested.

Fyavine threw her head back and cackled. It reminded him of the way Mariana laughed. He had thought it was a trait of the gods, but he was starting to wonder if he had simply never seen real laughter before. "That's rich! Self-control? Humans? Yeah right!" She laughed more, completely ignoring his burning glare.

"Okay, ha-ha, I have no self-control and I'm thousands of miles away from home because of it. It's all very funny," Thomas said.

Fyavine's cackling stopped and her smile fell away. All in one moment, she composed herself and frowned sympathetically at him. "Oh no, poor thing. What happened to you?"

Thomas could not answer her. For the first time in his life, he was meeting someone like himself, and she was expressing sympathy for his situation. She was not disgusted or shocked that he existed. She simply offered pure understanding, and he hadn't known he needed it so badly until that moment. "Um... I, uh... my..."

"You don't have to tell me if you don't want to. I get it," Fyavine said, placing a gentle hand on his shoulder.

"I want to," he blurted. "I've never met anyone like you before."

"A lesbian?" she asked with a pleasant laugh.

"What?" Thomas asked again.

"A gay woman," she said.

"There's a different word for that?" Thomas asked.

Fyavine nodded happily. "Yes," she said. She was smiling about it. She was *happy* to be this way.

"How do you...?" Thomas trailed off, still unable to find the words to discuss being gay. He didn't know how to finish the question. *Be happy? Love yourself?* Would she even know the answer?

"I'm not going to answer any gross questions, Felix."

"Wh—" Thomas suddenly realized what she had thought he asked and felt his face burn. "No! That's not what—I'm—I don't want to hear about that!" He turned away and hid his face behind one hand. "Dei, Fyavine."

Fyavine giggled like life wasn't a waking nightmare. "Sorry, babe. You'll understand once you start to come out to the world."

Thomas looked at her through his fingers. He couldn't imagine a version of himself that proudly let people know he was gay. "I don't know if I can do that."

Fyavine frowned and tilted her head. She grabbed the hand

he hid behind and folded it in both of hers. "Felix... The world is a scary, evil place," she said softly. "There are so many of us hiding in plain sight. People won't let us be here unless we make it clear we're here to stay. Do you get what I'm saying?"

Thomas nodded. "Yes, but I'm not brave enough."

"You're very brave. You're still here, and that's all it takes."

Thomas looked into her big golden eyes, wondering how she knew he didn't want to be here. Maybe she didn't know. She wouldn't be calling him brave if she knew how fast he would take the easy way out. "I don't want to be brave anymore," he admitted.

Her face fell. "Oh, you poor baby." She pulled him in by his hand and wrapped him in her arms, holding him against her chest. "The world is a better place with you in it. You know that, don't you?"

Thomas had no words. He didn't know how to answer her. The definite answer was no, but she didn't want him to say that. He sighed and listened to her heartbeat. She didn't make him answer but continued to hug him. She somehow knew what he needed to hear and to feel. Maybe she had been here before too.

The sound of sniffling echoed through the wide room. Thomas sat up and stared across the aisle into the other cell. They weren't alone. Thomas squinted, searching the dark corner of the other cell to see their fellow inmate.

"Hello?" he asked. The sniffling stopped. Thomas finally saw the dark shape of the other prisoner, and the shape was very small. A child? "Are you all right?"

Fyavine covered her mouth with her hand. "Gods, there's a child in here? You humans are terrible."

The child started crying.

"Hey, don't cry," Thomas said nervously. He had never been very good with children. Or feelings. "It's going to be okay." He stood up and approached the bars of the cell.

The young girl wiped her nose on her arm. "I'm scared."

Thomas was scared too, but he didn't think agreeing with her was going to help anything. "What's your name?"

The child hesitated. "My mama told me not to talk to strangers."

"That's very good advice, but I think you can make an exception considering the circumstances," Thomas said.

"Huh?"

Thomas scratched his head. How did anyone talk to children? It was impossible. "My name is Felix. I'm from Tinera."

The child sniffled again. "My name is Ametta," she said quietly.

"Ametta?" Thomas thought out loud. This young girl was Faya's daughter. How had he not realized that? How many imprisoned children could there be in one city? "Is your mother named Faya?"

"Yes," Ametta said cautiously.

"I know her. She's looking for you."

Ametta's attitude changed from despondent fear to cautious excitement. She approached the bars of her cell and watched Thomas with wide eyes. "You know my mom?" she asked in a small, quiet voice.

Thomas nodded at her. "I do. And I know she's not going to leave here without you."

Ametta grinned at him.

"You know that girl?" Fyavine asked.

Ametta gasped. "Is that a siren?" she asked quietly.

Thomas frowned at Fyavine, who folded her arms together and stared at the floor. "No, she's not a siren. She's a mermaid," Thomas explained. "She's my friend."

Ametta stared silently at Fyavine, refusing to speak.

"You're a magus, aren't you?" Thomas asked Ametta, trying to change the subject.

Ametta silently tucked her hands under her arms. She didn't

want to tell Thomas that she was a magus, but Thomas already knew the answer. Ametta was smart not to trust Thomas. Evidently, he was the biggest enemy of the magi.

"I'm on your side, Ametta," he said.

Ametta stared at him with wide eyes. "Are you a magus?"

"Well, no, but two of my best friends are. Can you use your magic in here?"

Ametta shook her head. "Not really."

That may have been for the best. A flame-throwing six-year-old in a confined area would be dangerous. "That's okay. We can get out of here without magic."

He pressed his face against the cool bars of his cell trying to think of an escape plan. There were five other cells in the room: three across from him and two to the left of him. This section of the building was in poor condition, which was obvious from the wobbly bricks that stuck out from the wall outside his cell. All of the bricks inside his cell were in perfect form, of course.

"Maybe if I can get myself to fall in love with the lock on this door, it'll disappear," Thomas joked.

Fyavine scoffed. "You're hilarious."

"You're right, that wouldn't work. It would falsely accuse me of crimes before I could get away," he said.

"Yikes, what happened to you?" Fyavine asked.

Thomas frowned at his feet. He was getting a little too comfortable with Fyavine. "Definitely not... that."

"Right."

The door at the far end of the room opened with a loud clunk. A soldier strolled across the room and stopped in front of Thomas. "You said your name is Felix Warren?"

"Yes."

"I've been told to release you." The soldier pulled a ring of keys off her belt and shuffled through them until she found the right key. "Come with me," she said, sticking the key into the lock of his cell door.

Thomas couldn't believe his luck. Maybe it was in the name after all. He hurried to think of a way to rescue Fyavine and Ametta with this miraculous opportunity. Thomas remembered being in the soldier's position when he had unlocked Faya's cell in the brig and wondered if he could pull off the same trick. Surely, he could not successfully trap a trained soldier. Faya had caught Thomas off guard, and it had been so surprising that he had not been worried about the keys in his hands. Maybe it would be the same for this soldier.

The soldier opened his cell door and pulled Thomas out. Thomas silently cursed at himself. At this point, Faya would have already locked the woman inside the cell. Thomas quickly snatched at the keys and miraculously retrieved them. He stared at the soldier for a moment, not believing that he had managed to steal the key ring.

"Hey! What do you think you're doing?" The soldier came at Thomas, but Thomas jumped back. The soldier's expression darkened. With a focus that was absent before, she grabbed Thomas and pushed him into the door of Ametta's cage. Thomas dropped the keys to the floor, surprised at how easily he had been subdued. "Why are you fighting me? I came to release you."

"Oh, you came to *release* me," Thomas said sarcastically.

The soldier believed that Thomas was just stupid and pushed Thomas behind her. "Stay there." She turned to search the floor for the keys, then looked into Ametta's cell. "Little girl, give me those."

Ametta clutched the key ring in her hands tightly with a determined look on her face. She was like a small, cute version of Faya. Thomas smiled encouragingly at her. "No!" Ametta said.

The soldier sighed angrily. "If you give me those keys, I'll let you out."

Ametta raised her eyebrows and looked at Thomas for approval. Thomas shook his head urgently.

"No!" shouted Ametta. She raised her right hand in the air, balled in a fist. It began to smoke.

The soldier took a step back, bumping into Thomas as she did. Thomas pushed her forward again. Before the soldier could decide whether to run, Ametta lobbed a ball of fire at her, setting the cuff of her pants on fire.

"Whoa! You're on fire!" said Thomas unhelpfully.

The soldier scowled at Thomas as she stomped her foot against the ground.

Behind the soldier, Fyavine slipped the enchanted bracelet onto her wrist and pushed herself from the bench on her new human legs. She carefully toddled to the open door of the cell. While the soldier was distracted by the fire at her feet, Fyavine grabbed her by the shoulders and pulled her into the cell, using the momentum of the pull to push herself outward. She gripped the bars of the cell door desperately, then pushed the door shut. She leaned against it precariously, relying on the door to keep the soldier locked up as much as to keep herself standing.

"Hey!" the soldier yelled.

"Sorry! There's water in there for the fire!" Fyavine said, squeezing her eyes shut.

"Ametta," Thomas said quickly, kneeling to her level. "Give me the keys."

Ametta thrust the ring of keys into his hands. Thomas locked the cell door as the soldier dunked her foot into the murky bucket of water. The sound of the lock caught the soldier's attention again.

"Hey! Let me out of here!" The soldier ran to the cell door with the bucket stuck to her foot.

Thomas ignored her and inserted the key into the lock on Ametta's door. The door swung open with ease. Ametta grinned at him and ran out. Thomas took Fyavine by the hand and slowly guided her away from the prison cell.

"THE PRISONERS ARE LOOSE!" yelled the soldier in the direction of the exit. "THEY ARE ESCAPING!"

Ametta stared at Thomas with fear. Fyavine held onto him with a death grip. Thomas shoved the ring of keys into his pocket and dragged Fyavine to the wall, kicking at the loose brick that had looked so promising from inside his cage. It didn't budge. Thomas tried not to look worried for Ametta and Fyavine's sake, but he didn't see any way out of this situation. The soldier continued shouting. The only way out was through the front of the building full of soldiers.

The luck of his name had run its course.

BRENTON

Thomas had never been in trouble like this before. He had been expelled from Blackwater Academy for arson and assault against another student. Since the Southworths were the only witnesses to the alleged assault, Thomas's parents had not believed it. However, there was evidence of the fire. Charles's scorched belongings made a solid case against Thomas in both allegations, so Thomas found himself back in his bed on the very same night he had committed his crimes.

Thomas's parents refused to talk to him about it. They didn't believe the Southworths, and that was all that mattered. In their eyes, the worst thing Thomas had done was get expelled from Blackwater Academy. Tuition was non-refundable upon expulsion, and Blackwater tuition was not cheap. Thomas had been sentenced to the confines of his bedroom, but he didn't think it was much of a punishment. He wouldn't have wanted to leave anyway.

On a particularly quiet night one week after his return, Thomas was watching pedestrians shuffle through the icy streets from his open window. The cold winter air had a harsh bite, but Thomas didn't care. People-watching was the most relaxing of the limited solitary activities he cycled through. He enjoyed imagining how easy their lives must be.

The people slowly drifted by, occasionally stopping to admire the large gate and expansive garden that sat between them and Thomas. Eventually, their eyes wandered up to his window and they hurried away, embarrassed that they had been caught staring. Thomas didn't mind. He wished he could tell them to stay.

Eventually, a figure stopped on the other side of the gate and peered into the garden as though the Hambleton house were his destination. There was something familiar about the person, but he was too far away to recognize. He gripped the bars of the gate and peered into Thomas's open window. After a few moments, the figure released the gate and gave a small wave in Thomas's direction. Thomas instantly knew who it was.

He pushed himself away from the window, regretting that Charles had seen him. Thomas yanked the bottom of the open window down hard as he could, slamming the window shut with an ear-splitting crack. The window somehow remained intact. He yanked the curtains shut with trembling hands. Charles wouldn't even let Thomas look out of his window in peace. It wasn't fair. Thomas clenched his jaw shut hard enough for his teeth to hurt. His eyes welled with tears, and he tried to convince himself it was from the pain in his mouth.

A quiet knock at the door announced the arrival of an unwelcome visitor. The door softly opened and closed as someone entered the room. Thomas stayed facing the drawn curtains of his window.

"Thomas?" his mother called.

"Yes," he said in his best impression of someone who wasn't crying.

The sound of her soft footsteps came closer. Thomas quickly wiped the tears off his face and braced himself for an unpleasant conversation.

"Are you all right, darling?" she asked, tugging at his arm to turn him around. He looked at her, painfully aware that his misery was written on his face. His mother was a dainty woman with a kind face. Her long golden hair normally fell elegantly down her shoulders, but it was now tied up into a loose bun. She carefully watched him with crystal blue eyes. "I heard a loud noise."

Thomas shook his head dismissively and looked away. He knew his face would betray him if he tried to speak.

"Oh, come here," she said, pulling him into a warm hug.

He rested his head on her shoulder and let the tears return, confident she wouldn't see. In a moment of weakness, Thomas let himself be candid with his mother. "I saw Charles outside."

"Is that why you're crying?"

Thomas paused. "I'm not crying," he cried.

"It's okay," she said as she patted his back.

When Thomas finally thought he could speak without breaking down again, he said, "Can I tell you something?"

"Of course. You can tell me anything."

"You're not going to like it."

"Of course I won't like it. Not if it's making you sad."

She didn't understand. Thomas knew better than to tell her, but in that moment, it felt like the right thing to do. It took him a few long moments to find the courage to speak. "I love him."

His mother hesitated. "Who?"

"Charles."

His mother gently pushed him away and wiped the tears from his face. "Thomas, don't say that."

Thomas knew he should have stopped talking, but he didn't care anymore. He was miserable and he needed someone besides Charles to know. "But it's true."

"You're not saying that the Southworths were telling the truth about what happened?"

"*No,*" Thomas insisted. His mother sighed a breath of relief. "That is *not* true. Charles told me that he loved me too."

His mother tensed up. "Thomas, he was lying to you. You can see that, can't you?"

Thomas didn't know if Charles had lied to him, but he wanted to believe it was the truth. "I don't think he was."

"He doesn't love you. He doesn't even like you," she said. "He's a Southworth." Her words were a dagger that she twisted deeper into his heart with every word.

Thomas couldn't speak. He could only desperately shake his head. He didn't want to hear any more.

"He found your weakness and he used it against you. If he said he loved you, he was just trying to hurt you."

"Stop," Thomas pleaded.

"You're far too trusting, Thomas. You always have been."

Thomas regretted sharing anything with her. She had told him that he could tell her anything, but she hadn't promised to respond well to it. "Yeah," he agreed. She was right. He shouldn't have trusted Charles, and he shouldn't have trusted her.

"I think we should take you to see the doctor. Something is clearly wrong."

Thomas's heart beat hard. He didn't want to talk about this with a stranger. What could the doctor do for him? "I don't need to see a doctor. I'm not sick."

"You don't want to be like this forever, do you?"

Instead of answering, Thomas turned around to face the window again. He parted the curtains and peered through the crack to look at the gate. Charles was gone. His eyes wandered past the dimly lit streets to the black sea beyond, shimmering under white moonlight. Although it was late, the docks still bustled with activity. His imagination ran away with the fantasy of being a sailor. How nice it must be to explore the vast sea without a care in the world.

"I'll arrange something for tomorrow," his mother interrupted his daydream.

He quickly turned to face her. "No. I am not going to the doctor. I'm fine."

"The doctor will make you feel better," she said as she walked away. She stepped into the hallway and gently closed the door behind her without another word.

Why did she want to take him to the doctor? Did she think there was a cure for heartbreak? Or was it his love for Charles that she wanted to cure? Suddenly a void of panic replaced the air in his lungs. His father would know the truth soon, and Thomas would have to bear the weight of fresh disappointment. Memories of the past suffocated him while omens for the future urged him to be anywhere but here.

He snatched his crumpled coat from the bed and pulled it on, then he dug under his mattress for the silver cigarette case. He hated that he couldn't part with it, but not enough to leave it behind. Thomas yanked the curtains away from the window and pushed the wooden frame up. He stuck his legs out of the window and steadied himself on an icy hold of the house's exterior. The cold winter air froze his joints and hindered his movement, making his escape just as difficult as every other pointless thing in his stupid life.

A tall trellis to his left supported a mess of pale, drooping violet flowers. He gripped the sturdy metal grid and began his slow descent. There were several frightening moments when he thought the trellis would give out under him or when he almost lost his grip, but to his dismay, he survived the climb.

His feet eventually hit the solid cushion of damp grass at the bottom. Thomas pulled his coat around him, struggling to stay warm in the dead of the cold winter night. He shivered as he crossed the garden and slipped through the gates. The lake had been his happy place at Blackwater, but there was truly nothing better in life than the sea.

CHRATAN

"You don't think you could burn down this wall, do you?" Thomas asked Ametta as the shouts of the guards carried through the hall.

Ametta's eyes widened with excitement and then narrowed with determination. She held a hand up, creating a small flame in the air. She threw it at the wall, but it dissipated against the bricks. Ametta frowned up at Thomas.

Thomas shrugged. "Thanks for trying." He turned to Fyavine. "Do you have some kind of mermaid magic that can get us out of this?"

"Mermaid magic?" Fyavine repeated the words slowly.

"It was worth asking," Thomas grumbled.

The door at the end of the aisle burst open and a group of soldiers rushed in.

"Stop them!" shouted the soldier in the cell.

Thomas rolled his eyes. They couldn't be stopped if they weren't moving.

The soldiers rushed forward. Thomas stood in front of Ametta to create a barrier between her and the soldiers. "Felix?"

she asked. The sound of her scared voice broke his heart. He couldn't save her. They had gotten so far for nothing.

"Stay behind me," Thomas said.

"Felix," she said again, tugging on his shirt. He turned around. The brick wall was disintegrating into torrents of sand starting from the middle and working its way outward. Two blurry silhouettes stood behind the vertical river of sand. The soldiers stopped to watch the strange sight with fear and awe.

Thomas squinted through the sand and eventually recognized the silhouettes. It was Faya and Fiona.

"Ametta, take my hand," Thomas said, reaching his hand toward her. Ametta took his hand, and he dragged her closer to the wall. He held Fyavine's hand tighter. "Fiona! Faya!" he yelled.

"Felix?!" Fiona called back.

"What are you doing?" yelled the imprisoned guard. "Stop them!"

The soldiers hesitated but eventually ran toward Thomas and Ametta again. The opening in the wall grew wider by the second. A hand exploded through the sandy downpour and grabbed Thomas by the front of his shirt. Fiona pulled Thomas through the wall, and Thomas pulled Fyavine and Ametta through behind him.

Debris from the disintegrating wall fell over his head, into his face and mouth, and inside his shirt. He spat dirt out of his mouth and coughed from inhaling dust. He couldn't open his eyes. "Fiona?" he asked. He could still feel the pressure of a hand closed around the fabric of his shirt.

"Come on, we have to run."

"What just happened?" Fyavine demanded.

"I can't see," said Ametta, coughing as she spoke.

"Ametta!" Faya yelled from beside Fiona.

Thomas dusted his hands off on his pants and wiped the brick sediment off his face. He opened his eyes to see Faya pick up her daughter and hold her close as Ametta pawed at her face. "Mommy?" she asked.

"I'm here, baby."

"This is very sweet, but we have to *go*," Fiona said, dragging Thomas away from the wall. "You can introduce us all later."

"Wait, she doesn't know how to walk," Thomas said, just as Fyavine tripped and fell into his arms. "She's a mermaid."

Fiona stared at Fyavine for a moment, her eyes darting down to the bracelet on Fyavine's wrist. Fiona's face lit up. "It works both ways!"

"Come on, guys," Faya said, already starting down the road with Ametta in her arms. "They'll eventually overcome their fear of magic to catch us. Hurry up."

"I'll carry you," Fiona said to Fyavine, crouching in front of her. "Hang on tight."

Fyavine leaned forward in an attempt to reach Fiona without using her feet. She flopped onto Fiona's back and clung to her. Fiona stood, keeping Fyavine up by holding her legs steady around her waist. Fyavine stared at her legs with great discomfort.

"Ready?" Fiona asked.

Fyavine stared miserably at the ground below.

Fiona ran off without confirmation. Thomas followed. The soldiers inside the jail soon found their courage and exploded through the torrential downpour of sand to chase them, but his crew had already made it to the end of the street.

Faya spotted the soldiers and turned down a dark, narrow alleyway. Fiona nimbly followed. They had only run a short distance, but Thomas was already fatigued. He was grateful Fiona had volunteered to carry Fyavine. He wouldn't have made it.

Distant shouts pushed them deeper into the dark alleyway. Faya led them into the dark garden of a stranger's house and stood pressed against the wall, suppressing her heavy breaths despite her obvious need for air. They silently listened to the shuffle of footsteps and soldiers' shouts pass and fade. Even Ametta knew to stay quiet, burying her face against Faya's chest.

"We need to get out of this city," Fiona said.

"Oh really?" Faya asked in a flat tone.

Fiona rolled her eyes and glanced around the yard. "Does someone live here?"

Faya turned around and peeked through a dark window. She shook her head. "They're either dead or out."

"That's grim," Fiona said.

Faya raised her eyebrows in somber agreement and set Ametta down. "Are you okay, Ametta? Did anyone hurt you?"

"I'm okay," she said quietly.

Faya hugged Ametta again, squeezing her tight. "I was so worried about you. I love you so much."

"I love you too, mama," Ametta said.

Thomas watched the sight in awe. It was surreal to see a mother show her child so much love. His mother had hugged him before, but never like this. Was this how it was supposed to be?

Fiona lowered Fyavine to the ground and stretched her shoulders. Fyavine held onto Thomas for support while she watched Fiona stretch.

Fiona turned around and smiled at Ametta. "Are you going to introduce us, Faya?"

Faya finally released Ametta again and looked at Fiona, Thomas, and Fyavine one at a time. "Yes. Ametta, these are my friends, Fiona and Felix, and..." she stopped at Fyavine.

"Fyavine," Fyavine said.

Faya nodded. "This is my daughter, Ametta."

Ametta silently moved behind her mother, hanging onto the fabric of her skirt.

Fiona kneeled to Ametta's level and smiled warmly at her. "It's nice to meet you, Ametta."

"She's a little shy," Faya said with a smile. In the short time he had known her, Thomas hadn't seen Faya smile so much.

Fiona stood up. "That's good. All magi should be wary of strangers."

"Your name is Faya?" Fyavine asked. "I got everyone's name but yours," she said with a light laugh.

"Yes," Faya said, frowning as she looked away.

The tension in the air was thick. Faya did not like Fyavine. Thomas remembered the way the soldiers had treated Fyavine when they saw her tail. Maybe it was a common prejudice in Widow's Cove. It would make sense considering all the damage the sirens had done, but Fyavine was not a siren. She was a mermaid.

Thomas cleared his throat. "How did you know we were in there?"

Fiona gave a short laugh and scratched her head. "We were looking for Ametta. I was surprised to hear your voice on the other side of the wall."

"You have good timing," Thomas said. "They thought I was a magus."

Fiona sucked air in through her teeth. "Why? Did they scan you?"

"Oh, um... Yes. But it told them I wasn't a magus... I think. I mean, I'm not a magus, so obviously, that's what it said."

"Did you scan red?" Fiona asked, narrowing her eyes.

"No, yellow."

"Yellow?" Fiona said, leaning back. She exchanged a confused look with Faya. "I've never heard of that. The only readings I've seen are red and green. Their scanner must have been broken."

Thomas scratched his head. "Yeah, maybe." The soldier who scanned him seemed to think it was an appropriate reading. She asked him if he had come from a Hambleton ship. What could that possibly mean?

"It was probably just a weird shade of green. You're clearly not a magus," Faya said. "We should keep going. It'll be dark soon and I think we should depart as soon as we can."

Faya was right. There was not a trace of magic in him. He had never even thought about magic before meeting them. The color was probably just weird because he had the enchanted bracelet in his pocket at the time.

"Yeah, and we need to take care of your cuts, Felix," Fiona said, looking him up and down. "What happened to you?"

Thomas threw a wary glance at Faya, afraid to bring up the sirens around her. "Nothing. I'm fine."

"Not nothing," Fyavine said. "He was attacked by sirens trying to save me. He's covered in scratches."

Fiona raised her eyebrows at Thomas. Faya scowled at Fyavine. "I can make you something to help," Fiona said. "Let's get back to the ship."

Thomas smiled gratefully at Fiona. Her magic had already helped him in so many ways, he wondered why he ever thought magi were bad.

The group filed out of the alley the same way they had come. Fiona carried Fyavine again while Faya carried Ametta. Thomas trudged along behind them. They snuck through the back streets, careful not to draw attention to themselves as they maneuvered their way back to the docks.

As soon as they came close to the beach, the sirens' singing started again.

Fyavine released her grip around Fiona's shoulders and fell backward. Thomas ran forward and caught her before she hit the ground, but it was hard to keep a hold of her. He hadn't considered that she was still human, or that the sirens would start singing again.

She writhed in his arms, pushing him away and kicking the ground as she tried to reach the sirens. Not only was she causing a scene, but now the soldiers of the town knew where their escaped prisoner had gone. He was one of the only men in Widow's Cove who would reasonably be anywhere near the beach, so nobody else would be rousing the sirens.

"What's wrong with her?" Fiona demanded, trying to help Thomas hold back Fyavine. Thomas pulled the bracelet from Fyavine's wrist and watched as her golden tail whipped back into existence.

Fyavine immediately stopped struggling and rubbed her head. "Oh no... I'm sorry guys."

"We need to run," Thomas said to Fiona. Fiona nodded, then picked Fyavine up like a princess.

Faya stared transfixed at the sirens.

"Faya, let's go," Thomas said, grabbing her arm.

Faya stumbled forward a few steps but continued watching the sirens. Ametta stared at her mother with wide eyes.

"Faya!" Thomas yelled.

"What?" she asked, blinking once and staring at him like she was surprised to see him.

"Let's go!" he repeated, pulling her toward the docks.

"Oh!" Faya said, finally returning her attention to the situation at hand.

They ran as fast as the sand would allow. It didn't take long for the soldiers of Widow's Cove to catch onto the meaning of the sirens' singing. They spilled out onto the beachfront streets, scanning the shore for the criminals. As soon as they spotted Thomas's crew, they ran to catch up.

"Shit! Hurry!" Thomas yelled, pushing them from behind.

"You try carrying a mermaid through the softest fucking sand in the world!" Fiona snapped.

"They're chasing us!" Thomas said.

They scrambled onto the dock. The firm wood beneath their feet granted them the speed they needed to quickly board the ship. Faya and Fiona boarded the ship with their respective passengers, yelling at the ship to go. Thomas jumped in after them as the ship detangled itself from its ties to the dock. The ship floated away from Widow's Cove just as the soldiers caught up. Thomas exhaled a heavy sigh of relief.

Magic was amazing.

CHAPTER FOURTEEN

BRENTON

The streetlights grew brighter and less bleak, and the sounds of nautical activity danced around Thomas's head, increasing in volume as he came closer to the docks. The splashing of seawater against ship hulls and the chatter of noisy sailors calmed him, more so than the quietest of lonely nights he spent at home. The chilly breeze didn't feel quite so unfriendly out here in this lively atmosphere.

Despite his appreciation for the new environment, Thomas felt out of place. He knew that he stuck out in the crowd as a clean, nicely-dressed, young aristocrat. Most of the people wandering around were large, tough, weathered men. A few sailors turned their heads to glance at him as he passed by, but most of them did not care that he was there at all. The general lack of care for appearances was refreshing.

Thomas spent a few quiet moments watching the large ships bob against the waves. Most of the vessels at the dock were familiar to Thomas. Hambleton and Southworth were the two most widely used merchant fleets in the world, and the docks were filled with ships from both families. The too-familiar crow emblem glared down at him from every Hambleton ship, but more problematic to him was the Southworth logo. The sight of it made him nauseous. The navy-blue silhouette of a fox blared from the sails of Southworth ships. His nausea quickly turned to anger. Both emblems were ridiculous. Why would they choose land animals to represent their nautical businesses? Before his hatred could grow, he turned away from the sea to face the oceanfront shops.

Boisterous shouting and singing echoed out of a nearby tavern. Its rickety wooden door had been propped open, and Thomas wondered how they could stand to let the cold winter air inside. He approached the strange establishment to get a closer look.

The moment he stepped into the stifling, boozy room, he understood. The bar was filled with loud, drunk sailors. The inside was incredibly warm, the air heavy with the smell of alcohol. It was almost preferable to be outside, but something about this strange, loud place made him feel at home.

The journey to the front of the room was difficult, but after much slinking around and dodging of elbows, Thomas finally sat in what seemed to be the last empty seat at the bar. A burly man with shaggy hair and a long beard approached Thomas from behind the counter. The look on his face warned Thomas not to waste his time. "What are you havin'?" he asked.

"Um..." Thomas had never been in a place like this before. The only experience he had with alcohol had been as an outsider to the erudite discussions his father hosted with his colleagues. Drinking never looked like much fun to Thomas, but the people in this tavern seemed to be having a great time. Thomas looked to the drinks on his right and left as if he were cheating on a test for which he hadn't studied. They both looked similar; large glass mugs of amber liquid foaming over the edges and wetting the bar top beneath them. "One of those," he said, pointing at the mug to his left.

"One of these?"

For the first time since sitting down, Thomas noticed the person to his left. He appeared to be the same age as Thomas and looked strikingly similar to him too. His messy blond hair fell wherever it pleased, and his shirt was untucked with several of the buttons done in the wrong buttonholes. The biggest difference between them was the eyes. This stranger's bright aquamarine eyes had a life to them that Thomas had never seen in his own dull green eyes.

"You're not going to make it out of here!" the stranger yelled. They looked similar in appearance, but their demeanors were very, very different. This person was much more eager to be here, or anywhere.

"What do you mean?" Thomas asked as the bartender dropped the full glass on the bar top with a heavy thud and a foamy splash. The boy beside him didn't respond. He only grinned at the bartender, who watched Thomas impatiently. Thomas peered up at the intimidating man, unsure why he was being watched until the large man extended one broad hand toward Thomas for payment. "Oh. Sorry." Thomas dug in his coat pocket and retrieved a stack of bills. He removed the top bill and placed it on the counter, turning again to the boy beside him.

A look of awe struck his doppelgänger's face as he watched the bartender collect his payment and walk off. "That could have paid for *ten* drinks!" he exclaimed.

Thomas shrugged as he pocketed the money again. "He didn't give me a price."

The stranger's look of awe stayed glued to Thomas. "Who *are* you?"

Thomas sighed and shook his head. "Nobody." He lifted the

heavy mug and took a sip of the amber liquid. The taste was unpleasant and bitter, and it burned his tongue. The muscles in his face involuntarily tightened with disgust as he held the drink away from him. "This is terrible."

The boy beside him laughed heartily. "Seriously, who are you?"

Thomas rolled his eyes and tried to take another drink, finding it more unpleasant the second time around. He gave up and set the glass back on the counter.

"Fine, don't tell me who you are. At least give me your first name," said the stranger.

"Thomas."

"Nice to meet you, Thomas." The young man extended a cordial hand to introduce himself. Thomas reluctantly shook it. "My name is Felix. Felix Warren."

"Hmm," Thomas grunted. "It's a pleasure."

"You seem down," Felix commented, taking a drink from his large glass. "What's a rich kid like you doing in this part of town?"

"Trying to pretend I'm not a rich kid."

"You should have left the money at home," Felix joked.

"Yeah. Probably," Thomas said. After a short pause, he said, "Do you want it?"

Felix laughed again but stopped when he saw that Thomas wasn't laughing with him. "Are you serious?"

Thomas reached into his coat pocket again and pulled out the stack of bills. He tossed the pile on the counter in front of Felix. "It's all yours."

The same awestruck expression returned to Felix as he eyed the pile of money in disbelief. He swiped it off the counter and slid it into his own pockets, looking around to make sure no one saw. "Thank you!" he whispered loudly.

"You're welcome," Thomas said. "I would give you my entire life if it were possible."

Felix was quiet. Thomas had only been talking to him for a few minutes, but Thomas could already tell it was uncharacteristic for him to be anything less than loud. Thomas watched Felix to understand why he wasn't talking, but Felix only stared into his drink.

"Are you all right?" Thomas asked.

Felix blinked and looked at Thomas like he forgot Thomas was there. "Oh, no. Yes, I mean. No, I'm fine." He continued to stare intently at Thomas like he had more to say but remained silent. Thomas raised his eyebrows to draw it out of him. Finally, he asked. "Would you actually want to trade lives?" He paused. "If it were possible?"

Thomas gave a short laugh. It felt weird to laugh after everything he had been through in the last week, but it was a funny question. "You don't want my life. Trust me."

"I don't want *my* life." Felix sat back in his seat and crossed his arms. His eyes wandered over the wood of the bar top like he was watching a scene that wasn't happening. "What's so bad about your life, anyway? You have so much money you don't even have to worry about the price of your drink," Felix said. An air of irritation slipped into the tone of his voice that Thomas recognized as jealousy.

"You won't have to worry about that for a while."

Felix stared at him solemnly. "You don't want to tell me."

"Nope."

"Why not?"

Thomas felt his eyebrow twitch upward. Felix was terribly nosy. "Why do you expect me to tell you? You wouldn't tell me your darkest secret, would you?"

"Maybe. Do you want to know it?" Felix asked.

"Not really."

"Maybe I should tell you anyway. It might help you."

Thomas stared at Felix. "How in the world would your darkest secret help me?"

"Because I can get you out of this life if that's what you want. But we will have to trust each other," Felix said.

Thomas remembered what his mother had told him. He trusted too easily. He would be stupid to trust this stranger with his shameful secrets so soon after meeting him. Then again, everyone in Brenton would probably know soon. He searched Felix's face for signs of deceit but quickly gave up. Clearly, detecting lies was not something he was capable of.

"Are you going to kill me?" Thomas asked.

"What? No. Of course not."

"Damn," said Thomas, taking a big gulp of his drink. He dropped the mug carelessly against the bar top. He didn't understand why he continued drinking it despite its awful flavor.

"Wow, what happened to you?" Felix asked.

"Something terrible." Thomas didn't know why he was suddenly willing to share, but it didn't seem dangerous anymore.

"Look, Thomas. I would be risking everything to even tell you how I can help. So, if you want to get away, I just need to know what happened."

Thomas sighed and leaned against the bar. "Fine. You first."

Felix scanned the room again in a similar manner he had when he took Thomas's money. Thomas couldn't help but look around as well, wondering if Felix was watching for anyone specific. Thomas's distracted gaze fell on Felix again as Felix leaned in to talk, beckoning Thomas to lean in too. Thomas strained to hear Felix's quiet voice among the shouts of drunken sailors. Then, Felix spoke and completely changed Thomas's life forever.

"I'm a shapeshifter."

PANTHEA SEA

Fiona set Fyavine down near the mast and groaned. "I am *shocked* we made it out of there."

Faya set Ametta down, then peered around to the stern of the ship, where the sirens gargled their music through the ship's wake. Fyavine watched Faya warily. She threw a questioning look at Thomas. He shrugged.

"So, uh... What happened to you?" Fiona asked Fyavine. "I mean when you fell off my back and Felix caught you. What was that?"

"Oh," Fyavine said with a nervous laugh. "Yeah, that. Well, as you probably know, the sirens attract their human victims with a song that leads people to them based on whether or not they're attracted to women. I am attracted to women, so it works on me when I'm a human."

Fiona raised her eyebrows, then looked at Thomas. "Oh."

Thomas's face burned. He opened his mouth to say something, then shut it. He cleared his throat, then shoved his hands in his pockets. "I'm glad you're all right, Fyavine," he finally said.

"Yeah, me too," Fiona said, glancing at Faya. "Faya?"

Faya scowled at the dark water as the sirens faded away. The ship moved quickly, creating distance from the cove where the sirens lived. The sirens would not follow the ship much farther.

Faya turned around and glowered at Fyavine. "Why are you on our ship? You can swim."

"Uh—I'm... I don't want to become a siren again," Fyavine stammered.

"How many people have you taken?" Faya demanded, taking a step toward Fyavine.

Fyavine leaned back, unable to move from her spot on the

ground with her tail. Her mouth fell open and her eyes widened. "None," she said quietly.

Thomas tried to forget the sight of the corpses he had seen underwater. He would never tell Faya about it. Or Fyavine, for that matter. "Faya," Thomas said, standing between her and Fyavine. "She's not a monster. Please be nice to her."

"She is a siren," Faya said with a glare.

"She's a mermaid. Those mermaids are sick, and they don't know what they're doing," Thomas said.

"That's true. I don't remember being a siren," Fyavine said.

"They need our help," Thomas said.

"The sirens have taken *everything* from me. You may have forgotten, but I never will," Faya said to Fyavine.

"I can't think of a better reason to help," Thomas said. "Don't you want the sirens gone?"

Faya turned the glare onto him. "Of course I do."

"Faya, I have family too," Fyavine said. "I miss my parents and my siblings dearly. The last thing I remember is going to sleep for the night and then suddenly I was on a beach with Felix." She nodded in Thomas's direction. "I don't know where I am or how long it's been, and I've lost everything too."

Faya frowned at Fyavine.

"You're treating her the same way the unmagic treats you," Thomas said.

"This is *not* the same," Faya hissed at him.

"Yes, it is," he said, crossing his arms. "Fyavine as a person has done nothing to you. Even as a siren, I don't think she drowned any men."

Faya was silent for a moment. "We lost women too," she said quietly.

Fyavine covered her mouth with her hand. Her eyes brimmed with tears. "I'm so sorry."

Faya glared at Fyavine for a long moment, then shook her

head and walked away, taking Ametta with her to the lower decks.

Fyavine rolled over and buried her face in her arms. Her shoulders shook gently with silent tears.

Thomas sat beside her and placed a hand on her shoulder. "It's not your fault, Fyavine."

"I'm a murderer," Fyavine sobbed.

Thomas exchanged a worried look with Fiona. Fiona shrugged helplessly and sat on Fyavine's other side.

"No, you're not. That wasn't you," Thomas said.

"The only siren out there who would have taken a woman was *me*, Felix. I killed them."

"That siren wasn't you," Thomas said. "You wouldn't have done that."

"But I *did!*"

"Do you remember doing it?" Thomas asked.

"No..."

"Then it wasn't you. Besides, it could have been another siren."

"Who else would have done it?" Fyavine asked.

"Do you really think you were the only gay siren in the cove?" Thomas asked. "If I could find myself a boyfriend at a pompous, stuffy academy, then surely there are more of us out here than it seems."

Fyavine sniffled and turned to look at him. She nodded slowly. "Maybe you're right. I don't remember anything."

Thomas gave her a gentle pat on the shoulder, then noticed Fiona staring at him. He suddenly realized he had just admitted to having a boyfriend. He didn't mean to admit that to her so openly. How would she react?

"You were... You—" She tilted her head to one side and furrowed her eyebrows. Thomas swallowed hard, bracing himself for her question. "You went to an academy? Who *are* you?"

Cold fear flooded his veins. The question he had been dreading seemed easy to answer now. This was so much worse. He tried to play it cool with a shrug. Plenty of students at Blackwater were from relatively unknown families. It didn't mean anything. "Just a sailor," he said.

"But you were some kind of aristocrat?" Fiona asked, leaning forward.

"No..." Thomas said, unable to follow it up with a plausible lie.

Fiona arched an eyebrow, waiting for him to continue. He never did.

"What was your boyfriend like?" Fyavine asked, rolling over and propping herself up on her elbows to join the conversation.

Thomas was grateful for the subject change, despite his aversion to the subject itself. "I don't want to talk about him," Thomas said.

"What was his name?" Fyavine asked, completely ignoring his request.

Thomas glared at her. "Charles."

"You *were* an aristocrat!" Fiona said. "That's the name of a pompous ass if I've ever heard one."

Thomas laughed despite himself. "He is a pompous ass, but I'm definitely not. Pompous, at least. Maybe I am an ass," Thomas said.

Fiona giggled. "I don't think so, Felix. I don't know what this *Charles* guy did to you, but he's an idiot to let you get away. You're wonderful."

Thomas frowned and looked away. Everything she said was very kind and, honestly, unexpected, but it only worsened the guilty nausea that had been building in his stomach since he found out who the Hambletons really were. She wouldn't be saying any of these things if she knew. "Thanks, Fiona," he grumbled.

"So, where are we going?" Fyavine asked.

"Dufonn," Fiona said. "I need to find my brother."

"Is that anywhere near Wyvahe?" Fyavine asked.

Fiona shot Thomas a confused look. Thomas shrugged. "What's Wyv—what's that?" Fiona asked.

Fyavine sighed. "That's my hometown."

"Where is it?" Thomas asked.

"Just north of Agryqua, but you probably don't know where that is either," Fyavine said.

"Do you know where it is in relation to land?" Thomas asked.

Fyavine shook her head.

Thomas sighed. "Sorry, Fyavine. We'll find W—uh, we'll get you home."

Fyavine smirked at him. "Wyvahe. Thanks, Felix."

Thomas smiled sheepishly back. "Where will we go after we find your brother?" Thomas asked Fiona.

Fiona was quiet for a moment. "Let's not think too hard about the answer to that. There has to be a place for us."

Thomas frowned at her. He didn't believe there was anywhere in the world that would accept him as he was, but he was starting to see that the safe spaces for magi were dwindling by the day.

"Right..." Thomas stood up, remembering he had big news for Mariana about the sirens. "Well, I've got to..." Thomas trailed off. Fiona hadn't reacted well last time he claimed he was speaking to Mariana.

Fiona raised her eyebrows. "Yes?"

It had been a few days, and Fiona seemed more comfortable with him. Maybe if he was honest with her, she would believe him this time. "You know who Mariana is, don't you?" he asked.

Fiona crossed her arms. "Yes."

"Well... She's the reason I'm trying to help the sirens. She saved my life so I would help her because I'm immune," Thomas explained.

Fyavine gasped. "Mariana speaks to you?!" She pushed herself fully upright, flapping her tail once against the boards of the deck.

Thomas stared at her for a moment as he mentally adjusted to this strange world where everyone knew Mariana but him. "Yes," he said.

"Can I meet her?" Fyavine asked.

Fiona shot Fyavine a doubtful stare. "Why would you want to speak to a god? Don't you know that's horrible luck for mortals?"

"Hold on," Thomas interrupted, "you believe me?"

Fiona shrugged. "It's not unheard of. I'm just surprised Mariana would choose to talk to someone so..."

Thomas raised his eyebrows, daring her to continue.

"I don't mean any offense," Fiona backtracked, "but you didn't even know who she was."

"She only spoke to me because she was desperate," Thomas said. Fiona shrugged again and looked away, and Thomas realized Fiona was jealous. "Is it really bad luck to speak to a god?" he asked, now dubious of her warning.

"I don't care if it is. I want to speak to her," Fyavine cut in. "I don't think my luck could get much worse, anyway."

"You've been healed and pulled from the ocean. Do you want to test that luck?" Fiona asked.

Fyavine sighed heavily. "No," she grumbled.

Thomas pulled the shell bracelet from his pocket and handed it to Fyavine. "Here. You might be more comfortable on this ship as a human now that the sirens are gone," he said.

Fyavine took it from him, frowning as she examined the shells. "All right."

"Sorry. Maybe another time," Thomas said.

"No! Not another time!" Fiona said. "Do you want her to die?"

"Obviously not," Thomas said. "Do you really think I could die?"

"Maybe!"

Thomas looked at a cloud near the horizon as he considered her answer. Despite his frequent thoughts about death, some part of him hadn't let himself die in Chratan. His sudden will to live only made sense because dying meant giving up on the mermaids. The ideal outcome would be to die while helping them, but he wanted to help them *first*. Thomas shrugged. "All right. See you later," he said, heading toward the stern of the ship.

"Felix!" Fiona called after him, but he did not stop.

The ocean fell away from the rear of the ship in swift, bubbling waves. Thomas perched himself against the ship's railing, looking into the churning water. "Mariana," Thomas said.

White bubbles swirled in the sea below him, growing larger until a pillar of water propelled itself from the sea into the air and took the shape of a woman. Mariana leaned her humanoid body of water over the side of the ship. "Yes?" she asked.

"I have news for you," Thomas said.

Mariana's sapphire eyes lit up. "Wonderful! What did you find?"

"I, uh... I cured a siren," he said.

Mariana gasped. "How?"

Thomas told Mariana all about the encounter with Fyavine and how the enchanted bracelet turned her into a human.

"Wow! Good thinking," Mariana said.

"She wasn't completely human until she coughed up this weird black... thing. It looked like a shadow."

"A shadow?" Mariana asked.

"I thought it was a liquid until it slithered away. It almost looked alive. Is that possible?" Thomas asked.

Mariana rubbed her chin and looked at the horizon. "A shadow... a living shadow. Hmm..."

Thomas waited for her to reply for a long time, but she continued staring at the horizon. He checked to make sure there was nothing there, then frowned at her. "Mariana, is it bad luck to speak to you?" he asked.

Mariana finally looked at him again. "Of course not. Besides, you're the luckiest person I know."

Thomas scratched his head and tried to ignore the accusation. "Do things often go wrong for humans when they interact with gods?"

"It takes a lot for a god to talk to a human," Mariana said. "Most gods only interact with humans who have angered them. You have not angered me, so things will not go wrong for you. Probably."

"Probably?" Thomas asked.

"Probably."

"Okay... How many gods are there?" Thomas asked.

"Hundreds," Mariana answered.

Thomas couldn't believe her answer. How could there be so many gods? What were they gods of? "Who is Tetra?" Thomas asked, remembering his conversation with Fiona.

Mariana snapped, then pointed one finger in the air. "Tetra. I was thinking the same thing, Felix. It has to be her."

"What?"

Mariana's distracted gaze focused on him. "What?" she repeated back to him.

"Who is Tetra?" he asked again. "Is she the god of the number four?"

Mariana's serious demeanor cracked for a moment as she laughed at Thomas's question. "No, but she is a god of four elements."

As Thomas learned more about the world of the gods, he understood it less. "How?"

"A long time ago, when she was only the god of evil, she killed the gods of darkness, fear, and death to absorb their power. Tetra is the reason each of these elements seems so closely linked. They aren't, but she forces them to be."

Thomas silently absorbed the new information. "I didn't know gods could die," he said after a pause.

Mariana shook her head somberly. "She's dangerous."

"Why would she want to hurt mermaids? And men?" Thomas asked.

"I wish I knew," Mariana said. "To accuse her of any of this would be slanderous, but I wouldn't be surprised. We have to find out if she's behind it without alerting her. If you could speak to her directly, that would be best."

"How am I going to do that? You said it takes a lot to get a god to talk to a human," Thomas said.

"You've done it once before," Mariana said with a sly smile.

"You mean when I watched my crew die and then almost died myself? I am not willing to recreate that situation."

Mariana shook her head. "No, of course not. Your ship couldn't sail without the crew."

Thomas was surprised at the casual way Mariana spoke about human life, as though the people on this ship were only worth keeping alive because they were useful to her. "So, what should I do? Anger her?"

Mariana grinned. "Yes! Dark magic!"

"I can't do magic. I'm not a magus," Thomas said with an angry frown. Obviously, his life was not important to her either if she wanted him to anger the god of death.

She paused to look him over once with narrowed eyes. "Hm... Aren't there magi on the ship with you? Ask them for help."

"I'm not going to ask them to do *dark magic* for me," Thomas said.

Mariana raised one eyebrow. "Do you even know what *dark magic* is?" she asked, imitating the scornful way he said the words.

Thomas scoffed. He crossed his arms. "Well—no, but it sounds bad."

"Oh, does it?" Mariana asked.

Thomas rolled his eyes. "Fine. I'll ask them."

Mariana giggled. "I'm so glad I found you."

"Really?" Thomas asked. He couldn't imagine why she would say such a thing. He had not been much help to her at all and he had a bad attitude about everything.

Mariana nodded. "Tetra is going to be so disappointed when she meets you."

That sounded more like it.

Chapter Fifteen

"You're a *shapeshifter?*" Thomas asked, leaning away from Felix. He had never met a magus before. Weren't they dangerous? Maybe Felix did plan to kill him. Thomas decided he was okay with that, or whatever else Felix had planned, and he relaxed. His life couldn't get much worse.

Felix frowned at him. "That's right. Now tell me your secret."

Thomas felt nauseous at the thought of sharing his deepest shame with a stranger, a *magus* no less, but he had agreed to it and he couldn't deny that the stigma of Felix's secret rivaled his own. "Fine." He sighed, preparing himself to say it out loud. "I fell in love with the wrong person." Phrasing it in a tolerable manner helped him admit it aloud.

Felix laughed so hard he almost fell off his stool. "That's it?" he asked. "That's easy."

Thomas shook his head. "No, you don't understand."

Felix leaned forward. "Then tell me. We're not going to get anywhere if you sugarcoat it."

Thomas groaned. "All right." He took another bitter gulp of his drink, still not sure why he was torturing himself with it. "This person wasn't just wrong, but the *worst* person I could have possibly chosen."

"Well, Thomas, you don't *choose* who you fall in love with. You know that, don't you?" Felix asked.

Thomas sighed again. "Yes, that aligns with my experience. I have always had poor judgment but this was just downright stupid."

"Who was it?"

Thomas shook his head. "My biggest adversary and longtime childhood rival. Maybe you've heard the name *Southworth* before?"

"Southworth?" Felix's face wrinkled with his confusion, and then immediately fell. He stared at Thomas with big eyes. "Does that mean you're...?" he trailed off, choosing to take a drink instead of finishing the question.

"A Hambleton? Yes."

Felix nervously fiddled with the collar of his shirt, taking another shifty look around the room. "Thomas, I—I'm harmless, I promise."

"Honestly, it's okay if you're planning to kill me."

"No, no, I'm not like that, I swear," Felix pleaded.

"Relax, I'm just joking."

Felix shot him a worried look and then laughed. The laughter seemed a little too loud, but everything seemed a little too *something* lately. "I didn't know the Southworths had a daughter," Felix said.

Thomas groaned again and leaned his elbows on the bar top so that he could hide his face in his hands. "They do, but I'm not talking about their daughter," he grumbled.

A long silence passed between Thomas and Felix. "Oh," Felix

said. After another long silence, he asked, "You're talking about Charles?"

Thomas lifted his head from his hands to rest his bleary eyes on Felix again. "Yes." He hesitated. "How do you know his name?"

Felix shrugged. "I work on a Southworth ship." He took another drink. "I met Charles one time here in Brenton," he said and then shook his head. "He's an ass."

Thomas laughed, surprised at the comment. "Yeah. He is."

Felix scratched his head. "I, uh..."

"You think I'm a freak."

"No, I don't. I just don't know how well my plan is going to work now that I know who you are."

Thomas didn't believe him. Felix clearly didn't want to talk to Thomas anymore because he knew about Charles. "What did you have planned?" Thomas asked.

"I was going to suggest we trade lives. I could take your face, and you could take my place on the ship. But you wouldn't want to give up your fortune for the life of a sailor..." Felix laughed nervously.

"Are you kidding? That's all I've ever wanted. I love the sea."

"I'd have to be insane to trade places with you," Felix said.

Thomas scoffed. He was right. Felix didn't want to hear his secret. Nobody would want to live his life. "Yeah, but you would also be *insanely* rich."

Felix rubbed his chin as he considered it. "That's a good point. I do like money."

"What are you running from, anyway?" Thomas asked.

"Oh." Felix sighed and leaned back in his chair. "Nothing in particular. The sea life just isn't for me. I'd rather have my feet on solid ground, where they belong."

"You don't like the ocean?" Thomas asked.

"No," Felix said. "It's too wet."

Thomas laughed again. "Didn't you anticipate that?"

Felix narrowed his eyes at Thomas. "I know that water is wet. The truth is, the open sea makes me nervous. Especially with those new siren creatures around." He fidgeted uncomfortably in his chair.

"Really?" asked Thomas. "I've always dreamed of living on the open sea." He wasn't scared of sirens. Siren attacks were rare.

"Oh, that's funny," Felix said. "I've always dreamed of being wealthy."

Thomas laughed harder than he intended. The drink was getting to his head fast. "Then it sounds like we're a perfect match," he said. He stopped laughing. "Not—I don't mean—not like that," he backtracked.

Felix laughed with him. "Relax. I know what you mean."

"You're not my type, anyway. You're too nice. I bet you're honest, too."

Felix snorted. "Well, aside from all the form-changing and lying about my identity, yeah I'd say so."

Thomas laughed again. He felt dizzy. "Let's trade lives."

"All right," Felix said with a shrug, "I'll be a Hambleton."

"Yes! Thank you!"

Felix smirked at Thomas. "We've got some planning to do if we want to make this work," he said. "Nobody notices me on the ship. I think just the sight of a young blond guy will be enough for you to pass as me." Felix threw his shifty look around the bar one last time before jumping from his stool and gesturing for Thomas to follow.

Thomas slid off his stool as well, following Felix into the thick crowd of noisy sailors. He struggled to stay upright as he weaved through closely packed bodies in the spinning room. Felix had been right; Thomas might not make it out of here. Thomas didn't know where Felix was taking him, but he let it happen. Felix led him to a narrow staircase that opened into a small room lined with beds. "What is this place?" Thomas asked.

Felix laughed but stopped as soon as he saw the look on Thomas's face. "Oh. You're serious. This is an inn; people pay money to sleep here."

"Oh." Thomas scratched his head as he looked at the small, dirty beds around him. "People pay money for *this*?"

Felix laughed again. Thomas didn't understand why Felix laughed so much. Thomas hadn't been making any jokes. "Yeah, and this is one of the nicer inns," he said. "Now, take off your clothes."

"What?"

"You're not boarding the ship dressed like that," Felix said. "And I'm not strolling into your mansion dressed like this." He gestured downward at his ratty clothing.

"Can I at least have some privacy?"

Felix again laughed loudly and with disbelief. "Privacy? You're joking, right?" Felix found that, again, Thomas was not joking. He cleared his throat and spoke seriously. "Oh, okay. Well, you're going to have to get used to a lack of privacy if you want to be a sailor."

Thomas sighed and looked around the room. Even the shared room at the inn seemed cramped to him, and he knew that this was a large living space compared to the living quarters of a ship.

"Are you having second thoughts?" Felix asked.

"No," Thomas said firmly. He began to carefully unbutton his shirt with a decisiveness that had not been there seconds before. "It's good that we're the same size, otherwise this might not work," he said as he finished pulling his shirt off.

"Of course it would work. I fit any size," Felix said. In an instant, the sight of the person before Thomas changed from the still-unfamiliar face of Felix to the too-familiar face that greeted Thomas at every mirror. The sight of his face on another person startled him and he froze momentarily as he examined Felix. Felix ran his eyes over Thomas to observe his posture and mannerisms one more time before trying to impersonate them. Throwing his shoulders back and pointing his chin in the air with the perpetual frown Thomas knew too well, he imitated Thomas, *"It's good that we're the same size, otherwise this might not work."*

Thomas shuddered at the sound of his voice outside of his mouth. It made his skin crawl. "Ugh."

"*Ugh,*" Felix imitated him again.

"Stop that."

Felix watched Thomas carefully when he spoke and continued to adjust his posture, trying to perfect his dignified but broken appearance. After he got the posture down, he got to work on the facial expression, immediately abandoning every trace of happiness and doing his best to wear Thomas's exhaustion and heartbreak over his unhindered spirit.

Before long, they were in each other's clothes. Thomas was uncomfortable in his new baggy, messy wardrobe, but Felix looked himself over in a mirror on the wall, thoroughly impressed with his new style. Thomas wondered for a brief moment if he was making a terrible mistake.

"Tell me about yourself. How should I act in order to be convincing?" Felix asked.

Thomas thought for a moment before responding. "Act tired, like you haven't slept in weeks. And don't offer your opinion. Ever. They encourage it, but they'll never be happy with what you have to say."

Felix grinned with Thomas's face. "Anything important I need to know?"

Thomas told Felix about everything that happened between Charles and himself from the beginning of the school year to his escape earlier that night.

"Wow," said Felix. "What a disgusting person."

"Yeah. He'll probably try to apologize to you but *please* don't let him. Don't even let him talk to you if you can help it."

Felix flashed a mischievous grin. "This is my life now, Felix," he said to Thomas.

Thomas's frown did not subside. "What is that supposed to mean?"

"Nothing bad." Felix shrugged with Thomas's shoulders. "I just don't think he should get away with his bad behavior."

Thomas smirked, now understanding that Felix was his ally. "Whatever you think is appropriate," he said. "What about you?"

"What about me?"

"Is there anything I need to know?"

"Oh." Felix's eyes scanned the ceiling as if his memories were stored there. "Not really. Nobody knows I'm a shapeshifter so you wouldn't have to worry about that. I don't talk to the crew much, I think our interests clash." Felix's gaze dropped back down to Thomas. "Just keep to yourself and no one will even be able to tell the difference."

"I can do that," Thomas said. Felix fixed his eyes on Thomas's face, still studying his mannerisms. Thomas watched him struggle to adapt to his new life, noticing how much happier Felix looked than him despite his attempts to look sad. "You look better as me than I do."

Felix looked down at his new body and then back up to Thomas. "That's not true. You looked just like this a minute ago."

"No I didn't. I've never looked like that."

"What am I doing wrong?" Felix asked helplessly.

"Nothing." Thomas paused. "It might be a noticeable difference, but not one that will expose you. I'm sure everyone will be relieved to see you instead of me."

Felix eyed him with concern. "Thomas, you have to tell me what that means. I'm not going to get myself caught because of your cryptic teen angst."

Thomas sighed. "They will be relieved to see me happier. That's all I meant."

"Oh." Felix frowned. "I'm sorry."

Thomas shook his head. "It's fine. You should probably get going." Thomas approached Felix and dug in his coat pocket for the cigarette case, retrieving it and placing it back in his own newly possessed pockets. His fingers grazed the folded bills from the stack of money he had given Felix earlier. Because the money was in Felix's pockets, Thomas had it again. He couldn't get away from it.

"What was that?" Felix asked, clearly affronted by the sudden invasion of personal space.

"Nothing." He changed the subject. "My address, or should I say *your* address, is... well, it's the huge house at the top of the hill. The one with the giant gate. You won't miss it. Go in through the window. Two floors up, second from the left."

"Right. Thanks." A brief look of fear passed over Felix's face, but he shook it off to pass along his own information. "Your ship is a Southworth ship," Felix said, then paused. "Sorry." Thomas pursed his lips in a false smile of acknowledgment. "It's called *The Exchange III*. Dock two."

"*The Exchange III*? What happened to the first two?" Thomas asked.

"I know, right?" Felix grinned and gave him a playful pat on the shoulder as he walked past him toward the room's entrance. "Hopefully you never find out."

Before Felix could step out of the room and leave his life behind forever, Thomas stopped him. "Hey, Felix."

"It's Thomas," Felix said.

"Right... Thomas." The name felt awkward in his own mouth. It was familiar to his ears but a stranger on his tongue. "Thank you."

"Are you kidding me? Thank *you,*" Felix said. "People have tried to tell me I'm lucky my whole life, but now I think I finally believe them. I owe you."

"There's just one more thing I need to tell you," Thomas said.

"Yeah?"

"Don't trust the Southworths. No matter how nice they appear, they are liars, and they will completely destroy you if they think it would benefit them."

"I won't even give them the time of day," said Felix.

Thomas laughed softly. "You're going to fit right in."

PANTHEA SEA

Early afternoon had become late night after Thomas's conversation with Mariana. He didn't know how to start a conversation about magic. There was so much he didn't know about magic; it was impossible to find a starting point. It was like trying to find the end of a long, tangled thread.

Thomas stared into the rippling waves of the black sea, illuminated by the dull moonlight hiding behind thin clouds. He had been pacing the top deck for hours, trying to find a way to ask Fiona for help. Fiona and Fyavine had retreated to the galley when Thomas left them, and he hadn't seen them since.

Thomas stopped his compulsive lap halfway around the ship to stare at the hatchway. Dim orange light flickered from below, telling him the rest of the crew hadn't retired for the night yet. After the events in Chratan, they didn't seem as wary of him. Maybe it would be easier to talk about magic now.

He forced his feet to move down the narrow steps, pushing himself through the dark mid-deck until he reached the fore, where the galley was alive with conversation and... laughter? Suddenly the smell of warm food hit him.

Fiona stood by the large iron kettle, stirring the contents with an elegant twirl of her hand. Her long orange hair was tied back with a piece of string. She had been smiling when he walked in, but she grinned when she saw him. "Felix! You're back!"

Faya and Ametta sat on one side of a small, wooden table, and Fyavine on the other. Thomas was amazed Faya allowed it.

He must have stared at them for a moment too long because Faya said, "There's only one table. Would you like to sit with us?"

Faya and Fyavine clearly hadn't resolved their differences, but it was a start. Thomas nodded and tried to smile, but it didn't come easy to him. He gave up and dropped himself onto the creaky bench beside Fyavine.

"What did Mariana say?" Fyavine asked.

Without thinking, Thomas looked at Fiona. To his dismay, Fiona noticed the look and raised her eyebrows. "Are you doing magic?" Thomas asked.

Fiona laughed. "I'm not brewing potions over here if that's what you mean. Not everything I do is magic."

"What are you doing with your hand?" Thomas asked, raising his hand in the air to imitate the twirl of hers.

Fiona stopped twirling her hand and stared at it. "Oh." She cleared her throat and smiled. "I suppose I am doing magic, yes." A faint rosy blush crept across her cheeks. "I'm making soup, are you hungry?"

Thomas clutched his stomach as it growled noisily. "Dei, yes."

Fiona laughed merrily and continued stirring. "Well? What *did* Mariana say?" she asked.

"Oh, um..." Thomas glanced at Fyavine, who had been watching him the entire time. "She seems to think another god is involved."

"Oh?" Fiona fixed her brown eyes on him. "Which god?"

"Tetra."

Fiona's smile fell away. Her hand fell to her side, and the whirlpool of soup slowed without her magic. "Tetra? Why would she...?"

Thomas shook his head. "I don't know. I was hoping you could tell me more about her. Mariana didn't tell me much."

Fiona nodded and looked into the kettle. She chewed her lip, then nodded again like the first nod didn't happen. "Okay. I can tell you about Tetra. What would you like to know?"

Thomas glanced around the table as if Faya or Fyavine could tell him what to ask. He didn't know where to start. He cleared his throat. "Well—um... Who is she? Why would I have assumed you worshipped her as a witch?"

Fiona crossed her arms, glancing at Faya before speaking. "She's the god of darkness. Witches use darkness as a tool in magic, and it's often assumed to be some kind of *evil* magic, because Tetra is also the god of evil. We *do* have to make the occasional sacrifice to her, but they are few and far between. Only done when necessary."

"*Sacrifice?*" Thomas asked.

Fiona's gaze flattened. "It's not what you think. We don't kill babies and drink their blood, like you've probably heard. It's just a simple offering."

Thomas's face warmed. He hadn't meant to insult her. "Like what?" he asked.

"Like..." Fiona's gaze wandered to the ceiling, and she narrowed her eyes as she pondered the question. "Have you ever received something from a friend or family member that was very special to you? It could be a gift, or something you inherited, or even just something you hold dear to your heart that reminds you of someone or something important."

Thomas suppressed a grimace, struggling to keep himself from thinking about anyone specific or their cigarette case. "Yes," he forced himself to say.

Fiona nodded and continued, "To receive her blessing, you would need to conduct a ritual in which you offer that item to her. If she takes it, you have succeeded."

"She takes it? You've seen her?" Thomas asked.

Fiona laughed. "Gods, no. You absolutely *must* keep your eyes closed. I've heard horror stories about the way people have died when they keep their eyes open during a sacrificial ritual."

"People *die* from it?"

Fiona shook her head. "Not if they keep their eyes closed."

"For how long?" Thomas asked.

"If it's not gone within a few minutes, she won't help you."

"How does she help?"

Fiona rubbed her chin. "Maybe 'help' is the wrong word. It's really meant to keep her from actively ruining the dark magic. She likes to mess things up. This is the only way to guarantee it won't go wrong."

Thomas nodded. He was starting to get a good idea of who Tetra was. "What is dark magic?"

"It's magic done in the dark. Doing magic in the dark decreases the risk of any stray energy entering whatever magic you are performing. For example, energy from the sun can sometimes muddle the amount of magic you need to use, and sometimes it needs to be very precise. Other people walking around also pull at your energy in weird and unpredictable ways, so it's better to do it when the sun and everyone else are asleep."

"What about the moon?" Thomas asked.

"Why in the world would you be out when the moon is bright? Even as an unmagic, you should know better," Fiona said.

Thomas didn't know what to say. He had always been peripherally aware that it was dangerous to be outside on a full moon, but he never cared. The worst thing that could have happened to him was also the best thing. "You don't do dark magic on those nights?" he asked.

Fiona shook her head. "It wouldn't be dark magic."

"So why do you wear dark clothes if you don't worship Tetra?" Thomas asked.

Fiona rubbed the sleeves of her dark violet shirt. "Dark colors absorb more light. With the right enchantment, you can get your clothes to hold extra magical energy for you. Sometimes your body and soul aren't enough."

"Wow," Thomas said. "I had no idea."

Fiona smirked at him. "Witches don't give out this information freely. Some do, but they either get killed, or nobody listens. I'm hoping for the latter here."

Thomas laughed nervously. If Fiona knew who she was talking to, she would not be sharing this information. "I'm not going to kill you," he said. "I don't think I could if I wanted to."

Fiona frowned at him. "You could report us."

"That wouldn't kill you," Thomas said, throwing a desperate glance at Faya to confirm. Faya scowled at the table in front of her. He looked at Fiona again. "Would it?"

Fiona shrugged and turned around to continue stirring the contents of the kettle. "Nobody knows what happens to magi when they're taken away. I think they're killing us."

"No!" Thomas said. He couldn't believe that. He wouldn't.

Fiona glanced at him with raised eyebrows. "Wow, why are you suddenly so passionate about magi rights?"

"Are you kidding?" Thomas asked. "Nobody deserves to die for the way they were born."

Fiona smiled, thinly masking the pain in her eyes. "You'd be surprised how many people disagree with you."

Thomas looked at Faya again. She looked up this time and nodded grimly at him. Ametta watched her mother with wide, innocent eyes. How could anyone think a six-year-old child deserved to be imprisoned or killed? It was so backward, he wondered if there was a different famous Hambleton family doing this to people. It couldn't be his family.

Fiona took a deep breath and exhaled slowly. "Whatever they're doing, I'm glad to have one more unmagic on our side. You've obviously experienced a similar kind of adversity, so I know you understand."

Thomas frowned at Fyavine. She smiled weakly back. He wanted to appreciate Fiona's words more, but heavy guilt of the magi experience overwhelmed him.

"Adversity? What are you talking about?" Faya asked.

Thomas cleared his throat. "Nothing, um—"

"Felix had a boyfriend back home. Isn't that sweet?" Fiona said.

Faya cast a blank stare at him. Thomas couldn't handle even the mildest of her gazes, so he looked away. "Not if it caused him adversity," Faya said. "Are you all right, Felix?"

Thomas folded his arms together and frowned at the floor. "I, uh... I'm just... This is weird, you know, because... I—" He didn't know how to continue without sounding pathetic, so he just shook his head.

"We understand, Felix. Not everyone will, but we do," Faya said.

Fyavine gently cleared her throat. "Um, Fiona?" she said.

"Yes?" Fiona asked.

"I'm so happy that you and Faya are, you know, decent people, but you can't... I mean, you *shouldn't* share that information about someone unless you are sure they're comfortable with it."

Fiona gasped and held her hand to her mouth. "Oh gods, Felix. I'm so sorry!"

Thomas shook his head again. "It's fine. Let's talk about something else," he said, shooting a grateful look at Fyavine. She winked at him in response. It was a relief to know that everyone here wouldn't hate him for who he loved, but having that personal information suddenly revealed to the entire room felt like falling into the siren-infested ocean all over again.

"The food is ready," Fiona said, easily settling into a new topic. "Who's hungry?"

Everyone at the table muttered affirmatively. Fiona quickly served the group out of a set of wooden bowls, using magic to ladle the stew. Thomas stared in awe at the way she moved the liquid effortlessly and was suddenly overcome with a desire to learn how to do it himself.

Thomas turned around to face the table again, disturbed by the sudden, overwhelming appreciation for magic. Soup magic, of all things. It wasn't even the most impressive magic Fiona had done. Fiona set the steaming bowl in front of him and wedged herself beside Faya with her own dinner. Thomas lifted the spoon from the bowl and watched the broth drip down.

"Aren't you hungry?" Fiona asked, watching him play with his food from across the table as she shoveled a spoonful into her mouth. Everyone else devoured the stew like it was a race.

Thomas frowned and dropped his spoon back into the bowl. "Can I ask you a question about magic?" he asked.

"Of course," Fiona said around a mouthful of food.

"Would I, as an... *unmagic*... be able to make a sacrifice to Tetra?" he asked.

Fiona swallowed her food and frowned at him. "I suppose you could, but... why would you want to? It's dangerous and unnecessary."

"Mariana wants me to get her attention. It sounds like the best way I could."

Fiona looked away as she considered it. "I don't know... Tetra is extremely evil."

Thomas nodded. "I know."

Fiona watched him for a moment. "Okay," she said with a sigh, "I can help you, but you have to promise me you won't open your eyes."

"Sure," Thomas said, looking into his bowl. He didn't know if he could keep that promise. It would be so easy.

"Felix," Fiona said sternly.

Thomas looked up.

"Promise me," she said.

Thomas sighed. "Yeah, all right. I promise."

Fiona smiled, seemingly satisfied with his answer. "Good. Now, do you have something to offer her?"

Thomas looked into his bowl again, stirring the contents with his spoon. He nodded carefully. "I think so."

"You think so? Is it important to you? Is it going to be hard for you to give up? You have to be *sure* it's something she'll take. Something you can't let go of," Fiona said.

Thomas nodded again with more certainty. "Yeah," he said. "I'm sure."

BRENTON

Charles hadn't seen Thomas for an entire week. Every evening he walked past the Hambleton house hoping to catch sight of him in the window, but Charles had only seen him a couple times. The last time it happened, Thomas saw Charles and angrily retreated back into his room. Charles hadn't seen him since.

Thomas's obvious disdain for Charles didn't keep Charles away. Thomas was mad at him, and rightfully so. Charles was mad at himself, too. His stomach turned at the very thought of what he had done to Thomas. The mere memory of it incapacitated him daily. Even confronting his own reflection was a nauseating task. Obliging his father's demands was not worth the pain he caused to the only person he truly cared about. If only he could have seen that at the time.

Every night he stood at the massive gate outside the Hambletons' garden and peered at the dark, looming mansion. Tonight, under the white light of the full moon, the house was monstrous, looking down at him scornfully. Charles wanted to see Thomas more than anything in the world, but he knew he didn't deserve it.

He leaned his head against the bars out of desperation, praying to Dei, *just one more time, please.* His prayer was soon answered. The shuffle of footsteps to his right roused him from his inner turmoil and presented him with the familiar silhouette of Thomas, illuminated by the bright moonlight.

"Thomas!" Charles called out before he could stop himself. Thomas immediately turned on his heels and walked back in the direction from which he had come. Charles wrenched his frozen hands away from the gate and ran down the sidewalk to catch up with him. "Please, wait! I am so, so –"

"Don't!" Thomas turned again to face Charles. "I don't want to hear your apologies."

Charles was taken aback. There was something very different about Thomas. He was angry, of course, but it was a frustrated anger rather than the hatred and disgust Charles expected to see. Anger aside, Thomas was livelier than before.

"You're right, I don't deserve that privilege," Charles said. The rest of his words escaped him as he struggled to identify what was different about Thomas. Maybe it was being back in his hometown that breathed life into him, but Charles had seen him in Brenton many times before and he never looked like this.

"There is a lot that you deserve, and none of it is good," Thomas said.

"That's true."

"Stop agreeing with me," Thomas snapped.

"Okay." Charles paused, wondering if that qualified as an agreement. Thomas rolled his eyes. "Where have you been?"

"Avoiding you."

"Hm..." Charles didn't know what to say. In spite of the abundance of time he had been given to come up with words of comfort, he had none. All he had were pleas of forgiveness, which Thomas did not want to hear.

"Goodbye," Thomas said. He turned away and ventured back into the darkness.

"Wait, don't go," Charles begged.

Thomas stopped. "You know what?" he asked. Charles felt the knot in his stomach pull itself tighter. "Why don't you come with me?"

Charles blinked. Why would Thomas want him to follow? What did it mean? "Uh—" Charles said as he watched Thomas walk away again. "Where are you going?" Thomas continued walking, and Charles stumbled forward to close the distance between them.

"Don't worry, nobody will see us together."

Charles frowned at the ground as he walked. "Thomas, I'm—"

"Stop," Thomas interrupted.

"Right. Sorry." Charles winced. "I mean, not—I'm not sorry."

Thomas shot him a deadly glare. "I know you aren't."

Silence fell between them as they slowly made their way down the moonlit sidewalk. Charles stared at Thomas, scrutinizing everything about his appearance from his clothing to the way he moved. "Thomas, you seem..." he hesitated as he tried to find the right words. Thomas looked *happier*, but saying so would not end well for Charles. Somehow, Thomas looked wellrested, but also like he could fall asleep where he stood. That wasn't new. There was no proper word for what Charles was seeing, so he decided on, "Different."

Thomas was silent for a moment. "Different?"

Charles avoided specificity because an explanation eluded him. "Yes, different."

"I can't imagine why," Thomas said. Charles knew that he had hurt Thomas, but he didn't look hurt. He looked well. Charles had nothing to say, so he remained silent for the rest of the walk. Conversation with Thomas had been so easy before, but now it felt impossible.

They left the wealthy area of Brenton and entered the outskirts of town, which was filled with crumbling houses and shacks. The pitch-black void of the forest stretched behind the houses on the perimeter. Thick layers of tree branches above protected the forest floor from all moonlight. Thomas stopped at the edge of the forest wearing a sentimental smile. "Do you remember the time we spent together in the forest at Blackwater?"

"Of course I do."

Thomas flashed a sly smile at Charles. "Care to join me?"

Charles gawked at Thomas. "Are you insane?"

Thomas shrugged. "I guess I must be. It wouldn't be the craziest thing I've done tonight." Thomas took several steps into the forest and disappeared into the darkness. "Are you coming?" his voice called from the void.

"Are you going to kill me?" Charles asked. The question was intended as a joke, but Charles found himself wanting an answer.

Thomas laughed. "No, Charles. I would never hurt you."

Charles's heart ached because he knew it was true.

Silence called from the dark forest. Tree branches rustled overhead and whistled in the wind. Even the town behind him seemed quieter than usual. Charles took a deep breath and stepped into the forest after Thomas. The cold night felt even harsher under the blanket of darkness. "Thomas?" Charles asked. He couldn't see anything. He wasn't even sure he was following Thomas. "Hello?" The pathetic sound of his voice against the shadows made him wince. Why was he doing this? Was it worth it? He always seemed to ask that question too late.

A deep, close growl to his right paralyzed him. Charles forced himself to back away from the direction of the sound. He gazed fearfully into the pitch-black night. Another sinister snarl cemented him in place. "T—Thomas?"

Silence.

Suddenly, the dark form of something huge crawled toward him from behind a tree. It was hard to see any detail, but it looked like the deformed shape of a large human crawling on all fours. But it couldn't have been human. It was much larger. And hairier. If it stood up it would be at least twice his height. Its arms were disproportionately long. The aggressive snarling continued as it pulled itself toward him. Charles backed away as fast as his feet would let him until the stiff trunk of a tree stopped him. Once the creature had him cornered, it stood up and reared its head back, letting out a long, ear-splitting howl.

Oh shit. A werewolf.

He took off before the wolf could finish howling, running back to the safety of Brenton faster than he thought he was capable of. He wanted to think that being around other humans would keep him safe, but he had never heard of any human encounters with werewolves that ended well. Werewolves didn't care about being spotted when they were werewolves, only when they were human. He ran as fast as his feet would carry him. The heavy tearing of thick claws through grass and dirt thundered behind him. The wolf was close.

The comforting feel of the firm street beneath his feet encouraged him to keep running. The werewolf hadn't followed him out of the forest. It was odd, but Charles didn't stop to look back. He continued running up the hill closer and closer to the safety of his own home. Near the top of the hill, he lost his breath and had no choice but to stop. He looked back to find that he wasn't being followed anymore.

Charles thought he could see the shape of Thomas standing at the edge of the forest. And between his shaky gasps for air, he swore he heard laughter.

Chapter Sixteen

Charles didn't leave his house for two weeks after his encounter with the werewolf. He could only bring himself to hide under the safe cover of his blankets, ignoring all questions about his health and well-being. Nobody would understand him, and he didn't believe anyone cared. There was no chance he would see another werewolf until the next full moon, but werewolves weren't the only deadly creatures that lurked in the darkness at night. Some deadly creatures came out during the day, and he was not going to risk it.

Charles was ashamed of himself all over again. His lack of consideration for Thomas's well-being that night scared him more than the werewolf. What good were his apologies when his cowardice proved him wrong?

However, there was something strange about Thomas. If Thomas hadn't looked exactly like himself, Charles would have thought he was someone else. Thomas seemed to have completely disappeared before entering the forest, and then he was laughing at the edge of the forest after the werewolf was gone. He was *laughing*. Had Thomas played some kind of trick on him?

Whatever had truly happened, Charles had abandoned Thomas. He owed Thomas an apology. It didn't matter what kind of monsters waited for him beyond the safety of his bed; Thomas was more important than anything. Charles needed to let him know, even if he didn't want to hear it.

He rolled out of bed and staggered toward the door. His hand trembled as he reached for the doorknob. *You're a coward,* he told himself. One minor encounter with a werewolf and no injuries, but he was shaking from the mere memory of it. He forced himself to exit the room, groaning with self-loathing as he did so.

The journey to the Hambletons' house was not nearly as frightening as he had imagined it would be. Even as the sun dimmed overhead, the world around was peaceful and quiet. The Southworth and Hambleton houses weren't very far apart, but they weren't exactly neighbors. Ten minutes of walking brought Charles to the familiar garden gate. Thomas was nowhere to be seen, as usual. Charles sighed and leaned his head against the polished bars of the gate.

"Charles? What are you doing here?" asked the gentle voice of his sister, Rebecca. Rebecca and Charles were very similar in appearance. They both inherited their mother's striking dark hair and their father's calm, confident features, but Charles had always suspected Rebecca was smarter than him.

Charles quickly turned to face his sister and found, to his absolute horror, that she was not alone. The words he had prepared in response vanished as he watched Rebecca approach him hand-in-hand with Thomas Hambleton.

He tried to speak his lost words, stuttering until he found something to say. "I'm—I was just—It's—What are *you* doing here?" he said in a much more defensive tone than he intended.

He ran his fingers through his hair and stood up straight, glancing at Thomas intermittently.

Rebecca smiled at Thomas, who beamed adoringly back at her. "Thomas and I, uh..." she hesitated as she struggled to put her explanation into words. Charles felt his heart sink to the pit of his stomach as he waited for her to continue. "We've come to an agreement."

"An agreement?!" Charles asked, the pitch of his voice rising with panic. "What the hell does that mean?"

Rebecca tucked a long strand of brown hair behind her ear and said nothing. Thomas released Rebecca's hand and draped his arm around her shoulder, pulling her close. "I think what she meant to say was, 'Thomas and I are in a relationship.'"

Charles watched, heartbroken, as Thomas gently turned Rebecca's face to his and kissed her. Charles could have convinced himself that Thomas was using his sister to get back at him, but he knew Thomas well enough to recognize two things:

1. Thomas would never use someone else to get back at him and

2. Thomas enjoyed kissing Rebecca.

"But—but he's a Hambleton," Charles argued desperately. "Our parents will never be okay with this."

"You think so?" Thomas asked, holding Charles's gaze for several long seconds.

"I *know* so. It will never work," Charles said.

"I don't care," Rebecca said. "If our love is real, nothing can break us apart."

"That's right," Thomas said.

"You don't love her," Charles said, seething with jealousy.

"Charles! How could you say that?" Rebecca demanded.

"If he told you he loves you, he was lying," Charles said.

Thomas rolled his eyes. "Not everyone is as heartless as you."

Charles frowned at Thomas, at a loss for words. He was quickly losing control of his life, and his sanity was going with it.

Rebecca looked back and forth between Charles and Thomas. "What is going on between you two?"

Rebecca's question sparked intense anger in Charles. This was not fair. How could she be with Thomas, but he couldn't? "I'll tell you what's going on, Rebecca. He's a Hambleton and you're a Southworth. You were born to be enemies. You're out of your mind if you think this will last." Thomas grimaced at him. Rebecca winced. Charles was acting crazy, but he couldn't stop himself. "Don't you remember what he did to me?"

Thomas's eyebrows shot up and his mouth fell open. Charles couldn't believe the words had left his mouth. He had intended to apologize to Thomas, but he only made things worse. Why couldn't he just *be nice?*

Rebecca crossed her arms. "What did he do to you, Charles?"

Rebecca had witnessed Charles's descent into madness for the last month. Charles never explicitly admitted that he had lied about Thomas, but he knew Rebecca could tell. She could see that Thomas hadn't done anything, and now she was calling him out.

"He—He..." Charles didn't have an answer.

Rebecca waited for a response, but it never came. "That's what I thought."

"This has been fun," Thomas said, glaring at Charles. "But I'm going to go home now if you'll both excuse me." Before departing, he turned to Rebecca and kissed her one more time. He pushed his way past Charles and slipped through the tall gates. On the other side, he turned to Charles and quietly said, "Are you proud of yourself?"

Charles watched Thomas walk away through the lush garden of colorful flowers in shameful silence. When Thomas was out of sight, Charles stared at his feet, fighting the painful lump that grew in his throat. "I'm sorry, Rebecca," he said, but Rebecca had already started walking home. He stumbled forward, hurrying to catch up with her. "Rebecca, wait."

"What is the matter with you?" Rebecca asked, refusing to stop.

"I don't know, I'm sorry. I came to apologize to him. I don't know what came over me."

Now Rebecca stopped and scowled at him, closely examining his face. "Can I ask you something?" Charles shrugged with assent. "Why are you obsessed with Thomas?"

"What? I'm not—Thomas? I'm not obsessed—Why would you even ask that?" Charles stammered.

Rebecca raised one eyebrow. "You have visited the Hambletons' house more in the last month than you have in the last seventeen years combined, and even though he 'assaulted' you, you can't stop talking about him."

"Do I talk about him a lot?"

Rebecca sighed. "What is going on? Did something happen between you two?"

"Yes."

"Do you want to tell me about it?"

"No."

"Are you sure?" she asked. "It seems like it's bothering you."

Charles shook his head. "You wouldn't understand. I'll see you later," he said, turning to walk in the other direction.

"Where are you going?" Rebecca asked.

Charles shrugged. "Anywhere else."

Panthea Sea

"She's picky, Felix," Fiona said, dangling the silver cigarette case from between her thumb and forefinger. "Are you sure this is enough? Why is this thing so special to you?"

Fiona had agreed to help Thomas with the sacrifice, but they had to wait a few days to allow the moon to darken in the night sky. Four days after they spoke, the night was as dark as he'd ever seen it. In the middle of the night, Fiona dragged Thomas to the top deck to make an offering to Tetra.

Thomas and Fiona sat across from each other at the outer edge of a charcoal circle drawn onto the floorboards. Everything was dark except for the bright spatter of stars above and the dim orange light that flickered across the damp boards of the deck from a wide, dripping candle that sat at the circle's center.

"It's enough," Thomas said.

"Where did it come from?" Fiona asked.

"Why do you need to know?"

Fiona arched an eyebrow. "Honesty is important in magic, and we won't get anywhere by hiding things."

Thomas felt something twist in his stomach. He didn't want to lie to her, but he didn't want to tell her the truth. "It belonged to Charles," he finally said. "It was the only thing I brought with me when I left home, and I don't know why I can't get rid of it."

Fiona's critical frown softened behind the dim glow of the flame. "I think you know."

Thomas sighed. The candle's flame flailed wildly for a moment. "Let's just get this over with," he said. Fiona wouldn't be looking at him like that if she knew what Charles had done.

Fiona swapped the candle at the center of the circle with the cigarette case, then handed the candle to Thomas. "Take this."

Thomas cupped the candle in both hands and stared at the whipping flame. "What do I do with it?"

"Close your eyes and repeat after me," Fiona said, watching him closely.

Thomas closed his eyes. The orange light of the flame danced on the back of his eyelids.

"In darkness, I offer you a piece of my soul, my heart, and all the good it brings. Please take this cherished part of my life in exchange for peace," Fiona said.

Thomas opened his eyes. Maybe he *had* chosen the wrong item for this ritual.

"Close your eyes," Fiona said again.

Thomas had already made it this far. He sat across from Fiona, candle in hand and words prepared. He reminded himself that his sacrifice *was* perfect because he was trying to anger Tetra. He closed his eyes, and Fiona repeated the words for him again.

"Are your eyes closed?" Thomas asked.

"Yes," Fiona said.

Thomas repeated her words. The moment he finished speaking, the light from the candle went out. He unintentionally opened his eyes out of surprise. Fiona sat across from him with her eyes squeezed shut. The trail of smoke from the candle drifted into the humid ocean air. The cigarette case remained at the center of the circle.

Suddenly, the world around him went pitch black. He held his eyes wide open but could not see anything. Not even the stars. He knew he should close his eyes, but he didn't want to. He wanted to meet Tetra.

A low, sinister laugh crept up from all around him, building in volume until it was all he could hear. "Thomas Hambleton!" His name echoed around him in a cold, raspy growl. His skin prickled with goosebumps. He shivered. "I am delighted to finally meet you."

Thomas inhaled sharply. Could Fiona hear her? Or did Tetra only let Thomas hear her? He swallowed nervously. His hands were shaking. He had never been this scared before, but he didn't know why. Thomas cleared his throat, remembering the purpose of this meeting. "Tetra," he whispered.

"Your eyes are open, Thomas," she growled, then cackled. "Only a Hambleton would have the *audacity*." She hissed the last word.

"Don't," he pleaded.

"Oh, don't worry. She can't hear me," Tetra said. "Although... Maybe I should do the right thing and officially introduce you."

"No!" Thomas said.

"Felix? Are you all right?" Fiona asked urgently.

"I'm fine. Keep your eyes closed," Thomas said.

"Are your eyes still closed?" Fiona asked.

"Yes," he lied.

Tetra cackled sharply. Her horrible laughs echoed across the water in all directions. "You're lucky I don't like doing the right thing."

Something hard hit Thomas square in the chest. He fought back a grunt and clawed the area around him to find what had hit him. Finally, his hands found a small, rectangular box. Tetra laughed again when Thomas realized what it was. The cigarette case.

"I don't want your pathetic little token," Tetra said. "You can't offer me something you don't even want yourself. I want to *take* something from you. I'd be doing more good than harm taking that nasty thing off your hands."

Thomas closed his eyes and shook his head. He didn't want to believe his most valued item was merely a void of happiness.

"Why did you *really* summon me?" Tetra asked. "I know that massive idiot has enlisted your help. I don't think she even knows you're an adolescent. She doesn't know anything about humans." Tetra's frightening laugh crept around him again.

"I'm helping her with the sirens," Thomas forced the words out.

"Ah," Tetra said, dragging the sound out and toying with it like a cat with a mouse. "But you could be helping *me* with the sirens."

"It is you!" Thomas said, opening his eyes again. It made no difference. The world was still black.

"Of course it is!" Tetra said through her laughter. "Is that why you summoned me? Mariana didn't *know* that?" Tetra's laughter grew in volume.

"Why are you doing it?" Thomas asked.

Tetra stopped laughing and groaned. "Don't tell me you actually care. Thomas Hambleton doesn't care about magical creatures."

"I do care. You're hurting them."

Tetra let the cold silence linger for a long moment. "Your *magus* friend is scared out of her mind," she finally said, completely ignoring his response. "She should be. If only she knew who sat across from her..." Thomas knew Tetra wasn't talking about herself.

"It's not like that," Thomas said.

"What's not?"

Thomas kept his mouth shut. She was trying to trick him into saying his name out loud so that Fiona could hear.

"You're no fun. I thought you would be more like your mother," Tetra said.

"My mother?" Thomas asked.

"You can't run away from who you are. It's in your blood. You don't belong with these magi, and you know it," Tetra said.

"You're wrong," Thomas said. He had never felt more at home with anyone than he did with the people on this ship.

"Goodbye, Thomas Hambleton. Talk to me again when you've accepted your birthright." Her echoing laughter faded away as the darkness lightened. The night was brighter now that Tetra was gone. Starlight shimmered off the rippling waves in the distance. Fiona kept her eyes firmly shut; her eyebrows were knitted together with worry.

"Are you all right, Fiona?" Thomas asked.

"Were you talking to... Tetra?" Fiona asked.

Thomas's throat was dry. He swallowed, but it didn't help. "Yes."

Fiona opened her eyes and somehow looked more worried now that her face wasn't pinched shut. "What did she say?"

"She created the sirens."

Fiona shook her head. "Of course she did. Did she take your offering?"

Thomas scoffed. "No. She just wants to take things from people? She doesn't care what they are?"

"Yeah. She only cares if it's important to you. That's what I was trying to tell you."

Thomas lifted the cigarette case to examine it. The silver metal sparkled under the stars. "It is important to me. I can't part with it."

"Did your relationship end badly?" Fiona asked.

Thomas rubbed his face and frowned at her. "Why do you ask?"

"That thing is obviously important to you. The only reason I can imagine she wouldn't want to take it is if it causes you more pain in your possession than parting with it would," Fiona explained.

Thomas glared at the stupid silver box in his hand. That wasn't fair. Why couldn't anything be easy for him? Why wasn't he allowed to be happy?

Thomas stood up and walked to the edge of the deck. He held the cigarette case over the churning water, but his hand wouldn't listen when he told it to let go. He tried to force his fingers open one at a time, but they wouldn't move. Knowing the cigarette case was bad for him, he still couldn't do it. He swore he could hear the echoes of Tetra's laughter creeping through the darkness on the horizon.

Thomas sighed and shoved the cigarette case back into his pocket where he could keep it hidden away. Fiona pushed herself up and stood beside Thomas. "It's okay, Felix. It's never easy to let go of someone you love."

"I never said I love him," Thomas grumbled.

"You didn't have to."

Thomas glared at her.

Fiona shrugged. "Do you want to talk about it?" she asked.

"No. The last fucking thing in the world I want to do is talk about Charles Southworth."

"Southworth?" Fiona asked. Her eyes lit up. "Your boyfriend was a Southworth?"

Thomas covered his face with his free hand. He couldn't believe he had given away such a vital piece of information about his identity. "Yeah," he muttered.

"Wow... I'm happy to know you *are* on our side," Fiona said, elbowing him playfully.

Thomas frowned miserably at her.

"Sorry," she said, clearing her throat. "I just meant that—"

"I know what you meant," Thomas said. He leaned his elbows against the bulwark and buried his face in his hands. Now that Thomas knew who the Hambletons were to the world, it was no wonder Charles had given up on him so quickly. Charles had absolutely nothing to gain by being with Thomas. Thomas was the evil boy next door whom Charles had to hide from his parents because being seen with Thomas was *actually* bad. It wasn't just about their gender, and Charles wasn't just embarrassed or scared. He was right to do what he did. Anyone would have done it.

"Don't feel bad," Fiona said, patting his shoulder. "Everyone gets dumped."

"Why would you just assume *I* got dumped?" Thomas asked.

Fiona scratched her head and looked away. "Uh..." She looked at him again. "Well... Did you?"

Thomas sighed heavily. "It's complicated."

"Right," Fiona said.

Thomas leaned back and crossed his arms. "Fine. Yes. He is a perfect, beautiful, manipulative jerk who claimed that I assaulted him when his father saw us together because he was..." Thomas stopped himself, remembering that Charles probably wasn't embarrassed. Thomas was just unimportant and disposable. "Because he was better than me and he knew it."

Fiona scoffed. "That's disgusting. You don't honestly believe he's better than you after he did that?"

Thomas didn't know how to reply. He had evil in his blood as Tetra said. Maybe Charles was exactly what he deserved. Charles had done the world a service by hurting Thomas. "I don't want to talk about this, Fiona," Thomas said. "I would rather summon Tetra again than continue this conversation."

"Okay, but you don't believe that you're worse than *that*, do you? You're a wonderful person, Felix."

Thomas rolled his eyes. "You don't know me at all. You have no idea who I was before I met you."

"Who were you?" Fiona asked.

Thomas shook his head. "Goodnight, Fiona. Thank you for your help." He walked away, hoping Fiona would stop prying.

"Felix," Fiona said.

Thomas stopped and glared at her. "What?"

"I don't care who you were. I know who you are *now*. You're someone who tries to help the mermaids because no one else will, and you're someone who reunites imprisoned children with their parents. I don't think there's anything you could tell me that would change my mind about what you've already shown me."

"Really? What if I was a murderer?" Thomas asked.

"Ha! You're not a murderer," Fiona said with an amused grin.

"But what if I was?" Thomas asked.

"You're not a murderer," she said more seriously this time.

Thomas forced a smile, remembering Fiona's claim that Hambletons were killing magi. "Thank you," he said, then descended the hatchway. Fiona hadn't answered the question, but her answer told him all he needed to know.

BRENTON

Charles couldn't go home. There was no room for him there while his sister was around. He couldn't stand the thought of Rebecca and Thomas together. It wasn't fair. He had convinced himself that it never would have worked with Thomas because he was a Hambleton, not because he was a boy. Rebecca's relationship with Thomas proved him wrong, and he hated it. He didn't know what to do with the overflowing jealousy in his heart.

He wandered through the cold twilight streets, forgetting his fear of the creatures of the night. They could take him for all he cared. Nothing mattered anymore.

Charles watched his feet carry him through town. None of the passing sights interested him. There was only one thing on his mind. The consequence of his inattention hit him in the face as he ran directly into another person. He stumbled away and looked up to find the baffled face of a young blond boy. His heart skipped a beat for a moment, thinking it was Thomas, but he soon recognized that it was someone else. "Sorry, wasn't watching my step," Charles mumbled.

"Don't worry about it, Charles," the stranger said.

Charles froze, struggling to remember where he had met this person before. Was he from Blackwater? Why did this stranger know his name? "Sorry, have we met before?"

The boy's eyes widened briefly. Charles had seemingly offended him with his lack of recognition, but he struggled to care. "We met a long time ago," the stranger said. "My name's Felix. I worked on a Southworth ship for a while. We ran into each other at the docks once. I wouldn't expect you to remember me."

"Oh, Felix. Right." Charles didn't remember him. Felix stared at him with pursed lips. "You don't look like a sailor," Charles said, noticing his expensive attire. The outfit was oddly familiar.

"I'm not a sailor anymore."

"What business are you in? You're far too young to have made a name for yourself but you're dressed like you come from wealth," Charles said.

"You're awfully nosy."

"I'm sorry," Charles said. "You're right, that was impolite."

Felix smirked. "It's okay. Where are you headed at this hour?"

"Oh, uh..." Charles peered down the darkening path before him. "I don't know."

Felix frowned pityingly at Charles. It was an oddly knowing look as if Felix already knew why Charles was upset. "You seem down. Do you want to see where I go when I'm feeling down?"

"Okay," Charles said. He didn't have a destination in mind, and it didn't matter where Felix took him. It could be dangerous, but he didn't care.

"I'm scared of the sea, but I love watching it from the shore. Do you like the ocean?" Felix asked as he crossed the street in the direction of the sea.

Charles followed Felix across the road. "Not really."

Felix gawked at Charles. "But you're a Southworth! You don't like the ocean?"

"No. I'm not very fond of being a Southworth, either."

"Why not?" Felix asked. "You have wealth, power, fame, status, comfort... everything you could ever want."

"Not everything," Charles said.

"What's missing?"

"Never mind. You're right. I should be happy."

Felix was quiet for a moment as he continued walking. "Is it love?"

"No," Charles snapped.

"Because I happen to agree with you," Felix said, ignoring his answer.

"I wasn't going to say that."

"Have you ever been in love?" Felix asked.

"You're awfully nosy."

Felix laughed. "Sorry."

Charles glared at the sparkling black ocean in the distance.

"I fell in love for the first time very recently," Felix continued. "It's a nice feeling, but this girl is way too good for me."

"What makes you say that?" Charles asked with disinterest.

"She's perfect," Felix said with a dreamy smile. "She's beautiful, clever, kind, and... well, terrifying."

Charles laughed at the unexpected descriptor. "Terrifying?"

"I don't know," Felix said. "Something about her is just so damn intimidating. I can't stop thinking about her." He sighed. "But she doesn't know who I am."

"Oh..." Charles scratched his head. "Why don't you introduce yourself?"

Felix stared at Charles for a moment. "We are together, but she doesn't know who I really am."

Charles frowned at him. "Don't lie to her. Dishonesty is never the answer."

Before long, Charles and Felix stood together at the glittery seaside on the cold sand of the beach, a safe distance from the rolling waves. A soft winter breeze brushed against them, carrying the salty smell of the brisk sea with it. The bright splatter of stars across the black sky danced in bright scurrying lines on the surface of the water.

"So, you think I should tell her?" Felix asked.

"I don't know you or your situation. All I can say is that your relationship won't last if it's built on a lie," Charles said. "If you love her, don't lie to her, or about her. I lied and it ruined my only chance at happiness."

Charles admired the sparkling ocean waves. He had never really taken the time to watch the sea move before. It swelled and dipped as though it were a living, breathing creature. He thought about its unending activity through all hours of the day and night. It moved on, no matter what happened on Earth. The ocean didn't care about the trivial concerns of humans. Standing there in that moment with Felix, Charles found a new appreciation for the sea as more than a means to earn money.

"What happened?" Felix asked.

"What are you talking about?" Charles asked, keeping his eyes on the sea.

"Your love."

"I never said I was in love."

"If the answer had been no, you would have said no," Felix said.

Charles sighed and looked at his feet. "It's not a nice story."

"Love stories rarely are, if the story has an end."

Charles struggled to find his words. He didn't have a proper answer for Felix. "This person, I..." Charles started his explanation, finding each word more difficult to say than the last. "I loved," he hesitated, "*her* more than I ever thought I could love anyone." He took a deep breath. He didn't know why he felt the need to lie to this stranger, but he couldn't bring himself to tell the truth. "But she wasn't a conventionally appropriate choice for me."

"Who cares about convention?"

Charles stared somberly at Felix. "Everyone. And I care about what everyone thinks of me."

Felix nodded. "What happened?"

Charles shook his head. "She left me for my brother."

"Really..." Felix said in a flat tone.

Charles shot him a baffled look. "Yes. It was heartbreaking."

Felix raised an eyebrow. "At what point in that story did you lie and ruin your only chance at happiness?"

"At every possible point."

"I know you don't have a brother. Want to try again?"

"Not really," Charles said. "I guess I still care about a stranger's opinion of me."

"I'm not a stranger. We've met before."

"Yes. Once," Charles said.

"Right," Felix said. "Once."

CHAPTER SEVENTEEN

The next morning, Thomas was the first to awake. The sky was still dim and speckled with stars, but he wanted to have a conversation with Mariana before anyone could hear him talking to himself.

Thomas leaned over the side of the ship, feeling the cool morning wind whip his hair around his face. He peered into the water, seeing nothing but black sea splash against the hull.

"Mariana," he whispered. The water slipped by, unaware of his presence. He wondered if Mariana rested like humans did. Maybe she was asleep. "Mariana," he said, louder this time.

A particularly hefty wave bumped against the ship then crashed back into itself and bounced upward, taking the shape of the big watery woman he had learned to recognize. "Felix!" Mariana said with a grin. "It's lovely to see you!"

Thomas nodded once. "Right, yeah. You too."

"What can I do for you?" Mariana asked.

Thomas scratched his head and looked away. "I met Tetra last night," he said. How was he supposed to tell Mariana she was right about the sirens?

Mariana gasped. "You talked to her?"

"Yeah..."

"Well?" Mariana asked, leaning closer to him. "What did she say?"

Thomas took a step back. "She made the sirens. She seems to think it's pretty funny that you didn't already know that."

Mariana's pleasant demeanor instantly fell away. She rolled her eyes. "How would I have known that? It's not like she would tell me."

Thomas shrugged. "I'm not going to claim I know Tetra, but I can tell she finds it funny to mess with people. Did you know witches have an entire sacrificial ritual dedicated to her just so that she won't mess up their magic?" he asked.

"Yes, I did know that. Do you know what she does with that stuff?" Mariana asked.

Thomas raised his eyebrows. "What does she do?"

"She dumps it in the ocean!"

Thomas stared at her. He had never seen Mariana angry before. Tetra likely did not get along with many of the gods, but there was something about the way Mariana churned with anger that told him she got the worst of it. "She doesn't keep it?"

"No," Mariana said, crossing her arms. "I expressed my disapproval over her methods a long time ago and she decided then that I was the best place to get rid of her garbage."

Thomas scratched his head and stared at the horizon. He didn't think the items offered to Tetra were garbage, but Mariana didn't care. "So... now that we know it's Tetra, what do we do?" he asked.

"We have to stop her," Mariana said.

"How?"

Mariana rubbed her chin and stared at the sky. "Do you think you could get her to come back?"

"No. She didn't want my... garbage," Thomas said.

Mariana looked at him. "What did you offer her?"

"It doesn't matter," Thomas said, crossing his arms and looking away. "She did tell me to talk to her again when I've—" Thomas stopped himself, afraid to finish the sentence. Did Mariana know who he was?

Mariana raised her eyebrows, watching him patiently. "What? You have a way to get back in contact with her?"

"She seems to believe I'm inherently evil," Thomas said. "She said I could be helping her instead of you."

Mariana's expression darkened. "Don't. She'll offer you whatever you want, but she won't deliver. Think of the mermaids, Felix. They need your help."

Thomas's heart sank. Mariana didn't believe in him either. "I'm not evil, Mariana," he said quietly.

Mariana sighed. "I know that. You've been great, but aren't you, uh...?" She glanced up at the full sail overhead, displaying the Hambleton family emblem of the crow.

Thomas glared at the stupid family emblem on the sail. Mariana knew who he was. "How did you know that?" he asked, turning to face her again.

"You've only just met me, but I've known you for your entire life," Mariana said.

Thomas thought of all the times in his life when he would sit on the beach to get away from his suffocating life. It was the only place that made him happy, but apparently, he was being watched. "So, you think I'm evil too," he said.

"I've seen the things your family does to their fellow humans, and it is frightening," Mariana said.

"I didn't know about that until a few days ago. Nobody ever

told me," Thomas said. "Do you know what they're doing to magi?"

"I'm afraid not. I only know what happens at sea."

Thomas sighed and buried his face in his hands. "I didn't know," he said again.

Mariana placed a cold, wet hand on his shoulder. It startled him out of hiding his face. He stared at her. "I know you're not evil, Felix. Why do you think I said Tetra would be disappointed to meet you?"

Thomas dropped his hands. "That's what you meant?"

Mariana nodded. "But I think if you're willing to pretend to be evil, you could do a lot of good. Do you want to try?"

"Would I have to tell my crew who I am?" Thomas asked.

Mariana shook her head. "That's not necessary. You just need Tetra to believe you. She doesn't often like interacting with humans, so it's good that she wants your help. I can't tell if she wants you because you're a Hambleton or just because you're helping me, but either way, I think she'll be willing to hear you out again."

Thomas took a deep breath. He didn't want to accidentally hurt anyone in his attempt to trick Tetra, but he would pretend to be the person everyone expected him to be if it helped the mermaids. "Should I try to make another sacrifice?" Thomas asked.

"Hmm... I don't think she would come back if it didn't work the first time. She'll probably be suspicious if you try to talk to her again right away," Mariana said, staring into the dark water. "She has temples all over the world. Maybe you can try to find one."

"Do you know where they are?" Thomas asked.

"Yes, but I wouldn't be able to go with you. You can't exactly take me out of the ocean," Mariana said with a shrug. "Where are you headed right now?"

"York," Thomas said.

"Oh, Dufonn! Yes, she has a temple there. Maybe your witch friend can show you where it is."

"I don't want her to know our plan," Thomas said. "For obvious reasons."

Mariana nodded. "You don't have to tell her. She probably won't go into the temple with you, anyway. Most humans who know about Tetra are afraid of her."

Thomas nodded. "Yeah. Okay, I'll see if Fiona knows anything."

"Thanks, Felix. You may be right about bad luck when it comes to Tetra. Would you like me to make you immune to death before I go?"

"No," Thomas said with a scowl.

Mariana shrugged. "Let me know if you change your mind," she said, then splashed back into the dark waves.

Thomas already knew he would not change his mind.

BRENTON

"Charles," Rebecca's firm voice called out, dragging Charles out of restless sleep. He rolled over in his bed to glare at his sister, who stood over him.

"Ugh, what?" he asked, squinting at the bright light that beamed in from the open doorway.

"Dad wants to talk to you."

Charles sat up and rubbed his eyes. "What time is it?"

"It's noon. Do you do anything other than sleep?"

"Why should I?" Charles asked.

"Just get dressed. He's waiting for you in his study," Rebecca said.

"I'll be there in a bit," Charles grumbled. He watched Rebecca leave, then stared at the dark floor for a few minutes before he found the energy to dress.

What could his father possibly want to talk about? He didn't have much respect for Charles these days. It couldn't be anything good.

Charles shuffled through the halls of his home and wound up at the tall oak door of his father's study. He took a deep breath before rapping twice on the door and turning the handle to let himself in. The first person he saw was his father, standing tall and looking grim, as usual. Standing beside him was his mother, also looking grim, but unusually so. His stomach turned. This wasn't good.

He stepped inside and shut the door behind him, shooting a questioning look at his parents. Neither of them responded. Charles spotted Rebecca at the other end of the room sitting alone on a sofa.

"Charles," his father said with less disdain than usual, gesturing toward the sofa. "Have a seat." His tone was careful; the tone of a confident man who, for the first time in his life, was not sure how to proceed. It made Charles nauseous.

"Okay," Charles said, cautiously taking his place beside Rebecca. "What's going on?"

"How should I say this..." his father said quietly to himself.

Charles threw a desperate glance at Rebecca. Rebecca did not look at him. Charles looked at his mother for an answer, but her eyes stayed fixed on the floor.

"We received news last week that one of our ships never showed up at the port. *The Exchange III*. It has been presumed lost at sea, along with its crew," his father explained.

"Okay?" Charles asked. His father glared at him. "That's awful. It's a terrible loss," Charles backtracked carelessly, "But why are you telling me this? You didn't bother telling me about the first two."

His father nodded somberly. "As I'm sure you already know, Rebecca has been seeing," he sighed and pinched the bridge of his nose, "*Thomas Hambleton*." He said Thomas's name like it was a bad word.

Charles's heart skipped a beat at the sound of the name. He scratched his head. "Yeah?" he asked, trying not to sound jealous.

"As it turns out, she hasn't been seeing Thomas at all. Yesterday, 'Thomas' revealed to Rebecca that he is a shapeshifter named Felix," his father explained.

"What?" Charles asked. Was it possible that his father was talking about the same Felix he had met in the city? Charles thought about their conversation about lying and love, and it suddenly made much more sense. He was a magus? A shapeshifter? Where was Thomas?

"Felix and Thomas switched lives in late December. Felix has been living here in Brenton as Thomas, while Thomas has been out at sea. Naturally, the Hambletons sent Felix away when we told them."

Charles first felt relief that Rebecca hadn't been dating Thomas. Then he felt sorry for her for the same reason. "So, Thomas is gone," Charles said.

The room was quiet for a long time. "Charles," said his father. "Felix was a crew member of *The Exchange*. He was very lucky that he jumped ship when he did."

Charles stared at his father. His brain refused to make the connection. "Okay... So?"

His father sighed. "There was a time in your life in which you were close friends with Thomas. I thought you would want to know what happened to him."

Charles looked at his mother, hoping she had a better answer for him. "I'm so sorry Charles," she said quietly.

"I don't understand," Charles said, now trying Rebecca. She fixed her eyes on the wall. He looked at his father again.

"Thomas Hambleton is dead."

Charles shook his head. "No," he said. His heart pounded in his chest. The air in the room suffocated him. "That can't be true. You're lying." Charles stood up.

"Why would I lie about this?"

"I don't know! Why do you lie about anything? All it does is hurt people and—and—gets them killed!" Charles stared desperately at his parents as he realized what he had just admitted. His eyes burned with tears that quickly spilled over onto his face. He hid his face in his hand. "This is your fault," he muttered behind his palm.

"Charles," his father warned.

"You know why he left," Charles said, lifting his head. He didn't care if they saw him cry. "I didn't want to hurt him, but you *made* me."

"I didn't make you do anything."

"Yes, you did. You know he wasn't just my friend."

"Charles. *Stop*," his father demanded.

"I loved him," Charles sobbed.

"That's enough," his father said, approaching Charles. "The relationship you had with Thomas was unhealthy and unnatural, and you know that to continue pursuing it would ruin our family. I only gave you an opportunity to end it. It was *your* decision."

"No it wasn't," Charles cried, taking a step away from his father. His hand trembled as he rubbed tears off his face. "How did you manage to lose the same ship *three times*? Why wouldn't you alter the course if you had already lost two ships on that route?"

"That route has been safe for the last one hundred years."

"It obviously isn't safe anymore! Are you stupid?" Charles yelled.

A sharp pain struck Charles's face, and he fell to the ground on his hands and knees. It took him a moment to realize his father had hit him. Charles watched the floor collect his tears as he rubbed the side of his stinging face.

"Alfred!" his mother yelled, running to Charles's side. She kneeled beside him, pulling him up into a tight embrace.

"Do not *ever* talk to me like that," Alfred said, ignoring his wife. "Do you understand?"

Charles lifted his head to scowl at his father. "I *hate* you."

Alfred glowered at Charles. "You're lucky your mother is here." He redirected the scathing look at his wife before turning to leave the study.

His mother hugged him tighter. "Are you all right?"

He rested his head on her shoulder and sobbed. He shook his head, unable to speak.

Rebecca eventually joined them on the floor. "Charles," she said softly. "I'm so sorry."

"Thomas—" Charles struggled through his shuddering gasps for air. "Is dead... because of me."

"He chose to leave," Rebecca said.

Charles sat back and wiped the tears from his face, but it was as futile as bailing water out of a fully submerged boat. "I'm never going to see him again. I'm never going to hear his voice, or hold his hand, or... see his smile." Charles covered his face with his hands and continued sobbing. "And—I'll never be able to apologize to him."

His mother gently pulled his hands away from his face and wiped his tears with a handkerchief. "It's not your fault."

Charles pushed her hands away. "Stop lying to me. I know what I did." He looked at his sister. "Rebecca... I'm sorry."

"Don't worry about me," Rebecca said, patting him gently on the arm.

"You lost him too," Charles said.

Rebecca shook her head. "No... Not really."

Charles hid his face in his hands again and continued crying. Rebecca never really had Thomas. The Thomas he knew was gone almost as soon as they got back to Brenton. The real Thomas probably hadn't even heard his weak attempts at an apology, which would have been better than nothing. Nothing was all he had now, and all he would ever have.

Chapter Eighteen

By midday, the entire crew was awake and going about their business. There wasn't much to do operationally thanks to Fiona's enchantment, so everyone struggled to find ways to occupy their time.

Faya and Ametta practiced their magic together on the upper deck. Thomas had never been fond of children, and Ametta was no exception. The biggest difference between Ametta and every other child was that Ametta shot flames from her hands when she was upset. Thomas was learning to appreciate magic, but he was terrified of Ametta.

To Thomas's surprise, Fyavine sat nearby and watched Faya and Ametta practice. Did Faya know she was watching? Didn't she hate Fyavine?

Faya turned to look at Fyavine and smiled. "What did you think of that?"

Fyavine clasped her hands together. "You two are amazing! Your fire is so beautiful!"

Faya laughed. Thomas had never seen her look quite so happy before. It must have been her reunion with Ametta, or maybe it was her ability to freely do magic without fear of imprisonment. "Thank you, Fyavine," she said.

Thomas sat down beside Fyavine, and Faya finally noticed him. "Oh! Hi Felix," Faya said.

"Hi Faya," Thomas said. He looked at Fyavine. "Hi, Fyavine. You're getting along with Faya?"

Fyavine smiled and looked away. She shrugged. "I asked her to show me her magic because I don't get to see fire very often. It's so pretty."

Thomas raised his eyebrows and looked at Faya. Faya shrugged. "I understand now, Felix. I was not being very nice to her. I'm trying to make up for it."

Thomas smiled. "I'm happy to hear that. Fyavine's great, isn't she?"

Faya nodded. "She is."

Fyavine giggled and tucked a long piece of dark curly hair behind her ear. She smiled at Thomas. "You're too kind."

Faya watched them with her hand resting on Ametta's head. "I heard that you had quite an encounter last night. Are you all right?" Faya asked.

"Where did you hear that?" Thomas asked.

Faya arched an eyebrow.

Thomas immediately felt stupid. The only person who could tell her was Fiona. "Yeah, I'm fine. Tetra didn't want my offer."

"Why not?" Faya asked.

"She just didn't want it," Thomas said. "I need to talk to her again, though. Do you have any idea how I could do that?"

"I don't mess with the gods. Especially not the god of darkness," Faya said, demonstratively igniting a plume of fire in her open palm. "Dark magic is not my thing."

Thomas turned to Fyavine. "Do you know anything about Tetra?"

"I'm afraid not. Sorry, babe," she said, patting him on the back.

"Fiona would be more than happy to answer your questions," Faya said shooting a knowing look at Fyavine. Fyavine giggled.

"What does that mean?" Thomas asked. "Why are you laughing?"

"Oh, come on," Fyavine said. "You haven't noticed? She loves helping you."

Thomas rolled his eyes. "She would help anyone. Besides, she knows I'm... gay."

"That doesn't matter," Fyavine said. "I crush on straight women all the time." She made brief eye contact with Faya, who smiled when Fyavine looked away.

"What does that mean?" Thomas asked. "Straight?"

Fyavine grinned at him. "People who aren't gay."

"Oh," Thomas said, glancing at Faya. He remembered the way she stopped to listen to the sirens every time they were around. "Are you straight, Faya?"

Faya shrugged. "I don't think anyone is completely straight."

Thomas raised his eyebrows. "Really?"

"Yeah," Faya said. "Men and women aren't that different."

Thomas did not feel that way at all. He didn't know it was possible to be attracted to more than one gender. He could hardly handle one *person*. "What about the sirens?" Thomas asked. "Do you think I'm not completely gay? They don't affect me at all, and I've never been attracted to a woman. What about all the women in your town? They're not affected either."

"I'm not affected by them," Faya said casually.

"Yes, you are," Thomas said, unable to contain a laugh as he answered her. "You stop to listen every time. You're barely responsive when you get that dazed look in your eyes."

Faya's face fell. She looked back and forth between Thomas and Fyavine. Fyavine rested her hand against her mouth with a wide smile on her face. "Really?" Faya asked.

"You haven't noticed?" Thomas asked.

Faya shook her head, then frowned at Ametta. "That's not good."

"I don't remember what happens when I'm enchanted by them either," Fyavine said. "It was a lot like *being* a siren. I didn't remember any of it," Fyavine said with a smile she couldn't seem to put away.

Thomas rubbed his chin. "Interesting." He frowned at Faya. "I thought having a crew of women would make this easier."

Fyavine giggled. "It's not that simple, unfortunately."

"Yeah," Thomas said with a sigh. "I see that now."

"That explains the lapses in time I've been experiencing all year," Faya said. "I thought someone had cursed me."

Fyavine threw her head back and cackled gleefully. "Faya! You're joking!"

Faya laughed with her. "I guess I should have known."

Thomas stood up. "I'll let you get back to your practice," he said. "I'm going to find Fiona."

"Bye, Felix!" Faya and Fyavine said in unison, then they both laughed again.

Thomas was relieved Faya had gotten over her mermaid prejudice. Faya and Fyavine seemed to be very good friends now.

Thomas found Fiona in the galley. She sat at the table, drawing something in an old leather-bound book. She lifted her pencil and stared at it like she didn't understand it.

"Hi, Fiona," Thomas said, approaching the table. "What are you doing?"

Her face lit up when she saw him. "Hi, Felix!" She turned the notebook toward him so he could see the drawing. "I'm designing my next tattoo. It would help me cast a spell to breathe underwater. I thought it would be useful to design the permanent version while we're at sea, especially considering the recent incidents."

"The sirens?" Thomas asked.

Fiona shrugged. "Yeah."

"They wouldn't drown you," Thomas said.

Fiona smiled at him and set her pencil down. "No, but I am a little worried about Fyavine. I would hate for her to jump overboard as a human. She'd be the first mermaid to die by drowning."

"That's nice of you," Thomas said, sitting down at the table across from her. Fiona really would help anyone.

"I'm just trying to keep us safe," Fiona said. "What are you up to? How do you feel after meeting Tetra? I haven't seen you all morning."

Thomas had been lying in the net beneath the bowsprit all morning. He needed some time alone to gather his thoughts after the events of the previous night. They still weren't gathered.

"I'm all right. A little offended she didn't take my offering, but I'll get over it. I've been rejected before."

Fiona giggled. "Charles is an idiot."

Thomas shrugged and frowned at the tabletop. "No, he's very smart."

"I don't care how 'smart' he is, breaking up with you was downright stupid."

Thomas laughed quietly and scratched his face. Maybe Faya and Fyavine were right. "Anyway, I wanted to ask you a few more questions about Tetra. Is that all right?" he asked.

Fiona closed her notebook and pushed it aside. "Sure. What would you like to know?"

"When we get to York, I want to visit Tetra's temple. Can you show me where it is?" Thomas asked.

Fiona frowned. "Why would you want to do that?"

"I need to talk to her again."

Fiona shook her head. "I don't think you should try to seek her out anymore. Nobody visits Tetra's temple and returns the same."

"I have to do it to help the mermaids. If I don't do it, who will?" Thomas asked. "They're suffering, and we are the only people in the entire world who know the cause. Please help me."

"I know it's important to you, but you have to consider your own safety. It may not be worth it," Fiona said. "You could die."

"I don't care," Thomas admitted.

Fiona raised her eyebrows. "You don't... care? About dying?"

"No," Thomas said. "I almost died in Chratan. I fought for my life because I didn't want to let the world down, but when we did the sacrifice, I opened my eyes. I wanted to see Tetra."

Fiona's eyebrows pinched together. "You did?"

Thomas nodded, swallowing to fight back the rising sadness. He had never been so honest about this with anyone. "I don't want to be alive," he said quietly. "I would give my one sad life to save thousands of lives worth living."

"Felix... Your life is worth living too."

Thomas shook his head. "You have no idea how I feel, Fiona."

Fiona tilted her head to one side. "Is it because of Charles?"

Thomas rubbed his eyes, refusing to let them leak his feelings. "No. I don't know. Maybe," he said, lowering his hands. "I've felt this way my entire life, but now it's worse than ever. If I can give my life doing good for the world, it would be a win for us all."

Fiona reached one hand out to squeeze his hand. "Felix. I meant what I said last night. You are an amazing and selfless person who gives up so much just to help others. It would be a huge loss for the world if you were gone."

Thomas withdrew his hand and shook his head. Fiona wouldn't be saying that if she knew who he was.

"I told you not to open your eyes because I care about you," Fiona said, "and I'm disappointed that you broke your promise."

Thomas stared at her. "What?" He hadn't considered that breaking his promise to her would cause *her* pain.

"I wanted to make sure you would get through the ritual safely. I helped you because you promised me you wouldn't open your eyes, and I made you promise because I don't want to lose you. We're friends, aren't we?"

Thomas had never believed his death would affect the people around him, but Fiona was sitting here telling him the opposite. "Y—yeah," he muttered. " Sorry."

"You don't need to apologize," Fiona said. "I'm sorry you're not feeling well, but things will get better. I promise."

"How can you promise that?" Thomas asked.

"Because it has to get better."

Thomas watched her carefully, wondering if she understood how he felt. But how could she? She was so happy all the time. "Are *you* all right, Fiona?"

Fiona forced a smile. "I'm really scared."

"Scared of what? Tetra?" Thomas asked.

Fiona shook her head. "I would give everything to Tetra just to know what happened to Finnlay. I'm terrified he's..." She tugged at a strand of hair and started twirling it in knots. "I don't know. Wherever he is, I hope the sirens don't get him, and I hope the Hambletons don't hurt him."

"Finnlay? Is that your brother?" Thomas asked.

Fiona nodded.

"They won't hurt him. He'll be okay," Thomas said.

Fiona stopped tugging on her hair and looked up. "How can you possibly know that?"

Thomas couldn't answer her. He should have known the Hambletons better than anyone on the ship, but he was starting to think he never knew his family that well at all. He wouldn't have thought his parents would hurt people just for being magi, but it took running away from home for him to learn that they might be killing people.

Suddenly he understood Fiona's answer to him. There could only be one answer because no other answer was tolerable. "Because he has to be okay."

Fiona's eyes welled with tears. She rubbed her face and sighed. "Felix, I don't want to show you where Tetra's temple is. I couldn't bear another loss, and telling my suicidal friend where the god of death lives is not a risk I'm willing to take. I'm sorry. If there's any other way I can help you, I would love to, but this is not something I can help you with."

"Please tell me," Thomas said. "I promise I won't intentionally get myself killed."

Fiona shook her head. "You've already shown me that's a promise you can't keep. I'm sorry, but I'm not going to tell you."

Thomas was annoyed, but Fiona was right. He probably wouldn't be able to keep that promise. "All right. Thanks, Fiona." He stood up to leave.

Fiona stood up with him. "Felix," she said.

Thomas stopped.

"Tetra isn't kind to her visitors. If she knows you want to die, she'll make you suffer another way. She's been known to go after her victim's friends and families. You don't want that to happen, do you?"

Thomas shrugged. "I don't have friends or family. It'll be all right."

"What about us?" Fiona asked, twirling her index finger in the air to point at the people on the upper deck.

Thomas frowned at her. "Tetra likes me," he said. "She won't do that."

Fiona raised her eyebrows. "What gives you that idea? Did she tell you that?"

"No, but... Don't worry, Fiona. It'll be all right."

"It better be," Fiona said.

BLACKWATER ACADEMY – ONE MONTH EARLIER

After the incident with Thomas, the Southworths had not allowed Charles to return to school until there was confirmation that Thomas would not be returning either. The Hambletons had tried to appeal Thomas's expulsion, but upon the discovery that Thomas was dead, it was pretty clear he would not be returning.

Charles's parents finally let him return to Blackwater Academy in mid-February. The term was already in full swing by that time, and Charles found himself with a lot of catching up to do. It was impossible. Due dates came and went without even a passing glance at the work. The majority of his day was spent face-down at his desk, and then at night on his bed. He had lost any and all ability to fake happiness. There was not an ounce of it left in him.

Other students at the school had heard a distorted version of the incident with Thomas, which was, coincidentally, closer to the truth. The rumor was that Charles and Thomas were secretly in love, but because of their rivalry, their parents wouldn't let them be together. His apparent depression only worsened the rumors, and nobody seemed to care about the news that Thomas was dead. It just made everything funnier for them. Charles wanted to die anytime he heard someone talk about it, but lately he felt that way regardless of what he heard.

Professor Redmond's shrill voice rang through his ears on a dull Wednesday morning. Charles didn't know what she was lecturing about, and he didn't care. There was only one thing on his mind, and it was the same thing that had been on his mind for weeks. It wasn't fair. Why did it have to be Thomas?

"Hey," a harsh voice whispered from directly behind him. "Southworth."

Charles didn't move. He didn't want to acknowledge the student behind him. Whatever they were going to say to him wouldn't be good.

"What's wrong? Do you miss *your boyfriend*?" the voice taunted him.

Charles said nothing. Several other students nearby laughed. Slowly, he peeled himself off his desk and faced the front of the classroom. Professor Redmond shot a wary glance in his direction but continued lecturing.

"I think he does," another voice whispered.

Charles couldn't even argue with them, because they were right. He tried to focus on the information at the front of the room, but tears blurred his vision. He quickly rubbed them away, but not before the other students saw.

"Oh my god, he's *crying*."

Charles's anger boiled over, and he whipped around to face them. "Shut up!"

"Mr. Southworth!" Professor Redmond yelled from the front of the room. The students behind Charles burst into laughter. "That's enough!"

Charles was fuming. The professor had no right to yell at him when he had only defended himself. "You're right. It *is* enough," Charles repeated, now standing up.

"*Mr. Southworth*. Sit down!" Professor Redmond scolded.

Charles ignored her. He faced the students behind him, who watched him with smirks. "Thomas is dead. It's not funny."

"It is funny," said the student. "That monster got what he deserved. I'm surprised you don't agree, Southworth."

"No," Charles said, struggling to steady his voice. "He didn't deserve to die."

"Why do you care? Is it because you *loved him?*" another student taunted.

"Yes!" Charles yelled. "Is that what you want to hear? Yes, I loved him!"

The classroom fell silent. Up until now, his love for Thomas had only been a rumor. Deep down he knew he had said something he couldn't take back, but he didn't care.

"*Gross,*" someone loudly whispered from the other side of the room. Several students snickered.

Charles shook his head and wiped tears off his face. He never understood why his peers thought it was funny that he liked boys, and he didn't understand why it was funnier to them now that the only boy he had ever loved was dead.

"Mr. Southworth," Professor Redmond scolded him. She pointed a sharp finger at the door. "Go to the headmaster's office."

"Me? The entire classroom is tormenting me and *I'm* in trouble?" Charles asked.

"You're being inappropriate and disruptive," she said.

"Should I be laughing too, professor?" Charles asked.

"*Go.*"

Charles picked a book up from the desk of the student that sat behind him and threw it at the wall. "Fuck you," he said to the student.

"I bet you would."

"Mr. Southworth!" Professor Redmond yelled.

"Fuck you, too!" he yelled at the professor as he left the classroom. He paused in the hallway. The headmaster's office was to the left. He turned right and hurried through the wide hall, down the empty stairs, and out the courtyard door.

He ran across school grounds until he was at the edge of the lake. He stopped to catch his breath and doubled over with his hands on his knees. Tears blurred his vision as he looked at the familiar landscape. The wind shook leaves from the trees and sprinkled them across the surface of the water. The fragrant smell of flowers on the wind broke his heart with the memories it carried. He wiped the tears from his eyes again and stared across the lake to the distant isolated shore where he had spent many evenings with a person he would never see again.

Thomas's death was the worst thing that had ever happened to him, and nobody cared. It was a joke to his peers. His father had hurt him for being upset over it. How could anyone ever understand? He had never felt so alone in his life.

His legs felt weak, and his body heavy. He dropped himself to the wet ground and let himself cry into the mud. Everything was his fault. He hated himself so much that it made him sick. He deserved to be laughed out of the classroom. Thomas had died so that Charles could maintain his family's reputation, but in the end, he didn't have Thomas or his reputation. Absolutely everything was ruined because of him. Charles resigned himself to lying in the cold mud. The icy sting of water seeped through his clothes, but he didn't move.

Time had no meaning. Each agonizing second that passed took him further from his last moment with Thomas. The thought hurt more when he remembered how unpleasant that moment had been.

Charles didn't know how long he had been lying in the mud staring at the gray clouds before a dark silhouette blocked his view. It was his father, Alfred. It must have been hours.

"Charles," Alfred said.

Charles didn't respond. He didn't even look at Alfred.

"Why are you like this?" Alfred asked.

"I don't know," Charles said with a hoarse voice.

"Do you have any idea what you've done?"

"I don't care."

Alfred sighed. "Get up."

Charles slowly rolled over and pushed himself up. He staggered in place and squinted at Alfred. "Why are you here?"

"Everyone knows you lied."

"They already knew. They've been harassing me since I got here."

"Look at you. You're disgusting," Alfred said. He swiped at the mud on Charles's shoulder but gave up when he realized it was futile. He released a disappointed sigh. "I don't understand why you can't keep your shameful urges to yourself."

"Why are you here?" Charles asked again. "Isn't today Wednesday? Or is it Friday?"

"I withdrew you from Blackwater. You have embarrassed me for the last time."

The news did not affect Charles. Charles thought he should feel something, but he didn't. He remembered how miserable he had been at Blackwater with the constant, relentless reminders of Thomas, and decided that it was probably best for him to leave. He nodded.

"I'm putting you to work on a ship. Nobody will recognize you out at sea."

The open ocean. Thomas's final resting place. Maybe his ship would get lost too. "Okay."

"'Okay?' That's all you have to say?" Alfred asked.

Charles shrugged. His shoulders were so heavy.

Alfred shook his head as he turned to leave. Charles stumbled behind to follow. "I wish you had never been born," Alfred muttered.

Charles didn't know if Alfred had intended for him to hear, but he answered anyway. "Me too."

Chapter Nineteen

On a cold, early morning Thomas stood at the bow of the ship watching the dark shore of York slowly come into view. The crew had been at sea for weeks, and the journey was finally coming to an end. Thomas pulled his coat around himself tightly and shivered. There had to be a temple to Tetra here. Even in the peak hours of daylight, there was no sun. It was hidden by the thick layer of clouds.

"Isn't it beautiful?" Fiona asked.

Thomas hadn't heard her approach. "This rainy, gloomy city?"

"Yeah," Fiona said with a grin.

Thomas shrugged. "It's cold."

"It's not that cold," she said, her breath evaporating on the air in a twirling cloud.

Thomas shot her a sideways glance, then stared at the water again. "Can I ask you something, Fiona?"

Fiona smiled at him. "Yes?"

"Have you figured out where you'll go after this? Are you

going to stay here? In this city full of people who hate you?" Thomas asked.

Fiona shook her head. "I don't know. I just want to find my brother. I'll think about that later."

"What happened to him?"

"I wish I knew," she said with a sigh. "When my friend turned us in for doing magic, we got separated in the pursuit. I haven't seen him since."

"I'm sorry."

"Why are you sorry? It's not your fault."

Thomas tried not to react. She had no idea how close their separation came to being his fault. "How do you plan on finding him?"

"I've been trying to figure that out," Fiona said. "If he was sent away like I was, how will I ever know?"

Thomas considered the question. "Maybe there's a record of it somewhere."

"A record?"

"You were arrested, weren't you? Wouldn't there be a record of your arrest?" Thomas asked.

Fiona stared at him for a moment before a smile spread across her face. "You're a genius!"

Thomas shook his head. "No," he said, but Fiona had already taken off across the deck, shouting for everyone to join her in the captain's cabin. Thomas forced his frozen feet from the boards of the deck to follow her.

Thomas ambled into the cabin where Fiona was already digging through the contents of the chest, presumably to find ingredients for some kind of enchantment. He sat at the wooden chair beside the table as he waited for the rest of the crew to assemble. Eventually, Faya dragged Ametta into the room. Fyavine clung to Faya for warmth. They all sat on the bed together.

"What's wrong, Fiona?" Faya asked.

"Just a minute," Fiona answered distractedly with her head still buried in the chest. Faya looked at Thomas. Thomas shrugged.

Finally, Fiona turned around to address her crew, Faya's enchanted cloaking necklace dangling in one hand and her other clutching a wooden bowl. "Thank you for joining me," she began. "As some of you already know, my brother and I were separated here in Dufonn. I was shipped away on a Hambleton ship, but I don't know what happened to him. I'm trying to stay optimistic, but..." she trailed off, but quickly brought herself back to the conversation with a façade of cheeriness. "I'm trying to stay optimistic," she repeated, setting the bowl and necklace on the table. Wilted white flowers filled the bowl.

Faya pulled Ametta closer to herself and squeezed her tight. "I'm sorry to hear that, Fiona. I'm sure your brother is fine."

Thomas didn't say anything. As a Hambleton, he should have known exactly what happened to Fiona's brother, but he didn't. Anything could have happened to Finnlay. Thomas fixed his eyes on the table in front of him. They still didn't know he was a Hambleton, and if they ever found out, he would probably not be welcome anymore.

"Thank you," Fiona said. "I may be able to find out what happened to him if I can find a record of our arrest, but I may need help. I completely understand if none of you are comfortable. I can do it by myself if necessary."

"I'll help you," Thomas immediately offered. The guilt of his name weighed on him, and he would do anything to make it right with his crew, even if they never found out who he was.

"Thank you, Felix," Fiona said.

The sound of his fake name sent an ache through his heart. As he grew to care more about his crew, this lie became more difficult to live. But there was no way he could tell them the truth.

"Of course," he said.

"I would love to help you, Fiona, but I don't want to leave Ametta alone," Faya said.

"I'll stay here and watch her," Fyavine said. "I don't know how much help I would be with my limited mobility anyway."

"Are you sure?" Faya asked Fyavine.

Fyavine rested her head on Faya's shoulder and smiled at Ametta. "If Ametta's okay with it, of course."

Ametta grinned hopefully at her mother "Can I stay here with Fyavine?"

Faya smiled at Ametta and then kissed the top of her head. "Of course, baby." She pulled Ametta close and nodded at Fiona. "You helped me find Ametta. I'll help you find your brother."

"Thank you, Faya," Fiona said.

"What's the plan?" Thomas asked.

Fiona looked into the bowl of flowers on the table. "I'm afraid if I show my face in town again, I might be recognized. I still have Faya's cloaking charm, but I think I need something more powerful this time. I want to repurpose it into an invisibility charm."

"Do you have everything you need?" Faya asked.

"I think so. The only thing I'm missing is the social aspect. I'm not sure we have it among us," Fiona answered.

"Social aspect?" Thomas asked, completely enveloped in this new piece of information about magic.

"Yes. Some recipes require an act or circumstance related to its function, but it isn't always available. In this case, we are dealing with invisibility, so the social circumstance is related to hidden identity. I don't suppose any of you have a secret to share, do you?" She gave a short, nervous laugh.

Thomas felt like he was drowning all over again. He sat back in his chair and tried his hardest not to look guilty. If he wanted to help Fiona, he would have to ruin his friendship with her and everyone else on the crew.

"I won't blame you if you do. We were all strangers when we met. If this applies to any of you, please don't tell me now. Just acknowledge that you can help, and I can start the process. Please."

Despite the frigidity of York, Thomas felt sweat form on his forehead. He knew that he had to do this for Fiona, but it would ruin everything. He stared at the ground, trying to work up the courage to admit that he had been lying. His hands trembled, and he shoved them into his coat pocket to hide his fear. He took a deep breath to speak, but someone else beat him to it.

"That applies to me," Faya said.

Everyone in the room stared at Faya. Thomas was overcome with relief, soon followed by a fresh wave of guilt for continuing to keep his secret in the face of a perfect opportunity to confess.

"Oh!" Fiona said. "Thank you, Faya. I will get started." She promptly reached for the necklace and began pulling the old ingredients from the braided rope. Thomas took this as his cue to leave, quietly slipping out of the room without another word.

The harsh, biting air attacked his face as he quickly crossed the length of the ship to create as much distance between himself and his crew as possible. His eyes burned with hot tears of guilt, and he rubbed them away to escape the feeling. He stared at the cloudy gray horizon and wondered how he managed to feel out of place no matter where he was in the world. The horizon offered an imaginary escape, but it was always out of reach. Where he stood now had once been the horizon he longed for, and everything was still the same.

"Felix!" Mariana called. The name stung his ears.

"Yes..." Thomas replied.

"Are you crying? What's wrong with you?" Mariana asked. "Are you dying?"

"No," Thomas said.

"I don't often speak to humans, so I struggle to understand your emotions. I have noticed you cry a lot, and I have been observing other humans to see what it means. I have concluded that it is an expression of grief. What are you grieving?" Mariana asked.

"I don't cry that much," Thomas said. "And I'm not grieving anything. Not right now, anyway. I feel guilty."

"Guilt!" Mariana exclaimed. "Humans are so strange. What are you guilty of?"

Thomas glanced over his shoulder to make sure he was alone. It was a risk to verbally acknowledge his lies, but he appreciated the effort Mariana had put in to understand him. She deserved to know. "I've been lying about my name," he whispered.

"Hambleton?" Mariana asked, glancing around the ship.

Thomas nodded. "And I lied to you about my first name."

Mariana shook her head. "No, you didn't. You told me the first time we met. Your name is Thomas."

"What?" Thomas was dumbfounded to discover that she had been listening to him. "Why haven't you been calling me by my real name?"

Mariana shrugged. "You introduced yourself as Felix first. I just assumed that was the name you preferred. Was I wrong?"

Thomas shifted his gaze from Mariana to the horizon again, seriously considering his answer. The difficulty of the question surprised him. "I don't know. I don't like my name, but I'm starting to hate Felix just as much."

"Should I call you Thomas?" Mariana asked.

Thomas shrugged. "I guess so. It's not like anyone will hear you."

Mariana watched him quietly for a moment. "I don't understand where your guilt is coming from," she said. "You don't know what your family is doing to magi, so clearly you haven't been participating. Why do you feel bad?" Mariana asked.

"Because I have been lying to everyone. If they find out, they are going to hate me."

"That's irrational," Mariana argued. "You haven't done anything."

"They don't know that."

"Then tell them."

"They won't believe me," Thomas said. "You don't understand, Mariana."

Mariana exhaled a bubbly sigh. "I'm sorry, Thomas. I'm trying."

Thomas watched her carefully, wondering why she suddenly sympathized with him. "Why?"

"Because I appreciate everything you're doing for me. I haven't met very many humans in my time, but among them, you are the most selfless. You deserve to receive the sympathy you give."

Thomas felt the tears coming back, and he turned away from Mariana so that she wouldn't see. The effort was wasted, however. Mariana followed him and sat directly in his line of sight. "Are you feeling guilty again?"

"No," Thomas said, rubbing his eyes. "Was there a reason you wanted to talk to me?"

"Yes! Since your friend won't show you the way to Tetra, I figured out how I can travel with you instead." Reaching somewhere deep below her, she retrieved an old glass vial from the sea and set it on the edge of the ship for Thomas to look at. It was covered in slimy green algae and plugged with a dark brown cork that Thomas imagined was just as slimy as the rest of it.

"You want me to put you inside this vial?" Thomas asked, plucking the dirty glass vial from the ledge and eyeing the murky green seawater inside.

"I am already in here," she said. "Just carry that with you, and I'll be wherever you are."

"Oh... Okay, thanks," he said, carefully slipping the filthy vial into his coat pocket.

"To visit Tetra, you should wear dark clothing. Otherwise, she won't believe you're on her side."

Thomas looked down at the long black coat that covered a lighter ensemble. "Is this enough black?"

Mariana eyed his outfit. "No."

Thomas tugged at his shirt, wondering where he could find black clothes.

"When you are in the temple try not to be scared, because she will use your fear against you. There is nothing to be afraid of as long as I'm with you, so do not lose that," Mariana said, pointing at the vial hidden in his pocket.

"All right."

"It's best to visit at night. Do you think you will be ready by tonight?" she asked.

"Yes."

"Great. I'll see you then," Mariana said. Instead of vanishing abruptly like usual, she said, "Bye, Thomas!"

Her goodbye caught Thomas off guard. "B-bye," he stuttered. Mariana gave a quick wave and then became one. Thomas waved awkwardly after her.

He turned around and was suddenly face-to-face with Faya. A cold shock struck him at the sight of her. How much had she heard? "Faya!"

"Felix."

Thomas looked around the deck in search of the others. It appeared they were all still in the cabin. "Are you all right?" Thomas asked.

"That's what I came to ask you. You left very fast."

Thomas felt his nerves tangling in his stomach. "I'm fine," he said quickly.

"Good," she said. "You seemed nervous in there."

"I haven't been feeling well," Thomas said. It wasn't really a lie.

"I offered to help because I wanted to spare you the shame." Faya refused to say anything more. She was trying to get the truth out of him. She deserved to know, but Thomas wasn't ready to share.

"Thank you," he finally said.

"I knew it. Who are you?"

Thomas shook his head.

"You can tell me. I promise not to tell the others," Faya said.

"You would hate me if you knew."

"I bet you thought that about your other secret too," Faya argued.

"Please stop," Thomas begged. "I promise I'm not a bad person. I haven't done anything wrong. I am Felix Warren, and I will continue to be Felix Warren for the rest of my life. It doesn't matter. Please don't ask me again."

Thomas stepped around her in an attempt to end the conversation, but Faya followed him. "You've only made me more curious. It can't possibly be that bad."

Thomas shook his head again, afraid to condemn himself any more than he already had. He grabbed the handle of the captain's cabin door and pulled it open. The room was warm and happy, sitting in stark contrast with the cold, dead air outside.

"Where have you been?" Fyavine asked from the bed, holding Ametta in her lap.

"We were just talking," Faya said, taking her seat beside Fyavine and Ametta again.

"Did you finish the enchantment?" Thomas asked, sitting down against the wall near the door.

Fiona's head popped up from her workspace to answer him. "Just about! Actually, now that you're back, Faya, it's almost time to share your secret. Are you comfortable sharing with everyone?"

"I don't think it would be fair to put a question in their mind without giving it an answer," Faya said. Thomas could see her look at him from the corner of his eye, but he refused to return the look.

"All right. Come over here, please," Fiona said. Faya stood and picked up Ametta from the bed. "You don't need to bring Ametta. It would be better if it was only you."

"It's about her," Faya said.

"Oh." Fiona paused. "Is she able to tell me herself?"

Faya set Ametta down in front of Fiona and whispered something to her. Ametta nodded and faced Fiona. Fiona picked up the necklace and held it in her hands. "Go ahead, Ametta," Fiona said.

"My name is Fiametta Leon," Ametta said with pride.

Fiona stared in shock. "Is that it?"

Faya nodded.

"I don't know if that's enough. Is there a reason you didn't tell us her full name?" Fiona asked.

"I thought this ship already had enough *F* names. But the number may still be the same." Her eyebrow twitched at her last comment. She was certainly talking about Thomas.

The secondhand confession triggered something in the necklace that Fiona had laid out. A white light glowed from the crevices in the braiding, and then the light died.

Fiona scratched her head. "*Something* worked," she said, shooting a baffled look at Faya. She draped the necklace around her neck and asked, "How do I look?"

Thomas hadn't even seen her disappear. One moment she

was in the room, and the next she was merely a disembodied voice.

"You don't," Faya said.

"It's working?" Fiona's excited voice asked from nowhere. Thomas could imagine the grin on her face that she always wore when her magic was successful.

"It's working," Thomas said.

"Great! This should be quick. We'll be in and out of there in no time," Fiona said.

Thomas rolled his eyes. It was impossible for things to be quick and easy, and Fiona should have known that by now. Fiona pulled the charm over her head, reappearing before them as inconspicuously as she had disappeared. "Everyone get ready. I'll meet you on the dock in ten minutes," she said, turning to clean up the mess she had made on the table.

Fyavine, Faya, and Ametta filed out of the room while Thomas stayed behind with Fiona. Without a word, he slid past her to look into the chest at the spare clothes they had gathered from the sailor's belongings, which had been serving the entire crew for the duration of the trip. They had most recently raided it for warm clothing.

Thomas peered inside. It was a disaster. Nobody bothered to fold anything, and Fiona had also decided to store her magical potions and other ingredients inside the chest. He tugged at every dark article of clothing he could find, pulling everything else out with it and making a mess on the floor.

"What are you doing?" Fiona asked.

"Changing clothes."

"Why?"

"I don't understand how you *lived* here. It's freezing," he said as he pulled off his coat, and then his lighter-colored top layers.

Fiona scoffed at him. "It's not that cold. Where are you from again? Tinera?"

"Yes." Thomas threw a navy long-sleeved shirt over the longsleeved undershirt he still had on.

Fiona watched him hastily pull black pants up around his waist and fasten them with a belt. "What are you doing?" she asked again with more suspicion.

"I already told you. I'm changing."

"Why are you changing into dark colors?"

"Dark colors absorb more light. I'm cold," he said, pulling on his overcoat again.

"There is no sunlight in Dufonn." Fiona paused. "You're going to visit Tetra's temple, aren't you?"

"How would I do that? I don't even know where it is," he said, reminding Fiona she had refused to help him.

"Don't go, Felix. It's an evil place."

Thomas threw her a sideways look. "Have you been there?" he asked.

"No amount of money would tempt me to set foot near that horrible place."

"I'm not doing it for money," he said, throwing his old clothes back into the chest. He turned to look at Fiona. "I have to do this."

Fiona nodded reluctantly. "Felix..." she said, wringing her hands together.

Thomas stuck his hands in his coat pockets to fight off the cold. "Yes?" he asked.

She looked into his eyes. "Do you remember what I said when you asked me to help you?"

"You said a lot of things," Thomas said.

Fiona nodded. "Yeah, I did. But most importantly I said that I care about you, and I don't want to lose you," she said.

Thomas shook his head. "I'll be fine," he said. He found it hard to believe that Fiona cared about him after their short time together. She definitely wouldn't care if she knew his real name.

"I hope you mean that," Fiona said, watching him carefully.

"Yeah, I mean it. I'll see you on the dock, Fiona," Thomas said, turning to leave before Fiona could say anything else.

He meant what he said, but his definition of *fine* was much different from hers.

CHAPTER TWENTY

Three minutes of waiting felt like hours to Thomas as he stood on the frosty wood planks of the docks of York. Flecks of ice hit his face with the aggressive force of the wind. Thomas crossed his arms to preserve his warmth, but the cold air seemed to blow right through him. Faya stood beside him with her arms crossed, glaring at their ship, unbothered by the icy gales.

"Y-you're n-not—cold?" Thomas asked. He struggled to talk through his shivering.

Faya shrugged. "I'm good at creating heat."

"What's t-taking her so long?"

"Maybe she doesn't want to come out because she's cold."

Thomas mockingly scoffed at the suggestion, as Fiona had done to him earlier. "It's not that cold."

Faya shot him a wary look, then smiled when she realized he was joking.

Fiona finally departed the ship to join Thomas and Faya. "Sorry, I lost track of time," she said, just as unbothered by the cold as Faya. "Let's go!"

"How far is it?" Faya asked, walking in step beside Fiona. Thomas followed behind them, struggling to move his limbs that had gone numb.

"Not far. It's that tall black building over there." Fiona pointed to a sea of tall black brick buildings.

"Okay..." Faya said.

The docks in York were much larger and busier than any other city Thomas had ever been in. Sailors bustled past them, casting angry but curious looks in their direction. Everything was darker in York, and not just because of the overcast skies. As the group approached the end of the dock, Thomas could see that the locals wore darker shades of clothing, and their houses were built with dark wood or black bricks. Tetra seemed to have a stronger hold on this place than he thought.

The ocean waves rolled quietly over the rocky shore, which didn't surprise him; Mariana didn't seem very fond of Tetra.

As they walked through the city, the familiar and painful smell of cigarette smoke drifted in the air. Thomas sped up to walk beside Faya. "Are we almost there?" he asked, trying to focus on something other than that smell.

"It's just up here." Fiona gestured ahead of them to a wide brick building that extended above them for three stories. The bricks of the building were an ashy black, and the doors were made of dark brown wood.

"Everything in York is so..." Thomas hesitated as he tried to find the right word. "Gloomy."

"Yeah," Fiona said, stopping in front of the heavy wooden doors of the peacekeeping office. "Are you ready?"

"What's the plan?" Faya asked.

"Here we go." Fiona threw the invisibility charm around her neck and vanished from sight. "Can someone open the door for me?" her disembodied voice asked from an indeterminable location.

Thomas approached the door and yanked on the handle to hold it open for Fiona and Faya. Faya nodded at him as she entered the building. Thomas waited several seconds to allow Fiona to enter before walking inside himself.

The interior of the building was as cold and impersonal as the exterior. A single black desk sat facing the door from the opposite side of the room. An older bearded man waited in the chair behind the desk, examining them for any signs of trouble. His eyes were tired and wary like he had been watching this scene for years, and he probably had. "What do you need?" his deep, gruff voice scratched its way across the room.

"I think I'm lost," Thomas said. Fiona had not given them a plan, so he decided to wing it. "I just arrived here from Tinera. I was told to ask for Mr. York." He tried feigning incompetence in the most nonsensical manner he could think of.

The officer raised a skeptical eyebrow at Thomas, and to Thomas's surprise, he said, "Do you have an appointment?"

"N-no," Thomas stuttered, looking at Faya desperately. Faya stared back at him in awe.

"Let me see if he's available." The man stood, pushing his chair away from the desk as he rose. His stature made the desk and chair seem small. The man exited through a dark wooden door set into the wall behind him.

"How did you know there was a Mr. York?" Faya asked.

"I didn't. I was trying to sound stupid."

"Great job, Felix!" the distant voice of Fiona called from somewhere in the room.

"I didn't do anything," Thomas said.

"It doesn't matter," Fiona said, "We're going to have a chance to look in the back."

The man returned quickly, standing in the doorway and gesturing down a narrow, dimly lit hallway. Thomas slowly approached the doorway and peered through the frame. "Will she be joining you?" The man shot a harsh look at Faya.

"Yes," Thomas said as he stepped through the doorway.

Faya messed with the heel of her shoe for a moment to buy time for Fiona as the man held the door open for her. He loudly cleared his throat. Faya looked up quickly like she was surprised to see him. "Oh, I'm sorry," she said, and stepped through the doorway.

"Last door on the right," the man said before shutting the door and cutting off all further communication.

"Did you make it through, Fiona?" Faya whispered.

"Yes, thank you," Fiona's quiet voice answered.

Thomas stared at the closed door in amazement. Faya pushed him forward. "Let's go. I don't want to be in here any longer than we need to be."

"Right," Thomas said, leading the group toward the office. As he stood before the door, Thomas took a deep breath and shot one last apprehensive look at Faya before knocking on the sturdy door that served as a barrier between them and the knowledge Fiona had been missing for too long.

Thomas turned the handle and stepped inside. Mr. York sat behind his desk, quietly watching Thomas and Faya. He did not seem like a typical member of the peacekeeping force. The man in the front office was bulky and aggressively tempered, but Mr. York was relatively slender and seemed to have a very patient disposition. Not many people would allow a confused teenager to interrupt their workday without an appointment. His calm brown eyes watched Thomas and Faya carefully. He sat behind a wide mahogany desk in a high-backed chair, giving him a sense of great importance to the functioning of not just this office, but the entire city of York. Maybe it was just his name.

"Good afternoon," he said. "My name is Ivan York. How may I help you?" He gestured to two seats in front of his desk.

Thomas and Faya sat down. Ivan's dark, searching eyes fell on Thomas and remained there as he waited for a response. Thomas got the strange feeling that Ivan could read his thoughts. He felt himself tense at the invasiveness of Ivan's gaze.

"We are lost," Thomas said. "Do you have a map we can look at?"

"Didn't you ask to speak with me specifically? You could have asked anyone for directions."

Thomas didn't know how to answer. "Do you have a map?" he asked again.

Faya hid her face in her hand and sighed.

The pages of a large book of documents lying on a table behind Ivan began to silently turn on their own. Ivan eyed Faya for a moment. "I certainly do." He began to turn to the table behind him where Fiona was invisibly searching for information on her brother.

"We don't need to look at a map," Faya said quickly. "Can you tell us how to get to the marketplace?"

Ivan turned to face Faya again. He glanced between her and Thomas a few times before his dark eyes landed on Thomas again. "Have we met before?" he asked Thomas.

Thomas shook his head. "I'm from Tinera."

Ivan narrowed his eyes and leaned forward. "The marketplace is three blocks east of here," he said carelessly, then paused. "What did you say your name was?" he asked Thomas again.

"I didn't. My name is Felix."

The book behind Ivan closed silently. Another book opened.

"What's your last name?" Ivan asked.

"Warren."

Ivan sat back in his chair and examined Thomas. "Felix Warren. From Tinera," he said. The tone of his voice made

Thomas nervous. "There's something terribly familiar about that."

Thomas stared at Ivan, desperately trying not to react. Did Ivan know about Felix? Had he been caught? "It must be a common name," Thomas said quietly.

Ivan rifled through a stack of pages lying on his desk. He paused to read something, then let the stack of papers fall back in place. He folded his hands together and shot a blank look at Thomas. "Not as common as you'd think."

The pressure of panic squeezed Thomas's lungs. "You would be surprised."

Ivan nodded. "It takes a lot to surprise me," he said. "But I *am* surprised. I truly didn't believe you were still alive, Thomas."

Thomas stood up. "I think you have me confused with someone else." He grabbed Faya's hand and pulled her up with him. "Let's go."

"Wait," Faya protested.

Ivan stood up too. "You're not going to leave without your friend, are you?"

Thomas hesitated. He had almost forgotten about Fiona. How did Ivan know she was there? A page from the book of documents removed itself and then vanished. Fiona must have found her brother.

"Did he call you Thomas?" Faya asked.

Thomas ignored her.

"Let's go!" Fiona's voice whispered as it ran past them. The door flew open, and the sound of footsteps ran through. Faya ran after her, followed by Thomas.

They ran through the hall but didn't get very far before Ivan yelled after them. "If you stay, I'll let your friends go."

Faya stopped, but Thomas pushed her forward. "Run!" he said to her. Thomas didn't believe Ivan. Thomas had met many men like him, and he knew that Ivan would do everything in his power to arrest all of them. And he *really* didn't want to go back to Brenton.

Thomas dragged Faya through the door at the end of the hall hoping that Fiona was following. He felt like he was suffocating, and not just from the physical exertion. Ivan knew exactly who he was. Ivan regularly arrested magi and sent them away. Of course he knew the Hambletons. Of course he recognized Thomas.

They quickly ran through the building, avoiding the officer at the front desk and ignoring his angry demands. Thomas hardly watched his step as he tried to process what had just happened. Felix had definitely been caught. That was the only reason Thomas would be assumed dead and connected to Felix's name. Was he okay? What had they done to him?

The piercing cold greeted them as they left the building. Thomas pulled Faya to the right of the building down a dark, narrow street. He dragged her down the street until it curved out of the sight of the peacekeeping office and the docks came into view at the other end. They stood at the junction of two streets as they tried to understand what had just happened.

"Thomas?" Faya asked.

Thomas instinctively looked up at the sound of his name, and only realized why it was a mistake when he saw Faya's eyes widen. His reaction to the name was damning.

"Your name is Thomas?" Faya asked.

"No," he lied. He didn't know why he bothered. Faya had already figured it out.

Faya sighed and shook her head. "Fiona? Are you here?"

No response.

"We have to go back for her," Thomas said. "You know what, you should stay here. My punishment probably won't be as harsh if they catch me."

"Why?" Faya demanded.

"Because I'm not a magus," he said. The truth was that Thomas's family could buy his way out of anything, but he couldn't tell her that.

"I'm here," Fiona's voice said quietly from nearby. Suddenly, Fiona stood where her voice had come from. Her hands tightly clutched the rope necklace and the paper she had stolen. Her wide eyes were cast downward.

"Oh, thank Dei. Why didn't you say anything?" Thomas asked.

"I'm sorry, I..." She turned her sad gaze onto the paper. Without saying anything else, she offered it to Thomas.

Thomas's eyes scanned the information on the page. At the center was a rough sketch of a young man with curly hair and freckles. He looked like Fiona. She had found her brother's file. His name was printed above his picture: Finnlay Ferguson. Below his photo the word *wanted* had been crossed out in red ink. Beside the cross-out, someone had written *found and processed.*

Thomas looked up from the page to see Fiona burying her face in her hands. "I'm so sorry, Fiona." He didn't know what else he could say. There was nothing else to say. He hardly noticed when Faya snatched the paper from his hand so that she could read it too.

"What does 'processed' mean? He might be okay," Faya offered.

Fiona ripped her hands away from her face to shoot a deadly glare at Faya. Her face was wet with tears. "It means he's *dead*, Faya. He's not okay. He's dead."

Thomas didn't know what *processed* meant. He was heartbroken for Fiona, but he was also frustrated that he couldn't even use his experience as a Hambleton to console her. "Did you happen to see your own file? I bet yours says the same thing," Thomas said. It was all he had for her.

"Maybe it does, but I *would* be dead if it weren't for the sirens. Faya and I were *very* lucky." Her voice grew louder and more frantic.

"You don't know that," Thomas said.

"Yes I do! You have no idea! You don't have any idea what it's like to be a magus, Felix. You don't live in constant fear of the Hambleton family like the rest of us do," Fiona shouted.

Thomas didn't know whether he wanted to laugh or cry at the statement. He had likely been living in fear of the Hambletons far longer than Fiona had.

"They are vile, wretched, disgusting people. If I ever meet a single one of them, I swear to the gods, I will kill them! I hate them, Felix! I hate them!" Fiona sobbed.

Her declaration made Thomas nervous. Fiona had clearly missed the revelation that his name wasn't Felix. When Fiona found out his full name, she might actually kill him. "I bet I could find a Hambleton ship," she muttered, and before either Thomas or Faya could stop her, she ran in the direction of the docks.

"Fiona! What are you doing?" Thomas yelled.

Before Thomas could even consider chasing Fiona, Faya went after her. Thomas struggled to close the gap, and only managed to catch up with them at the docks. Fiona had already stolen a half-empty bottle of whiskey from the hands of a drunk sailor who lay face-down on a barrel and stuffed the enchanted necklace into the neck of the bottle.

"*Ablight!*" Fiona said. The bottle trembled in her hand before the rope sticking from the neck of the bottle came to life with bright fire.

"Fiona! Stop!" Faya yelled, snatching the bottle from her hands and extinguishing the flame with her own magic.

"Are you insane?" Thomas asked Fiona. "What if someone saw you doing magic?"

"Let them see!" Fiona yelled, tears streaming down her face. "Maybe if I get caught again, I'll have my chance to meet a Hambleton in person!" She turned to face the passersby who had stopped what they were doing to watch her meltdown. "I'm a magus! Come take me away!" she yelled. Nobody moved. The entire crowd was uncomfortably silent and still.

"*Fiona!*" Thomas said. "Stop yelling."

"I hate them, Felix. I hate the Hambletons. I will avenge my brother if it takes me the rest of my life. I swear I will," she sobbed.

Thomas had nothing to say to her. It hurt him to watch one of his closest friends suffer because of the actions of his own family, but there was nothing he could do or say to make it better. He only had the words to make it worse.

Unfortunately, the words found him first.

The drunk sailor stood up. He tapped Faya on the shoulder and pointed at the bottle in her hands. "Excuse me, that's mine," he said.

The sight of the sailor paralyzed Thomas. The mess of dark hair that fell over his face, the beautiful hazel eyes, the very shape of his silhouette. It was a drunken, haggard, tattered version of Charles.

Thomas could not move. He could only watch Faya pull the charred enchantment from the neck of the bottle and shove it into Charles's hands with disgust. "Thank you," Charles muttered ungratefully, and then his eyes landed on Thomas.

Charles's entire demeanor changed. The sight of Thomas sobered him. His eyes widened, his eyebrows shot up in desperate relief, and his mouth hung open. The bottle fell from his fingers and clattered dully against the wooden planks, but he didn't seem to notice or care.

"No," Thomas muttered, taking a step back and shaking his

head. "Don't." Thomas desperately hoped Charles understood that he didn't want to be recognized.

Charles didn't get it.

"Thomas!" Charles said. "You're alive?"

CHAPTER TWENTY-ONE

Nausea overwhelmed Thomas at the sound of Charles's voice around his name. He couldn't tell if it was disgust, fear, or something else he didn't want to acknowledge. Charles staggered toward Thomas and forced a sloppy hug on him. "I can't believe it," Charles cried, and squeezed all of the air out of Thomas's lungs, forcing Thomas to inhale the strong smell of alcohol and cigarettes. It worsened the sick feeling in his stomach.

Thomas shoved Charles away. "Get off me!" he yelled. Charles stumbled backward, unfazed.

"You said your name wasn't Thomas," Faya said, glancing between Thomas and Charles.

He could lie about being mistaken for a Thomas once, but not twice. He frowned at Faya and opened his mouth to speak, but he had nothing to say.

Fiona stared at Thomas. Her face was still wet with tears. "Your name isn't Felix?"

"Felix?" Charles asked. "You took his name too?"

Thomas shot a scathing glare at Charles. "How do *you* know

Felix? Did you turn him in? I bet you fucking told him you loved him first, didn't you?"

"Thomas…" Charles said, shaking his head. "I'm so—"

"Fuck you!" Thomas yelled. "Don't apologize to me! What are you even doing here? Go away!"

Charles took a step toward Thomas. Thomas took a step back. "I didn't turn him in," Charles said. "What did you expect was going to happen? He's a magus who traded lives with a Hambleton."

Thomas's chest felt tight. He had been so caught up in his anger that he hadn't considered the consequences of talking to Charles. He shook his head, not daring to look at Faya or Fiona. "I didn't know," he said quietly.

Charles squinted at Thomas. "You didn't know what?"

Thomas forced himself to look at his friends, who stared at him slack-jawed.

"*You…?*" Fiona said, furrowing her brow. "Are a *Hambleton?*"

"I didn't know," Thomas said, struggling to contain his own tears. He couldn't handle the pain of losing these people who had grown to be like family to him. The kind of family he had never had. "I didn't know about any of it. I'm so sorry."

Fiona and Faya continued staring at him. Thomas took a step back. It was too much. Charles was here in Dufonn. Fiona and Faya knew he was a Hambleton. He couldn't deal with either situation individually, and he definitely couldn't deal with them at the same time.

So he didn't. He turned and ran down the dock.

"Thomas, wait!" Charles shouted after him. Charles's light footsteps followed behind Thomas as he cut through the bitter afternoon wind.

"Go away!" Thomas yelled.

Charles easily caught up to Thomas and stood in front of him to stop him from running. "Thomas, please stop for just a second!" Charles said. "I can't believe you're really here. I thought you were dead."

"I wish I were. Leave me alone," Thomas said, stepping around Charles to continue walking.

"Please, you have no idea what I've been through."

Thomas stopped and whirled around to face Charles, who was, to Thomas's dismay, very pleased to see him. "I don't care! I don't want to hear you whine about how you had to face the consequences of your own actions for the first time in your life."

"Please, just give me two minutes. I'm so happy to see you. This is like a dream. No—this is like waking up from a nightmare."

Thomas scowled and gritted his teeth. "I wish someone would wake me up."

Despite Thomas's harsh words, Charles smiled at him. The same nausea from before gripped Thomas, and he recognized that it wasn't fear or disgust. It quickly turned into hot frustration that he still got butterflies at the sight of Charles. He wanted to hate Charles so badly, but he just didn't.

"Thomas, I am so—"

"No," Thomas said, turning around again. He walked away as he spoke. "Do *not* apologize to me." Maybe he could hate Charles.

Charles ran to catch up with Thomas, walking in step beside him. "Please hear me out."

"No. Your two minutes are up."

"It hasn't been two minutes yet."

"I don't care."

"Felix gave me hell," Charles continued anyway. "I don't know what you told him, but it must have been bad because I definitely got what I deserved."

"I told him the truth." Thomas stopped walking again once they had reached the end of the dock. He stood in a messy patch of grass away from the main road, watching Charles. For the first time since their reunion, he was interested to hear what Charles had to say. "What did he do to you?"

Charles told Thomas that he was chased by a werewolf, which he had decided was probably Felix. He also told Thomas about Felix's relationship with Rebecca, and how much worse it was to watch Thomas date his sister than to be chased by a werewolf.

"Your sister?" Thomas asked. "How did they manage that? I'm surprised she didn't claim he was assaulting her as soon as they were seen together."

Charles sighed sadly. "Thomas... I regretted saying that the moment the words left my mouth."

"Then why didn't you do something about it?" Thomas demanded. The familiar warmth of tears filled his eyes again, but he didn't bother trying to hide it anymore. "I still can't believe you would turn on me as quickly as you did. I wouldn't have even considered it if it had been my father."

"I—"

"No. Stop. Do you know what I don't understand more than anything? Do you know what question has been killing me every single day since I left Brenton?"

Charles shook his head guiltily.

"I don't understand why you would go out of your way to tell me that you loved me if it wasn't true."

Charles reached for Thomas's hand, but Thomas swatted him away. "It was true," Charles said.

Thomas shook his head. "No. You wouldn't have done that to me if you loved me."

"I did love you. I still do."

"Stop," Thomas cried as tears fell down his face. "Don't say that. You're a liar."

Charles reached toward Thomas to wipe the tears away, but Thomas pushed his hand away again. "I am a liar," Charles said.

"I lied to you and I lied about you, but I didn't lie about that. I'm so–" he stopped himself. "I regret everything. I wish we had never become friends. For your sake."

Thomas nodded, wiping his face with the sleeve of his coat. "Me too," he sobbed. "Loving you was the worst thing that ever happened to me." Thomas quickly turned around and walked away from Charles. He hated that Charles could see how hurt he was. He took deep breaths to calm himself and continued trying to dry his face with his sleeve.

His feet hit the cobblestone path that led into town, but he stopped immediately when he realized that he didn't know where he was going. The sun hadn't set yet, but even if it had, Mariana had never told Thomas where Tetra's temple was. Fiona surely wouldn't tell him now.

Thomas turned around to look at the docks as he thought about Fiona and was surprised to find that Charles hadn't followed him this time. He was still standing where Thomas had left him, drilling a pained look into a wooden crate beside him. His eyes darted up when he noticed Thomas watching him. The pain on his face turned to hope as he waited for Thomas to acknowledge him.

Thomas knew he should turn around and keep walking. He knew better than to invite Charles back into his life. But his feet wouldn't move. His body listened to his desire to be around Charles more than its need to be away from him. His autonomy completely disappeared as he beckoned Charles to follow him again.

Charles looked behind himself, as though Thomas were looking at someone else. There was no one else. There was no one else in the entire world who knew what Charles knew about Thomas and still wanted to be part of his life. Thomas nodded impatiently, and Charles jumped at the opportunity to be with him again.

Although he had invited Charles to follow, Thomas didn't wait for him to catch up before walking away. He turned to cross the grass in the direction of the beach. It wasn't long until he heard Charles's footsteps behind him. "Why are you in Dufonn?" Thomas asked.

"My father sent me away."

Thomas dropped himself onto a grassy hilltop that sloped downward into the rocky beach. He patted the space beside him impatiently to urge Charles to sit. Charles obliged with ease. "Why?" Thomas asked.

"I couldn't focus. I failed out of school. He got tired of seeing me cry all the time."

Thomas stared at Charles as he processed the information. Was he telling the truth? Would he really cry in front of his own father? Thomas had never seen Charles cry before. Was he capable of crying? "You're lying," Thomas said. Even if there was no logical basis for the accusation, he had a statistical advantage.

Charles sighed and held his head in his hands. "You're right. I didn't fail out of school. He withdrew me. In my defense, I was also failing."

"I don't understand."

Charles lifted his head and stared at Thomas. For a brief moment, Thomas felt guilty for his harsh attitude. "What?" Charles asked.

"Why were you failing?"

Charles raised his eyebrows at Thomas and stared at him for several seconds before answering. "Because my best friend died."

"Walter?"

Charles threw him a puzzled look. "You."

Thomas threw the puzzled look back at him. "Me?"

"Yeah, you."

Thomas sat in silence for a few moments as he considered their friendship. "We're not friends," he decided aloud.

Charles frowned at him. "What are we?"

Thomas had to think for a long time to find the right answer. "Bad at keeping a secret."

The familiar sound of Charles's laughter surprised Thomas. It made him feel all right for a moment, until he remembered what Charles was laughing at. "I forgot how funny you are," Charles said.

Thomas shrugged and frowned at the horizon. "You didn't have to forget." The sea had almost completely swallowed the dim, hazy patch of light that the residents of Dufonn called the sun. A murky blanket of shimmering cloudlight illuminated the distant border of the sea. The dim light would soon sink below the horizon, and Thomas would have to leave. There was a good chance he would never see his magi family again. He hoped more than anything that they would find a safe place to live and avoid whatever atrocity his own family was committing.

Suddenly, it occurred to Thomas that Charles might know exactly what that atrocity was. "Charles..."

"Thomas."

Thomas struggled to feel annoyed at the tone of Charles's voice. "Do you know what my family is doing? To magi?"

Charles hesitated. "I know some of it."

Thomas watched him closely, waiting for an explanation, but Charles's expression only grew more surprised by the second.

"Thomas, you don't know?" Charles asked.

"Why didn't you tell me?"

"How do you not know?"

"I don't know." Thomas folded his arms together. Every time he thought about how little he knew about his own family, he felt incredibly stupid.

Charles sighed and looked away. "I suppose it makes sense that they wouldn't tell you about it," he said quietly.

"Why?" Thomas asked leaning closer.

Charles stared longingly at Thomas for a moment before averting his eyes again to look out across the sea. "There is a rumor about you. Do you remember the first time you sat with us in the dining hall? When Walter tried to ask you a question?"

"Yes."

"He was going to ask about a rumor that I told him. I heard it from my mother, but she told me not to tell anyone. I was stupid enough to tell Walter, who can't keep his stupid mouth shut."

"What was the rumor?" Thomas asked impatiently.

"Well, uh..." Charles shot Thomas an apprehensive look. "Is it possible that you're... um..."

"What?" Thomas demanded. "You already know that I'm gay. What could be worse than that?"

"Gay? What is that?"

Thomas hesitated, unsure how to define it. "It's us. We're gay."

"Oh," Charles said with surprise, then a sly smile slid across his face. "What could be better?" he asked with a wink.

"Almost anything," Thomas growled. "What was the rumor?"

Charles looked away, then picked at the grass by his feet. "Is it possible that you're... a magus?"

There was a short pause, and then Thomas laughed. "No. That's ridiculous."

Charles shrugged. "My mother seems to think you are."

"I am not a magus. I would know if I were."

Charles looked Thomas in the eyes. "Would you?"

Thomas thought about it. How could he know whether he had an ability if he never had the opportunity to use it? He knew almost nothing about magic, so how would he know how to test the theory? Ametta seemed pretty proficient in magic for as young as she was, but she had her mother to show her. Maybe his own magic was stunted because nobody had shown him how to use it. If Ametta inherited her magic from her mother, then would that mean that one of Thomas's parents was a magus too?

If he were a magus, would that explain the reading he got in Chratan? He didn't know what it meant to scan yellow, but he certainly hadn't scanned green. "I don't know," Thomas said quietly. There were too many questions in his head, and he didn't have anyone to answer them.

"Sorry, Tommy. I wish I could tell you more."

"My name is Thomas," he said again. "You don't know anything else? You don't know what they're doing to magi?"

"Oh, uh..." Charles stared at Thomas for a moment before continuing. "Yeah. They process magi into what they call a 'rehabilitation camp' and then take their magic away."

"They take their magic away? How?"

"I'm not sure."

"What happens after that?"

"They are brainwashed into believing that magic is bad for them and the world, and then they are given jobs aboard Hambleton ships as crew members," Charles explained.

Thomas quietly processed the new information. It was a relief to hear that his family wasn't murdering anyone. He wished he could tell Fiona that her brother was okay, but Fiona would probably not believe him. Thomas remembered the crew of the Hambleton ship that had thrown themselves to the sirens so that he could have a working ship, and came to the horrible realization that he was the only Hambleton to ever cause the death of magi. He groaned and held his head in his hands. "That's not so bad."

Charles shrugged. "It's not great. I assume you've seen the ships' crews. They're not the happiest crowd."

"I'd probably be depressed too if I had that kind of power taken from me."

Charles stared at him for a long time. "Thomas, you *are* depressed."

Thomas scowled at him. "I'm depressed because the only

person I ever loved completely destroyed me to make his father happy."

"You were depressed before that happened."

Thomas could not believe the lack of remorse in his answer. "You know me so well," he said dryly. "Why didn't you ever ask me about this? How did it never come up?"

Charles shrugged. "I did try to talk about magi, but you said it had nothing to do with us. I thought you were just avoiding the subject."

Thomas closed his eyes and exhaled. "Dei, no wonder you gave up on me."

"I—that's not it, Thomas. I didn't give up on you. I didn't care about that."

Thomas shook his head. "You should have cared. You should have continued hating me if you really believed I was that kind of person. Why were you okay with it?"

Charles stared at him in awe. Thomas looked away. "You *want* me to hate you?" Charles asked.

"No!" Thomas said. "I mean, I don't care how you feel about me, but I don't want to believe you're the kind of person who would look the other way when someone you love is doing something bad." Thomas shook his head. "What am I saying? Of course you would."

"I don't understand... Doesn't that show you that I would love you no matter what?" Charles asked.

Thomas glared at him. "No. It shows me how little you care about the well-being of the world when it gets in the way of what *you* want."

Charles stared at him for a long moment, then sighed and looked away. "You're right. I was being selfish, but I do love you."

"You don't love me," Thomas said. "You knew there was no future with me. That's why you couldn't answer me when I asked. You didn't want a future with Thomas *Hambleton*."

"Of course I did," Charles said.

Thomas shook his head. "That's easy to say now, isn't it?" He looked at the darkening horizon and found Mariana waiting for him at the shore.

"Thomas!" she called out, running across the beach to sit on his other side. Thomas watched in awe. *Mariana was capable of leaving the ocean?* Suddenly he remembered the vial of seawater in his pocket, and it made sense. "You've had a crazy night," she said, peering around him to examine Charles, who was still talking to Thomas. Thomas wasn't listening. "Is that your boyfriend?"

"What? No. He is *not* my boyfriend," Thomas said. Why was that Mariana's first guess? As far as he could remember, he had never told her about Charles.

"What?" Charles interrupted himself to ask. "Who are you talking to?"

"He is very beautiful. Now I understand why you've been crying so much," Mariana said.

"I don't cry that much," Thomas said quietly so that Charles wouldn't hear him. He turned to face Charles, who had a look of puzzled amusement on his face. Charles obviously heard him. "I'm talking to a god named Mariana. She doesn't want you to see her."

"Is she talking about me?" Charles asked.

Thomas watched Charles carefully. "You don't think I'm crazy?"

Charles shrugged and smiled slyly at Thomas. "Maybe you are, but if your imaginary friend is talking about me, that means you're thinking about me."

Thomas stood up quickly and scowled at Charles. "She's not imaginary. I don't think about you."

"You're a bad liar," Charles said, staring dreamily at Thomas.

"I have to go. Don't follow me," Thomas said as he began to walk away.

"Where are you going?" Mariana and Charles said in unison. Mariana said it mockingly, while Charles said it with desperation.

Thomas chose to answer Charles. "I'm going to speak with another god, but not about you."

Charles pouted playfully. "I bet I'll come up in conversation."

Thomas rolled his eyes. "Goodbye, Charles. Have a nice life. Or don't. I don't care." He turned to leave.

"Wait—" Charles said, pushing himself up to chase after Thomas again. He grabbed Thomas's arm to keep him from walking any further. "This isn't the end, is it?"

Thomas yanked his arm away. "What did you expect? Did you think we would sail back to Brenton together and live happily ever after?"

Charles shrugged sheepishly.

"No," Thomas said, turning to leave again, hoping that Charles would give up his pursuit.

"Thomas, wait," Charles begged. "There's one more thing I have to say."

Thomas sighed angrily and faced Charles again. "What."

"I really do love you. I wouldn't be here if I didn't. I'm so happy you're alive."

Thomas glared at him. "You already said that."

Charles nodded. "I don't want you to think I was lying."

Thomas stared at Charles with a mixture of hatred and reluctant adoration. As much as he hated to admit it, it was nice to see Charles again. "I have something of yours," Thomas said.

"You do?"

Thomas nodded. He stuck his hand into the pocket of his pants and felt the smooth metal of the cigarette case. It had been empty for a long time, but Thomas still carried it with him everywhere. He didn't understand why he couldn't part with it, but now seemed like the right time. He hesitated as the case reached the edge of his pocket, but he eventually forced himself to pull it out and present the expensive accessory to Charles.

Charles took it from him with curiosity, turning it over in his hands. "Why do you have this?" he asked, flipping the case open and looking inside.

"I stole it."

Charles examined Thomas for a moment before his eyes fell down to the case in his hands again. "What happened to the cigarettes?"

"It was empty when I found it."

Charles smirked at him. "No it wasn't. You *have* been thinking about me."

Thomas frowned at Charles and shook his head. "I'm not the one who ended our relationship." He tugged on the drawstring of his shirt, struggling to admit his last thought. "I really loved you, Charles. I would have given you my whole future."

Charles's smug expression fell away. He frowned at the cigarette case, snapping it shut. "I'm so sorry," he said.

"Goodbye. Don't follow me," Thomas said. He started to turn, but stopped himself before Charles was out of sight. "I'm serious."

"I won't," Charles said softly. "Goodbye, Thomas."

CHAPTER TWENTY-TWO

Thomas quickly walked away from the wet, rocky beach, not daring to look behind him. Charles might consider it an invitation. Thomas sighed, and a plume of winter steam rose through the air in front of him. The stinging nip of the day had become the harsh bite of night. He folded his arms close to himself to stop his shivering, but it made no difference. "M—Mariana?" Thomas chattered into the darkening evening air.

"Yes?" Mariana's bubbly voice came from behind him. She had been following him, but Thomas was too focused on creating distance between Charles and himself to ask her any follow-up questions about Tetra's temple.

"Am I going the right way?"

"You're going to Tetra's temple, remember?" Mariana answered as though Thomas were deliberately asking a stupid question.

"Yes, obviously. Where is it?"

"I'll lead the way," she said, passing Thomas to walk in front of him. "You didn't tell me you had a boyfriend. He was cute."

"He is *not* my boyfriend, and he is *not* cute."

Mariana shot him a skeptical look. Thomas rolled his eyes, trying not to look guilty.

Suddenly it occurred to him that he had never told Mariana he was gay. "Wait a second, you don't think it's weird that we're both boys?"

"Why would I?"

"I don't know. Some people think it's unnatural."

"It's not unnatural at all. Every animal species has same-sex pairings. Who cares if it is, anyway? Clothes are unnatural, boats are unnatural, mirrors are unnatural, but that doesn't stop anyone from using them. Humans are silly," Mariana said. She talked about human behavior as though her opinion as a god was not life-changing.

Thomas was silent for a long time. There was no denying that he was different, but Mariana treated it like it wasn't a bad or embarrassing way to be. "Thank you," he said.

"What? Why? I should be thanking you. Isn't this why you've been able to help me with the sirens?"

"Yes."

"Well then, thank *you*," Mariana said, turning around to grin at him.

He smiled back. "You're welcome. Not that I really had any choice."

"You had a choice! Your other choice was to die on that ship!"

"No, you wouldn't let me. I would have been okay with that. You forced me to help you."

Mariana scoffed. "I can't force you to do anything, Thomas. You didn't even want a reward. You only decided to help me out of the goodness in your heart."

"Ugh," Thomas groaned. "There is no goodness in my heart. And I didn't say that. I do want a reward." Thomas stopped walking, refusing to continue until they came to an agreement. They were near the forest's edge. Mariana eagerly looked into the black forest, unable to move on without him because she was restricted to a short radius around the vial of seawater in Thomas's pocket. She couldn't walk too far away without disappearing.

"What would you like?" Mariana asked impatiently. "Immortality? I can give you that right now."

"No. Why do you keep offering that? No. Absolutely not," Thomas said. He couldn't think of anything worse than living an immortal life. The limited number of years he already had seemed like too much. He considered what else Mariana might be able to offer, and it was suddenly very clear what he should ask for. "I want you to help me save the magi from my family. I don't think I can do it alone."

"Really?" Mariana asked. "That's what you want as your reward?"

"Yes, why?"

Mariana shrugged. "Not many people in the history of humanity have ever had an opportunity like this. You can have almost anything you want, and you're using it to help others? You're a strange human."

"It's the only thing I want," Thomas said.

"All right, I can help you with that. It's the least I can do after everything you've done for me." Mariana grinned. It was strange to hear her acknowledge the difficulty of his trials after months of thankless effort.

Thomas nodded with approval and continued following her into the forest's entrance. The darkness of the forest was overwhelming. Nothing but pitch black shadow waited beyond the trees, but dim twilight still shrouded the city behind him.

"Can you see anything?" Thomas asked.

"Yes. The temple is very close."

"I can't see anything in that direction," Thomas pointed into the woods. His hand got lost in the forest's darkness as he threw it in front of him.

"Aw, should I hold your hand?" Mariana joked.

Thomas sighed. Normally, he wouldn't acknowledge the question, but this time he thought he might actually need to hold her hand. "If it would help," he grumbled.

Mariana giggled as her ice-cold grip enveloped Thomas's hand. It felt like he had stuck his hand into a bucket of ice water. Thomas involuntarily sucked air through his teeth. The cold of the water burned like fire against his hand. "What's wrong?" Mariana asked, pulling him forward.

"Your hand is as cold as ice," Thomas said through chattering teeth.

"We're almost there."

Thomas squeezed his eyes shut to dispel the pain, and it soon stopped. He opened his eyes to the same sight that he saw on the back of his eyelids: nothing. He momentarily wondered if he had died from the cold, but he could still feel the cold pressing against the rest of his body. "Mariana?" Thomas asked into the thin air.

"We're here. Now, repeat after me," Mariana said. "*Mortem, Mali, Metus, et Tenebras. Lux mea, sic nos occurrere.*"

"Uh... What?"

"Do you really need me to repeat it?"

"Yes. What language is that?"

Mariana shrugged. "Some language humans seem to think the gods speak. It is not the first language we spoke, nor is it the only language. Let's try it again."

Mariana repeated the phrase for him several times, but he could not remember the entire sentence. He didn't understand how Mariana expected him to get it after only hearing it once.

She impatiently broke the sentence into fragments, and he repeated it slowly with poor pronunciation.

It seemed to be good enough, because the heavy darkness around them lifted and Thomas could finally see his surroundings. Before him was a tall, smooth black stone with a narrow entrance carved into it. Words had been carved around the doorway, which Thomas recognized as the first four words in the sentence Mariana had just said to him ten times. The narrow entryway revealed a steep staircase that led deep underground. It was dimly lit by small torches attached to the wall.

"I'm going to leave you now," Mariana said. "Tetra will not be happy to see me. Pretend you are here to help her, but listen to me, Thomas. This is very important. Do not be scared of her, or she will use your fear against you."

"Great, now I'm scared that I'll be scared."

"I'll be here if you need me," Mariana said, and then evaporated into mist.

Thomas peered down the deep stairwell. He heard Fiona's voice in his head saying *it's an evil place.* It did seem like an evil place so far, but he wasn't worried. He had blindly lived with evil his entire life. He probably wouldn't even notice.

Thomas took a deep breath and stepped into the dark temple. His shoes crunched against the thin layer of frost that lined the top step. His hand shot out to steady himself against the ice-cold wall.

When he reached the bottom, an endless hall stretched ahead of him, lit by the same dim torches as the staircase. He looked behind him to find that the torches had gone out as he passed them. All that remained of the entrance was a dim point of darkening twilight at the top of the stairs.

Thomas could feel his heart beat faster, and took a deep breath to calm himself before he continued down the narrow hall. The crunching of ice beneath his feet was the only sound inside the tunnel. The darkness seemed to defy logic, closing around the light of the torches as much as possible without extinguishing them. With every step he took his fear intensified. His skin prickled and his heart beat fast. He got the feeling that someone or something was following him, but there was only darkness behind him. Anything could have been in there.

Thomas began to run, his heart rate quickening with his pace. The sound of his heavy, panicked breathing now joined the crunch of his footsteps. He remembered Mariana's warning: *Do not be scared of her, or she will use your fear against you.*

He forced himself to stop. There was probably nothing following him. He was only scared because he was approaching the source of all fear. He took several long, deep breaths and tried to relax. As his anxiety lessened, the darkness around him eased up. Finally, he could see the end of the tunnel. He slowly approached the hallway's outlet, breathing slowly to remain calm.

The hallway led into a large, circular chamber, with five archways that exposed individual chambers. A large lantern hung above the portal to each room, illuminating familiar words carved into the stone frames. The rooms to his left were labeled *Mortem* and *Mali.* The rooms to his right were labeled *Metus* and *Tenebras.* On the opposite wall from the entrance was the largest chamber, displaying the large name *Tetra* carved above it. A diamond shaped symbol with concave edges and a hollow center decorated the foot of each doorway.

Thomas slowly walked into the room as he took in the unusual surroundings. The room was very dark, lit only by the dim lanterns that highlighted each of Tetra's names. Because of the pressing darkness, Thomas did not notice the wide circular platform at the center of the room. He clumsily tripped over its ledge and stumbled onto it. He worried that the shock of tripping over the unseen platform would trigger the spiraling fear he had managed to control in the tunnel, but something caught his sight before he could begin to worry. A tall humanoid silhouette of darkness stood at the center of the platform.

It could only be Tetra.

Her appearance was much different from Mariana's. The sight of her was extremely disorienting. She looked like a shadow but existed without a surface to project herself from. Her edges blurred into the darkness around her. There was no beginning or end to her. She had long black hair that floated around her in spiraling black tendrils. To Thomas's surprise, she smiled with a mouth full of razor-sharp white teeth.

Looking into her face evoked a primal fear in Thomas. He could only look at her for a few seconds before he had to look away. The fear he felt in her presence was so strong he could taste it on his tongue.

"Well, well, well…" Her voice was smooth and cold like the metal of Charles's cigarette case, but unpleasant like the resentment Thomas felt when he looked at it. "Thomas Hambleton. You've decided to join me."

Thomas said nothing.

"I am pleasantly surprised. I didn't think you had it in you," Tetra said. "Or did you come here for something else? Something I know you've wanted for a long time…"

Thomas couldn't think of anything he had wanted for a long time. For all of his life, there had never been much he couldn't have if he really wanted it. The only thing he could imagine wanting consistently was death, and suddenly it made sense. Tetra was the god of death. "That's not why I'm here," Thomas forced himself to say.

"Are you sure? It's only natural to be afraid," she said, disappearing in a wisp of shadows and instantly reappearing at his side.

Thomas jumped and yelled out in alarm, then tugged at his shirt in an attempt to recompose himself. As much as he had wished for death in the past, he couldn't leave this world. Not yet. "I'm sure," he said. "I want to join you. Like you said, evil is in my blood."

Tetra grinned. "You made the right choice. You're much more useful serving me than you would have been serving Mariana."

Thomas didn't know what that meant. *Would have been?* Hadn't he already been serving Mariana?

"Don't be scared, Tommy. It won't hurt that much."

"What?" Thomas asked, taking a step away from her.

"Immortality. Isn't that why you came here?"

Thomas backed away so fast he almost fell over his own feet. "No! What?"

Tetra's sharp smile fell away. "Oh…" She leaned back, standing tall and towering over Thomas. "You're just as stupid as she is. You really haven't figured it out yet?"

"F—figured out *what?*" Thomas stammered.

"Tetra," Mariana's comforting and familiar voice called out from behind Thomas. Her ice-water grip closed around Thomas's arm and pulled him away. "What do you think you're doing?" she demanded as soon as Thomas stood safely at her side. Thomas shivered and hid behind her. He had never been so nervous in his entire life.

"What are *you* doing here?" Tetra demanded.

"What do you *think* I'm doing here?" Mariana said. "You're damaging my ecosystem!"

Tetra peered around her to look at Thomas. "Oh, I see…" she said with an angry frown. "You have no right to complain, *Mariana.* You're obviously after the same thing as me."

"You have no right to invade on my domain," Mariana said.

"I can do whatever I want. I am a god."

Thomas scoffed. "Mariana is a god, and she can't do anything," he muttered.

Tetra cackled into the air. "This human is funny. I can see why you want him as your eternal servant."

"Wait, what?" Thomas asked, looking at Mariana.

Mariana ignored him. "Is that what you're doing? You're trying to find a human to serve you?"

"Mariana?" Thomas asked. "Is that what you're doing with *me?*"

Tetra laughed her sinister laugh again. "How many times has she asked you if you want to be immortal?"

Thomas gawked at Mariana. She had offered him immortality more than anything else.

"That was not my plan, I promise. You said no, and I respect that decision," Mariana said.

"You *just*—" Thomas began to argue with her but stopped himself. Mariana clearly did not respect his decision to remain mortal, because she had continued asking him even after he said no. Anger coursed through him, overpowering the fear he felt in the presence of Tetra, but he decided this argument could wait for the sake of the mermaids and the magi. Thomas turned to Tetra. "Is that what you're doing?"

Tetra shrugged lazily. "Obviously. None of these sailors live up to my standards. Most of them die before they reach the bottom anyway, so I can't assess them properly."

"That's terrible!" Thomas said.

Tetra snickered. "Oh yes."

"You can't interfere with the other gods' domains. You are harming Earth life *and* sea life," Mariana said.

"I'll stop once I find the right man. Thomas knows what I mean," Tetra said to Thomas with a wink.

Thomas shook his head.

"You are going to stop *now,*" Mariana said.

"Fine. I'll stop," said Tetra.

Mariana and Thomas stared at Tetra. "Oh... That was easy," Thomas said.

"This has to be some kind of trick," Mariana said.

"No tricks," Tetra said with a grin. "I just happened to find the perfect person right here in this very temple."

"I am not going to be your eternal servant, Tetra," Thomas said.

Tetra grinned at Thomas. "As much as I admire your courage, your affinity for death, and your bloodline, I was not talking about you. Tell me something, Thomas. Did you feel like you were being followed on your way in?"

Alarm chased away the anger he felt toward Mariana. He looked at the entrance to see who or what had followed him in, but he only saw darkness. "Yes," he said, scanning the shadows.

"So, you're not completely stupid," Tetra said as she gestured at the doorway. "You don't have to hide anymore. We know you're here, why don't you join us?" The trembling silhouette emerged from the darkness to stand under the lantern of the *Tenebras* chamber. It was Charles.

That fucking idiot.

"Charles?!" Thomas yelled in a panic. "I told you not to follow me!"

Charles flinched at the sound of Thomas's voice. He had clearly succumbed to the overwhelming fear of the temple. "S-sorry," he stuttered.

"Come here," Tetra demanded. Charles obediently crossed the room to stand beside her. He threw a frightened glance at Thomas before fixing his eyes on the ground.

Tetra towered over Charles, grinning as she examined him. "Charles Southworth. You're just what I've been looking for. How do you feel about immortality?"

"Im-immortality?" Charles said. "As in, eternal life?"

"Oh, he's smart," Tetra said, lowering herself to his level. She took his face in her large clawed hand, turning it left and right to get a better look at him. "Charming, charismatic, handsome, ambitious... He's perfect! Don't you agree, Thomas?" Tetra turned to Thomas and flashed her horrible smile at him as she dug her sharp claws into Charles's face. Charles winced but did not dare fight back.

"Let go of him," Thomas demanded.

"Answer the question," Tetra replied with an angry frown.

"No. He's far from perfect," Thomas said, keeping his eyes on Charles. It was hard to watch Tetra hurt him, but he couldn't let himself look away. If something bad happened to Charles here, Thomas would not be able to live with himself.

Tetra shrugged. "The traits you find objectionable are the traits I prefer." She released Charles from her grip and smiled at him. He rubbed his face where her nails had dug into his skin. "What do you say, Charles?"

"Thomas," Mariana whispered. "She will torture him if he says yes. If you love your boyfriend, don't let him accept her offer."

"He's not my boyfriend," Thomas insisted.

"Oh, okay. Let him suffer, then."

Thomas glared at her.

Charles flashed a frightened look at Thomas in search of an answer. Thomas shook his head.

Charles glanced at Tetra, but immediately turned away out of fear. "No," he said.

"No?" Tetra challenged him, placing one sharp finger under his chin, forcing him to look at her again. "Do you have any idea what you're turning down? You would be young forever. I could give you anything and everything you've ever wanted. You could regain the power you lost ten times over. Your father would respect you again. It would be as though nothing ever happened. All I would ask of you is a small favor every now and then."

Charles's fearful expression slowly melted away as he considered her offer. "A small favor?" Thomas hid his face in his hands and sighed. Charles hadn't changed. He never would.

"Nothing worse than the things you've already done," Tetra said.

Thomas couldn't bring himself to look at Charles. He couldn't watch Charles choose evil over everything else. Not again.

It felt like an eternity waiting for Charles to make his decision, but finally, his voice broke the silence. "No."

Thomas dropped his hands and stared at Charles. Did he say *no*? Why? Thomas had been sure Charles would accept Tetra's offer.

Tetra instantly became furious. She pushed Charles away, and he stumbled backward a few feet before falling down. He watched Tetra with horror as she lifted one arm in the air and summoned a swirling orb of dark crimson shadows. "You might want to rethink your answer." Her voice morphed into a deep, monstrous growl that brought back the intense primal fear Thomas had felt before.

Charles squeezed his eyes shut. "I have done terrible things in my life that I promised myself would never happen again. I would rather die than act that way again."

"Charles!" Thomas yelled. "Run! She is going to kill you!"

Tetra's sinister laughter echoed through the chamber, bouncing off the walls and across the room in a symphony of terror. The orb swelled larger in her palm. She reared her hand back to throw it. Charles remained frozen in fear beneath her.

"No!" Thomas's scream joined the cacophony of laughter. The sound of Thomas's footsteps beneath him was the first indication that he was running. His feet carried him faster in fear than his brain would ever willingly allow him to move, but he still wasn't fast enough. Tetra had already thrown her attack. Thomas leaped forward, shielding Charles's body with his own.

The feeling of a thousand white-hot needles stabbed every nerve in his body. The pain was so intense, he could not remember who or where he was. Nothing existed but agony for five eternal seconds, until it finally stopped with a welcome silence of the senses.

Thomas was finally at peace.

Chapter Twenty-Three

It took Charles a long, disorienting moment to understand that the force that had knocked him back had not been from Tetra's attack. Something else had knocked him down. Charles quickly realized it was Thomas from the sound of his voice. Thomas screamed like he couldn't hear himself. Charles had never heard anyone in such pain. It was the worst sound he had ever heard in his life.

Charles sat up, holding onto Thomas as he writhed in pain. Thomas's entire body was tense, until it wasn't. The screaming stopped when Thomas collapsed against Charles. Charles caught him and leaned forward, holding Thomas in his arms. "Thomas?" Charles gently shook him.

No response.

"Thomas," Charles said with desperation. His voice caught in his throat and his heart pounded in his chest. "Wake up." His voice shook as he spoke. This couldn't be happening. Charles pulled him upright, but his body was limp with a clumsy heaviness that couldn't be imitated by the living. No, he couldn't be...

Charles put his ear to Thomas's chest. He was not breathing. There was no heartbeat.

Thomas was dead. Again.

And it was his fault. Again.

"No!" Charles cried out. He held Thomas close, ignoring that his life was in imminent danger.

"Charles," Tetra called from above, sinking to the floor to be level with him.

He shut his eyes and held Thomas so tight that Thomas surely wouldn't have been able to breathe if he were alive.

"I can bring him back to life," Tetra said.

Charles shook his head. "I don't believe you."

"I am the god of death."

"You're evil!"

Tetra laughed again, sending a flood of terror through his veins. "Yes, but I'm telling the truth. If you let me bring him back, I will spare your life."

Let her? Why would Tetra want to revive him unless she gained something from it? She could only gain something from it if she planned to make Thomas her eternal servant.

Charles recalled a conversation from their time at Blackwater about a book they had read called *Eternality.*

Why would anyone seek out eternal life? I can't think of anything worse than living forever. Charles could hear Thomas's voice in his head as clearly as if Thomas were talking directly to him.

Charles examined Thomas's corpse. Tears stained his face. His eyebrows were pinched together in pain, and his mouth was forever stuck in the frown that Charles had long ago vowed to erase. Dei, how he'd messed that up. Charles wiped a tear from Thomas's face and brushed his hair away from his eyes. "I'm so sorry, Thomas," he whispered.

Thomas wouldn't want to live forever. He wouldn't even want to come back to life. It would be selfish of Charles to bring him back now, and Charles had hurt Thomas too many times with his own selfishness. The last thing he wanted to do was to take Thomas's peaceful mortality away from him. It was all he had left.

As hard as it was to give him up, Charles had to let him go.

"No," Charles said.

Tetra frowned. "Don't be stupid. I'm offering to bring the person you love back to life and let you live. Why would you turn that down?"

"He wouldn't want that."

"Isn't that what *you* want?"

"It doesn't matter what I want."

Tetra narrowed her crimson eyes at Charles and stared at him for several long, petrifying seconds. "You're right. It doesn't matter what you want."

She reached over Charles and pried Thomas out of his arms. As hard as Charles struggled to keep hold of Thomas, Tetra stole him from Charles with insulting ease.

"It doesn't matter what you want," she said again, holding Thomas up carelessly. Charles could barely stand to watch her wave his lifeless body around. "I'm going to bring him back anyway. He's going to be my servant for the rest of eternity, and he will have to do *everything* I tell him."

Charles pushed himself up. "No! Please, don't."

"You could have avoided all of this. You just had to say *yes*. You have a much greater capacity for evil. I'd rather have you." Tetra shrugged. "But you said no."

"Yes! You can have me instead! Please," Charles begged. "Please, leave him alone."

Tetra threw her head back and laughed maniacally as she dropped Thomas to the floor again. Charles lurched forward, but Thomas hit the floor before he could properly react. "Was that so hard?" Tetra said.

Charles could not look away from Thomas's crumpled body on the floor. How could he have messed up this badly? His heart was heavy with guilt. Thomas was dead, and the evilest entity to exist now had an evil human to serve her. Charles was going to suffer forever because he didn't listen to Thomas. He should have listened to Thomas from the very beginning.

At least Thomas wouldn't have to suffer.

Tetra approached him, and he tried to swallow his fear. He trembled as she reached her clawed hand toward him. Before Tetra could touch him, another large woman suddenly appeared beside Thomas's body. It was hard to make out any features in the darkness of the temple, but it was obvious by her silhouette that she was just as large as Tetra. Another god?

"Charles!" the new woman shouted.

Charles took a step back. "What? Who are you?"

"I'm Mariana. Listen to me, she can't have your soul unless you give it to her. She tricked you! Take it back!"

Tetra yelled out angrily and swiped her claws through Mariana, but it did nothing. Mariana's skin rippled, and Charles thought he could see bubbles floating upward from the slash marks.

"What the hell?" Charles whispered.

Tetra turned toward Charles with a menacing scowl. She lunged at him, but he dove away from her. Charles finally understood what Mariana meant. Tetra wouldn't have had Thomas as her servant unless he agreed to it. She had tricked Charles into giving away his soul. "I take it back! I won't serve you," Charles said before Tetra came after him again.

Tetra stopped where she stood, then turned to Mariana. "You salty bitch! I almost had him!" She moved toward Mariana, but instead of attacking, she hovered over Thomas's body. "Where are you?" Tetra asked, inspecting the corpse beneath her. She quickly located a vial of water and pulled it off Thomas.

"Charles, run!" Mariana shouted before Tetra launched the vial into the floor, sending damp shards of glass through the temple. As soon as the vial shattered, Mariana disappeared. Charles was alone with Tetra.

Tetra quickly moved toward Charles again and grabbed him before he could even consider running. "You're not going anywhere," Tetra hissed. "I'm going to *make* you say yes."

SOMEWHERE UNKNOWN

A cool, gentle breeze brushed over the pale sands of the warm beach. Clouds drifted overhead, casting pleasant shade whenever the sun came too close to unpleasant. Ocean waves gushed over the wet sand and then slowly retreated back into the crystal blue sea. The salty breeze carried the smell of petrichor and fresh flowers.

Thomas had never been anywhere like this in his life.

A pleasant hum from deep within him replaced the unbearable pain, which he was already forgetting. He looked around and found that he was completely alone in this unfamiliar place. Where was he? Had Tetra teleported him somewhere?

Thomas stepped forward into the cool ocean waves as they rolled across the sand. The temperature of the water was perfect. Nothing had ever given him quite a profound sense of peace as this beach. It didn't matter where he was. This was a happy place. For the first time possibly ever, Thomas was content.

"Thomas!" a distant voice yelled. It was familiar, but so faint he decided he must have imagined it. "Thomas!" the voice yelled again, louder this time. He turned around to inspect the area but found nothing. He was still alone. He shrugged and faced the ocean.

Mariana stood in the surf, watching him. "Thomas!" she yelled again. Of course. It was Mariana's voice.

Thomas smiled at her. "Mariana! You're here!" he said, then looked around again. "Where is *here*, exactly?"

"The afterlife. You're dead."

"Wow. I'm dead," Thomas said. The idea seemed natural to him, and not at all disturbing. "Why am I at a beach?"

"Your afterlife is an ideal environment for your soul to rest in until you are ready to move on. It's based on personal preference," Mariana explained, staring at the fabricated ocean. "I'm flattered, honestly." She grinned at him.

Thomas laughed an unfamiliar and genuine laugh. "I do love the ocean. I always have."

"Aww. The ocean loves you too," Mariana said, tilting her head to the side.

"What are you doing here?" Thomas asked. "Are you part of my ideal environment?"

Mariana giggled. "Oh stop it." Her pleasant demeanor became very serious, and she looked at the fake ocean again. "I'm sorry I didn't tell you that immortality came with eternal servitude. I would have told you beforehand if you had agreed to it."

Thomas frowned at her. "Oh. That's okay. It's too late for that now, anyway."

"You would have been perfect for me."

"Do you really believe that?" Thomas asked.

Mariana nodded with a proud smile. "Absolutely. Not only do you love and know me already, but you're a water elementalist, too."

This was news to Thomas. He stared at her with wide eyes. "I —I am?"

"You didn't know that?"

Thomas shook his head.

"Oh," Mariana said with a curious frown that only lasted a few seconds before she smiled at him again. "Let me show you!" She reached her ethereal hand into the depths of his undead chest, where his heart would have been if he were still alive. She retracted her hand and held up a spherical ball of pale blue energy that clung to Thomas with thin strands of light. The sphere had a hollow space at the center. A matching cylindrical shape orbited the sphere. "This is your soul." Mariana frowned as she observed the orb. "What did you do to it?"

"I didn't do anything," Thomas said, staring at the sight with awe. "Is it damaged?"

Mariana frowned at his soul for a long time. "You poor thing. No wonder you're always sad."

"I'm not sad right now."

"No, you wouldn't be. Your soul is here to rest, but not even the afterlife could fix this."

Thomas stared at his soul. He could feel the sadness creeping up on him again.

"Well, it *could*, but it would take a few lifetimes. It's a good thing you have me!" Mariana grinned at him before grabbing the cylindrical fragment and replacing it at the center of the sphere. She held her hands over the sphere and molded it back into a whole piece, then replaced his soul into his chest.

Thomas instantly felt different. He hadn't known it before, but he had always felt hollow at his core, the same as his soul. Now there was something there. Something he didn't know he had been missing.

"Mariana," Thomas whispered, clutching at his chest. "I had no idea. Thank you."

"Anything for you, Thomas." Mariana frowned at him. "I'm going to miss you."

"I'm going to miss you too," Thomas said with a sad smile. He rubbed his chest where Mariana had placed his soul as though he could feel its wholeness with his hands. He wanted to appreciate this feeling more.

"I'm sorry about Tetra. I wouldn't have asked you to talk to her if I had known she would kill you. She's not supposed to do that."

Thomas nodded as he recalled his last moments. "Did Charles make it out alive?"

Mariana's frown remained as she shook her head and gestured to the space behind Thomas. He whirled around to see the sight of Tetra's temple stuck in the air before him. "That's your final resting place," she said. For the first time since entering the afterlife, an unpleasant pang struck Thomas's heart. Charles kneeled before Tetra, holding his head and begging her to stop.

"What is she doing to him?" Thomas asked.

"Probably trying to convince him to be her servant the best way she knows how."

"How's that?"

Mariana frowned at the image suspended in the air. "Fear. She won't let him say no again. I don't want to think about what she'll do to him if he says yes."

"I didn't think you cared about human life," Thomas said.

Mariana shook her head. "Death happens every day. I don't think much of it because every living being will die, but it doesn't mean I don't care. Nobody deserves eternal suffering. Your boyfriend is not okay, Thomas."

"He's not—" Thomas stopped himself. "Mariana, please. You have to help him," he begged.

"I'm sorry, I can't."

"Screw the rules! The gods can't meddle with life, but Tetra just killed me, and now she's going to torture Charles. You can break the rules once, can't you?" Thomas yelled, surprised at the panic in his own voice.

"I would help if I could, but Tetra smashed the vial of me-water that you were carrying to prevent that from happening. I'm sorry."

Thomas stared helplessly into the floating image of his final resting place. His death would be for nothing. Absolutely nothing he had done in life or death would amount to anything. Charles would suffer forever. The sirens would continue to murder sailors. The Hambletons would continue to steal magic.

Thomas couldn't let himself die. He wasn't done yet.

"Is it too late?" he asked.

Mariana stared at him. "What?"

"To accept your offer?"

"You don't want that. You told me so yourself," Mariana said.

"You just repaired my soul. I can't die now!" Thomas pleaded. "Please, Mariana. Is it possible?"

"I don't know, Thomas. You've been dead for a while. I don't know if your body will wake up again."

"Can't you try?"

"Are you sure you want this? You will never die again, and you will have to do everything I ask of you for all of eternity. You can't take it back."

"I'm sure," Thomas said.

Mariana nodded. "Okay," she said, placing one hand over his heart. She shot Thomas one last probing look, to which he responded with an urgent nod. Mariana smiled, closed her eyes, and said, "Dei, grant me the power to create an unbreakable eternal bond that will bring this human into the Pantheon to serve me forever."

The permanence of her words frightened Thomas, but he could not let himself die with the amount of unfinished business that waited for him.

The pleasant hum inside him slowly ceased like a flame at the end of a drowning wick. Tetra's malicious laugh replaced the gentle sound of ocean waves. Thomas opened his eyes to find himself lying in an uncomfortable position on the cold, hard floor.

The pain of Tetra's deadly attack still lingered over Thomas's nerves. He couldn't move for a long time as his body adjusted to being alive again. Despite the extreme cold and the pain in his limbs, Thomas felt a comfort deep inside himself that hadn't been there before.

"Please stop," Charles begged. "Just kill me."

The comfort was dampened by the sound of Charles's desperate pleading. Thomas tried to move, but the effort of it sent a painful shock through his muscles. He collapsed onto the floor again, unable to help. He tried to speak but only managed to cough out a pitiful croak that got lost behind Tetra's laughter.

"I'm not going to kill you, Charles," Tetra said. "That would be too easy."

"Please," Charles cried.

Thomas slowly moved his head to look at Charles. Tetra watched Charles from a distance as he kneeled in front of her with his head in his hands, just like Thomas had seen from his afterlife. Mariana had mentioned that Tetra was using fear to persuade Charles. She must have been torturing him with his own thoughts. Knowing Charles's inability to confront fear, it was no wonder he was begging for death.

Thomas tried to move again with more success. He could only push his arm forward an inch. His body was still mostly dead.

"I just want to hear you say *yes*," Tetra said. "I know you know that word. You're a smart boy."

Charles shook his head. "Please stop," he begged.

"Just say yes!" Tetra yelled.

Thomas was amazed that Charles wouldn't give in. Thomas clawed at the ground in front of him but hardly moved. His body was so weak.

Tetra lowered herself so that her face was level with Charles's. "What are you going to do if you get out of here? Go home? Nobody wants you there. Especially not your father. He's going to be so disappointed if you ever make it back."

Charles shook his head with his eyes shut tight. "I don't care."

"Yes you do," Tetra said. "You care what everyone thinks, and you prioritize it over everything else."

"No..." Charles said in a small voice.

"There's nothing left for you in the mortal world. Nobody wants you around, and they never did. The only person who ever truly loved you is dead, and it's your fault," Tetra continued.

"Please," Charles begged, "I don't want to live..."

"I won't let you die, Charles. I'm going to keep you alive for as long as it takes," Tetra said.

"I'll never help you, Tetra," Charles said with a shaky voice. "You killed Thomas."

Who was this person? How could Charles stand up to *Tetra,* but not his father? Thomas managed to push himself into a sitting position, but neither Tetra nor Charles noticed him. He had never felt so ill in his life. He was afraid he would throw up if he moved again, but he forced himself not to.

"Oh, is that the problem?" Tetra asked. "You're sad about *Thomas?* The person you won't admit you love to anyone but him?"

"I love him," Charles finally said, looking up at Tetra through his tears. "I'm not afraid to admit it."

"You never have to admit it again. I can help you forget him," Tetra said.

Thomas didn't know his heart was capable of hurting over Charles in a new way.

Charles knit his eyebrows. "*Forget him?*" His eyes landed on Thomas, then widened. He opened his mouth to speak but stopped himself. He fixed his eyes on Tetra again. "Never."

Tetra whirled around to face Thomas. Her face twisted with ethereal anger when she saw him. "You're alive?!" she boomed.

Thomas stood up. The world spun beneath him, but he staggered toward Charles anyway. Charles jumped up when Thomas approached and caught him when he inevitably fell over. "Charles," Thomas groaned, clinging to Charles. "You have to get out of here." He felt pathetic. He thought he could save Charles, but he could barely walk.

"No. I'm not leaving you here," Charles whispered, holding Thomas steady.

"This is a pretty inconvenient time for you to decide you aren't a coward anymore," Thomas said. "Go!"

"Get away from him!" Tetra roared, throwing her hands in the air to summon another ball of death overhead.

Charles swept Thomas's legs out from under him and lifted him up. Before Thomas could argue, Charles ran toward the exit with Thomas in his arms.

"Charles!" Thomas yelled. "Put me down! Leave me here!" He watched Tetra from over Charles's shoulder. She slowly built up the dark energy in her hands that she had used to kill him minutes ago.

"No!" Charles said.

"Don't be stupid!" Thomas yelled. Tears burned his eyes. He was shocked at his own desperation, but he had made himself immortal for this, and Charles was about to get himself killed. "I came back to life for you," Thomas said. "Don't waste it trying to save me."

Charles looked at Thomas with wide eyes. "You—" He stopped himself, then looked forward again as he ran. "Nothing is wasted on you, Thomas," he said. "I love you so much."

Tetra threw her attack. Thomas rolled out of Charles's arms, pulling Charles down with him just as the death orb whizzed through the air inches above them. Thomas immediately pulled

Charles up again, refusing to let go of his hand as he ran for the exit. Charles followed close behind, holding onto Thomas just as tight.

Something as sharp as a cluster of needles and as hot as fire hit Thomas square in the back. He stumbled forward and nearly fell to the floor, but Charles caught him. The pain quickly fizzled away. Thomas soon realized Tetra had tried to kill him again, but he was still alive.

"Thomas!" Charles said, holding Thomas's face with his hand as he looked into his eyes with concern. "Look at me."

Thomas blinked hard and looked into Charles's eyes. "I'm fine," he whispered. "Keep running."

"I'm not leaving you—"

"So," Tetra's cold, dead voice cut through their conversation. Tetra loomed over them, suddenly standing between them and the exit. "You're immortal now?" She locked her invasive gaze on Thomas.

"Yes," Thomas said, positioning himself between Charles and Tetra.

"You don't really believe you can escape, do you?" Tetra asked with an amused smirk, peering around Thomas to watch Charles. Charles gripped Thomas's arm tightly. "It'll only be easier to convince him now that you're here."

Thomas was silent.

"Maybe if I can get you to scream loud enough, your boyfriend will give in," Tetra said.

"No!" Charles said.

"He's not my boyfriend," Thomas grumbled.

Tetra's dark laughter echoed off the walls. "I'm looking forward to having a human in the Pantheon."

This was a surprise to Thomas. He had assumed there were other human servants in the Pantheon already. "I'm the first?"

"You're the first." She grinned sharply at him. "Shall we?" she asked, then grabbed his arm with her clawed hand. A thin blue layer of light covered his arm where she held onto him. Thomas felt nothing. He watched her struggle against it, wondering if she was playing some kind of trick on him.

Tetra released his arm and shot him a glare so deadly it made his skin crawl. "So... I can't touch you." Her eyes locked on Charles. Her sickening smile widened. "But I can touch *him.*"

Thomas reached behind him to grab Charles's wrist just as Tetra slipped through the darkness and reappeared beside Charles. Thomas pulled Charles away, making a run for the exit, but Tetra caught Charles's other arm and stopped them from escaping.

Thomas turned around to place himself between Charles and Tetra again but stopped when he saw the protective blue light around Charles's arm. Charles stared at Tetra's claws around his wrist with wide eyes, not daring to move an inch. Thomas didn't understand. He had assumed the protection came from his association with Mariana, but why was it working for Charles too?

Thomas looked at his own grip on Charles. Could it be because Thomas was touching him? Charles would be safe from Tetra as long as they kept physical contact?

Thomas easily pulled Charles away from Tetra and into his arms. He could feel Charles trembling against him. "You can't have him," Thomas said.

Tetra snarled with the hatred and bloodlust of a thousand predators about to strike their prey. "I *will* have him," Tetra growled.

"You don't want him," Thomas said. "He's awful."

"I know, he's perfect," Tetra said.

Thomas held Charles tight. Charles hid his face against Thomas's neck. "If I *did* convince him to give his soul to you, would you stop creating sirens?" Thomas asked.

"What?" Charles hissed. "Thomas—"

Thomas glared at Charles. Charles stopped talking.

A horrible grin slowly grew across Tetra's face. "Oh, Thomas. I didn't know you had it in you."

"Would you?" he asked again.

"Yes, of course."

"What if I found you someone else? Someone better?"

Tetra's grin fell away. She sneered at Thomas. "You?"

"Yes, me," Thomas said with a shrug. "I found Charles, didn't I?"

Tetra nodded pensively. "You certainly did. We do have the same taste in men..."

Thomas grimaced. "Yes," he agreed.

"And all you want is for me to stop turning the mermaids into sirens?"

"That's all I want."

A sickening smile spread across her face. "I like that offer."

Thomas wasn't sure he heard her correctly. "You'll stop right now?"

"Right this very moment," Tetra assured him, extending a hand forward. "Shake on it, Thomas Hambleton. You owe me a human soul."

Thomas hesitated as he reached forward to shake her hand.

Tetra pouted at him. "What's wrong, Thomas? Having second thoughts? I don't mind making more sirens to help me find a cold-hearted man. I'm sure they would be just as effective as you."

Thomas suppressed another grimace and shook his head. "No," he said. He shook her cold, corpse-like hand, keeping Charles close to him as he did. Tetra grinned at him. He felt nauseous at the sight of her smile, like he had just done something terrible. Like he had just promised something he would not be able to deliver.

"Thank you, Thomas." She gestured toward the wall where

the exit chamber sat waiting for him, now well-lit with the torches that had extinguished themselves on the way in. "I'm looking forward to meeting the poor soul you decide deserves to spend eternity with me."

Thomas felt immediate guilt. There was no way he would be able to condemn anyone to eternity with Tetra. He nodded at her meekly, trying not to let the thought show on his face. He had finally fixed Mariana's problem at a steep price for himself. Thomas said nothing as he dragged Charles toward the exit. Their feet crunched against the frosty stone floor of the narrow hallway.

They silently walked through the long tunnel until the main chamber was no longer visible. Thomas stopped, still holding Charles's hand firmly in his own. "Are you okay?" Thomas asked.

Charles swept him up in a big hug. Thomas leaned into it, wrapping his arms around Charles. "I am so sorry," Charles said, burrowing his face against Thomas's neck. "Are *you* okay?"

"I think so."

Charles leaned away from Thomas but continued holding him by the shoulders. He stared at Thomas for a long time. "So, you're...?" he started to ask, but never finished the question.

Thomas looked away. "I didn't want my death to be for nothing."

Charles frowned in response. He didn't speak for a long time. "You gave your life for me... twice?"

Thomas nodded and stared at his feet. The reality of the situation finally hit him, and his heart broke for the afterlife he would never see again. "I told you not to follow me," he said quietly.

"I'm sorry," Charles said again. "I didn't think Mariana was real. I didn't believe you were actually going to talk to a god, but I believed that you believed it. I saw you walk into the forest alone, and I was afraid..."

Thomas sighed. He knew he looked strange when he talked to Mariana, but he didn't think it would be his undoing. "I understand," he whispered.

"You're not upset?"

"I don't think I will ever not be upset with you."

Charles let out a short laugh and pulled Thomas into another hug. Thomas sighed and rested his head against Charles's shoulder. As irritating as he was, it was nice to be with him again.

"Let's get you back to your ship," Thomas said, trying to find a reason to let him go.

"Come with me," Charles said, hugging him tighter.

"Are you sure you want to be seen with me?" Thomas asked.

Charles buried his face into Thomas's neck and sighed. The hot air from Charles's lungs flowed around Thomas's neck and down his back, causing goosebumps on his skin. "I'm sorry you even feel the need to ask that," Charles said. He punctuated his apology with a kiss against Thomas's neck.

The kiss sent a shock through Thomas, starting at his neck and ending at his fingertips, which he curled into the fabric of Charles's shirt. "Damn it, Charles," Thomas whispered, pushing him away.

"I'm sorry."

Thomas looked Charles in the eyes and saw the familiar, perfect rehearsed face of regret. Thomas knew he didn't regret anything. If Charles had the opportunity to kiss him again, he would. "You drive me crazy. I know you aren't sorry, and that makes me so angry," Thomas fumed. "But what makes me even angrier is how much I enjoy it. After everything you put me through and after traveling across the world to get away from you, I still *fucking* love you."

Charles's remorseful façade cracked, and his perfect smile peeked through. It wasn't practiced, and it wasn't fake. Charles's smile was genuine, and Thomas finally realized that Charles hadn't lied to him. Not about one thing, at least. Charles really did love him.

"You love me?" Charles asked.

"Is that not obvious?" Thomas asked, gesturing down the dark passageway.

Charles peered into the dark cavern for a moment before his gaze fell on Thomas again. He nodded somberly and then gently took hold of Thomas's hand. "Thank you. I owe you my life. I owe you everything." He lifted Thomas's hand and kissed it.

A similar shock paralyzed Thomas's hand. Thomas pulled his hand away and shook it to rid of the feeling. "I knew you weren't sorry."

"I can't help myself, Thomas. I adore you. It's taking all my restraint not to kiss you right now," Charles said.

"Why can't you ask first?"

Charles watched Thomas carefully for a moment. "Can I kiss you?"

"No."

Charles narrowed his eyes at Thomas. "Wh—" he stopped himself. "Fine. That's what you want."

"Thank you."

Charles offered his hand to Thomas. "Let's go home."

Thomas smiled at the show of restraint. Charles had finally listened to him. He took Charles's hand and walked with him in silence down the remainder of the dark passageway, until finally they saw the dim light at the end of the tunnel.

CHAPTER TWENTY-FOUR

The biting cold of the winter air embraced Thomas as he stepped into the dark forest, hand-in-hand with Charles. The forest was eerie and still. It was too dark to see much more than black shadows haunting the edges of his vision.

Faint whispering echoed from their left, raising the hair on the back of Thomas's neck.

Charles squeezed his hand tight. "Come on, Thomas. Let's get out of here," he whispered.

"Thomas?!" A bright flash of yellow light blinded him for a moment before it settled into a steady flame. Behind the flame were the dimly lit faces of Faya and Fiona. Faya held the flame up, peering over the fire in search of him.

"F—Faya! Fiona!" Thomas said. He took a step back. "What are you doing here?"

Fiona urgently grabbed Faya's arm. "It's him! He's okay!" she said. She lifted her hand in the air and whispered, *"Ablight."* A bright flame ignited in her palm. She held it up and ran toward Thomas.

Thomas took another step back. There was no way she was here to help him. She had declared earlier in the night that she would kill a Hambleton if she ever met one, and now she knew he was a Hambleton.

Fiona stopped in front of Thomas, staring at him with concern in her bright eyes.

"Fiona..." Thomas said. "I didn't mean any harm, I promise."

Fiona shook her head and smiled sadly. "I'm just glad you're okay. We were so worried about you."

"You—you were?" Thomas asked.

"Of course," Faya said, intercepting their conversation. "Let's get back to town. There is something evil in this forest, and I don't think we should stay much longer than we need to."

Fiona nodded and took off in an unexpected direction. Faya followed her.

Thomas stared at them as they walked away. Had they not heard the news? Did they know who he was? He shook off the confusion and quickly followed them, dragging Charles behind. He was shocked that Faya and Fiona were not only okay with being near him, but they were actually *concerned* about him.

"We've been looking for you since you ran off. Fiona somehow knew you would be here, but we couldn't get into the temple," Faya said as he caught up to them.

"Wh—I don't understand," Thomas said. "You were looking for me? Why?"

"Because we love you!" Fiona said.

"You—You know who I am, don't you?" Thomas finally asked.

"Yeah. We know who you are," Fiona said, swatting a leafy branch away from her face. The forest gradually lightened as they distanced themselves from Tetra's temple. The sounds of the distant docks grew louder as the pale moon shone brighter through the tree branches overhead.

"You're our friend," Faya said. "You risked your life to help us find our families knowing we are magi. Your name is not important. We know who you *really* are."

Thomas rubbed his burning eyes, trying to fight back tears. He had been so worried about what would happen when they found out he was a Hambleton, but he never expected this. They stepped onto the cobblestone street, blanketed in moonlight. Thomas stopped walking. "I'm sorry I lied to you," he said.

Fiona shook her head. "I'm glad you did. Honestly, I don't know if I would have given you a chance."

Faya nodded. "She's right Fe—Thomas... I would have done the same thing in your position."

"I didn't know about it when we met," Thomas said quickly. "About what we're—*they're* doing to magi. I only just learned what they're actually doing from—" Thomas turned to look at Charles. "From him."

Fiona glanced at Charles before resting her hopeful gaze on Thomas again. "Does that mean you know what happened to my brother?"

"Oh, uh... He should be fine. I mean, he's definitely fine," Thomas said, glancing at Charles. Charles nodded.

Fiona released a heavy sigh of relief, then covered her face with her hands. "Thank the gods." She uncovered her face again. "What are they doing? What happened to him?" She looked at Charles for the answer, her eyes briefly falling to their interlocked hands.

Thomas also looked to Charles for the answer, painfully aware that Charles knew more about the Hambleton family than Thomas knew himself. Charles straightened up, looking back and forth between Fiona and Thomas. He cleared his throat. "Well, I don't know about your brother specifically, but they're removing magic from magi and forcing them to work on Hambleton ships," Charles said.

Fiona gasped and covered her mouth. Faya grimaced.

"That's horrible!" Fiona said.

Thomas nodded grimly.

"You *really* didn't know about this?" Faya asked Thomas.

"No, I really didn't," Thomas said.

Fiona tilted her head and frowned at him. "How is that possible?"

"I think it's because I'm... uh..." He looked at Charles again. "Your mother was right about me," Thomas said, extremely uncomfortable admitting his discovery in front of two real magi.

Charles's eyes widened. "It's true?" he asked. "You're a magus?"

Thomas winced at the word *magus* like it was a curse. He looked at Fiona and Faya. "Nobody ever told me."

Faya and Fiona exchanged a surprised look. "*You?*" Faya asked. "I mean no offense, but... *you?* The kid who was afraid of magi just a few months ago?"

Thomas nodded guiltily.

"How could you *not* know something like that?" Fiona asked.

"My magic was taken a long time ago," Thomas said. "Mariana just gave it back to me."

Fiona stared at him in awe for a moment. "How did it feel?"

"What?" Thomas asked.

"To have no magic?"

Thomas shook his head. "It happened so long ago; I don't even remember. All I can say is now I don't feel so... hollow. I've always felt empty inside, but I feel a lot better now."

Fiona covered her mouth and watched him. Thomas looked at the ground, unable to handle the pity in her eyes. "Thomas, can I give you a hug?" Fiona asked.

Thomas looked at her again. "What? Why?"

"Well, because... Don't you need a hug?" Fiona asked.

Thomas struggled to control his face. Maybe it was her magic, but Fiona had managed to completely override the calm that had settled in him with just a question. Something bubbled up from within, escaping in the form of burning tears. He nodded, letting go of Charles's hand to rub his eyes.

Fiona wrapped him up in her arms, squeezing him tight. Thomas melted into her. He hadn't realized how much he needed a real hug. Charles had just hugged him, but that was different, somehow. "Are you all right?" Fiona asked.

"I think so," Thomas muttered.

"It's okay if you're not," Fiona said. "You've been through a lot."

Thomas shook his head, still resting against her. "I'm not," he cried. It was all he could say. He continued crying on Fiona, unable to get any words through the river of tears.

Fiona squeezed him tighter as he cried. "Everything will be okay," she said quietly. "It doesn't feel like it now, but it will be."

Thomas shook his head but still couldn't speak, thinking about the eternity he couldn't escape.

"Who is this?" Faya finally asked.

Thomas peeled himself off Fiona and dried his tears with his sleeve. Faya eyed Charles, while Charles frowned at Fiona, not caring to introduce himself.

Thomas stepped away from Fiona. "This is Charles," he said, struggling not to sound resentful. "*Southworth*," he added. "Charles, this is Fiona and Faya. They are the reason I'm still alive."

Charles finally looked away from Fiona to smile at Faya. "Nice to meet you," he said.

Faya raised her eyebrows. "Southworth?" she asked. "As in, *Southworth*?"

"Charles?" Fiona asked. "As in, *Charles*?"

"Yes, those are my names," Charles said.

A brief silence lingered as Faya and Fiona processed this information. Fiona spoke first. "You should be ashamed of yourself, *Charles*," she said.

"Fiona, it's okay—" Thomas started, but Fiona lifted one finger in the air to stop him without even turning to look at him.

"Thomas deserves so much better than you," Fiona continued.

Charles crossed his arms and narrowed his eyes. "And I suppose you think he can find that with *you?*" he asked, eyeing her up and down in the same judgmental way he used to use on Thomas.

"Charles..." Thomas said in a scolding tone. Charles ignored him. Thomas couldn't believe Charles was jealous of Fiona. He should have known better than anyone that Thomas wasn't interested in her.

"He could find it with almost anyone else. You're a bad person," Fiona said.

"You're clearly jealous," Charles said.

"Yeah! I am!" Fiona said. "We aren't all lucky enough to find someone as kind and caring as Fe—uh... Thomas, but somehow *you* found him and tricked him into loving you just so you could break his heart. He deserves someone who cares about him as much as he cares about *everyone else.*"

Thomas felt his face burn. He hadn't expected Fiona to admit to being jealous of Charles, but it was obviously the only way to get Charles to listen. Charles's jealous pout melted away, leaving behind the same defeated look he had on his face when Thomas had left him at the beach earlier in the night. His sad gaze landed on Thomas and stayed there.

Charles nodded slowly. "You deserve better. I'm sorry."

Thomas shook his head. "It's not enough, Charles."

"I will do anything to make it better," Charles said. "Absolutely anything."

Thomas wanted to believe Charles's beautiful lies, but Fiona was right. Charles was not good for him. Thomas would rather be alone than suffer in love, but he had no willpower around Charles, and Charles was relentlessly charming and handsome. There was nothing Charles could do to make it better. Thomas would never recover with Charles around.

"Do you mean that?" Thomas asked.

Charles nodded. "I'll do anything you want. Just name it."

"Leave me here," Thomas said.

The hope in Charles's eyes vanished. "Leave you?"

"Go back to your ship. I'll go back to mine," Thomas said. "We're better off going our separate ways."

Charles reached for Thomas but stopped himself. "Is that really what you want?" he asked.

"I'll never feel better if you're always around to reopen the wound," Thomas said.

"Right, but... Are you sure?" Charles asked.

"You said you would do anything," Thomas reminded him.

Charles stared at him for a long moment. "Okay." He took a hesitant step back, watching Thomas as though waiting for Thomas to change his mind. After another stretch of silence, he said, "I love you, Thomas."

Thomas nodded, unable to meet his eyes. "Yeah. I know."

"Okay... good," Charles said, then turned to leave.

Thomas watched Charles's silhouette slowly disappear into the early morning fog. Thomas could hardly believe his own eyes. Charles Southworth would finally leave him alone.

"I'm proud of you, Thomas," Fiona said.

Thomas forced himself to look from Charles to Fiona. "Why?" he asked.

"It's incredibly hard to cut out the bad people in your life. Especially people you love."

Thomas shook his head. "I don't—" He looked into the fog

again, knowing there was no point in lying to her. Lying only caused problems. "We should leave before we get arrested again," he said.

Fiona nodded with a tired smile before stepping onto the icy street. Thomas and Faya quietly followed her. The frozen breeze blew in from the seafront and washed the pleasant scent of salty morning air over them. The harsh sting of the cold was no longer painful, but a lovely reminder that he was still alive.

The world was so beautiful, and Thomas had never noticed before.

As they approached the docks, the tops of the ships' masts slowly came into view. The brick buildings parted to make way for the sparkling ocean, littered with ships. Thomas stopped at the end of the street and looked out at the dark sea. He had seen the ocean many times before, but this was the first time he had seen her since giving his soul to her for eternity. This was the beginning of something that would never end.

The docks were mostly empty apart from the few drunk sailors stumbling through the darkness after a long night. The taverns around them were beginning their closing duties as late night became early morning. The cold breeze assailed them as they stepped onto the docks, vulnerable to the wind without the protection of buildings to keep them warm.

"Thomas!" Mariana's bubbly voice called from somewhere beneath him. Thomas looked at his feet and saw the movement of water between the planks of the dock.

"Mariana!" he called back.

Seawater dripped upward through the wooden planks and formed the familiar shape of Mariana directly in front of Thomas. She grinned at him. "I'm so happy you're still alive!"

"Thanks, I uh... I guess I am too," Thomas said, surprising himself with his answer.

"I'm glad to hear that," Mariana said. She glanced back and forth between Fiona and Faya, who were frozen in place staring at Mariana. "Hello!" Mariana said.

Thomas watched his friends for a moment and then whipped back around to examine Mariana. "Can they see you?"

Mariana shrugged. "Yes."

"Finally," Thomas said. Mariana was starting to understand him. "Fiona, Faya, this is Mariana. Mariana, this is—"

"It's wonderful to meet you!" Mariana interrupted him.

Fiona and Faya remained still. "You're real?" Faya finally asked.

Mariana grinned at Faya. "Of course!"

"This is bad luck..." Fiona muttered.

"Nonsense," Mariana said, waving the thought away. "I won't hurt you."

"Did you need something, Mariana?" Thomas asked in an attempt to spare Fiona and Faya from Mariana.

"Well, yes. I would like to know what happened with Tetra," Mariana said.

"Oh..." Thomas said. The nausea he felt in the temple returned to him. "She told me she would stop infecting the mermaids."

"Really?" Mariana asked eagerly. Her expression immediately soured. "Why?"

"We... uh... made a deal."

Mariana watched him closely. "You made a deal with Tetra?"

Thomas scratched his head and looked away. "I told her I would find her an eternal servant," he muttered.

Mariana was quiet for an uncomfortably long time. "Thomas... Do you have any idea what you've done?" she finally asked.

"I've done exactly what you asked me to do," Thomas said.

The words came surprisingly easy to him, fueled by a new and unfamiliar energy.

"If she gets herself a servant, she could destroy the entire world!" Mariana said.

"Well then it's a good thing I get to choose, isn't it?" Thomas asked. "The mermaids are safe. That's what you wanted."

Mariana appeared taken aback. She stared at Thomas with wide eyes and said nothing. "That is what I wanted, but if you give her what *she* wants, we could have a much bigger problem on our hands," she said.

"I did the best I could!" Thomas said. Mariana watched him with curiosity. He took a step back, surprised at the wide range of emotions he suddenly felt. Did everyone else feel this much all the time? "Do you have any idea what I sacrificed to help you?" Thomas asked, unable to stop himself.

"You didn't do that just for me," Mariana said.

"Why did you find me in the afterlife? Was it to ask me one more time if I wanted to be immortal?" Thomas asked.

"I found you to say goodbye, Thomas. Because I care about you," Mariana said.

"Whoa, what?" Fiona asked.

"You knew I had unfinished business," Thomas said.

"Everyone has unfinished business when they die. Dying is not a choice. Even when it is, it isn't," Mariana said. "I'm sorry you've been led to believe that the people close to you are secretly out to get you, but I genuinely wanted to help you, Thomas. I was prepared to step away and let you move on because that's what you asked me to do."

Fiona and Faya watched them argue uncomfortably. Thomas glared at Mariana, lacking a response. She was right. She *did* ask him three times if he was certain he wanted to become immortal.

"I have never been friends with a human before, but I consider you my friend," Mariana continued. "I wouldn't hurt you, and that includes binding your soul to mine eternally without your explicit consent. I'm sorry you regret it, but I didn't trick you, and I can't take it back."

Thomas opened his mouth to speak but found he had nothing to say. He closed his mouth and turned away, trying to hold back more tears. Now that his soul was whole, he could feel again, but it was all too much. "You're right. I'm sorry. I can't even die right," Thomas said.

"You died just fine," Mariana said, "and you came back to life better than anyone ever has."

Thomas rubbed his eyes and laughed. "That's one way to look at it."

Mariana smiled at him. "You'll learn how to look at things that way too. Just give it some time. Things will get better," Mariana said.

Thomas nodded and wiped his tears on his sleeve. "Okay." He smiled at Mariana, amazed at the ease with which it came to him.

"Wait, wait, wait..." Fiona said, waving both hands in the air to stop the conversation from progressing. *"What?"*

"What?" Thomas said.

"What do you mean *what?*" Faya interjected. "You died?"

"Yes."

"And then you came back to life?" Fiona asked.

"Yes."

Fiona hesitated. "And you're immortal?"

Thomas shrugged with a queasy frown. "Yes."

Fiona and Faya exchanged a look. "Wow," Faya said. "Rough night."

Thomas scoffed. "It's been a rough *life*," he said, but instantly felt ashamed, knowing that he had it better than most people in the world. Only after becoming a sailor did he realize how little other people had in comparison, and he was complaining about... what? Being sad? Living forever? He shook his head. "I'm sorry. I didn't mean that. It's just hard to be... I don't know. Never mind."

"You have nothing to apologize for," Fiona said. "Sure, you probably grew up in a giant castle and never had to worry about money, but honestly... you might be the unluckiest magus in the world to be born a Hambleton."

Thomas smiled at her, grateful for her generous perspective. "Maybe, but If I hadn't been born a Hambleton, I never would have met you two. I consider myself very lucky."

Fiona laughed. "You have no idea how relieved we are to know there's a good Hambleton in the world."

Thomas didn't know what to say. He nodded. "I have to do something to help. I have to go home."

"I'll go with you," Fiona said. "I bet I'll find Finnlay if I do."

Faya pursed her lips and looked away. "As much as I don't want to bring Ametta right into the heart of this issue, I owe you. I'll go too."

"You don't have to put yourself at risk for me, Faya," Thomas said. "I understand you want to keep Ametta safe."

Faya shook her head. "I want to help you. Ametta will be fine. I would die before I let anything happen to her again."

Thomas nodded. "Thank you, Faya." He turned to Mariana again, who had been watching them with interest. "Are you ready to help me?" he asked.

Mariana bowed her head. "I'm a god of my word. I am indebted to you, Thomas Hambleton."

Thomas sighed with relief. "Thank you," he said to the group. "You don't know how much I appreciate all of you."

"Of course, Thomas," Fiona said.

Faya squeezed his shoulder gently. "Let's get you back to Tinera."

"Yeah," Thomas said. He sighed and stared at the deep violet horizon. It was strange to him to think that the world had always been so beautiful, but he had never been able to see it. Thomas got the sudden, overwhelming sense that he had been far, far away from home for far too long. He still felt that there was no place for him in the world, but for the first time in his life, he felt a very real possibility that he could make one. "I'm ready."

End

ACKNOWLEDGMENTS

I have to start off by thanking my family. I couldn't have written this book without your lifetime of support and love. Thank you for always cheering me on and believing in me every step of the way. I love you guys.

Christa, thank you for being my first fan and for reading my manuscript three whole times. Your gentle and constructive feedback helped me shape this story into its best version. I appreciate that you were honest with me even when it was hard. I wouldn't have actually started believing the story was good if it weren't for you.

Amy, thank you for being my author sister. (Everyone read *Playing Witch* by Amy Suddarth!) You are one of the kindest and most supportive people in my life, and I am grateful that you always have words of encouragement when I need them.

Dana, thank you for being my twin soul. You make me feel less alone in the world because I know I can count on you to feel the same way about everything. Except for puns.

Scott, thank you for growing up with me and being my best friend from the start. I am grateful that you are good at staying close even though you're all the way out there in Florida.

Mom, I couldn't have thrived in this world without your support. Thank you for always being there for me and for loving me through everything. I wouldn't be the person I am today without you.

Dad, thank you for always supporting me no matter what I

chose to do in life. You are the reason I love the ocean enough to write a book about it. I wish you were here to see it get published. I love you and miss you very much.

Thank you to all of my friends who got excited for me when I told you about this project and demanded to read it. I appreciate every single one of you.

Finally, I want to thank my cat, Neena. You were by my side for the years of daydreaming that went into creating this world. I'm very grateful for the seventeen years I had with you, and I miss you every day.

About the Author

When not imagining fantastical worlds, Bryn is listening to music, researching apocalypse scenarios, and trying to keep sunflowers alive. This is their first novel, with many more planned for the future. Bryn lives in Arizona but really wishes they didn't. Visit their website at www.brynsuddarth.com or follow them on Instagram and TikTok for updates.

instagram.com/bryns_writing
tiktok.com/@bryns_writing

BRYN SUDDARTH
SERVANT
OF
FEAR